Thea Sti
3 IN 1

PAPERCUTZ

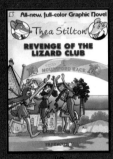

Thea Stilton

3 IN 1

By Thea Stilton

"The Secret of Whale Island"

"Revenge of the Lizard Club"

"The Treasure of the Viking Ship"

PAPERCUTZ

New York

THEA STILTON 3-in-1 #1

Geronimo Stilton and Thea Stilton names, characters and related indicia are copyright, trademark, and exclusive license of Atlantyca S.p.A. All rights reserved. The moral right of the author has been asserted.

Based on an original idea by Elisabetta Dami.

"The Secret of Whale Island"
Original Title: "Il Segreto dell'Isola delle Balene"
© 2008 Edizioni Piemme S.p.A., Italia
Text by Thea Stilton
Editorial Coordination by
Lorenza Bernardi and Patrizia Puricelli
With the collaboration of Serena Bellani
Artistic Coordination by Flavio Ferron
With the assistance of Tommaso Valescchi
Editing by Katja Centomo and Francesco Artibani
Editing Coordination and Artwork Supervision by Stefania Bitta and Maryam Funicelli
Script Supervision by Francesco Artibani
Script by Francesco Artibani and Caterina Mognato
Design by Giada Perissinotto
Color by Giulia Basile and Ketty Formaggio
Art by Cristina Giorgilli and Raffaella Seccia
With the assistance of Michela Battaglin and Marta Lorini
Cover by Giada Perissinotto (design), Raffaella Seccia (art), and Giulia Basile (color)

"Revenge of the Lizard Club"
Original Title: "La Rivincita del Club delle Lucertole"
© 2008 Edizioni Piemme S.p.A., Italia
Text by Thea Stilton
Text Coordination by Lorenza Bernardi and Sarah Rossi (Atlantyca S.p.A)
Editorial coordination by Patrizia Puricelli and Serena Bellani
Artistic Coordination by Flavio Ferron
With the assistance of Tommaso Valsecchi
Editing by Yellowhale
Editing Coordination and Artwork Supervision by Stefania Bitta and Maryam Funicelli
Script Supervision by Francesco Artibani
Script by Francesco Artibani and Caterina Mognato
Design by Arianna Rea
Art by Raffaella Seccia and Michela Frare
Color by Giulia Basile
With the assistance of Michela Battaglin and Marta Lorini
Cover by Giuseppe Faccioto (design and art) and Daniele Verzini (color)

"The Treasure of the Viking Ship"
Original title: "Il Tesoro della Nave Vichinga"
© 2009 Edizioni Piemme S.p.A., Italia
Text by Thea Stilton
Text Coordination by Lorenza Bernardi and Sarah Rossi (Atlantyca S.p.A.)
Editorial coordination by Patrizia Puricelli and Serena Bellani
Artistic Coordination by Flavio Ferron
With the assistance of Tommaso Valsecchi
Editing by Yellowhale
Editing Coordination and Artwork Supervision by Stefania Bitta and Maryam Funicelli
Script Supervision by Francesco Artibani
Script by Francesco Artibani and Caterina Mognato
Design by Claudia Forcelloni
Art by Michela Frare
Color by Giulia Basile, Alessandra Bracaglia, and Vanessa Santato
With the assistance of Michela Battaglin and Marta Lorini
Cover by Claudia Forcelloni (design), Michela Frare (art), and Giulia Basile (color)

© Atlantyca S.p.A. – via Leopardi 8, 20123 Milano, Italia – foreignrights@atlantyca.it
© 2018 for this Work in English language by Papercutz.
www.geronimostilton.com
Stilton is a name of a famous English cheese. It is a registered trademark of the Stilton Cheese Markers' Association.
For more information go to www.stiltoncheese.com

Editorial supervision by Alessandra Berello and Chiara Richelmi (Atlantyca S.p.A.)
Translation - Nanette McGuinness
Lettering and Production - Big Bird Zatryb
Original Editor – Michael Petranek
Editorial Intern- Spenser Nellis
Assistant Managing Editor – Jeff Whitman
Jim Salicrup
Editor-in-Chief

ISBN: 978-1-54580-140-6
Printed in China
March 2018

Papercutz books may be purchased for business or promotional use.
For information on bulk purchases, please contact Macmillan Corporate and Premium Sales Department at (800) 221-7945 x5442.

Distributed by Macmillan
First Papercutz Printing

THE SECRET OF WHALE ISLAND

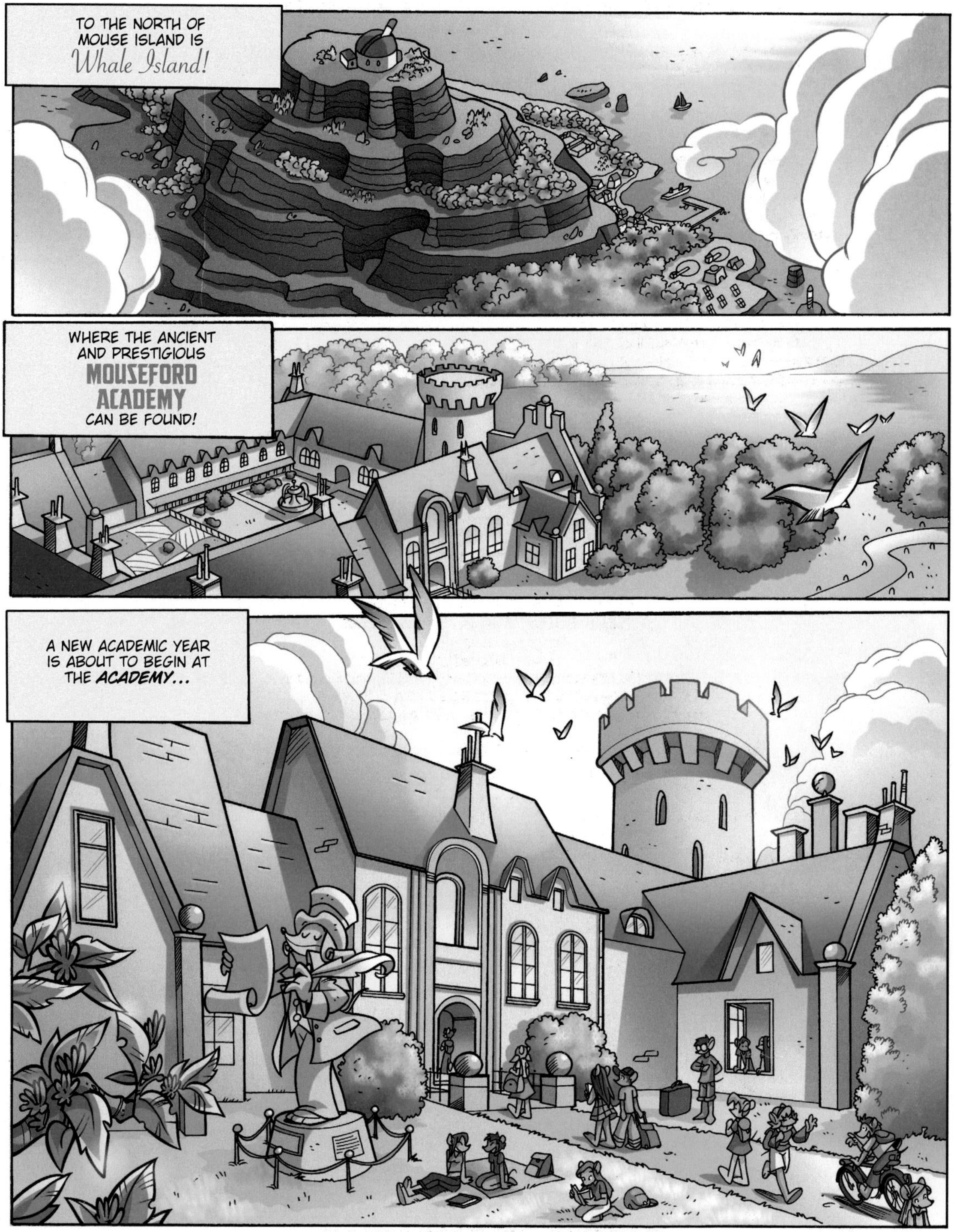

TO THE NORTH OF MOUSE ISLAND IS *Whale Island!*
WHERE THE ANCIENT AND PRESTIGIOUS **MOUSEFORD ACADEMY** CAN BE FOUND!
A NEW ACADEMIC YEAR IS ABOUT TO BEGIN AT THE ***ACADEMY...***

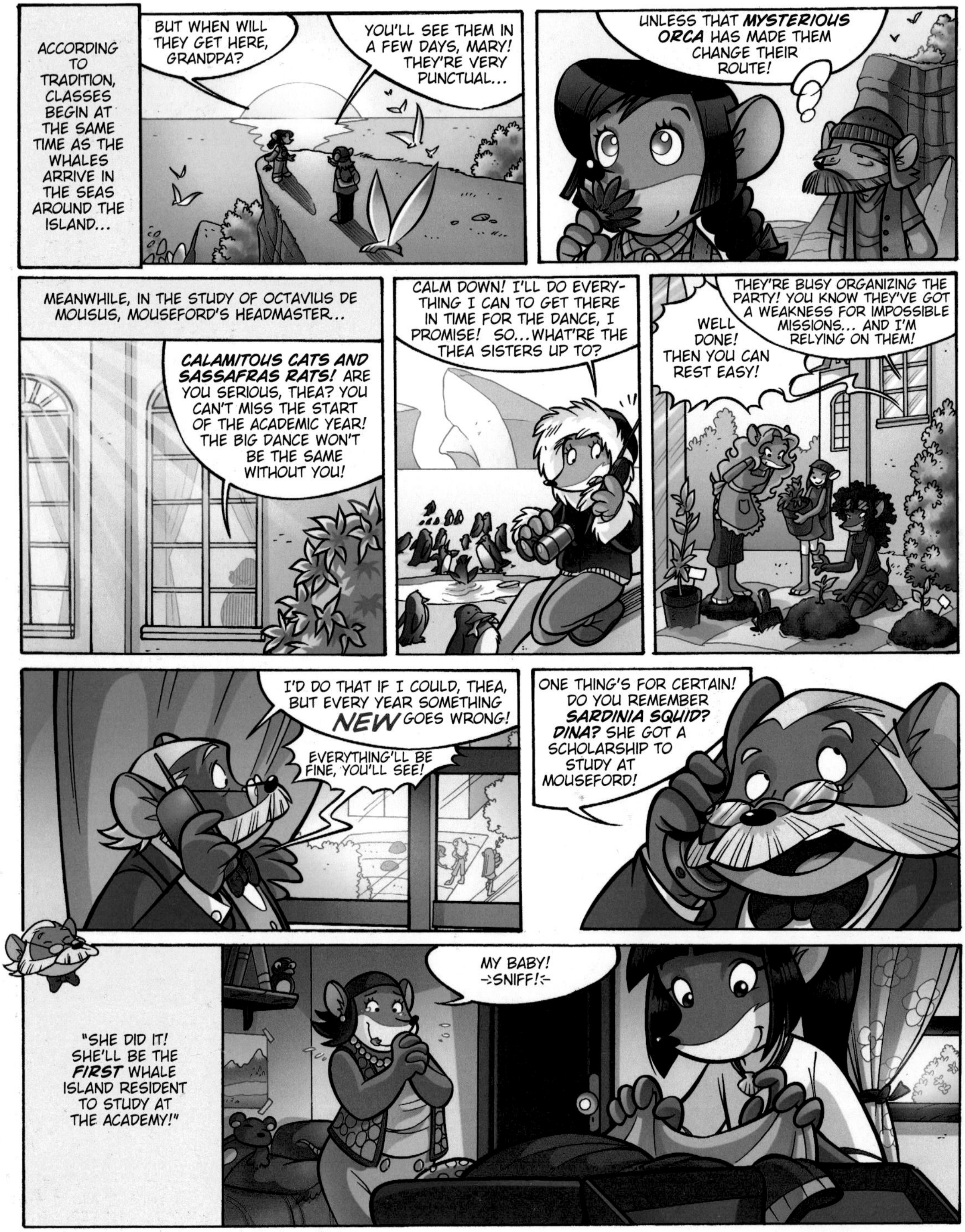
ACCORDING TO TRADITION, CLASSES BEGIN AT THE SAME TIME AS THE WHALES ARRIVE IN THE SEAS AROUND THE ISLAND...
BUT WHEN WILL THEY GET HERE, GRANDPA?
YOU'LL SEE THEM IN A FEW DAYS, MARY! THEY'RE VERY PUNCTUAL...
UNLESS THAT MYSTERIOUS ORCA HAS MADE THEM CHANGE THEIR ROUTE!
MEANWHILE, IN THE STUDY OF OCTAVIUS DE MOUSUS, MOUSEFORD'S HEADMASTER...
CALAMITOUS CATS AND SASSAFRAS RATS! ARE YOU SERIOUS, THEA? YOU CAN'T MISS THE START OF THE ACADEMIC YEAR! THE BIG DANCE WON'T BE THE SAME WITHOUT YOU!
CALM DOWN! I'LL DO EVERY-THING I CAN TO GET THERE IN TIME FOR THE DANCE, I PROMISE! SO...WHAT'RE THE THEA SISTERS UP TO?
THEY'RE BUSY ORGANIZING THE PARTY! YOU KNOW THEY'VE GOT A WEAKNESS FOR IMPOSSIBLE MISSIONS... AND I'M RELYING ON THEM!
WELL DONE! THEN YOU CAN REST EASY!
I'D DO THAT IF I COULD, THEA, BUT EVERY YEAR SOMETHING NEW GOES WRONG!
EVERYTHING'LL BE FINE, YOU'LL SEE!
ONE THING'S FOR CERTAIN! DO YOU REMEMBER SARDINIA SQUID? DINA? SHE GOT A SCHOLARSHIP TO STUDY AT MOUSEFORD!
"SHE DID IT! SHE'LL BE THE FIRST WHALE ISLAND RESIDENT TO STUDY AT THE ACADEMY!"
MY BABY! -SNIFF!-

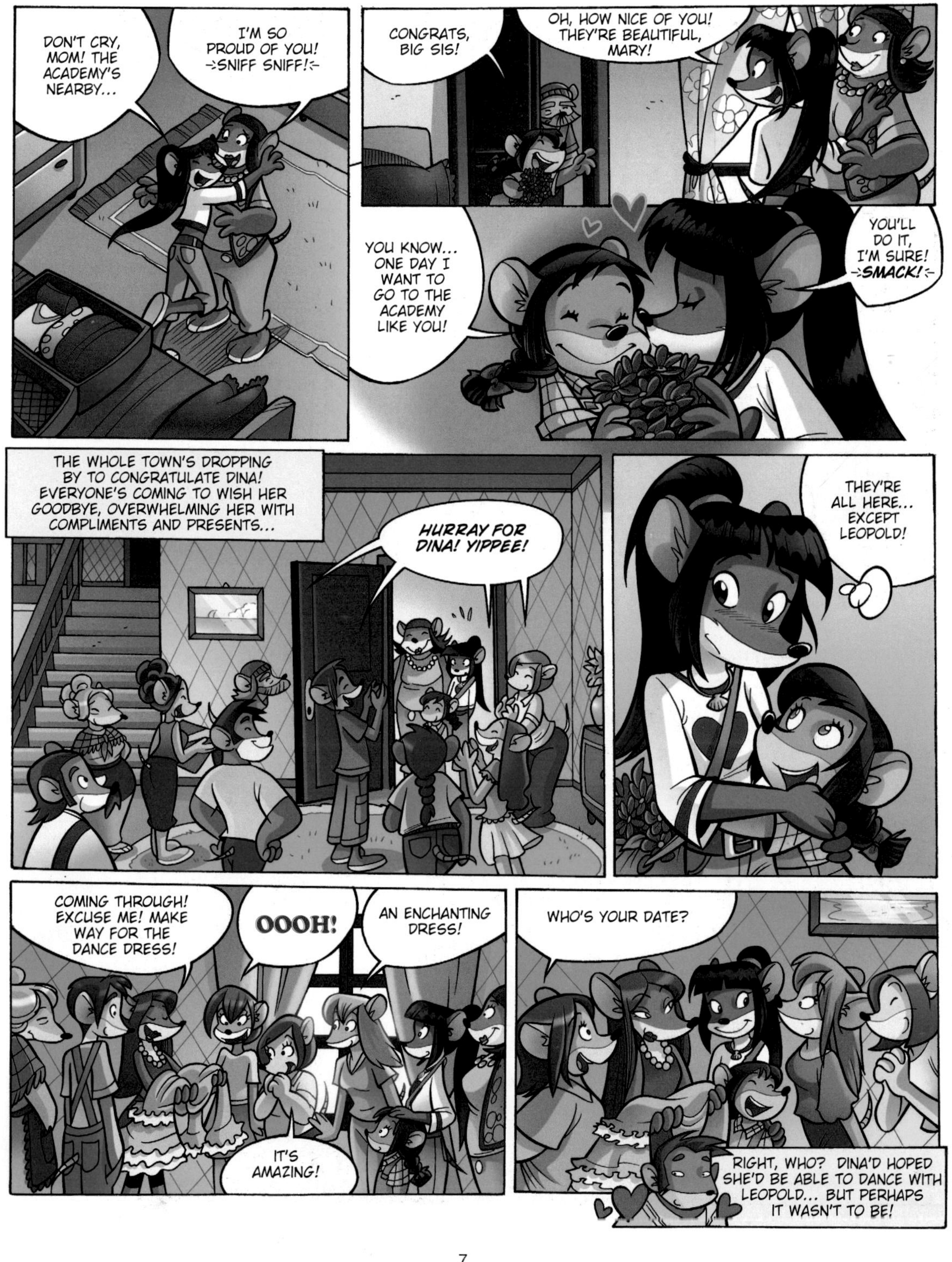

DON'T CRY, MOM! THE ACADEMY'S NEARBY...
I'M SO PROUD OF YOU! -SNIFF SNIFF!-
CONGRATS, BIG SIS!
OH, HOW NICE OF YOU! THEY'RE BEAUTIFUL, MARY!
YOU KNOW... ONE DAY I WANT TO GO TO THE ACADEMY LIKE YOU!
YOU'LL DO IT, I'M SURE! -SMACK!-
THE WHOLE TOWN'S DROPPING BY TO CONGRATULATE DINA! EVERYONE'S COMING TO WISH HER GOODBYE, OVERWHELMING HER WITH COMPLIMENTS AND PRESENTS...
HURRAY FOR DINA! YIPPEE!
THEY'RE ALL HERE... EXCEPT LEOPOLD!
COMING THROUGH! EXCUSE ME! MAKE WAY FOR THE DANCE DRESS!
OOOH!
AN ENCHANTING DRESS!
IT'S AMAZING!
WHO'S YOUR DATE?
RIGHT, WHO? DINA'D HOPED SHE'D BE ABLE TO DANCE WITH LEOPOLD... BUT PERHAPS IT WASN'T TO BE!

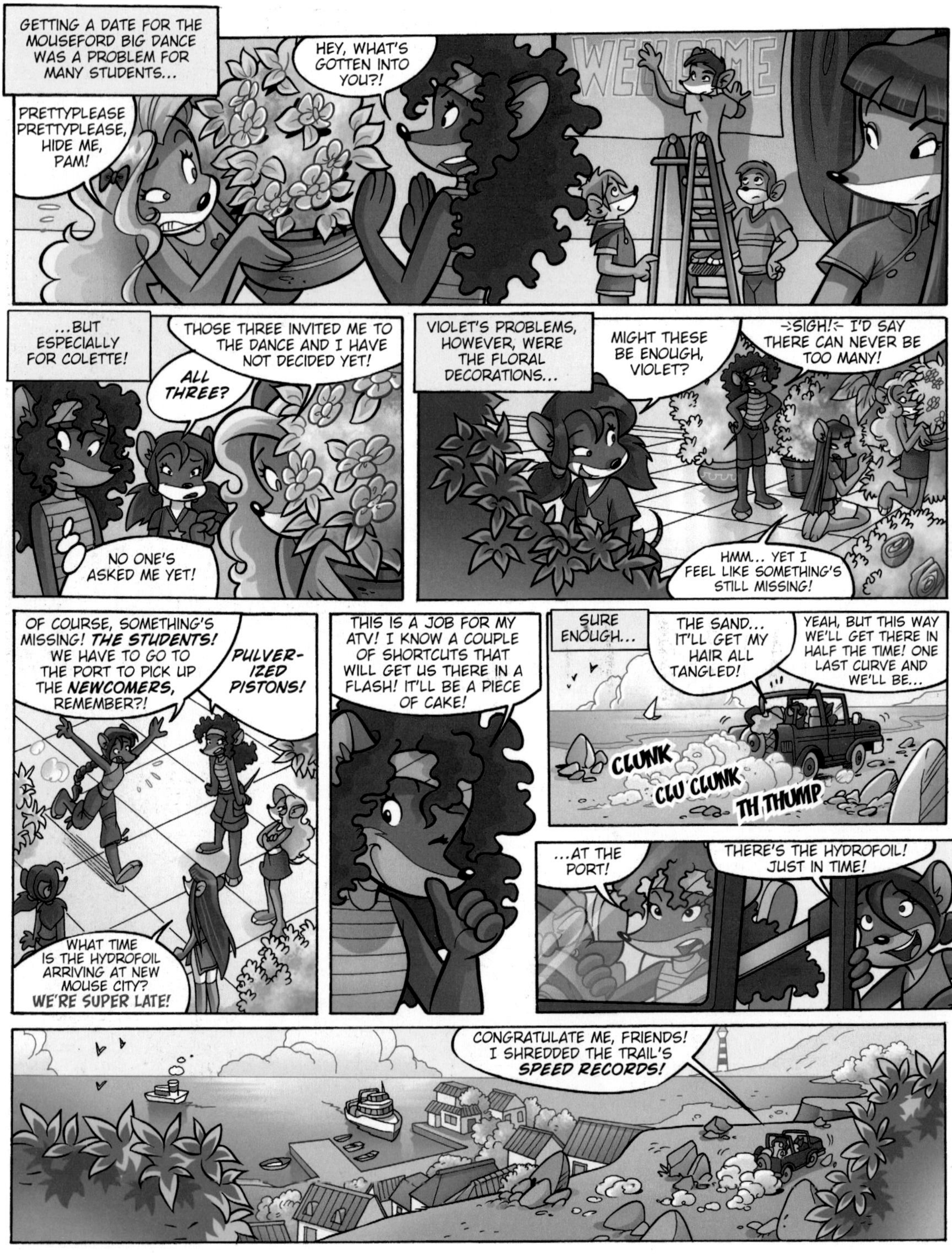
GETTING A DATE FOR THE MOUSEFORD BIG DANCE WAS A PROBLEM FOR MANY STUDENTS...
PRETTYPLEASE PRETTYPLEASE, HIDE ME, PAM!
HEY, WHAT'S GOTTEN INTO YOU?!
WELCOME
...BUT ESPECIALLY FOR COLETTE!
THOSE THREE INVITED ME TO THE DANCE AND I HAVE NOT DECIDED YET!
ALL THREE?
NO ONE'S ASKED ME YET!
VIOLET'S PROBLEMS, HOWEVER, WERE THE FLORAL DECORATIONS...
MIGHT THESE BE ENOUGH, VIOLET?
-SIGH!- I'D SAY THERE CAN NEVER BE TOO MANY!
HMM... YET I FEEL LIKE SOMETHING'S STILL MISSING!
OF COURSE, SOMETHING'S MISSING! THE STUDENTS! WE HAVE TO GO TO THE PORT TO PICK UP THE NEWCOMERS, REMEMBER?!
PULVERIZED PISTONS!
WHAT TIME IS THE HYDROFOIL ARRIVING AT NEW MOUSE CITY? WE'RE SUPER LATE!
THIS IS A JOB FOR MY ATV! I KNOW A COUPLE OF SHORTCUTS THAT WILL GET US THERE IN A FLASH! IT'LL BE A PIECE OF CAKE!
SURE ENOUGH...
THE SAND... IT'LL GET MY HAIR ALL TANGLED!
YEAH, BUT THIS WAY WE'LL GET THERE IN HALF THE TIME! ONE LAST CURVE AND WE'LL BE...
CLUNK
CLU CLUNK
TH THUMP
...AT THE PORT!
THERE'S THE HYDROFOIL! JUST IN TIME!
CONGRATULATE ME, FRIENDS! I SHREDDED THE TRAIL'S SPEED RECORDS!

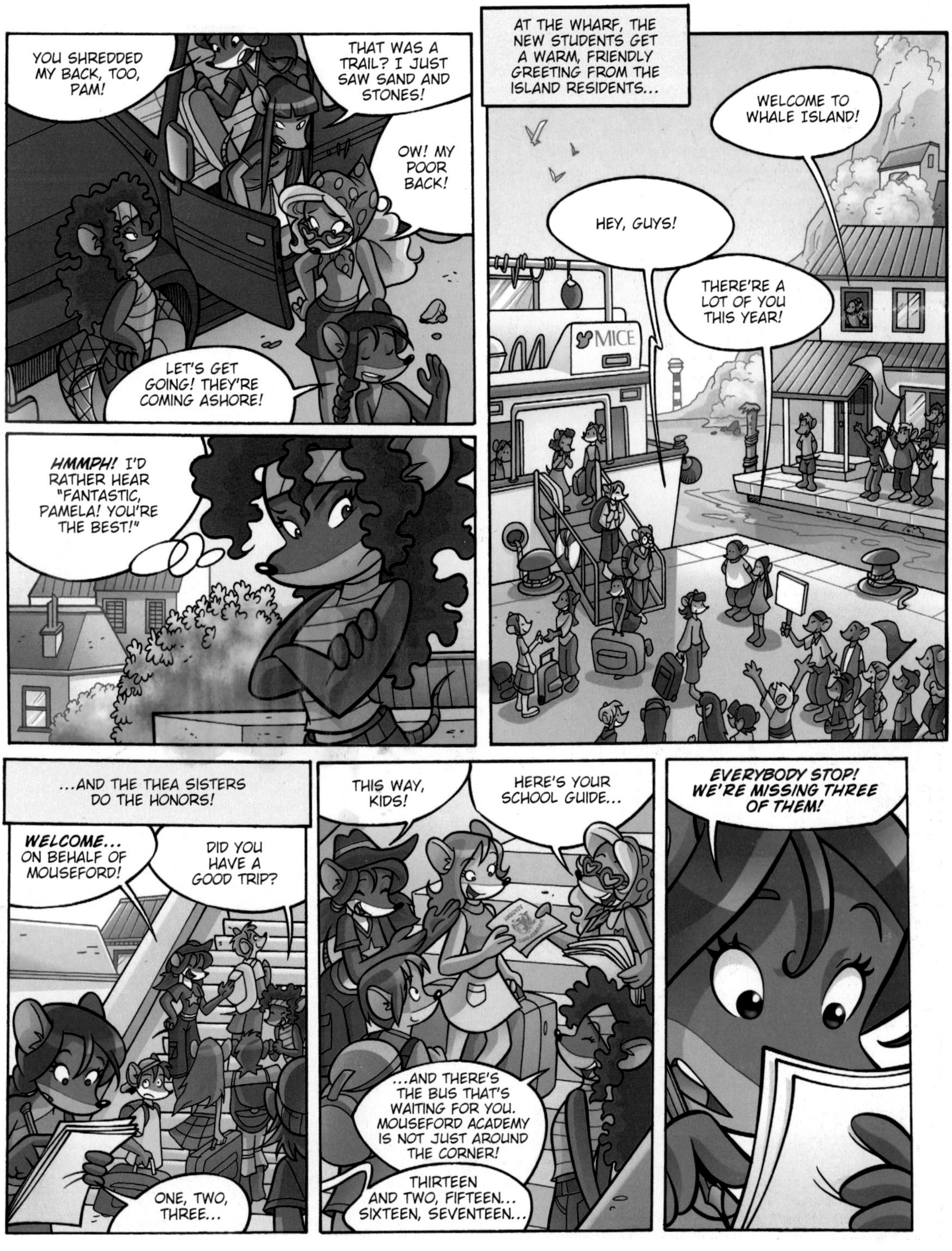
YOU SHREDDED MY BACK, TOO, PAM!
THAT WAS A TRAIL? I JUST SAW SAND AND STONES!
OW! MY POOR BACK!
LET'S GET GOING! THEY'RE COMING ASHORE!
AT THE WHARF, THE NEW STUDENTS GET A WARM, FRIENDLY GREETING FROM THE ISLAND RESIDENTS...
WELCOME TO WHALE ISLAND!
HEY, GUYS!
THERE'RE A LOT OF YOU THIS YEAR!
MICE
HMMPH! I'D RATHER HEAR "FANTASTIC, PAMELA! YOU'RE THE BEST!"
...AND THE THEA SISTERS DO THE HONORS!
WELCOME... ON BEHALF OF MOUSEFORD!
DID YOU HAVE A GOOD TRIP?
ONE, TWO, THREE...
THIS WAY, KIDS!
HERE'S YOUR SCHOOL GUIDE...
...AND THERE'S THE BUS THAT'S WAITING FOR YOU. MOUSEFORD ACADEMY IS NOT JUST AROUND THE CORNER!
THIRTEEN AND TWO, FIFTEEN... SIXTEEN, SEVENTEEN...
EVERYBODY STOP! WE'RE MISSING THREE OF THEM!

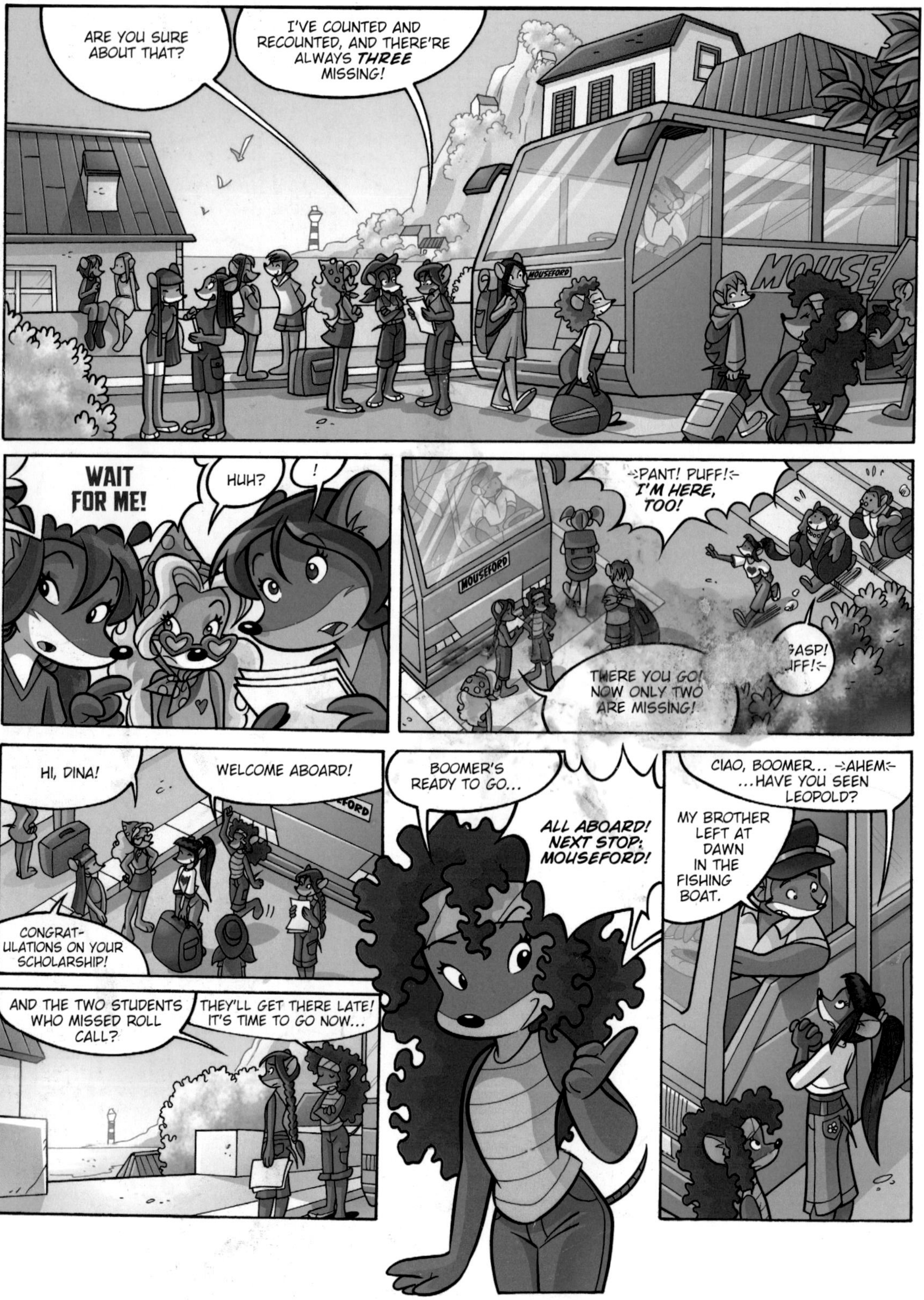

ARE YOU SURE ABOUT THAT?
I'VE COUNTED AND RECOUNTED, AND THERE'RE ALWAYS THREE MISSING!
MOUSEFORD
MOUSE
WAIT FOR ME!
HUH?
!
–PANT! PUFF!– I'M HERE, TOO!
MOUSEFORD
–GASP! PUFF!–
THERE YOU GO! NOW ONLY TWO ARE MISSING!
HI, DINA!
WELCOME ABOARD!
CONGRAT-ULATIONS ON YOUR SCHOLARSHIP!
BOOMER'S READY TO GO...
ALL ABOARD! NEXT STOP: MOUSEFORD!
CIAO, BOOMER... –AHEM– ...HAVE YOU SEEN LEOPOLD?
MY BROTHER LEFT AT DAWN IN THE FISHING BOAT.
AND THE TWO STUDENTS WHO MISSED ROLL CALL?
THEY'LL GET THERE LATE! IT'S TIME TO GO NOW...

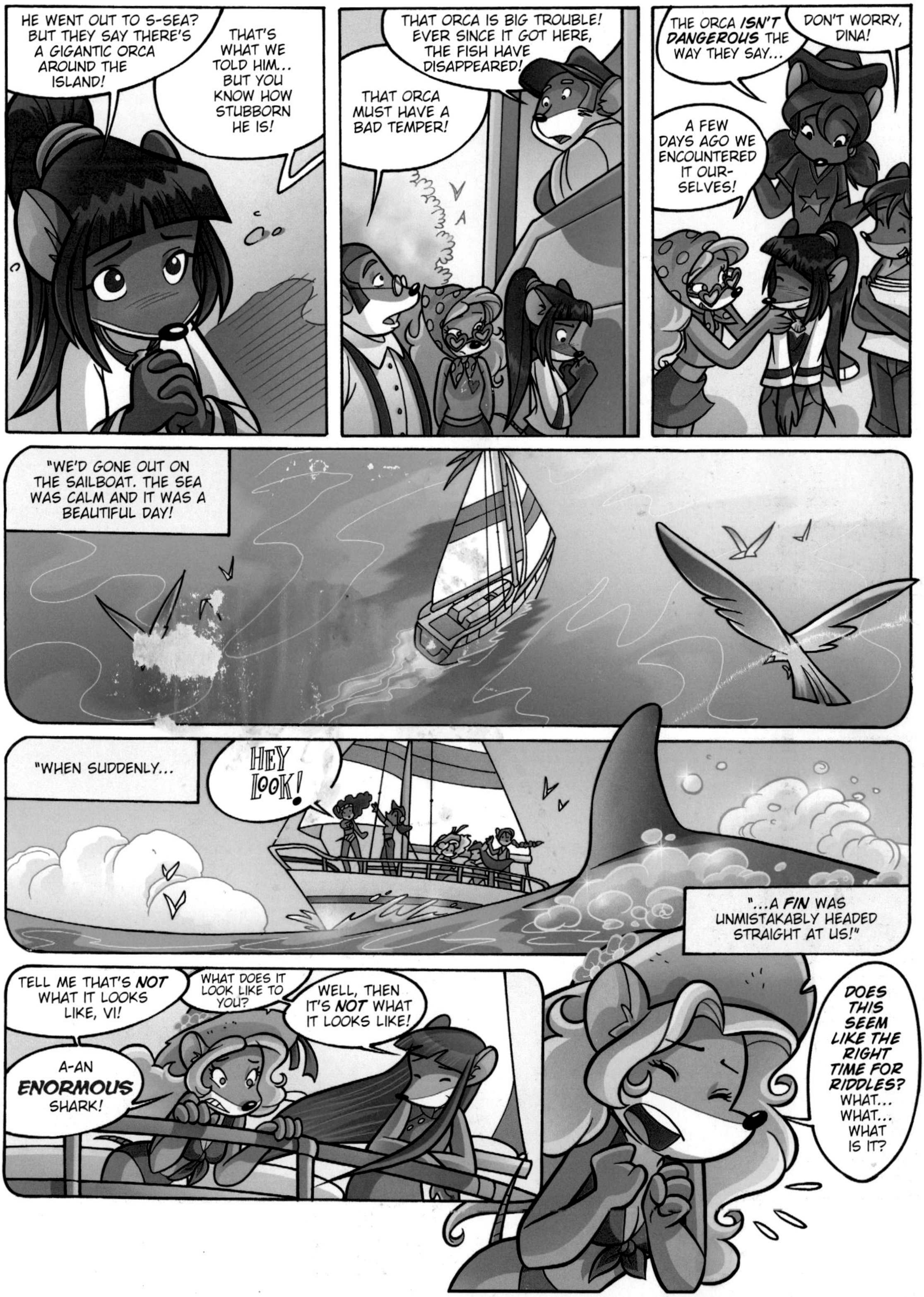

HE WENT OUT TO S-SEA? BUT THEY SAY THERE'S A GIGANTIC ORCA AROUND THE ISLAND!
THAT'S WHAT WE TOLD HIM... BUT YOU KNOW HOW STUBBORN HE IS!
THAT ORCA IS BIG TROUBLE! EVER SINCE IT GOT HERE, THE FISH HAVE DISAPPEARED!
THAT ORCA MUST HAVE A BAD TEMPER!
THE ORCA ISN'T DANGEROUS THE WAY THEY SAY...
DON'T WORRY, DINA!
A FEW DAYS AGO WE ENCOUNTERED IT OURSELVES!
"WE'D GONE OUT ON THE SAILBOAT. THE SEA WAS CALM AND IT WAS A BEAUTIFUL DAY!
"WHEN SUDDENLY...
HEY LOOK!
"...A FIN WAS UNMISTAKABLY HEADED STRAIGHT AT US!"
TELL ME THAT'S NOT WHAT IT LOOKS LIKE, VI!
WHAT DOES IT LOOK LIKE TO YOU?
WELL, THEN IT'S NOT WHAT IT LOOKS LIKE!
A-AN ENORMOUS SHARK!
DOES THIS SEEM LIKE THE RIGHT TIME FOR RIDDLES? WHAT... WHAT... WHAT IS IT?

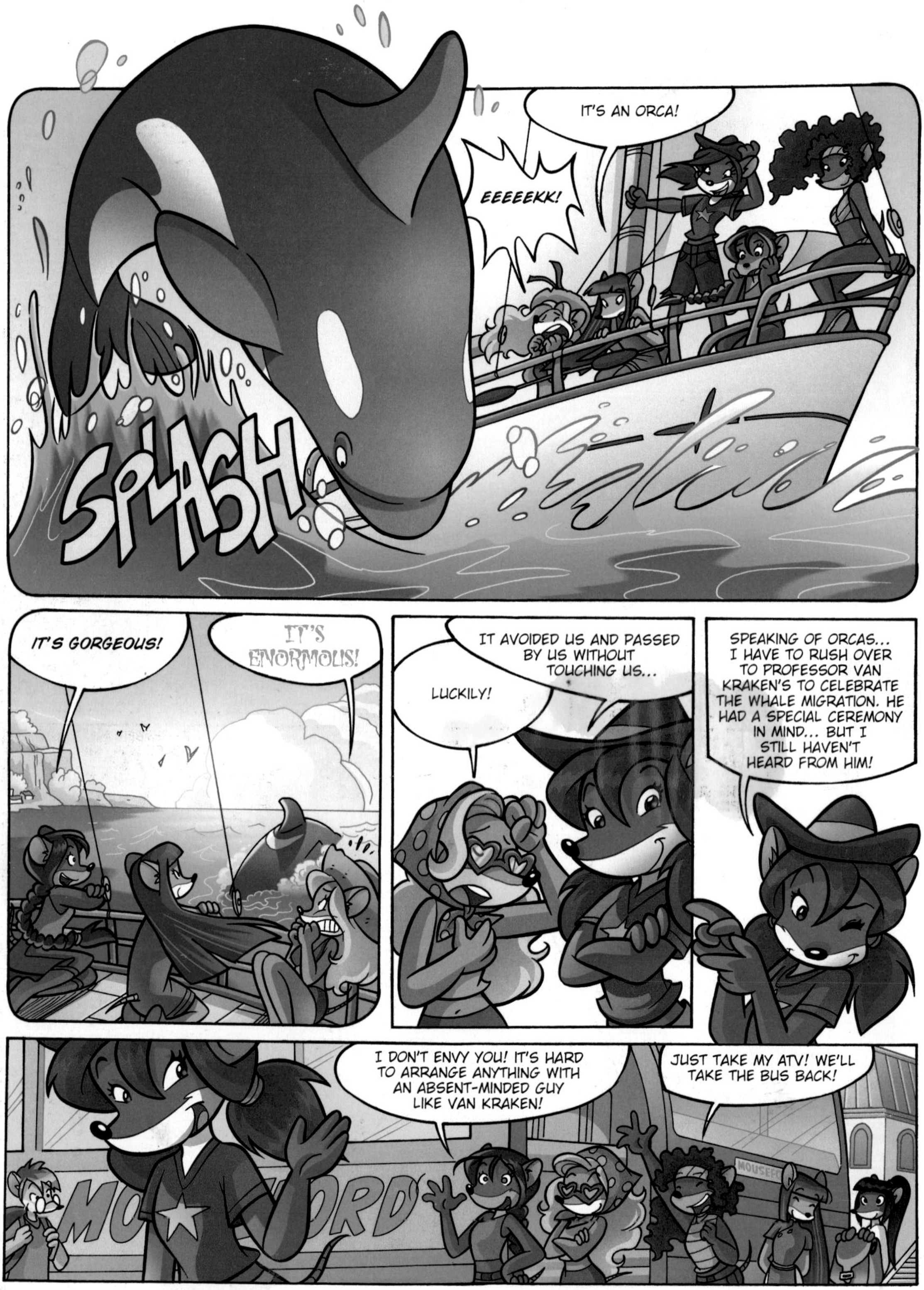
IT'S AN ORCA!
EEEEEKK!
SPLASH
IT'S GORGEOUS!
IT'S ENORMOUS!
IT AVOIDED US AND PASSED BY US WITHOUT TOUCHING US...
LUCKILY!
SPEAKING OF ORCAS... I HAVE TO RUSH OVER TO PROFESSOR VAN KRAKEN'S TO CELEBRATE THE WHALE MIGRATION. HE HAD A SPECIAL CEREMONY IN MIND... BUT I STILL HAVEN'T HEARD FROM HIM!
I DON'T ENVY YOU! IT'S HARD TO ARRANGE ANYTHING WITH AN ABSENT-MINDED GUY LIKE VAN KRAKEN!
JUST TAKE MY ATV! WE'LL TAKE THE BUS BACK!

THE MARINE BIOLOGY LAB IS THE UNDISPUTED REALM OF PROFESSOR IAN VAN KRAKEN.

I HOPE THE PROFESSOR'LL HAVE A DEFINITE PLAN IN MIND!

BUT TO ALL APPEARANCES, THE PROFESSOR HAS SOMETHING ELSE TO THINK ABOUT!

...LET'S JUST TAKE A LOOK... INSERT OBJECT A1 INTO SUPPORT Y23...

⇒GASP!⇐ BUT-- BUT WHAT HAPPENED IN HERE?

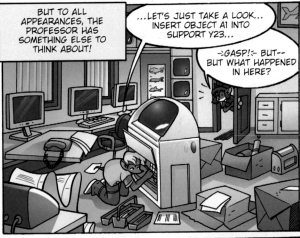

HEY, THERE! ISN'T THIS WONDERFUL? THIS IS THE **NEWEST EQUIPMENT**, COURTESY OF DE VISSEN, INC.!

?!

WHAT BRINGS YOU OVER HERE, NICKY?

THE CEREMONY, PROFESSOR! THERE'S NOT MUCH TIME LEFT!

THE CEREMONY? OH, *THE CEREMONY*--BUT, OF COURSE! I WAS JUST WORKING ON IT!

RIGHT... BEFORE THE NEW "TOYS" ARRIVED!

I REMEMBER THERE WAS A PROBLEM WITH THE WHALES' ROUTE! I WAS ABOUT TO GO OUT INTO THE SEA IN THE BATHYSCAPHE WHEN...

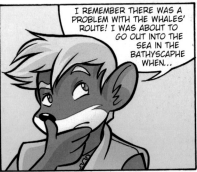

WAP

...WHEN THE TRUCK WITH THE BOXES OF EQUIPMENT CAME!

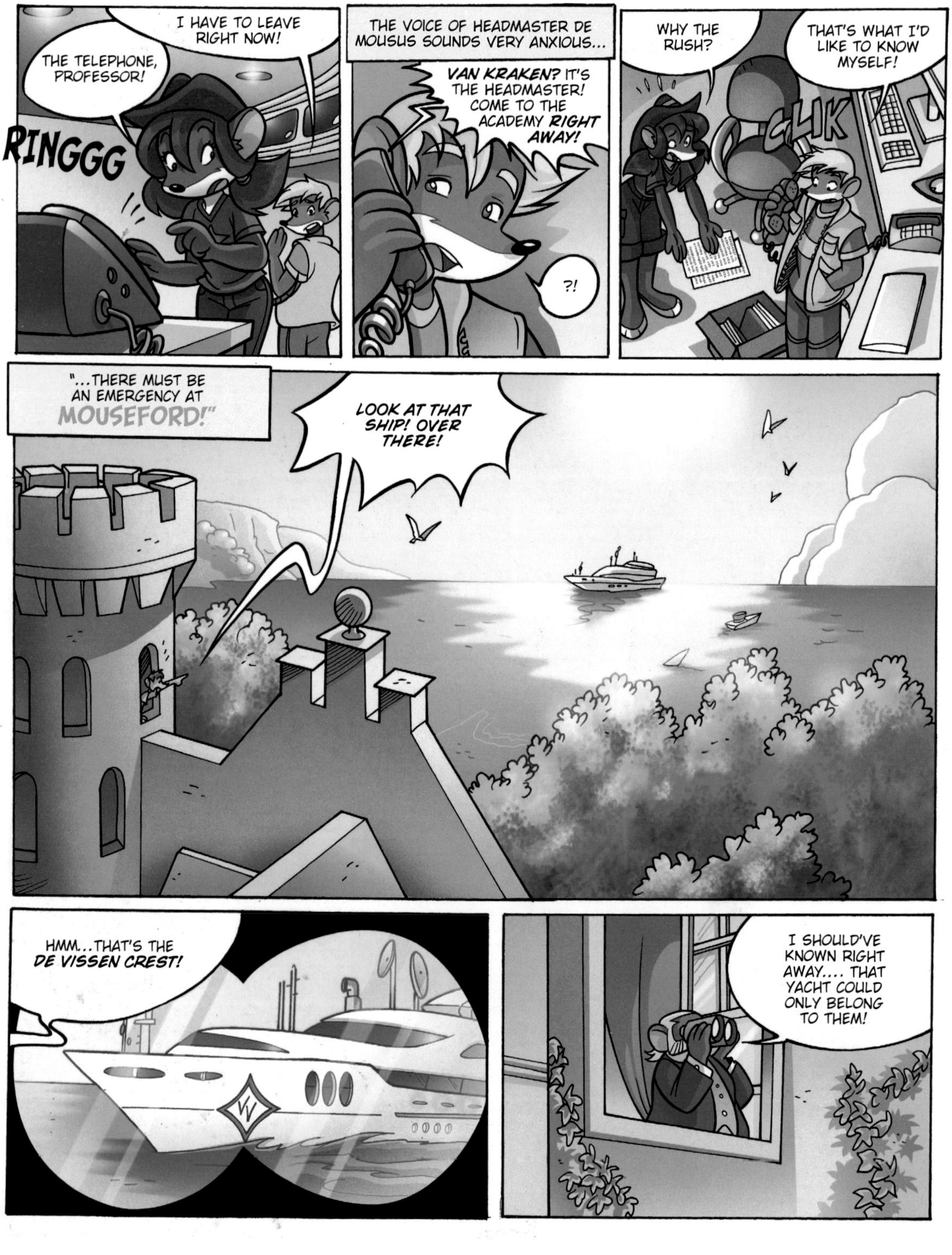

THE TELEPHONE, PROFESSOR!
RINGGG
I HAVE TO LEAVE RIGHT NOW!
THE VOICE OF HEADMASTER DE MOUSUS SOUNDS VERY ANXIOUS...
VAN KRAKEN? IT'S THE HEADMASTER! COME TO THE ACADEMY RIGHT AWAY!
?!
WHY THE RUSH?
THAT'S WHAT I'D LIKE TO KNOW MYSELF!
CLIK
"...THERE MUST BE AN EMERGENCY AT MOUSEFORD!"
LOOK AT THAT SHIP! OVER THERE!
HMM...THAT'S THE DE VISSEN CREST!
I SHOULD'VE KNOWN RIGHT AWAY.... THAT YACHT COULD ONLY BELONG TO THEM!

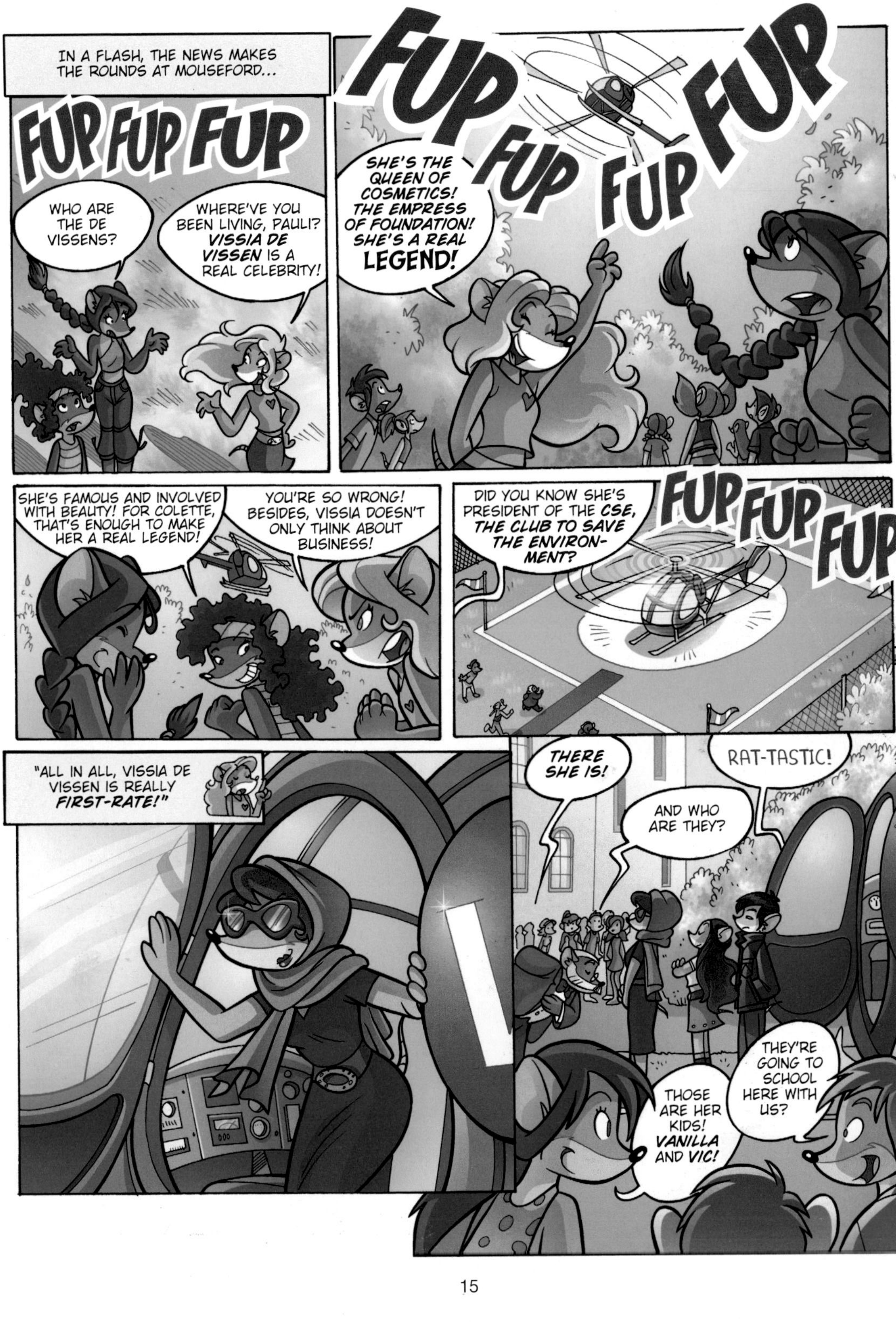

IN A FLASH, THE NEWS MAKES THE ROUNDS AT MOUSEFORD...
FUP FUP FUP
WHO ARE THE DE VISSENS?
WHERE'VE YOU BEEN LIVING, PAULI? VISSIA DE VISSEN IS A REAL CELEBRITY!
FUP FUP FUP FUP
SHE'S THE QUEEN OF COSMETICS! THE EMPRESS OF FOUNDATION! SHE'S A REAL LEGEND!
SHE'S FAMOUS AND INVOLVED WITH BEAUTY! FOR COLETTE, THAT'S ENOUGH TO MAKE HER A REAL LEGEND!
YOU'RE SO WRONG! BESIDES, VISSIA DOESN'T ONLY THINK ABOUT BUSINESS!
DID YOU KNOW SHE'S PRESIDENT OF THE CSE, THE CLUB TO SAVE THE ENVIRONMENT?
FUP FUP FUP
"ALL IN ALL, VISSIA DE VISSEN IS REALLY FIRST-RATE!"
THERE SHE IS!
RAT-TASTIC!
AND WHO ARE THEY?
THEY'RE GOING TO SCHOOL HERE WITH US?
THOSE ARE HER KIDS! VANILLA AND VIC!

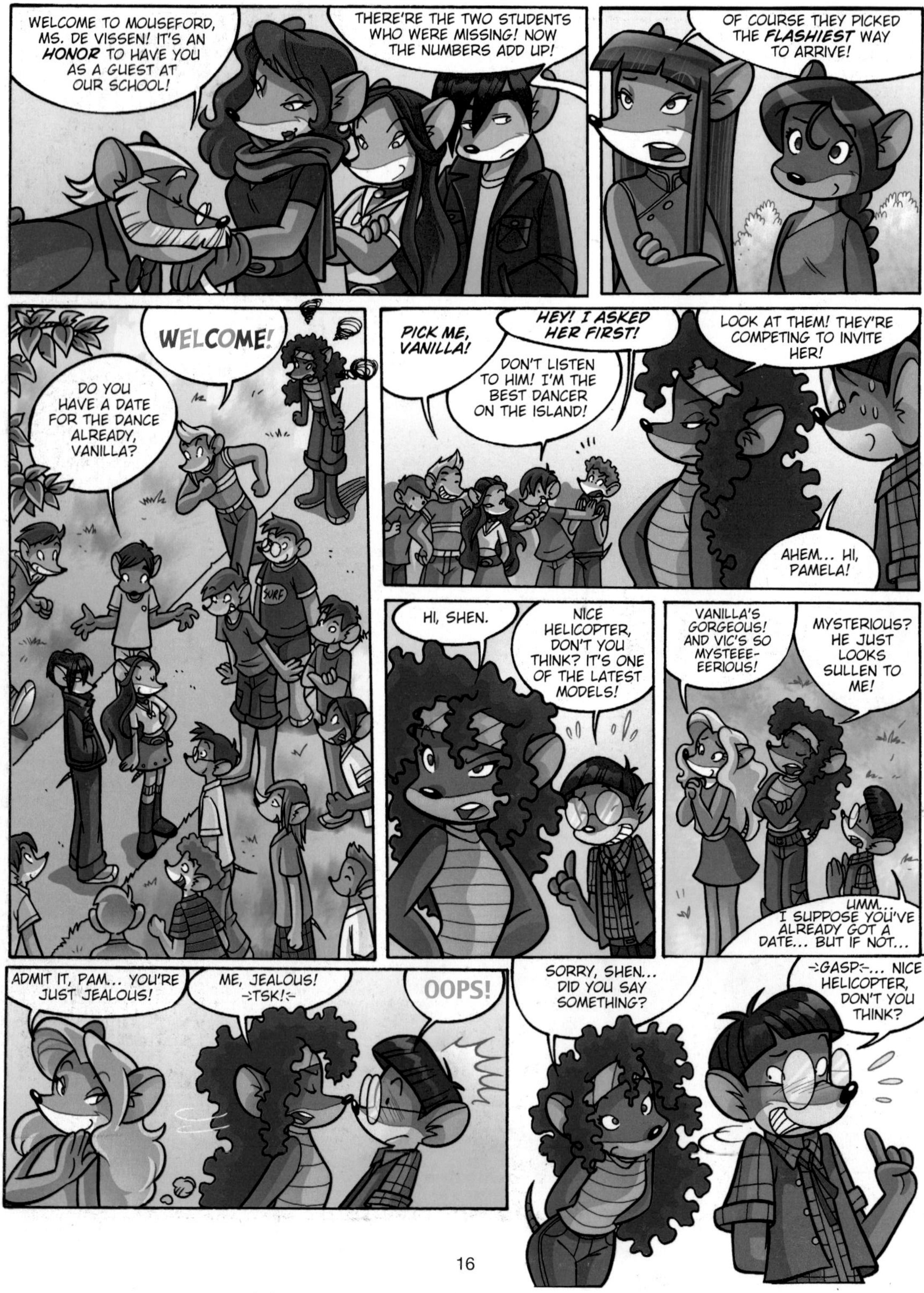

WELCOME TO MOUSEFORD, MS. DE VISSEN! IT'S AN **HONOR** TO HAVE YOU AS A GUEST AT OUR SCHOOL!
THERE'RE THE TWO STUDENTS WHO WERE MISSING! NOW THE NUMBERS ADD UP!
OF COURSE THEY PICKED THE ***FLASHIEST*** WAY TO ARRIVE!
WELCOME!
DO YOU HAVE A DATE FOR THE DANCE ALREADY, VANILLA?
PICK ME, VANILLA!
HEY! I ASKED HER FIRST!
DON'T LISTEN TO HIM! I'M THE BEST DANCER ON THE ISLAND!
LOOK AT THEM! THEY'RE COMPETING TO INVITE HER!
AHEM... HI, PAMELA!
HI, SHEN.
NICE HELICOPTER, DON'T YOU THINK? IT'S ONE OF THE LATEST MODELS!
VANILLA'S GORGEOUS! AND VIC'S SO MYSTEEE-EERIOUS!
MYSTERIOUS? HE JUST LOOKS SULLEN TO ME!
UMM... I SUPPOSE YOU'VE ALREADY GOT A DATE... BUT IF NOT...
ADMIT IT, PAM... YOU'RE JUST JEALOUS!
ME, JEALOUS! -TSK!-
OOPS!
SORRY, SHEN... DID YOU SAY SOMETHING?
-GASP-... NICE HELICOPTER, DON'T YOU THINK?

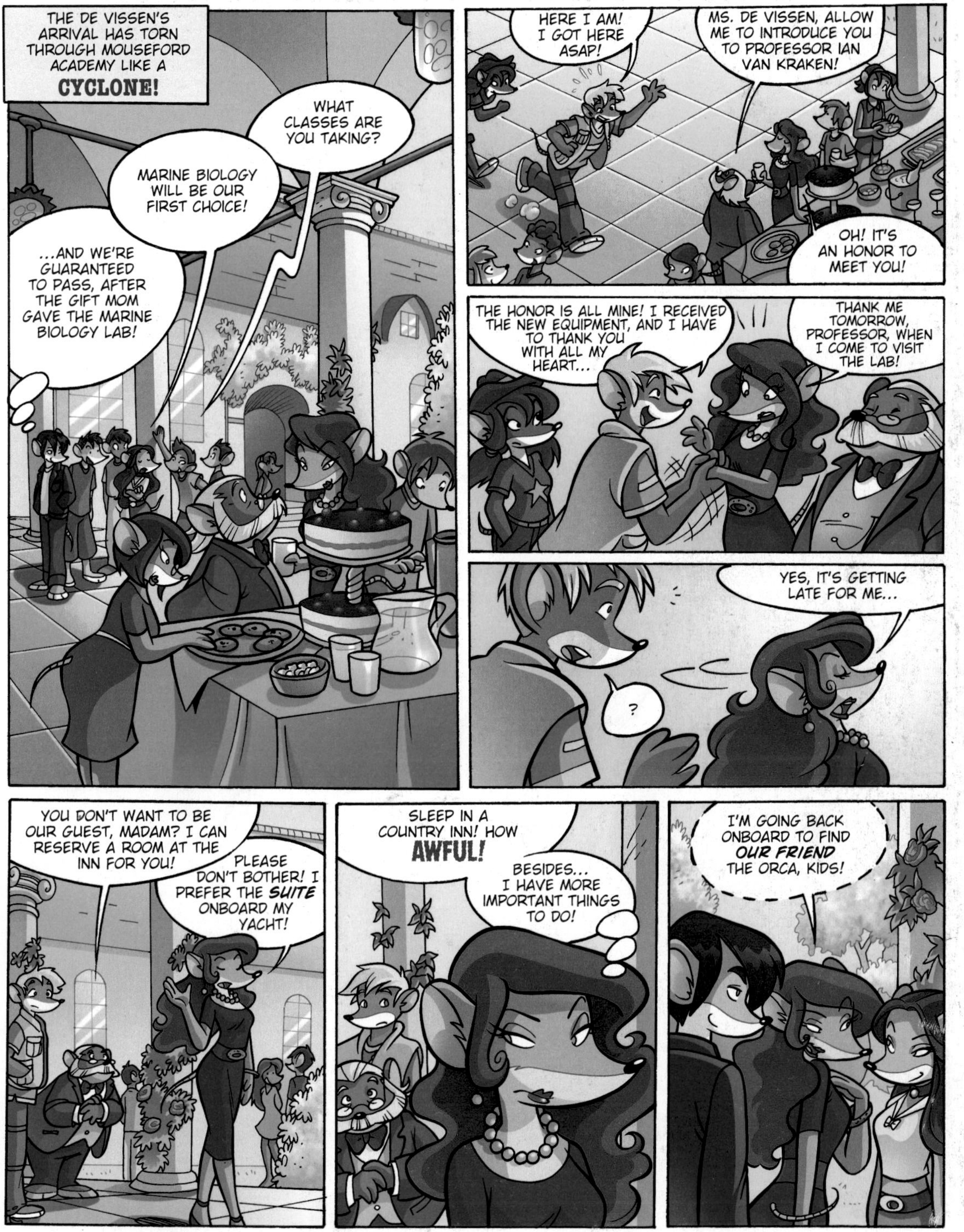
THE DE VISSEN'S ARRIVAL HAS TORN THROUGH MOUSEFORD ACADEMY LIKE A CYCLONE!
WHAT CLASSES ARE YOU TAKING?
MARINE BIOLOGY WILL BE OUR FIRST CHOICE!
...AND WE'RE GUARANTEED TO PASS, AFTER THE GIFT MOM GAVE THE MARINE BIOLOGY LAB!
HERE I AM! I GOT HERE ASAP!
MS. DE VISSEN, ALLOW ME TO INTRODUCE YOU TO PROFESSOR IAN VAN KRAKEN!
OH! IT'S AN HONOR TO MEET YOU!
THE HONOR IS ALL MINE! I RECEIVED THE NEW EQUIPMENT, AND I HAVE TO THANK YOU WITH ALL MY HEART...
THANK ME TOMORROW, PROFESSOR, WHEN I COME TO VISIT THE LAB!
YES, IT'S GETTING LATE FOR ME...
?
YOU DON'T WANT TO BE OUR GUEST, MADAM? I CAN RESERVE A ROOM AT THE INN FOR YOU!
PLEASE DON'T BOTHER! I PREFER THE SUITE ONBOARD MY YACHT!
SLEEP IN A COUNTRY INN! HOW AWFUL!
BESIDES... I HAVE MORE IMPORTANT THINGS TO DO!
I'M GOING BACK ONBOARD TO FIND OUR FRIEND THE ORCA, KIDS!

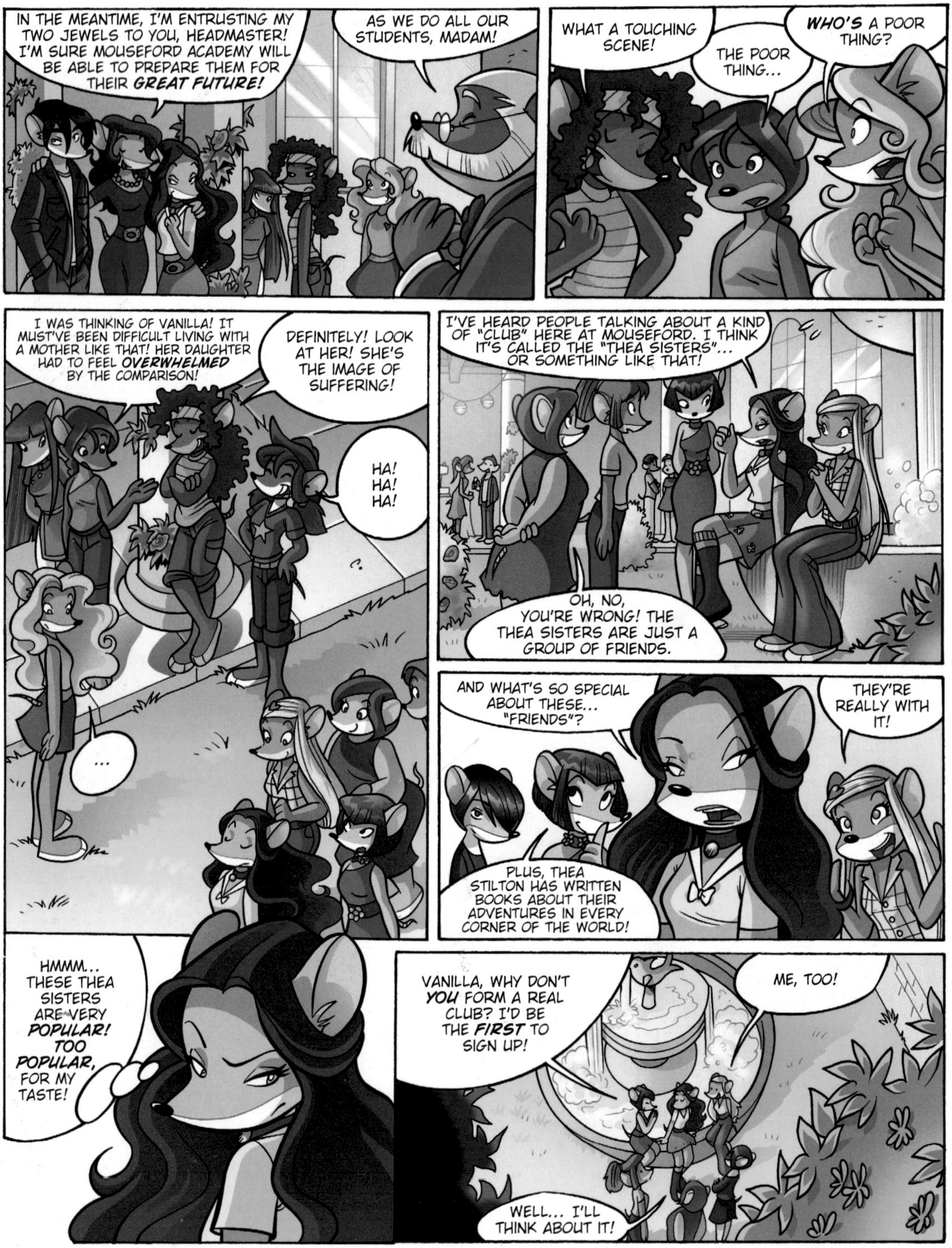

IN THE MEANTIME, I'M ENTRUSTING MY TWO JEWELS TO YOU, HEADMASTER! I'M SURE MOUSEFORD ACADEMY WILL BE ABLE TO PREPARE THEM FOR THEIR GREAT FUTURE!
AS WE DO ALL OUR STUDENTS, MADAM!
WHAT A TOUCHING SCENE!
THE POOR THING...
WHO'S A POOR THING?
I WAS THINKING OF VANILLA! IT MUST'VE BEEN DIFFICULT LIVING WITH A MOTHER LIKE THAT! HER DAUGHTER HAD TO FEEL OVERWHELMED BY THE COMPARISON!
DEFINITELY! LOOK AT HER! SHE'S THE IMAGE OF SUFFERING!
HA! HA! HA!
...
I'VE HEARD PEOPLE TALKING ABOUT A KIND OF "CLUB" HERE AT MOUSEFORD. I THINK IT'S CALLED THE "THEA SISTERS"... OR SOMETHING LIKE THAT!
OH, NO, YOU'RE WRONG! THE THEA SISTERS ARE JUST A GROUP OF FRIENDS.
AND WHAT'S SO SPECIAL ABOUT THESE... "FRIENDS"?
THEY'RE REALLY WITH IT!
PLUS, THEA STILTON HAS WRITTEN BOOKS ABOUT THEIR ADVENTURES IN EVERY CORNER OF THE WORLD!
HMMM... THESE THEA SISTERS ARE VERY POPULAR! TOO POPULAR, FOR MY TASTE!
VANILLA, WHY DON'T YOU FORM A REAL CLUB? I'D BE THE FIRST TO SIGN UP!
ME, TOO!
WELL... I'LL THINK ABOUT IT!

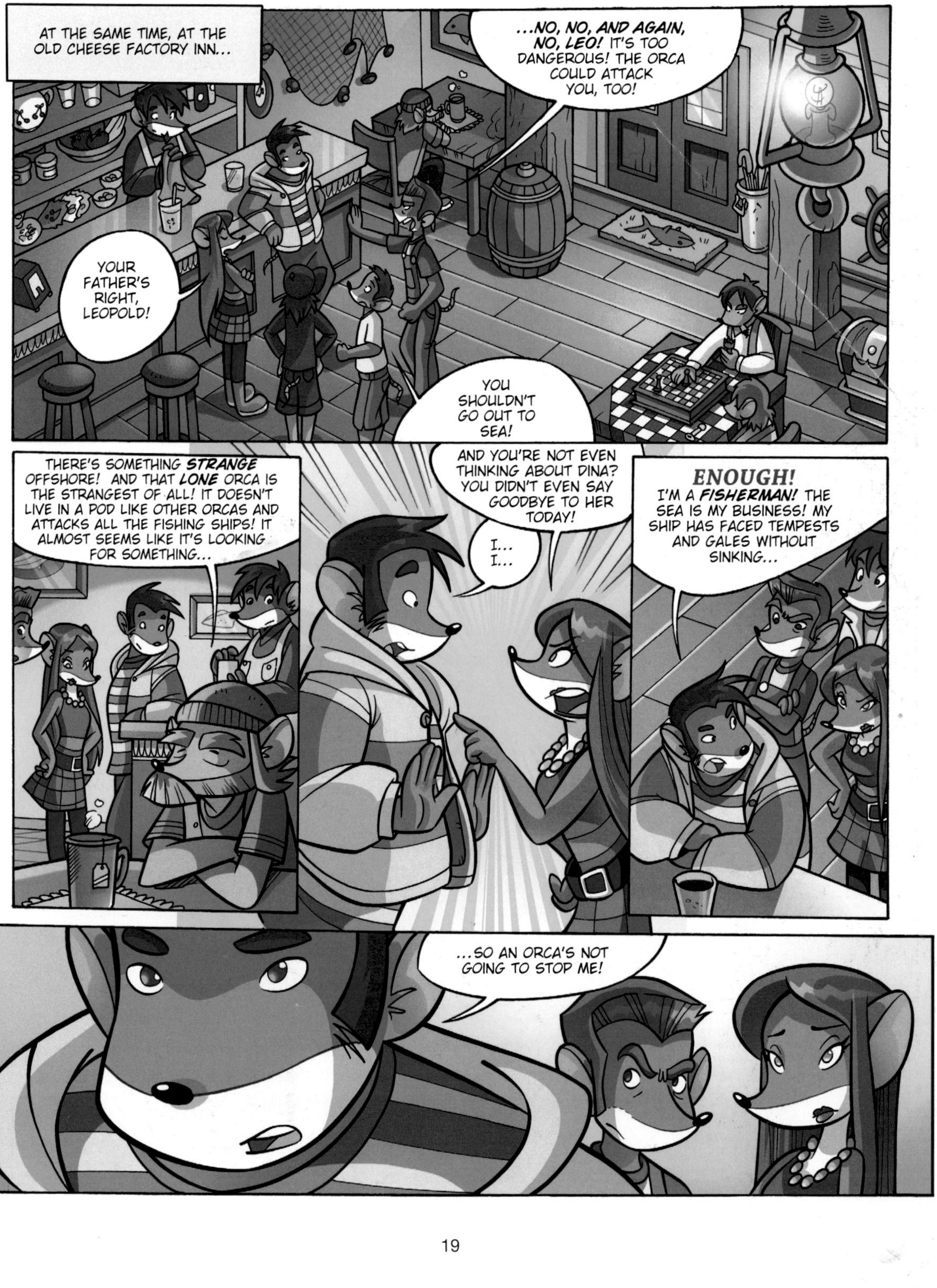

AT THE SAME TIME, AT THE OLD CHEESE FACTORY INN...
...NO, NO, AND AGAIN, NO, LEO! IT'S TOO DANGEROUS! THE ORCA COULD ATTACK YOU, TOO!
YOUR FATHER'S RIGHT, LEOPOLD!
YOU SHOULDN'T GO OUT TO SEA!
THERE'S SOMETHING STRANGE OFFSHORE! AND THAT LONE ORCA IS THE STRANGEST OF ALL! IT DOESN'T LIVE IN A POD LIKE OTHER ORCAS AND ATTACKS ALL THE FISHING SHIPS! IT ALMOST SEEMS LIKE IT'S LOOKING FOR SOMETHING...
AND YOU'RE NOT EVEN THINKING ABOUT DINA? YOU DIDN'T EVEN SAY GOODBYE TO HER TODAY!
I... I...
ENOUGH! I'M A FISHERMAN! THE SEA IS MY BUSINESS! MY SHIP HAS FACED TEMPESTS AND GALES WITHOUT SINKING...
...SO AN ORCA'S NOT GOING TO STOP ME!

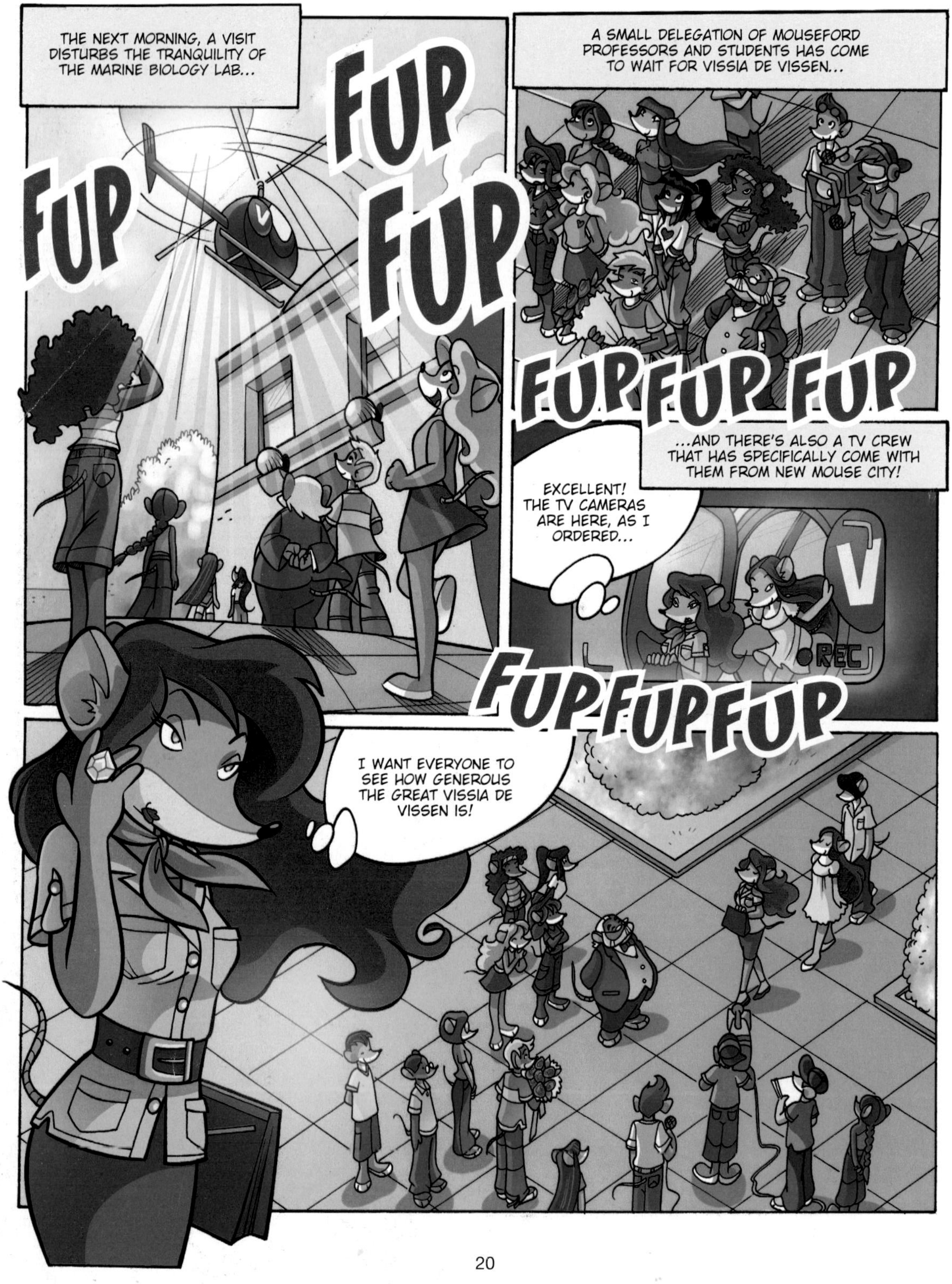
THE NEXT MORNING, A VISIT DISTURBS THE TRANQUILITY OF THE MARINE BIOLOGY LAB...
FUP
FUP
FUP
A SMALL DELEGATION OF MOUSEFORD PROFESSORS AND STUDENTS HAS COME TO WAIT FOR VISSIA DE VISSEN...
FUP FUP FUP
...AND THERE'S ALSO A TV CREW THAT HAS SPECIFICALLY COME WITH THEM FROM NEW MOUSE CITY!
EXCELLENT! THE TV CAMERAS ARE HERE, AS I ORDERED...
V
REC
FUP FUP FUP
I WANT EVERYONE TO SEE HOW GENEROUS THE GREAT VISSIA DE VISSEN IS!

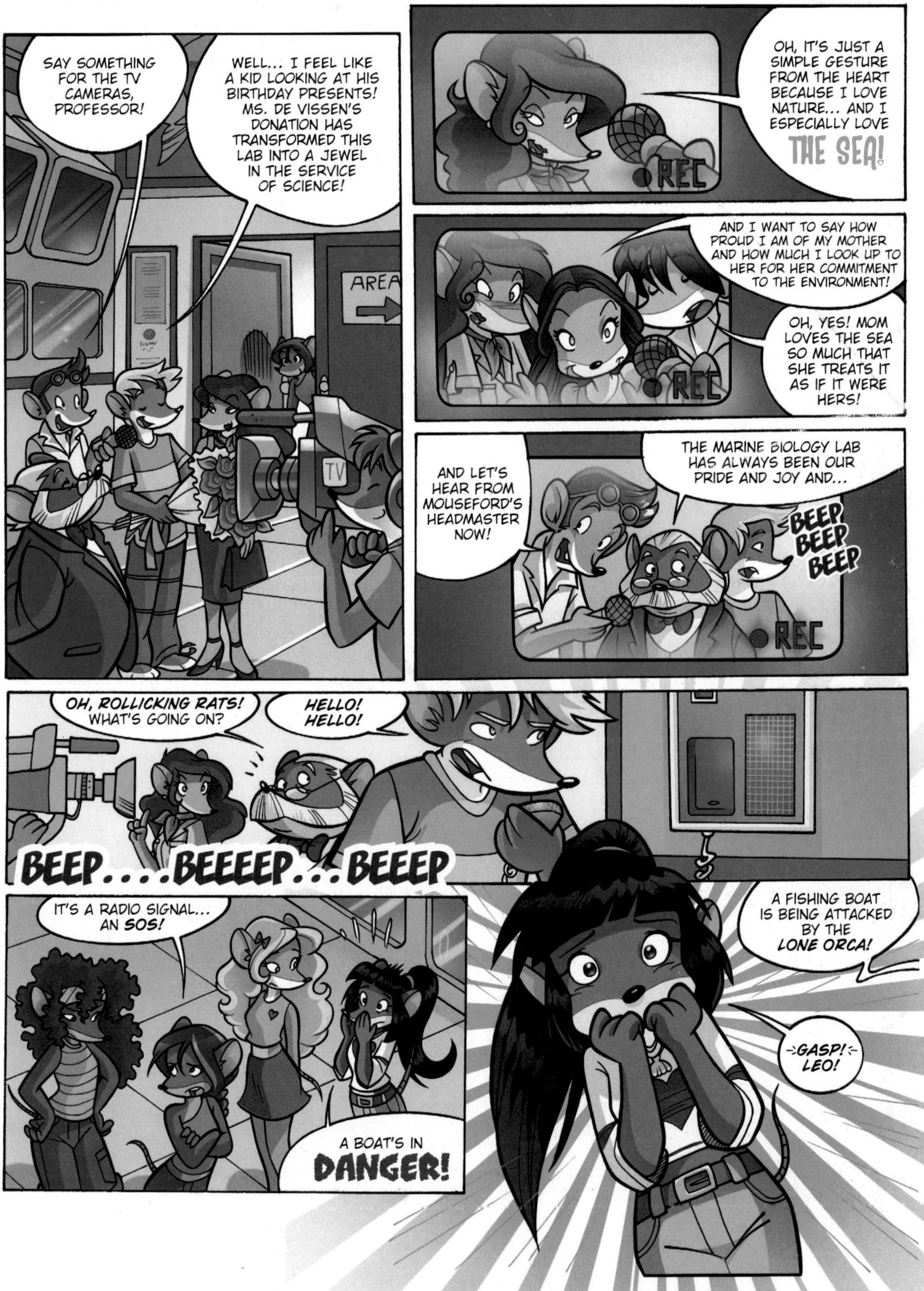
SAY SOMETHING FOR THE TV CAMERAS, PROFESSOR!
WELL... I FEEL LIKE A KID LOOKING AT HIS BIRTHDAY PRESENTS! MS. DE VISSEN'S DONATION HAS TRANSFORMED THIS LAB INTO A JEWEL IN THE SERVICE OF SCIENCE!
AREA
TV
OH, IT'S JUST A SIMPLE GESTURE FROM THE HEART BECAUSE I LOVE NATURE... AND I ESPECIALLY LOVE THE SEA!
REC
AND I WANT TO SAY HOW PROUD I AM OF MY MOTHER AND HOW MUCH I LOOK UP TO HER FOR HER COMMITMENT TO THE ENVIRONMENT!
OH, YES! MOM LOVES THE SEA SO MUCH THAT SHE TREATS IT AS IF IT WERE HERS!
REC
AND LET'S HEAR FROM MOUSEFORD'S HEADMASTER NOW!
THE MARINE BIOLOGY LAB HAS ALWAYS BEEN OUR PRIDE AND JOY AND...
BEEP BEEP BEEP
REC
OH, ROLLICKING RATS! WHAT'S GOING ON?
HELLO! HELLO!
BEEP....BEEEEP...BEEEP
IT'S A RADIO SIGNAL... AN SOS!
A BOAT'S IN DANGER!
A FISHING BOAT IS BEING ATTACKED BY THE LONE ORCA!
GASP! LEO!

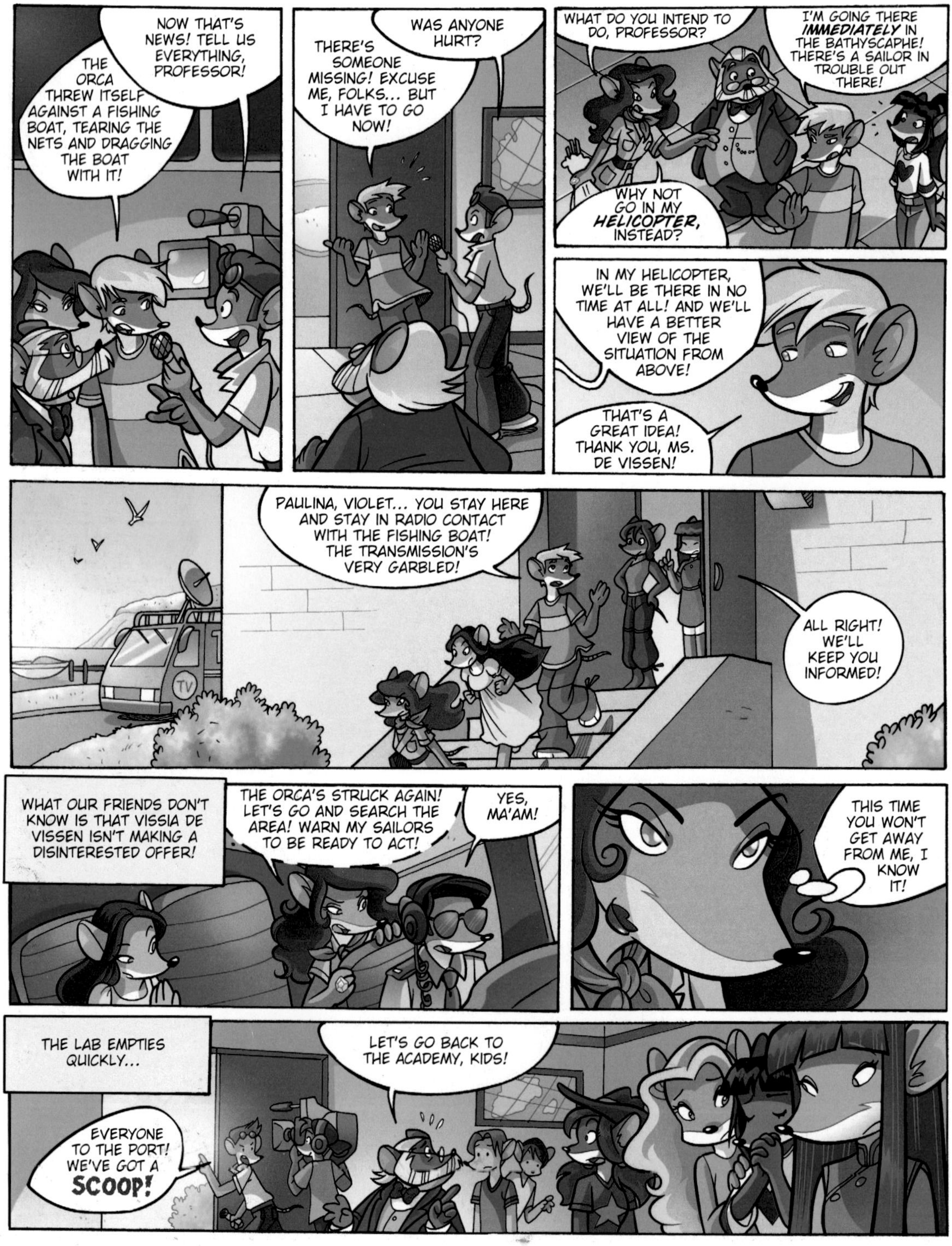

NOW THAT'S NEWS! TELL US EVERYTHING, PROFESSOR!
THE ORCA THREW ITSELF AGAINST A FISHING BOAT, TEARING THE NETS AND DRAGGING THE BOAT WITH IT!
WAS ANYONE HURT?
THERE'S SOMEONE MISSING! EXCUSE ME, FOLKS... BUT I HAVE TO GO NOW!
WHAT DO YOU INTEND TO DO, PROFESSOR?
I'M GOING THERE IMMEDIATELY IN THE BATHYSCAPHE! THERE'S A SAILOR IN TROUBLE OUT THERE!
WHY NOT GO IN MY HELICOPTER, INSTEAD?
IN MY HELICOPTER, WE'LL BE THERE IN NO TIME AT ALL! AND WE'LL HAVE A BETTER VIEW OF THE SITUATION FROM ABOVE!
THAT'S A GREAT IDEA! THANK YOU, MS. DE VISSEN!
PAULINA, VIOLET... YOU STAY HERE AND STAY IN RADIO CONTACT WITH THE FISHING BOAT! THE TRANSMISSION'S VERY GARBLED!
ALL RIGHT! WE'LL KEEP YOU INFORMED!
TV
WHAT OUR FRIENDS DON'T KNOW IS THAT VISSIA DE VISSEN ISN'T MAKING A DISINTERESTED OFFER!
THE ORCA'S STRUCK AGAIN! LET'S GO AND SEARCH THE AREA! WARN MY SAILORS TO BE READY TO ACT!
YES, MA'AM!
THIS TIME YOU WON'T GET AWAY FROM ME, I KNOW IT!
THE LAB EMPTIES QUICKLY...
LET'S GO BACK TO THE ACADEMY, KIDS!
EVERYONE TO THE PORT! WE'VE GOT A SCOOP!

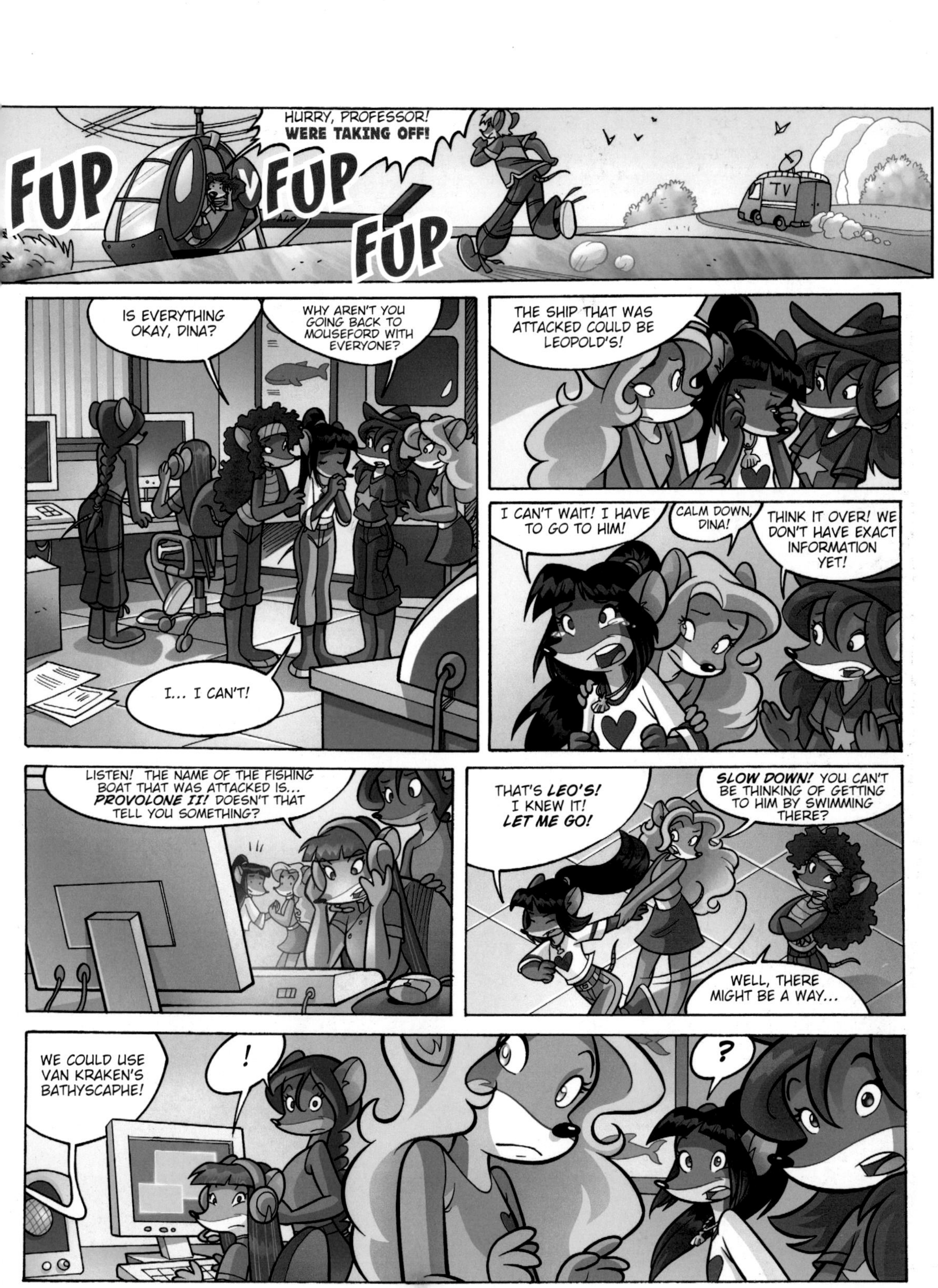

FUP
HURRY, PROFESSOR! WERE TAKING OFF!
FUP
FUP
TV
IS EVERYTHING OKAY, DINA?
WHY AREN'T YOU GOING BACK TO MOUSEFORD WITH EVERYONE?
I... I CAN'T!
THE SHIP THAT WAS ATTACKED COULD BE LEOPOLD'S!
I CAN'T WAIT! I HAVE TO GO TO HIM!
CALM DOWN, DINA!
THINK IT OVER! WE DON'T HAVE EXACT INFORMATION YET!
LISTEN! THE NAME OF THE FISHING BOAT THAT WAS ATTACKED IS... PROVOLONE II! DOESN'T THAT TELL YOU SOMETHING?
THAT'S LEO'S! I KNEW IT! LET ME GO!
SLOW DOWN! YOU CAN'T BE THINKING OF GETTING TO HIM BY SWIMMING THERE?
WELL, THERE MIGHT BE A WAY...
WE COULD USE VAN KRAKEN'S BATHYSCAPHE!
!
?

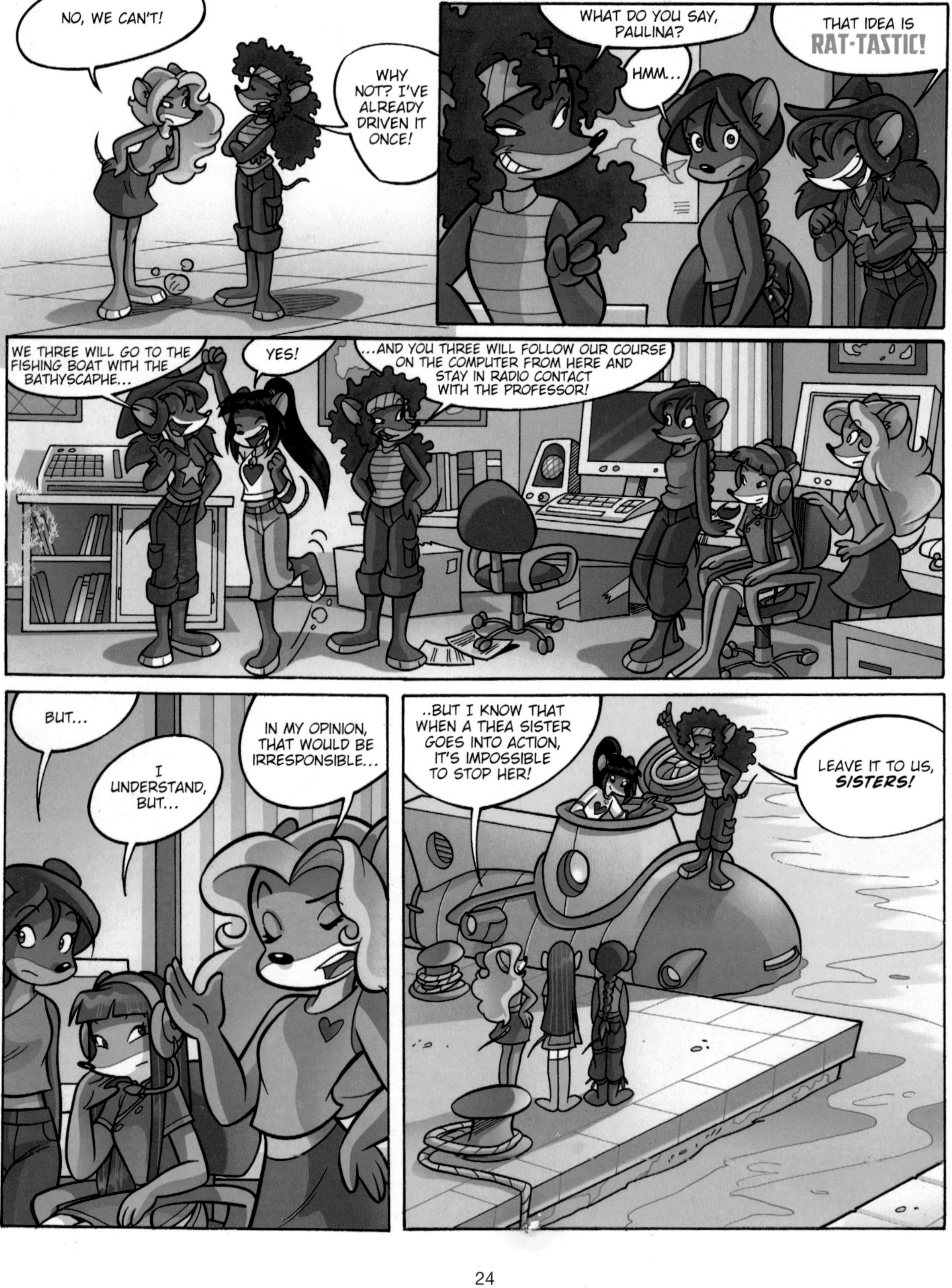
NO, WE CAN'T!
WHY NOT? I'VE ALREADY DRIVEN IT ONCE!
WHAT DO YOU SAY, PAULINA?
HMM...
THAT IDEA IS RAT-TASTIC!
WE THREE WILL GO TO THE FISHING BOAT WITH THE BATHYSCAPHE...
YES!
...AND YOU THREE WILL FOLLOW OUR COURSE ON THE COMPUTER FROM HERE AND STAY IN RADIO CONTACT WITH THE PROFESSOR!
BUT...
I UNDERSTAND, BUT...
IN MY OPINION, THAT WOULD BE IRRESPONSIBLE...
..BUT I KNOW THAT WHEN A THEA SISTER GOES INTO ACTION, IT'S IMPOSSIBLE TO STOP HER!
LEAVE IT TO US, SISTERS!

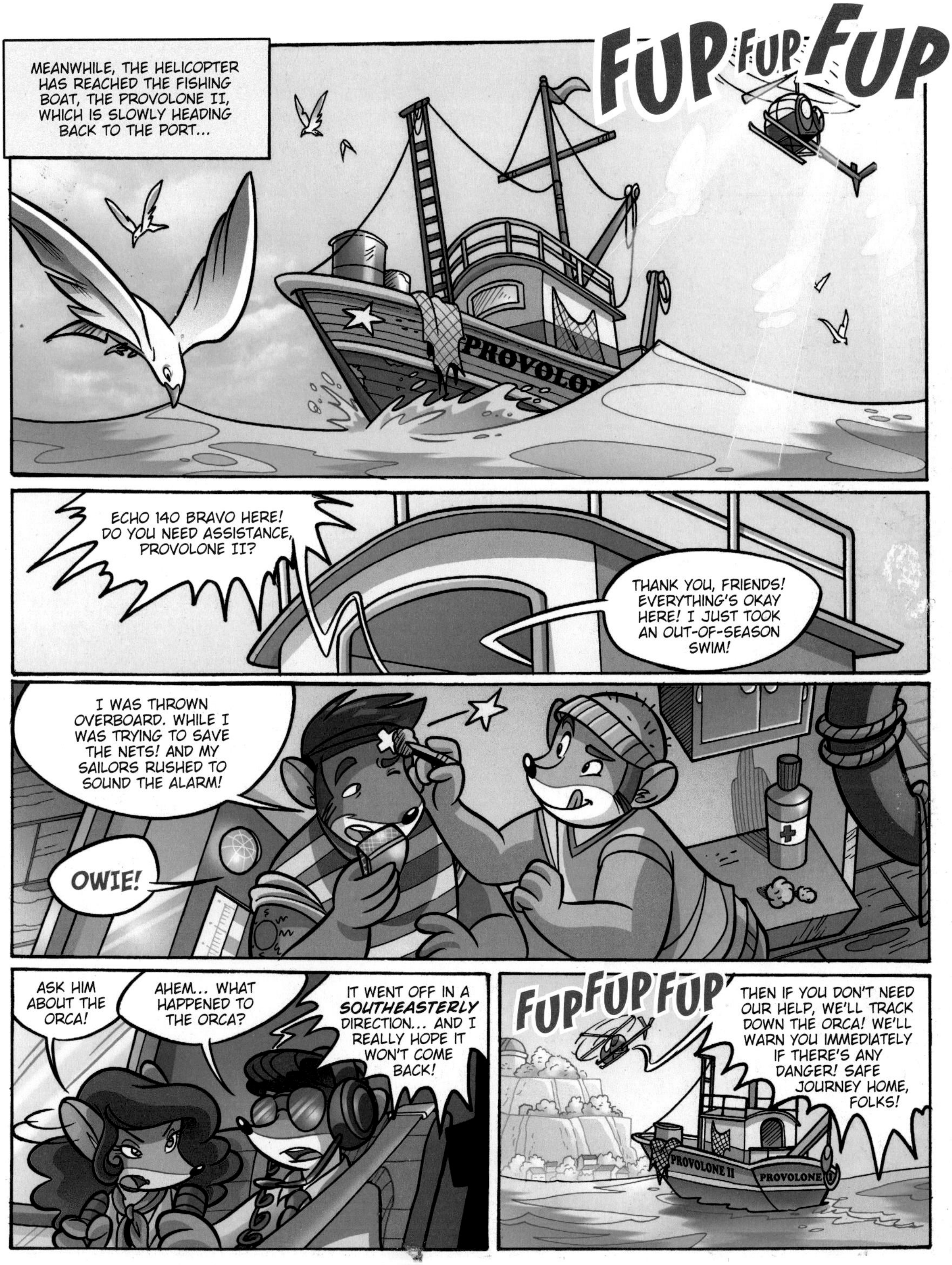

MEANWHILE, THE HELICOPTER HAS REACHED THE FISHING BOAT, THE PROVOLONE II, WHICH IS SLOWLY HEADING BACK TO THE PORT...
FUP FUP FUP
PROVOLONE
ECHO 140 BRAVO HERE! DO YOU NEED ASSISTANCE, PROVOLONE II?
THANK YOU, FRIENDS! EVERYTHING'S OKAY HERE! I JUST TOOK AN OUT-OF-SEASON SWIM!
I WAS THROWN OVERBOARD. WHILE I WAS TRYING TO SAVE THE NETS! AND MY SAILORS RUSHED TO SOUND THE ALARM!
OWIE!
ASK HIM ABOUT THE ORCA!
AHEM... WHAT HAPPENED TO THE ORCA?
IT WENT OFF IN A SOUTHEASTERLY DIRECTION... AND I REALLY HOPE IT WON'T COME BACK!
FUP FUP FUP
THEN IF YOU DON'T NEED OUR HELP, WE'LL TRACK DOWN THE ORCA! WE'LL WARN YOU IMMEDIATELY IF THERE'S ANY DANGER! SAFE JOURNEY HOME, FOLKS!
PROVOLONE II
PROVOLONE II

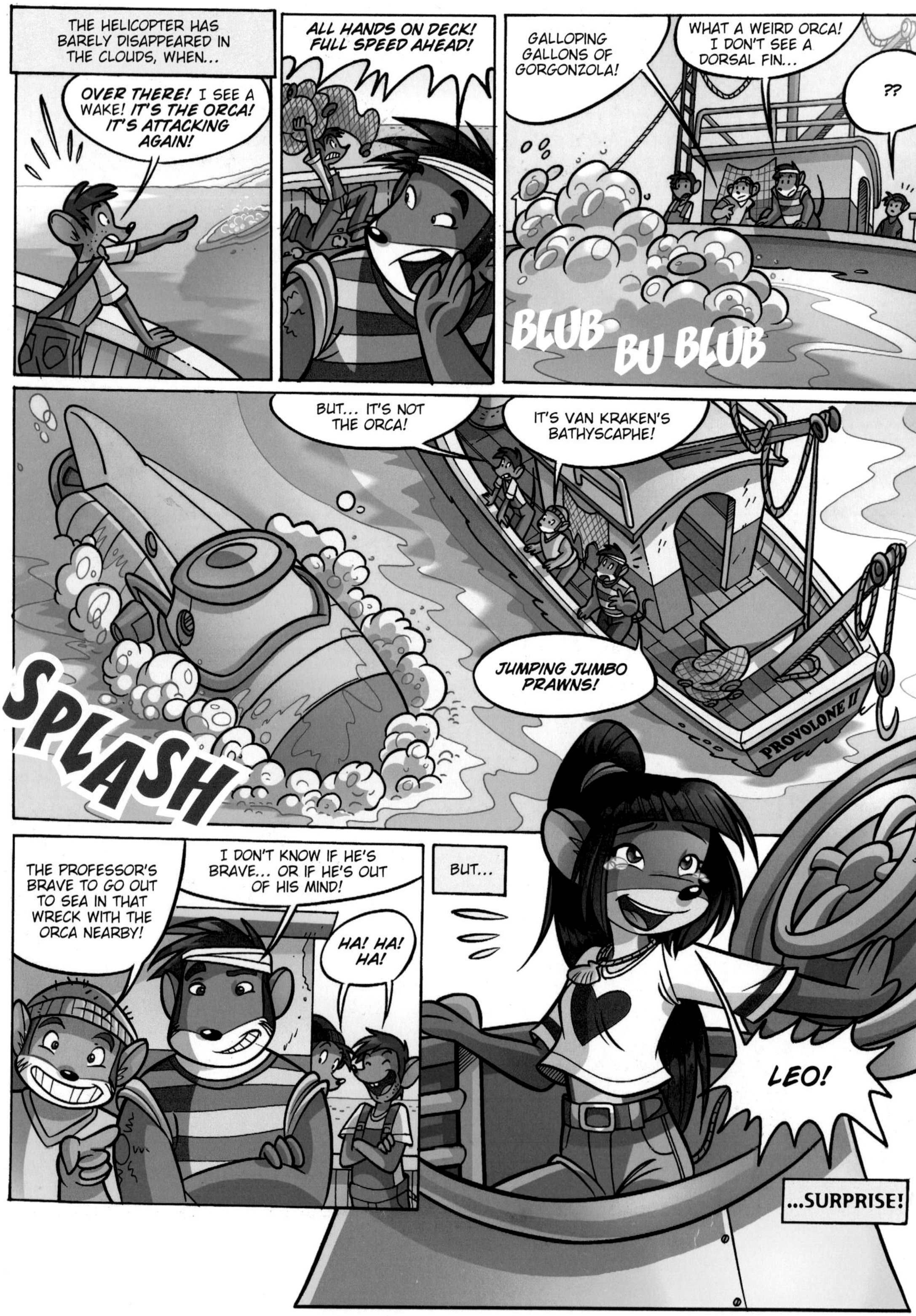
THE HELICOPTER HAS BARELY DISAPPEARED IN THE CLOUDS, WHEN...
OVER THERE! I SEE A WAKE! IT'S THE ORCA! IT'S ATTACKING AGAIN!
ALL HANDS ON DECK! FULL SPEED AHEAD!
GALLOPING GALLONS OF GORGONZOLA!
WHAT A WEIRD ORCA! I DON'T SEE A DORSAL FIN...
??
BLUB BU BLUB
BUT... IT'S NOT THE ORCA!
IT'S VAN KRAKEN'S BATHYSCAPHE!
JUMPING JUMBO PRAWNS!
SPLASH
PROVOLONE II
THE PROFESSOR'S BRAVE TO GO OUT TO SEA IN THAT WRECK WITH THE ORCA NEARBY!
I DON'T KNOW IF HE'S BRAVE... OR IF HE'S OUT OF HIS MIND!
HA! HA! HA!
BUT...
LEO!
...SURPRISE!

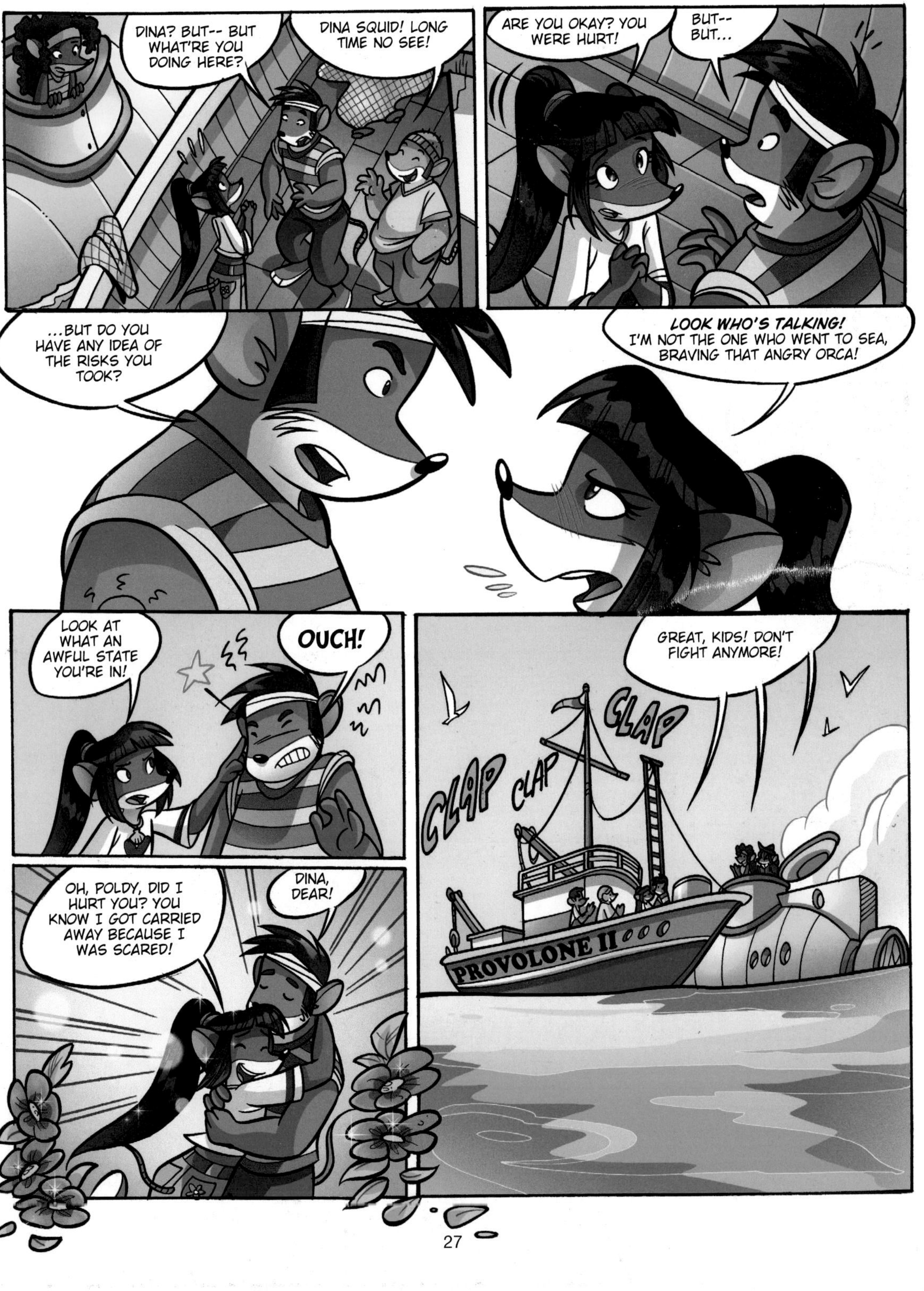

DINA? BUT-- BUT WHAT'RE YOU DOING HERE?
DINA SQUID! LONG TIME NO SEE!
ARE YOU OKAY? YOU WERE HURT!
BUT-- BUT...
...BUT DO YOU HAVE ANY IDEA OF THE RISKS YOU TOOK?
LOOK WHO'S TALKING! I'M NOT THE ONE WHO WENT TO SEA, BRAVING THAT ANGRY ORCA!
LOOK AT WHAT AN AWFUL STATE YOU'RE IN!
OUCH!
GREAT, KIDS! DON'T FIGHT ANYMORE!
CLAP CLAP CLAP CLAP
PROVOLONE II
OH, POLDY, DID I HURT YOU? YOU KNOW I GOT CARRIED AWAY BECAUSE I WAS SCARED!
DINA, DEAR!

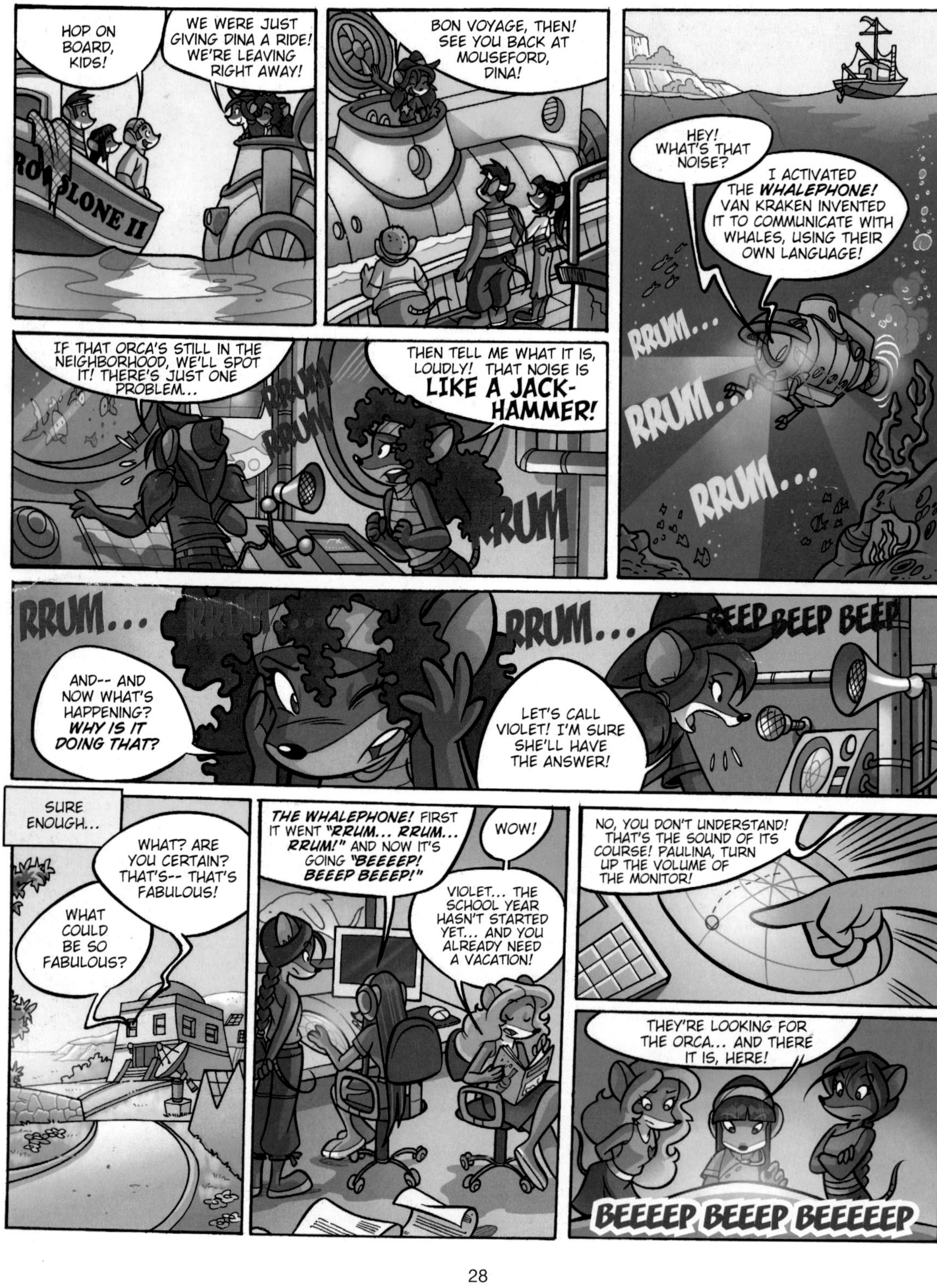
HOP ON BOARD, KIDS!
WE WERE JUST GIVING DINA A RIDE! WE'RE LEAVING RIGHT AWAY!
BON VOYAGE, THEN! SEE YOU BACK AT MOUSEFORD, DINA!
HEY! WHAT'S THAT NOISE?
I ACTIVATED THE WHALEPHONE! VAN KRAKEN INVENTED IT TO COMMUNICATE WITH WHALES, USING THEIR OWN LANGUAGE!
RRUM... RRUM... RRUM...
IF THAT ORCA'S STILL IN THE NEIGHBORHOOD, WE'LL SPOT IT! THERE'S JUST ONE PROBLEM...
THEN TELL ME WHAT IT IS, LOUDLY! THAT NOISE IS LIKE A JACK-HAMMER!
RRUM RRUM RRUM
RRUM... RRUM... RRUM...
BEEP BEEP BEEP
AND-- AND NOW WHAT'S HAPPENING? WHY IS IT DOING THAT?
LET'S CALL VIOLET! I'M SURE SHE'LL HAVE THE ANSWER!
SURE ENOUGH...
WHAT? ARE YOU CERTAIN? THAT'S-- THAT'S FABULOUS!
WHAT COULD BE SO FABULOUS?
THE WHALEPHONE! FIRST IT WENT "RRUM... RRUM... RRUM!" AND NOW IT'S GOING "BEEEEP! BEEEP BEEEP!"
WOW!
VIOLET... THE SCHOOL YEAR HASN'T STARTED YET... AND YOU ALREADY NEED A VACATION!
NO, YOU DON'T UNDERSTAND! THAT'S THE SOUND OF ITS COURSE! PAULINA, TURN UP THE VOLUME OF THE MONITOR!
THEY'RE LOOKING FOR THE ORCA... AND THERE IT IS, HERE!
BEEEEP BEEEP BEEEEEP

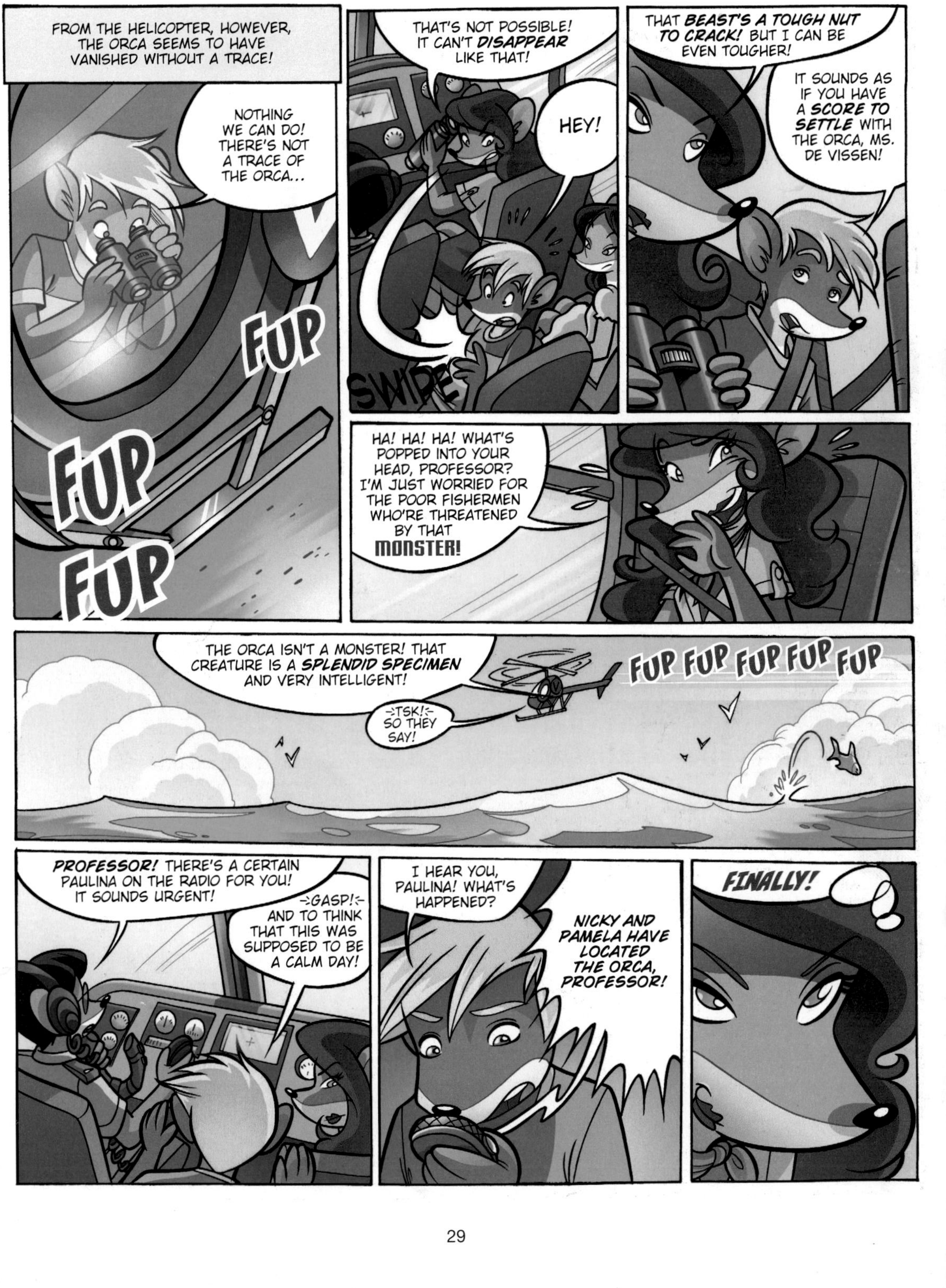
FROM THE HELICOPTER, HOWEVER, THE ORCA SEEMS TO HAVE VANISHED WITHOUT A TRACE!
NOTHING WE CAN DO! THERE'S NOT A TRACE OF THE ORCA...
FUP
FUP
FUP
THAT'S NOT POSSIBLE! IT CAN'T DISAPPEAR LIKE THAT!
HEY!
SWIPE
THAT BEAST'S A TOUGH NUT TO CRACK! BUT I CAN BE EVEN TOUGHER!
IT SOUNDS AS IF YOU HAVE A SCORE TO SETTLE WITH THE ORCA, MS. DE VISSEN!
HA! HA! HA! WHAT'S POPPED INTO YOUR HEAD, PROFESSOR? I'M JUST WORRIED FOR THE POOR FISHERMEN WHO'RE THREATENED BY THAT MONSTER!
THE ORCA ISN'T A MONSTER! THAT CREATURE IS A SPLENDID SPECIMEN AND VERY INTELLIGENT!
TSK! SO THEY SAY!
FUP FUP FUP FUP FUP
PROFESSOR! THERE'S A CERTAIN PAULINA ON THE RADIO FOR YOU! IT SOUNDS URGENT!
GASP! AND TO THINK THAT THIS WAS SUPPOSED TO BE A CALM DAY!
I HEAR YOU, PAULINA! WHAT'S HAPPENED?
NICKY AND PAMELA HAVE LOCATED THE ORCA, PROFESSOR!
FINALLY!

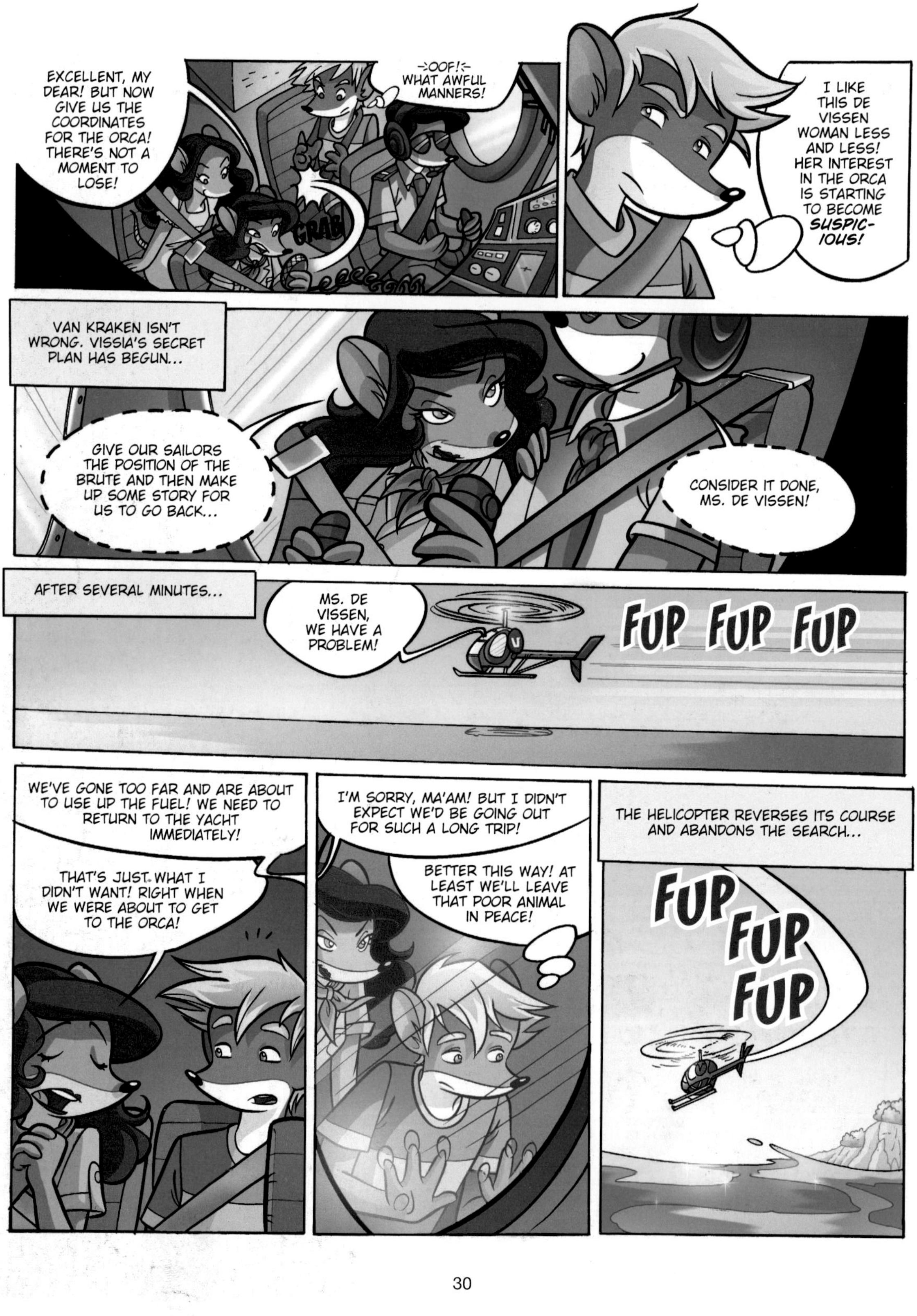
EXCELLENT, MY DEAR! BUT NOW GIVE US THE COORDINATES FOR THE ORCA! THERE'S NOT A MOMENT TO LOSE!
GRAB!
OOF! WHAT AWFUL MANNERS!
I LIKE THIS DE VISSEN WOMAN LESS AND LESS! HER INTEREST IN THE ORCA IS STARTING TO BECOME SUSPICIOUS!
VAN KRAKEN ISN'T WRONG. VISSIA'S SECRET PLAN HAS BEGUN...
GIVE OUR SAILORS THE POSITION OF THE BRUTE AND THEN MAKE UP SOME STORY FOR US TO GO BACK...
CONSIDER IT DONE, MS. DE VISSEN!
AFTER SEVERAL MINUTES...
MS. DE VISSEN, WE HAVE A PROBLEM!
FUP FUP FUP
WE'VE GONE TOO FAR AND ARE ABOUT TO USE UP THE FUEL! WE NEED TO RETURN TO THE YACHT IMMEDIATELY!
THAT'S JUST WHAT I DIDN'T WANT! RIGHT WHEN WE WERE ABOUT TO GET TO THE ORCA!
I'M SORRY, MA'AM! BUT I DIDN'T EXPECT WE'D BE GOING OUT FOR SUCH A LONG TRIP!
BETTER THIS WAY! AT LEAST WE'LL LEAVE THAT POOR ANIMAL IN PEACE!
THE HELICOPTER REVERSES ITS COURSE AND ABANDONS THE SEARCH...
FUP FUP FUP

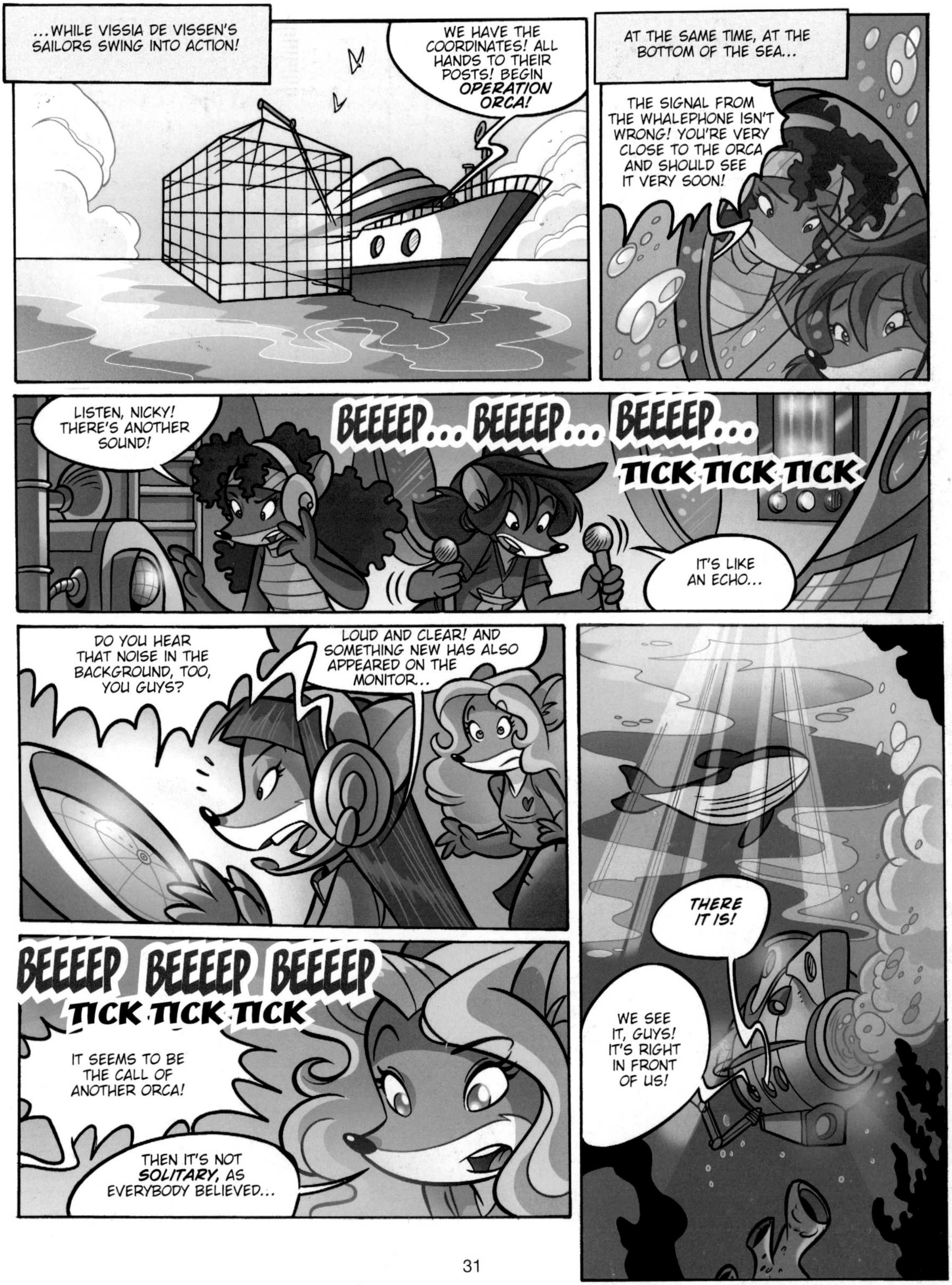

...WHILE VISSIA DE VISSEN'S SAILORS SWING INTO ACTION!
WE HAVE THE COORDINATES! ALL HANDS TO THEIR POSTS! BEGIN OPERATION ORCA!
AT THE SAME TIME, AT THE BOTTOM OF THE SEA...
THE SIGNAL FROM THE WHALEPHONE ISN'T WRONG! YOU'RE VERY CLOSE TO THE ORCA AND SHOULD SEE IT VERY SOON!
LISTEN, NICKY! THERE'S ANOTHER SOUND!
BEEEEP... BEEEEP... BEEEEP...
TICK TICK TICK
IT'S LIKE AN ECHO...
DO YOU HEAR THAT NOISE IN THE BACKGROUND, TOO, YOU GUYS?
LOUD AND CLEAR! AND SOMETHING NEW HAS ALSO APPEARED ON THE MONITOR...
BEEEEP BEEEEP BEEEEP
TICK TICK TICK
IT SEEMS TO BE THE CALL OF ANOTHER ORCA!
THEN IT'S NOT SOLITARY, AS EVERYBODY BELIEVED...
THERE IT IS!
WE SEE IT, GUYS! IT'S RIGHT IN FRONT OF US!

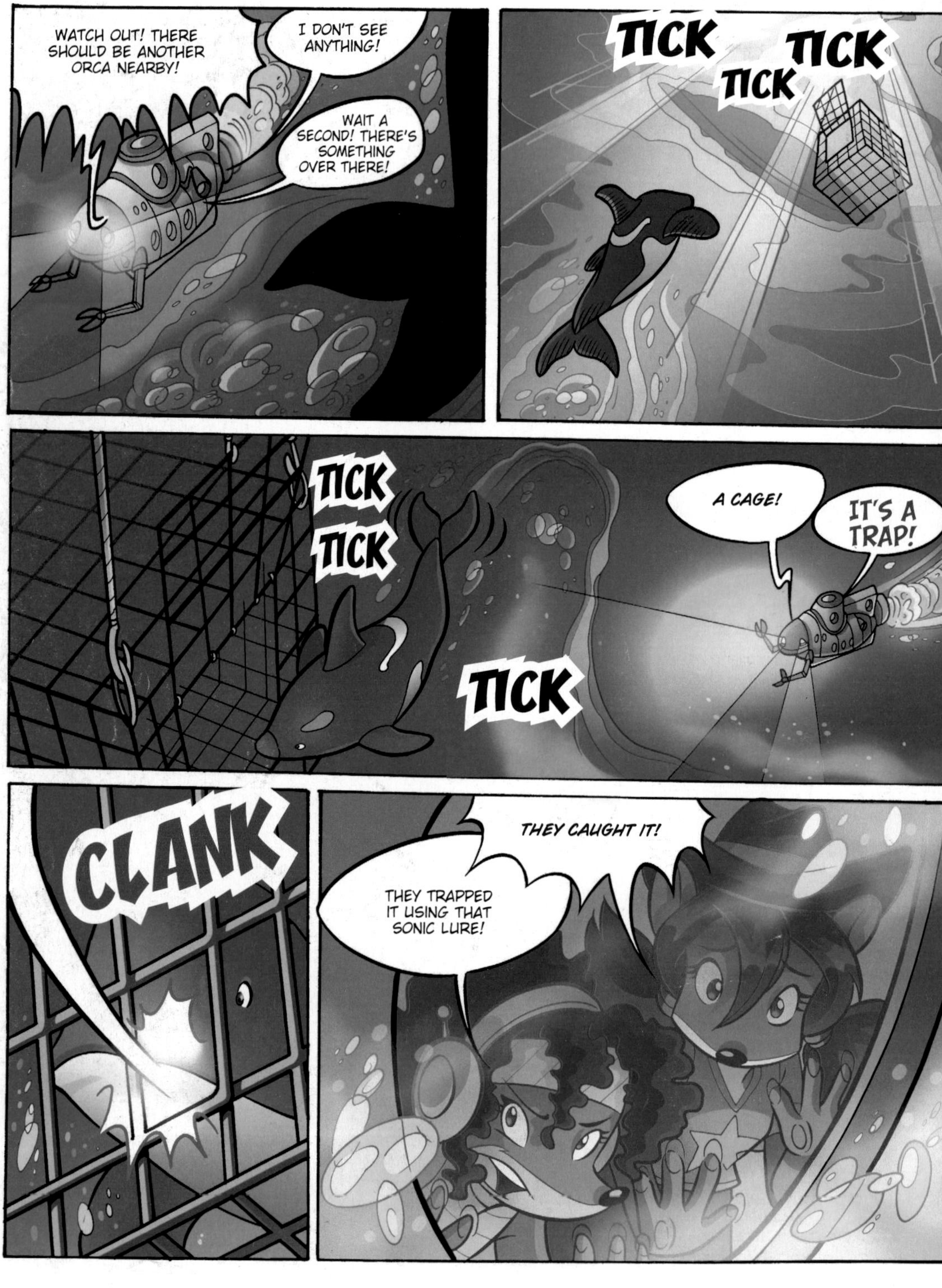
WATCH OUT! THERE SHOULD BE ANOTHER ORCA NEARBY!
I DON'T SEE ANYTHING!
WAIT A SECOND! THERE'S SOMETHING OVER THERE!
TICK
TICK
TICK
TICK
TICK
A CAGE!
IT'S A TRAP!
TICK
CLANK
THEY CAUGHT IT!
THEY TRAPPED IT USING THAT SONIC LURE!

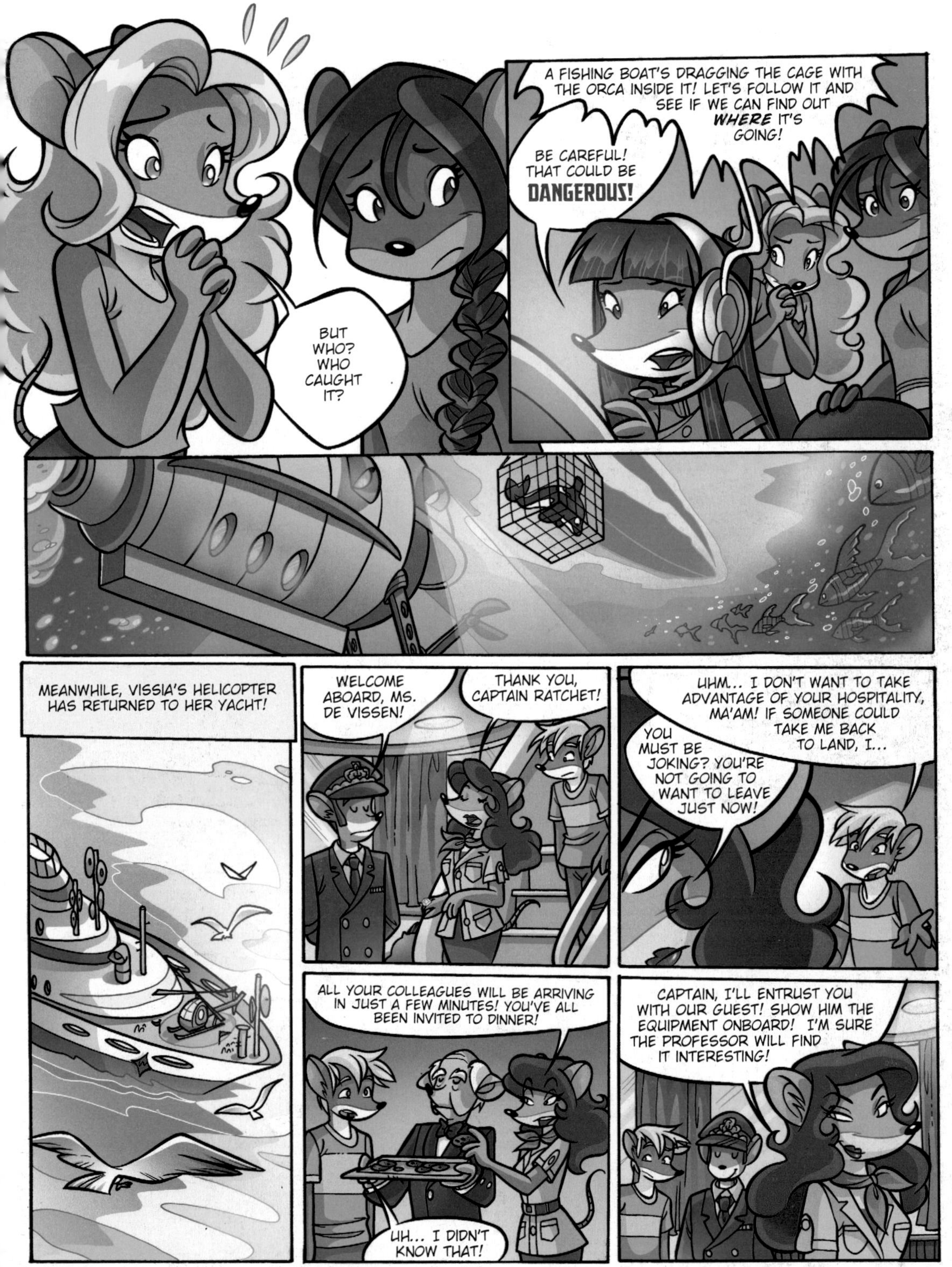

BUT WHO? WHO CAUGHT IT?
A FISHING BOAT'S DRAGGING THE CAGE WITH THE ORCA INSIDE IT! LET'S FOLLOW IT AND SEE IF WE CAN FIND OUT WHERE IT'S GOING!
BE CAREFUL! THAT COULD BE DANGEROUS!
MEANWHILE, VISSIA'S HELICOPTER HAS RETURNED TO HER YACHT!
WELCOME ABOARD, MS. DE VISSEN!
THANK YOU, CAPTAIN RATCHET!
UHM... I DON'T WANT TO TAKE ADVANTAGE OF YOUR HOSPITALITY, MA'AM! IF SOMEONE COULD TAKE ME BACK TO LAND, I...
YOU MUST BE JOKING? YOU'RE NOT GOING TO WANT TO LEAVE JUST NOW!
ALL YOUR COLLEAGUES WILL BE ARRIVING IN JUST A FEW MINUTES! YOU'VE ALL BEEN INVITED TO DINNER!
UH... I DIDN'T KNOW THAT!
CAPTAIN, I'LL ENTRUST YOU WITH OUR GUEST! SHOW HIM THE EQUIPMENT ONBOARD! I'M SURE THE PROFESSOR WILL FIND IT INTERESTING!

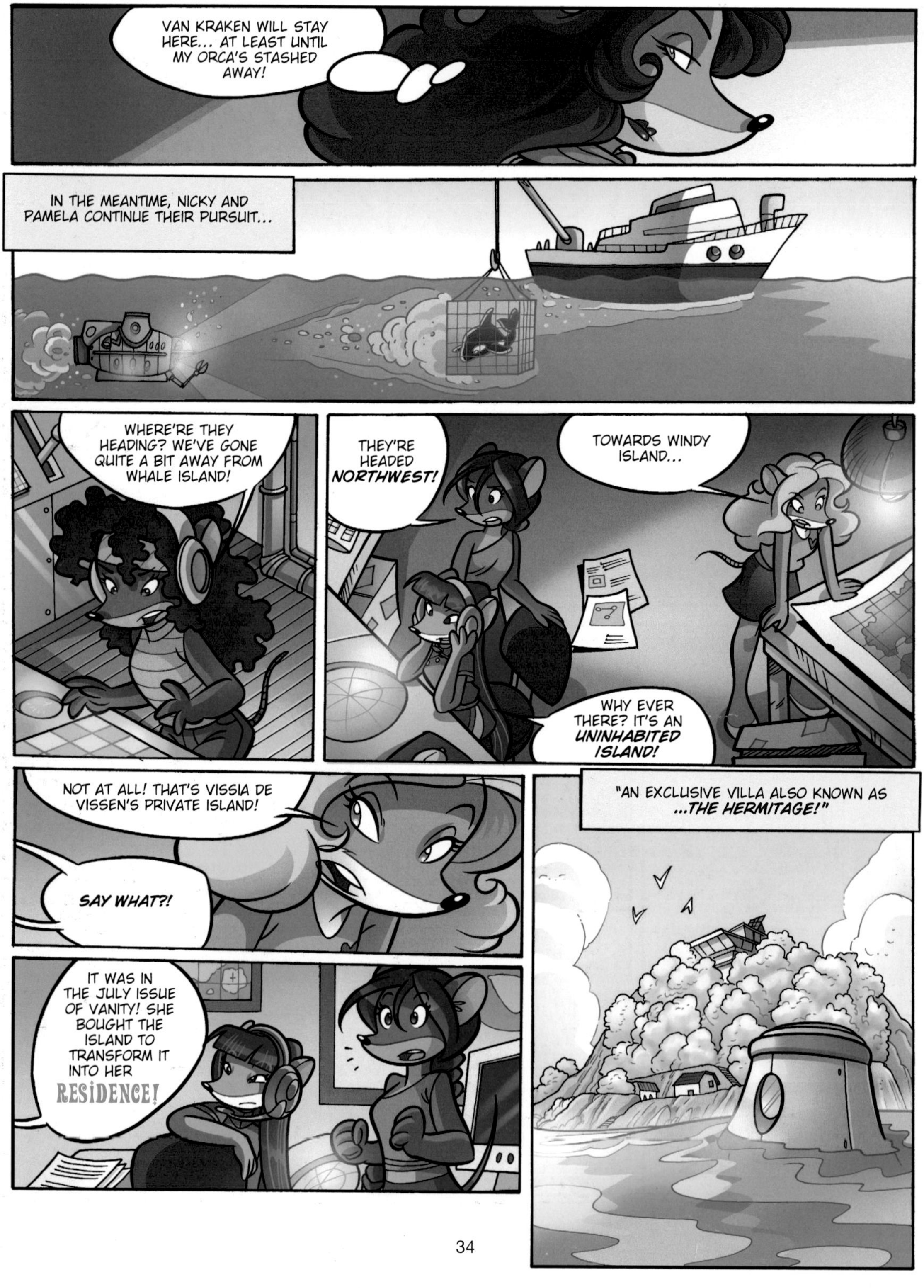
VAN KRAKEN WILL STAY HERE... AT LEAST UNTIL MY ORCA'S STASHED AWAY!
IN THE MEANTIME, NICKY AND PAMELA CONTINUE THEIR PURSUIT...
WHERE'RE THEY HEADING? WE'VE GONE QUITE A BIT AWAY FROM WHALE ISLAND!
THEY'RE HEADED NORTHWEST!
TOWARDS WINDY ISLAND...
WHY EVER THERE? IT'S AN UNINHABITED ISLAND!
NOT AT ALL! THAT'S VISSIA DE VISSEN'S PRIVATE ISLAND!
SAY WHAT?!
IT WAS IN THE JULY ISSUE OF VANITY! SHE BOUGHT THE ISLAND TO TRANSFORM IT INTO HER RESIDENCE!
"AN EXCLUSIVE VILLA ALSO KNOWN AS ...THE HERMITAGE!"

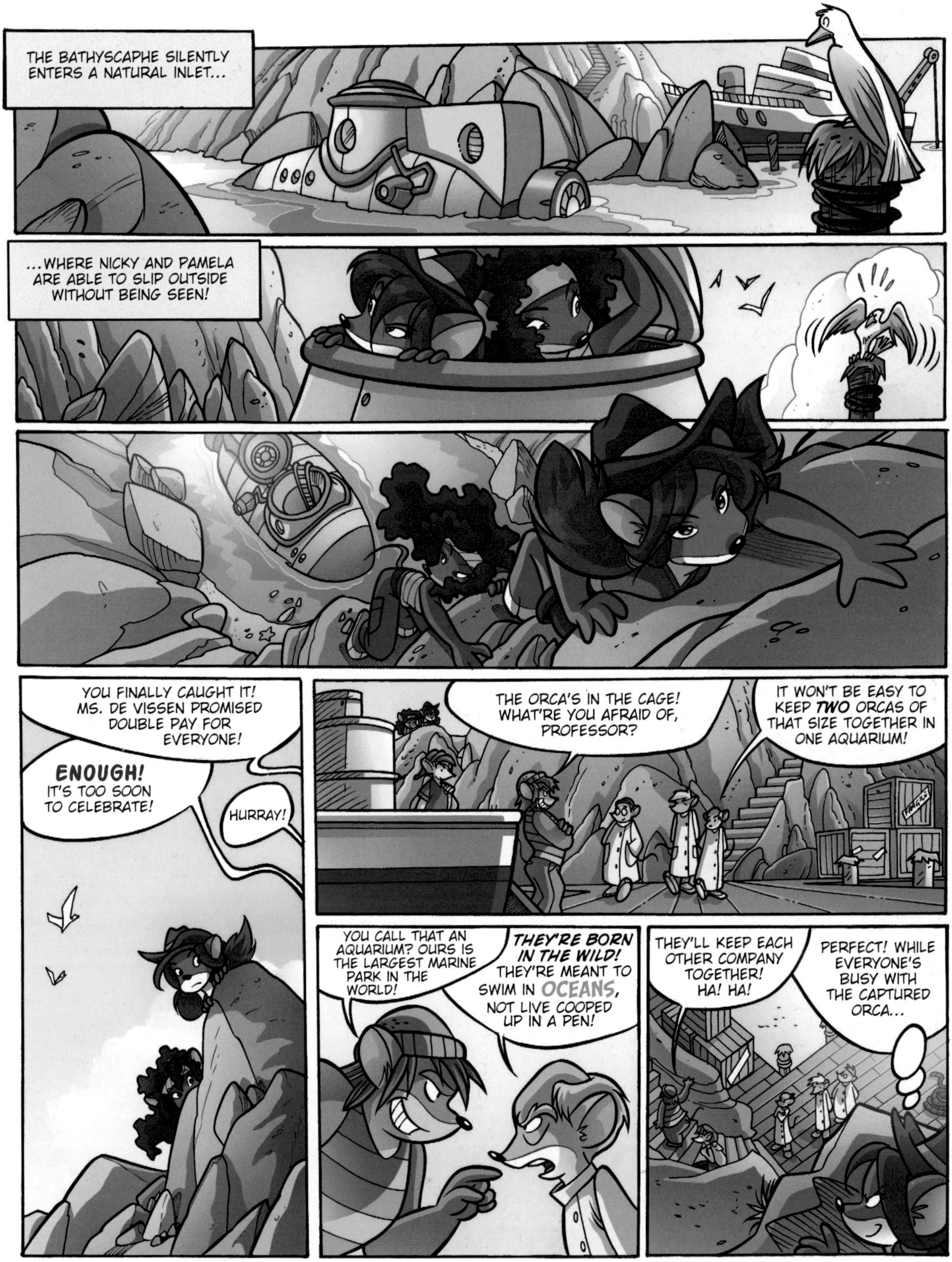
THE BATHYSCAPHE SILENTLY ENTERS A NATURAL INLET...
...WHERE NICKY AND PAMELA ARE ABLE TO SLIP OUTSIDE WITHOUT BEING SEEN!
YOU FINALLY CAUGHT IT! MS. DE VISSEN PROMISED DOUBLE PAY FOR EVERYONE!
ENOUGH! IT'S TOO SOON TO CELEBRATE!
HURRAY!
THE ORCA'S IN THE CAGE! WHAT'RE YOU AFRAID OF, PROFESSOR?
IT WON'T BE EASY TO KEEP TWO ORCAS OF THAT SIZE TOGETHER IN ONE AQUARIUM!
YOU CALL THAT AN AQUARIUM? OURS IS THE LARGEST MARINE PARK IN THE WORLD!
THEY'RE BORN IN THE WILD! THEY'RE MEANT TO SWIM IN OCEANS, NOT LIVE COOPED UP IN A PEN!
THEY'LL KEEP EACH OTHER COMPANY TOGETHER! HA! HA!
PERFECT! WHILE EVERYONE'S BUSY WITH THE CAPTURED ORCA...

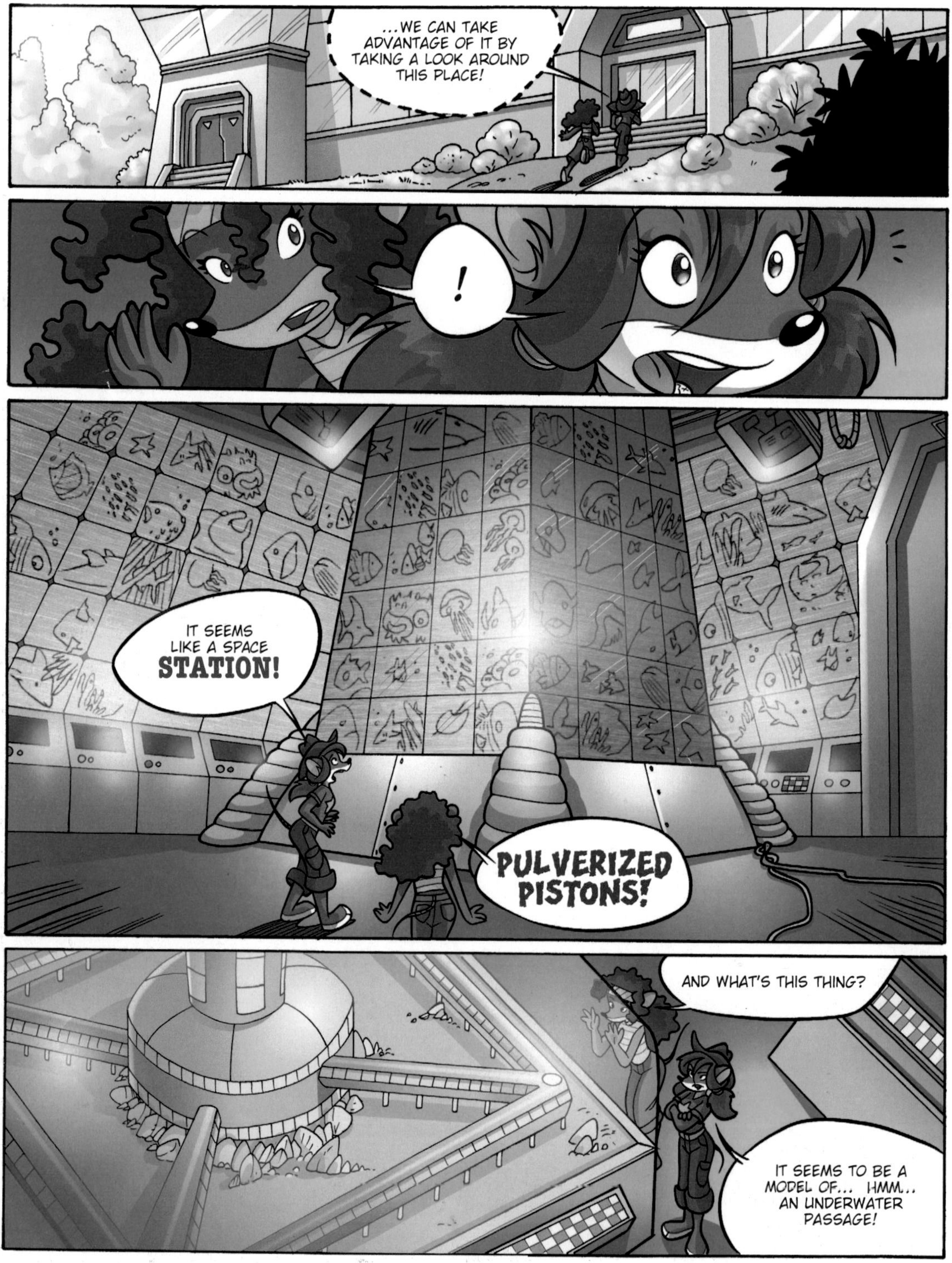
...WE CAN TAKE ADVANTAGE OF IT BY TAKING A LOOK AROUND THIS PLACE!
!
IT SEEMS LIKE A SPACE STATION!
PULVERIZED PISTONS!
AND WHAT'S THIS THING?
IT SEEMS TO BE A MODEL OF... HMM... AN UNDERWATER PASSAGE!

A HATCH OPENS UP AUTOMATICALLY AND...

WHOOSHHH

!

HEY! I KNOW WHAT THAT IS! IT'S AN *ANGEL SHARK**! A RARELY SEEN FISH THAT'S ON THE WAY TO BEING *EXTINCT*!

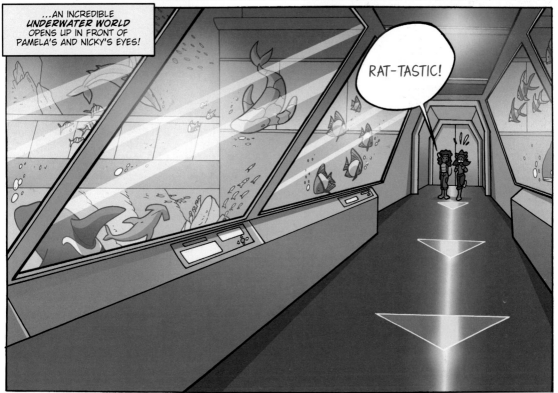

...AN INCREDIBLE *UNDERWATER WORLD* OPENS UP IN FRONT OF PAMELA'S AND NICKY'S EYES!

RAT-TASTIC!

* THE TWO WINGS OF THE ANGEL SHARK ARE ACTUALLY ITS PECTORAL FINS. IT LIVES ALONG THE COASTS IN TEMPERATE WATERS. DURING THE DAY IT SPENDS ITS TIME HIDDEN UNDER THE SAND, LEAVING ONLY ITS EYES SHOWING.

WE'RE IN A HUGE **AQUARIUM!** LOOK AT HOW MANY FISH THERE ARE!

MANY ARE **PROTECTED** SPECIES!

THAT MANTA RAY*, FOR EXAMPLE! BUT HOW WERE THEY ALL CAUGHT?

WE HAVE TO **BLOW THE WHISTLE** ON THE PEOPLE IN CHARGE OF THIS AND MAKE THEM **FREE** ALL THESE POOR ANIMALS!

LOOK OVER THERE, NICKY...

"THE ORCAS... THERE ARE **TWO** OF THEM!"

I'M REALLY CURIOUS TO SEE THEM TOGETHER!

YOU WON'T HAVE TO WAIT VERY LONG! I'LL OPEN IT UP!

SOMEONE'S COMING! LET'S HIDE!

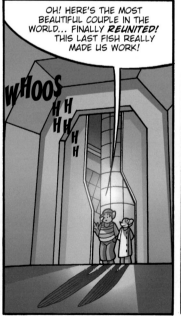

OH! HERE'S THE MOST BEAUTIFUL COUPLE IN THE WORLD... FINALLY **REUNITED!** THIS LAST FISH REALLY MADE US WORK!

WHOOS H H H H H

SAME THING! WHAT MATTERS IS THAT NOW THE OTHER ONE'S **CAGED,** TOO!

ORCAS AREN'T FISH! THEY'RE MAMMALS!

*A RELATIVE OF SHARKS, THE MANTA RAY IS THE LARGEST RAY IN THE WORLD. ITS "WING" SPAN CAN BE AS LARGE AS 22 FEET. IT LIVES IN TROPICAL WATERS, IN THE PACIFIC AND INDIAN OCEANS AND IN THE RED SEA. IT'S HARMLESS TO HUMANS AND FEEDS ON PLANKTON.

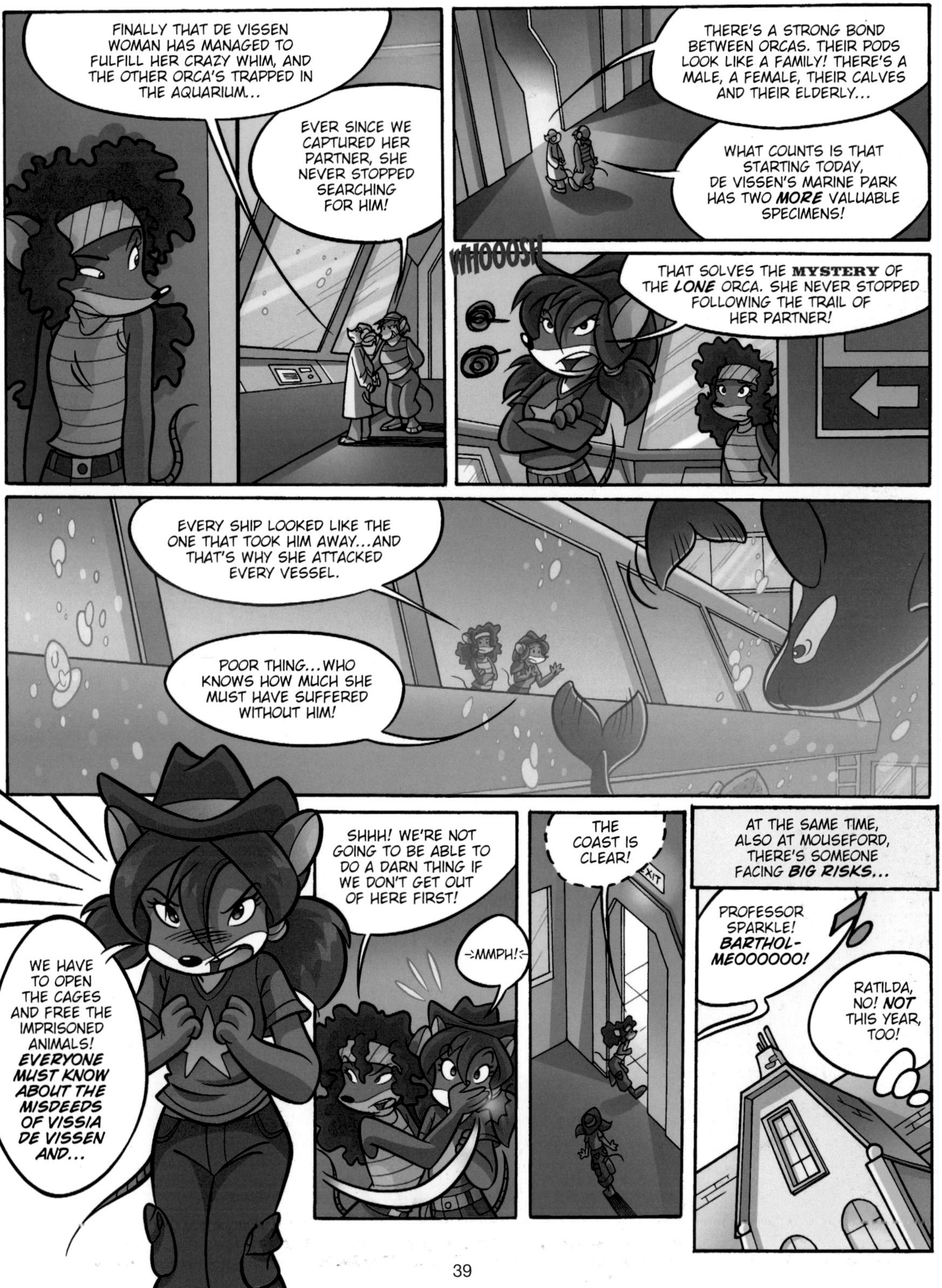
FINALLY THAT DE VISSEN WOMAN HAS MANAGED TO FULFILL HER CRAZY WHIM, AND THE OTHER ORCA'S TRAPPED IN THE AQUARIUM...
EVER SINCE WE CAPTURED HER PARTNER, SHE NEVER STOPPED SEARCHING FOR HIM!
THERE'S A STRONG BOND BETWEEN ORCAS. THEIR PODS LOOK LIKE A FAMILY! THERE'S A MALE, A FEMALE, THEIR CALVES AND THEIR ELDERLY...
WHAT COUNTS IS THAT STARTING TODAY, DE VISSEN'S MARINE PARK HAS TWO MORE VALUABLE SPECIMENS!
WHOOOSH
THAT SOLVES THE MYSTERY OF THE LONE ORCA. SHE NEVER STOPPED FOLLOWING THE TRAIL OF HER PARTNER!
EVERY SHIP LOOKED LIKE THE ONE THAT TOOK HIM AWAY...AND THAT'S WHY SHE ATTACKED EVERY VESSEL.
POOR THING...WHO KNOWS HOW MUCH SHE MUST HAVE SUFFERED WITHOUT HIM!
WE HAVE TO OPEN THE CAGES AND FREE THE IMPRISONED ANIMALS! EVERYONE MUST KNOW ABOUT THE MISDEEDS OF VISSIA DE VISSEN AND...
SHHH! WE'RE NOT GOING TO BE ABLE TO DO A DARN THING IF WE DON'T GET OUT OF HERE FIRST!
MMPH!
THE COAST IS CLEAR!
EXIT
AT THE SAME TIME, ALSO AT MOUSEFORD, THERE'S SOMEONE FACING BIG RISKS...
PROFESSOR SPARKLE! BARTHOL-MEOOOOOO!
RATILDA, NO! NOT THIS YEAR, TOO!

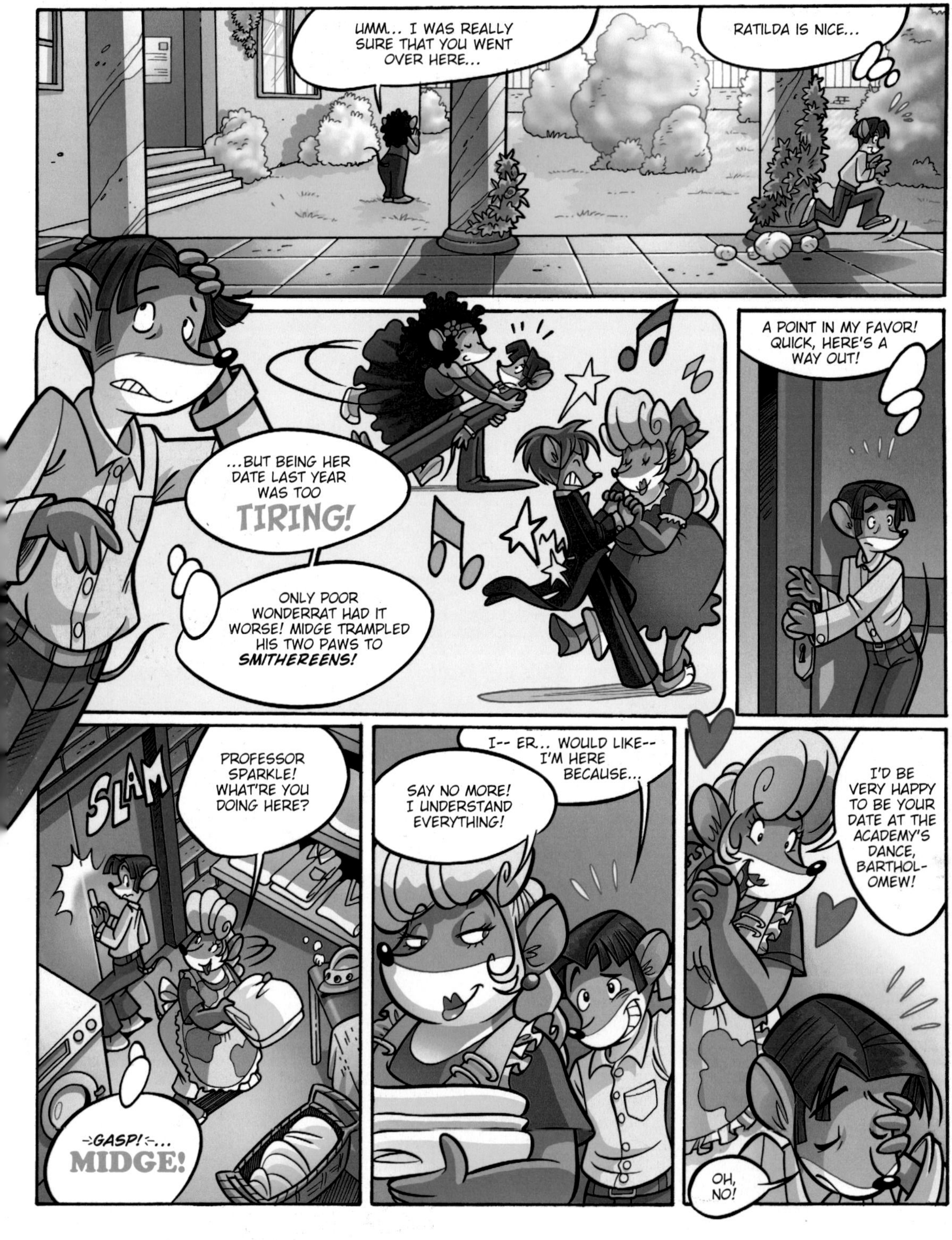
UMM... I WAS REALLY SURE THAT YOU WENT OVER HERE...
RATILDA IS NICE...
...BUT BEING HER DATE LAST YEAR WAS TOO TIRING!
ONLY POOR WONDERRAT HAD IT WORSE! MIDGE TRAMPLED HIS TWO PAWS TO SMITHEREENS!
A POINT IN MY FAVOR! QUICK, HERE'S A WAY OUT!
SLAM
PROFESSOR SPARKLE! WHAT'RE YOU DOING HERE?
GASP!... MIDGE!
I-- ER... WOULD LIKE-- I'M HERE BECAUSE...
SAY NO MORE! I UNDERSTAND EVERYTHING!
I'D BE VERY HAPPY TO BE YOUR DATE AT THE ACADEMY'S DANCE, BARTHOLOMEW!
OH, NO!

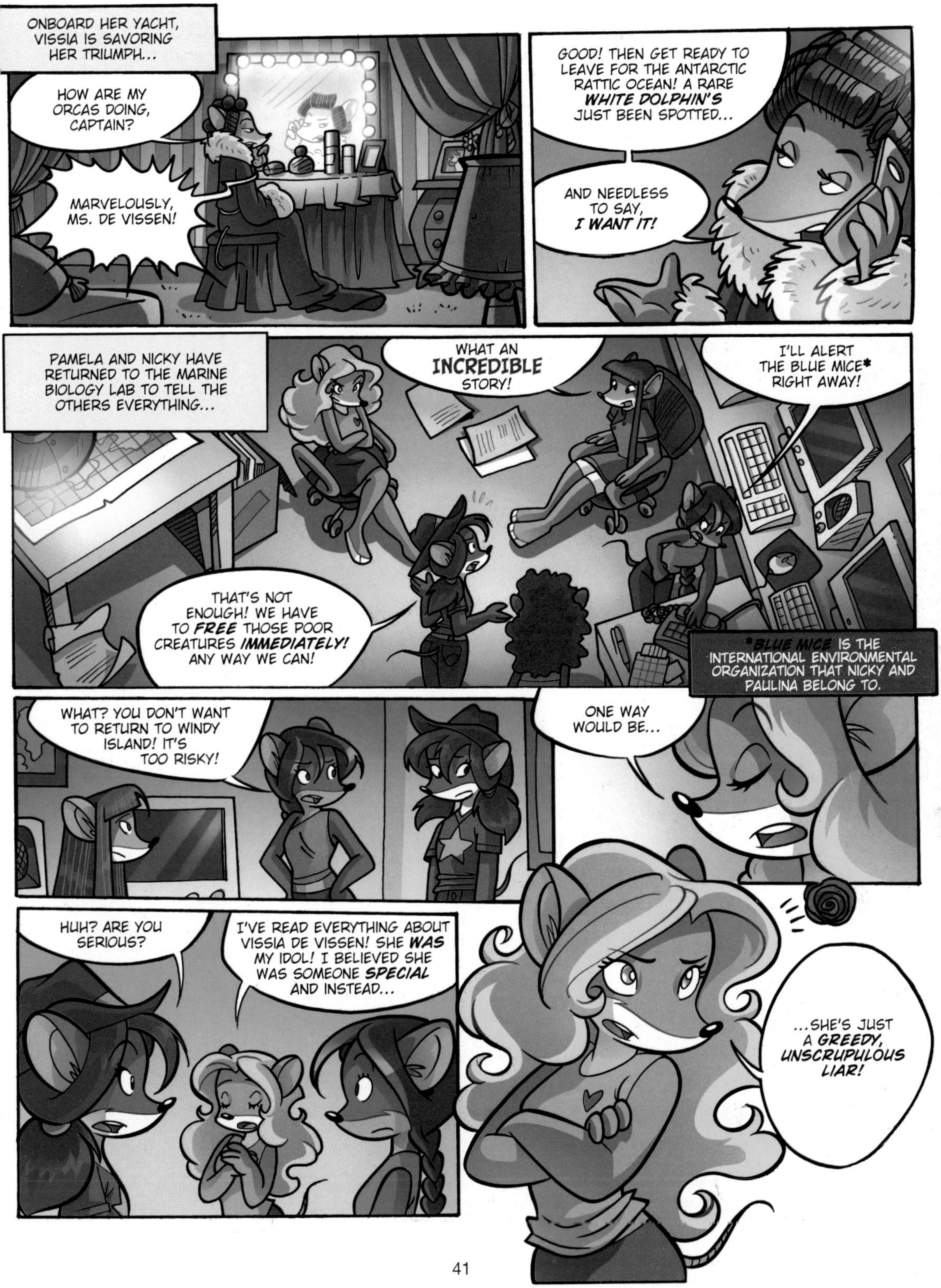
ONBOARD HER YACHT, VISSIA IS SAVORING HER TRIUMPH...
HOW ARE MY ORCAS DOING, CAPTAIN?
MARVELOUSLY, MS. DE VISSEN!
GOOD! THEN GET READY TO LEAVE FOR THE ANTARCTIC RATTIC OCEAN! A RARE WHITE DOLPHIN'S JUST BEEN SPOTTED...
AND NEEDLESS TO SAY, I WANT IT!
PAMELA AND NICKY HAVE RETURNED TO THE MARINE BIOLOGY LAB TO TELL THE OTHERS EVERYTHING...
WHAT AN INCREDIBLE STORY!
I'LL ALERT THE BLUE MICE* RIGHT AWAY!
THAT'S NOT ENOUGH! WE HAVE TO FREE THOSE POOR CREATURES IMMEDIATELY! ANY WAY WE CAN!
*BLUE MICE IS THE INTERNATIONAL ENVIRONMENTAL ORGANIZATION THAT NICKY AND PAULINA BELONG TO.
WHAT? YOU DON'T WANT TO RETURN TO WINDY ISLAND! IT'S TOO RISKY!
ONE WAY WOULD BE...
HUH? ARE YOU SERIOUS?
I'VE READ EVERYTHING ABOUT VISSIA DE VISSEN! SHE WAS MY IDOL! I BELIEVED SHE WAS SOMEONE SPECIAL AND INSTEAD...
...SHE'S JUST A GREEDY, UNSCRUPULOUS LIAR!

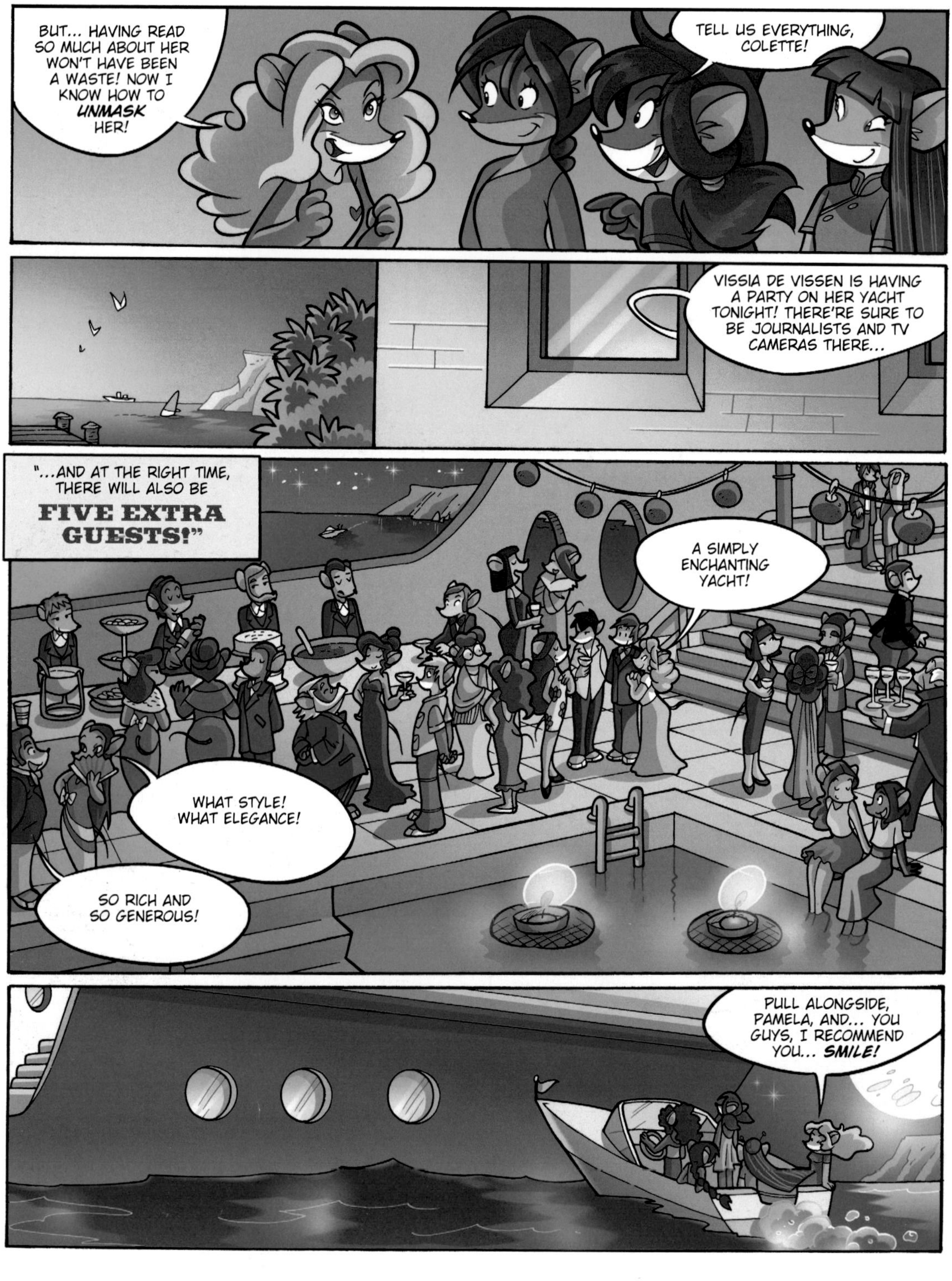
BUT... HAVING READ SO MUCH ABOUT HER WON'T HAVE BEEN A WASTE! NOW I KNOW HOW TO UNMASK HER!
TELL US EVERYTHING, COLETTE!
VISSIA DE VISSEN IS HAVING A PARTY ON HER YACHT TONIGHT! THERE'RE SURE TO BE JOURNALISTS AND TV CAMERAS THERE...
"...AND AT THE RIGHT TIME, THERE WILL ALSO BE FIVE EXTRA GUESTS!"
A SIMPLY ENCHANTING YACHT!
WHAT STYLE! WHAT ELEGANCE!
SO RICH AND SO GENEROUS!
PULL ALONGSIDE, PAMELA, AND... YOU GUYS, I RECOMMEND YOU... SMILE!

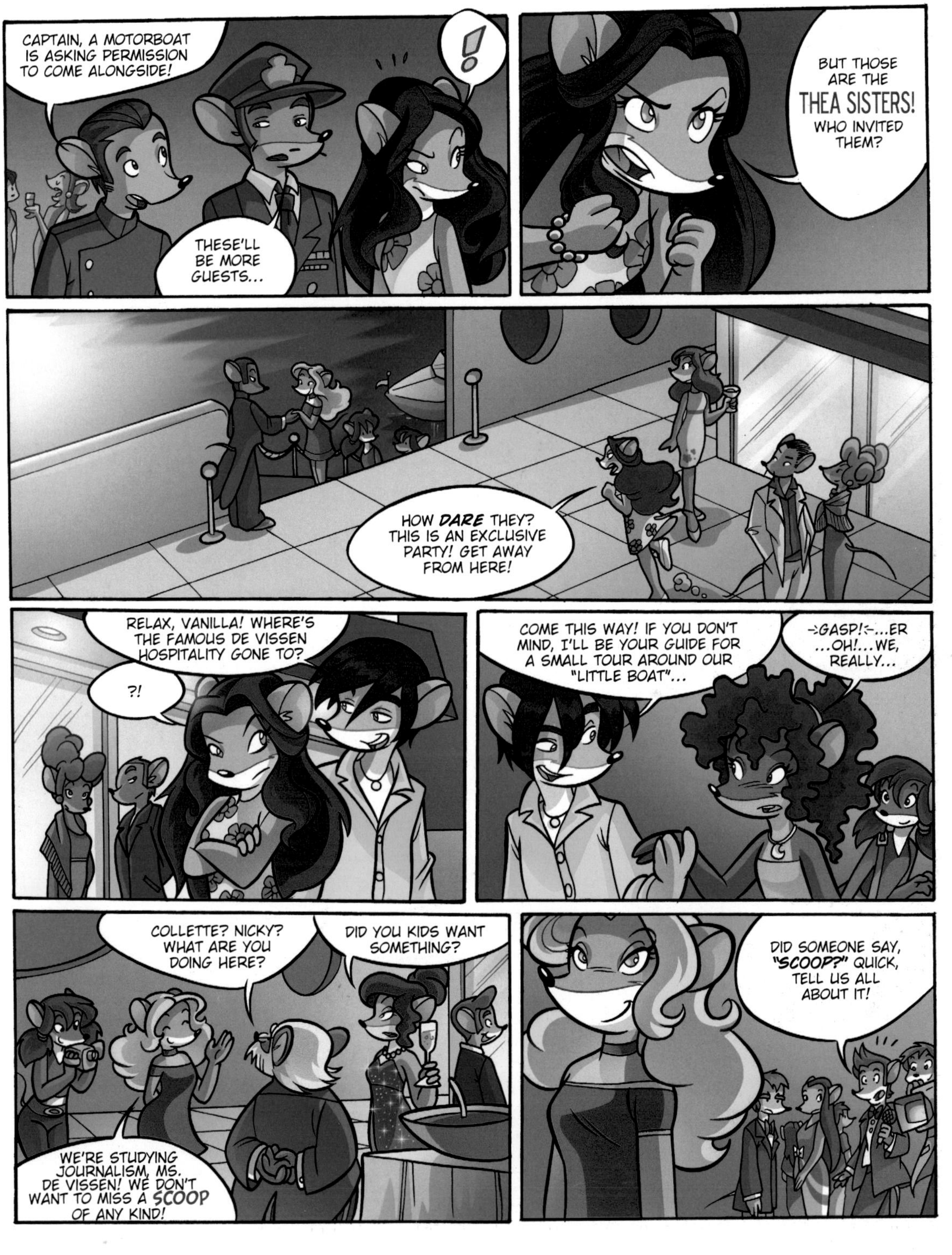
CAPTAIN, A MOTORBOAT IS ASKING PERMISSION TO COME ALONGSIDE!
!
THESE'LL BE MORE GUESTS...
BUT THOSE ARE THE THEA SISTERS! WHO INVITED THEM?
HOW DARE THEY? THIS IS AN EXCLUSIVE PARTY! GET AWAY FROM HERE!
RELAX, VANILLA! WHERE'S THE FAMOUS DE VISSEN HOSPITALITY GONE TO?
?!
COME THIS WAY! IF YOU DON'T MIND, I'LL BE YOUR GUIDE FOR A SMALL TOUR AROUND OUR "LITTLE BOAT"...
GASP! ...ER ...OH!...WE, REALLY...
COLLETTE? NICKY? WHAT ARE YOU DOING HERE?
DID YOU KIDS WANT SOMETHING?
WE'RE STUDYING JOURNALISM, MS. DE VISSEN! WE DON'T WANT TO MISS A SCOOP OF ANY KIND!
DID SOMEONE SAY, "SCOOP?" QUICK, TELL US ALL ABOUT IT!

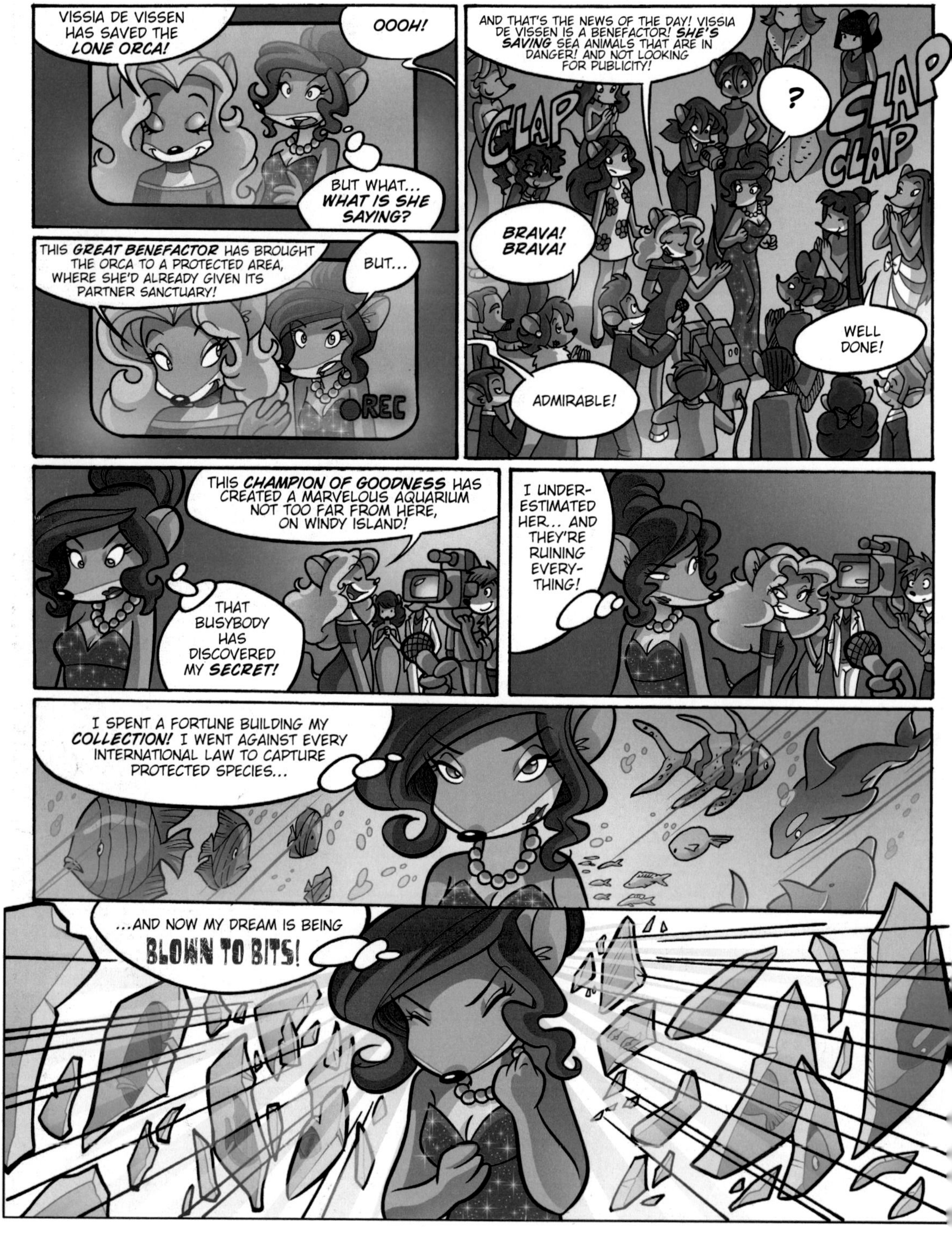
VISSIA DE VISSEN HAS SAVED THE LONE ORCA!
OOOH!
BUT WHAT... WHAT IS SHE SAYING?
THIS GREAT BENEFACTOR HAS BROUGHT THE ORCA TO A PROTECTED AREA, WHERE SHE'D ALREADY GIVEN ITS PARTNER SANCTUARY!
BUT...
REC
AND THAT'S THE NEWS OF THE DAY! VISSIA DE VISSEN IS A BENEFACTOR! SHE'S SAVING SEA ANIMALS THAT ARE IN DANGER! AND NOT LOOKING FOR PUBLICITY!
CLAP
?
CLAP
CLAP
BRAVA! BRAVA!
WELL DONE!
ADMIRABLE!
THIS CHAMPION OF GOODNESS HAS CREATED A MARVELOUS AQUARIUM NOT TOO FAR FROM HERE, ON WINDY ISLAND!
THAT BUSYBODY HAS DISCOVERED MY SECRET!
I UNDER-ESTIMATED HER... AND THEY'RE RUINING EVERY-THING!
I SPENT A FORTUNE BUILDING MY COLLECTION! I WENT AGAINST EVERY INTERNATIONAL LAW TO CAPTURE PROTECTED SPECIES...
...AND NOW MY DREAM IS BEING BLOWN TO BITS!

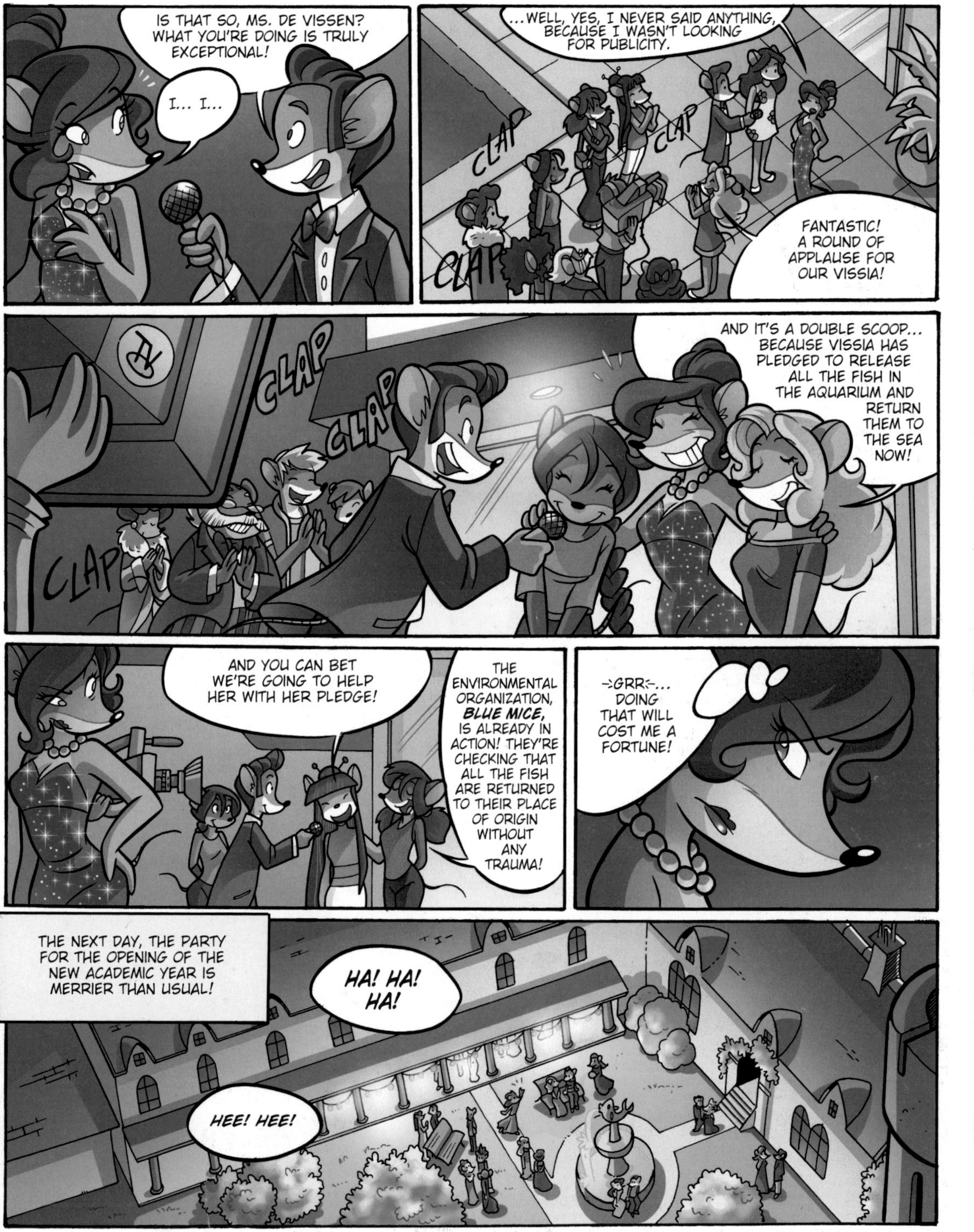
IS THAT SO, MS. DE VISSEN? WHAT YOU'RE DOING IS TRULY EXCEPTIONAL!
I... I...
...WELL, YES, I NEVER SAID ANYTHING, BECAUSE I WASN'T LOOKING FOR PUBLICITY.
CLAP
CLAP
CLAP
FANTASTIC! A ROUND OF APPLAUSE FOR OUR VISSIA!
CLAP
CLAP
CLAP
AND IT'S A DOUBLE SCOOP... BECAUSE VISSIA HAS PLEDGED TO RELEASE ALL THE FISH IN THE AQUARIUM AND RETURN THEM TO THE SEA NOW!
AND YOU CAN BET WE'RE GOING TO HELP HER WITH HER PLEDGE!
THE ENVIRONMENTAL ORGANIZATION, BLUE MICE, IS ALREADY IN ACTION! THEY'RE CHECKING THAT ALL THE FISH ARE RETURNED TO THEIR PLACE OF ORIGIN WITHOUT ANY TRAUMA!
GRR... DOING THAT WILL COST ME A FORTUNE!
THE NEXT DAY, THE PARTY FOR THE OPENING OF THE NEW ACADEMIC YEAR IS MERRIER THAN USUAL!
HA! HA! HA!
HEE! HEE!

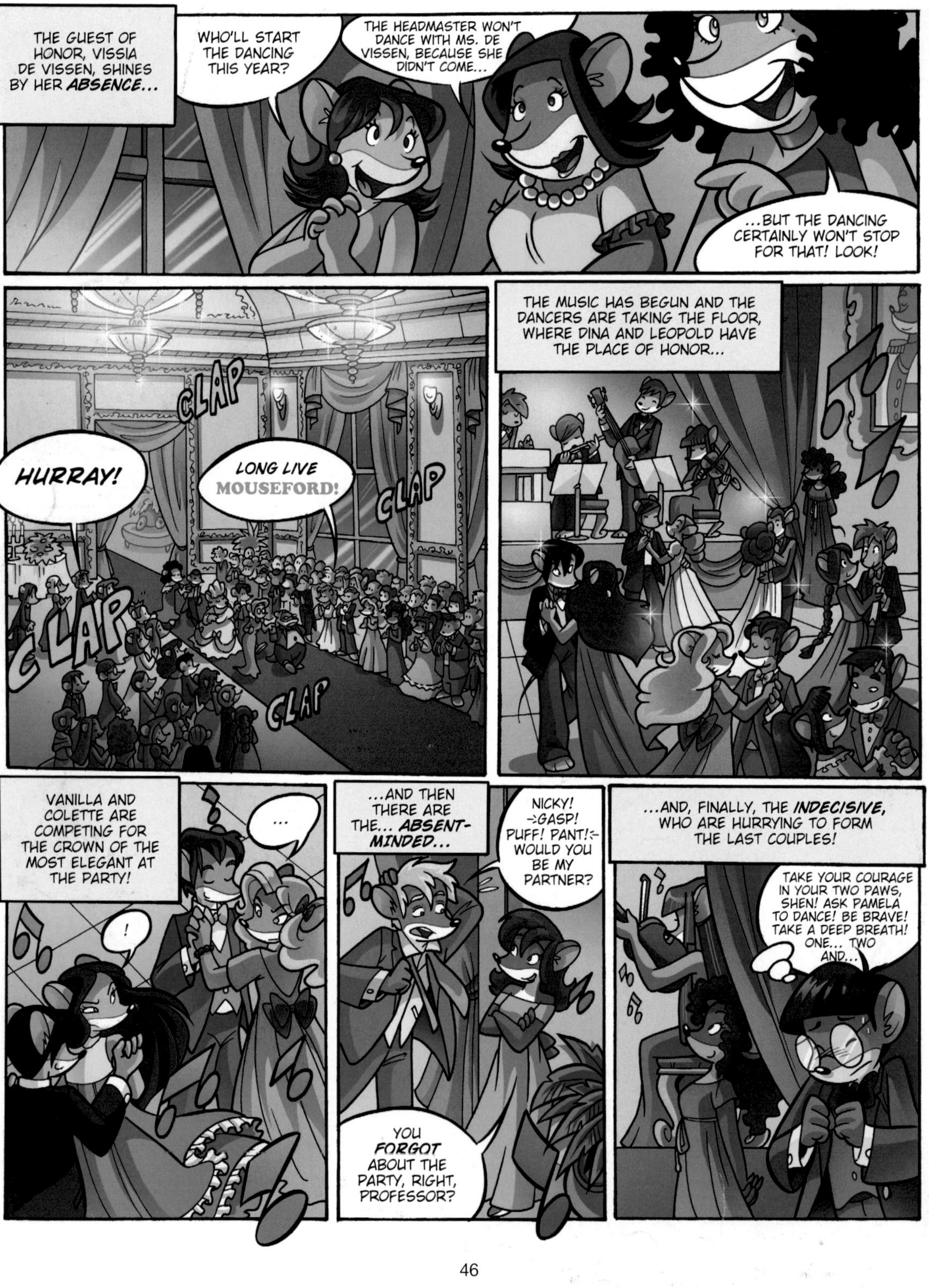

THE GUEST OF HONOR, VISSIA DE VISSEN, SHINES BY HER ABSENCE...
WHO'LL START THE DANCING THIS YEAR?
THE HEADMASTER WON'T DANCE WITH MS. DE VISSEN, BECAUSE SHE DIDN'T COME...
...BUT THE DANCING CERTAINLY WON'T STOP FOR THAT! LOOK!
CLAP
HURRAY!
LONG LIVE MOUSEFORD!
CLAP
CLAP
CLAP
THE MUSIC HAS BEGUN AND THE DANCERS ARE TAKING THE FLOOR, WHERE DINA AND LEOPOLD HAVE THE PLACE OF HONOR...
VANILLA AND COLETTE ARE COMPETING FOR THE CROWN OF THE MOST ELEGANT AT THE PARTY!
...
!
...AND THEN THERE ARE THE... ABSENT-MINDED...
NICKY! →GASP! PUFF! PANT!← WOULD YOU BE MY PARTNER?
YOU FORGOT ABOUT THE PARTY, RIGHT, PROFESSOR?
...AND, FINALLY, THE INDECISIVE, WHO ARE HURRYING TO FORM THE LAST COUPLES!
TAKE YOUR COURAGE IN YOUR TWO PAWS, SHEN! ASK PAMELA TO DANCE! BE BRAVE! TAKE A DEEP BREATH! ONE... TWO AND...

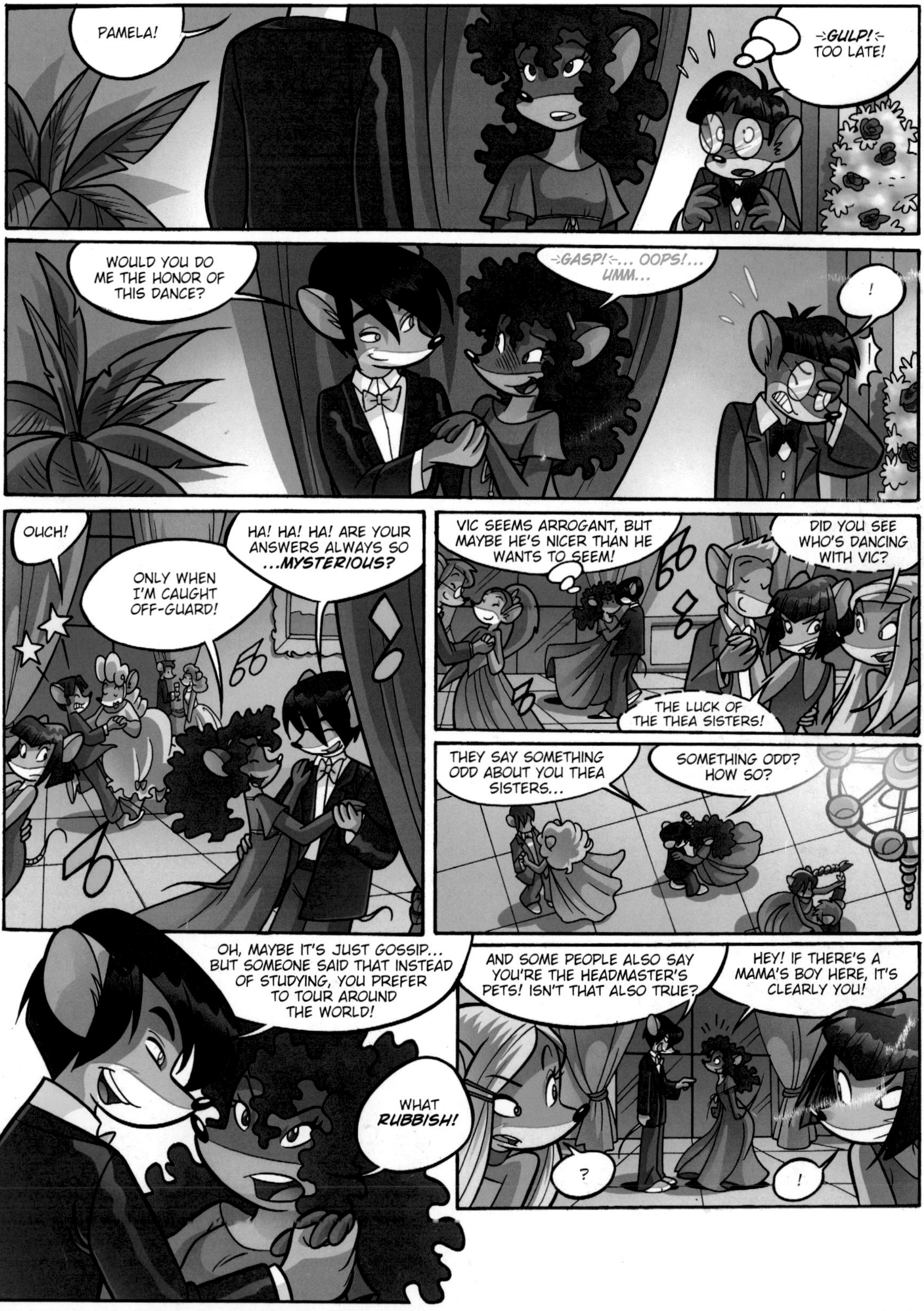
PAMELA!
-GULP!- TOO LATE!
WOULD YOU DO ME THE HONOR OF THIS DANCE?
-GASP!-... OOPS!... UMM...
!
OUCH!
HA! HA! HA! ARE YOUR ANSWERS ALWAYS SO ...MYSTERIOUS?
ONLY WHEN I'M CAUGHT OFF-GUARD!
VIC SEEMS ARROGANT, BUT MAYBE HE'S NICER THAN HE WANTS TO SEEM!
DID YOU SEE WHO'S DANCING WITH VIC?
THE LUCK OF THE THEA SISTERS!
THEY SAY SOMETHING ODD ABOUT YOU THEA SISTERS...
SOMETHING ODD? HOW SO?
OH, MAYBE IT'S JUST GOSSIP... BUT SOMEONE SAID THAT INSTEAD OF STUDYING, YOU PREFER TO TOUR AROUND THE WORLD!
WHAT RUBBISH!
AND SOME PEOPLE ALSO SAY YOU'RE THE HEADMASTER'S PETS! ISN'T THAT ALSO TRUE?
HEY! IF THERE'S A MAMA'S BOY HERE, IT'S CLEARLY YOU!
?
!

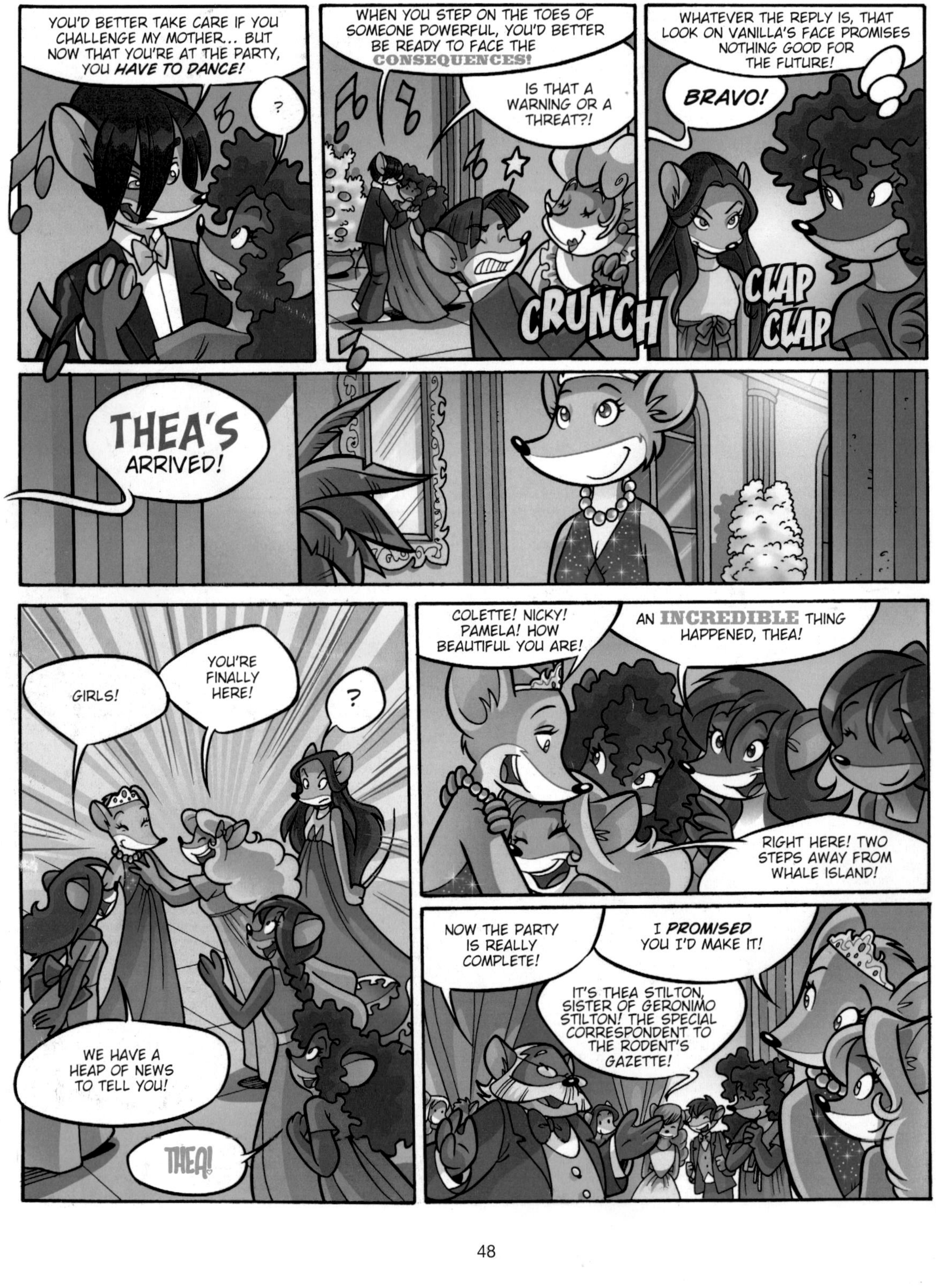
YOU'D BETTER TAKE CARE IF YOU CHALLENGE MY MOTHER... BUT NOW THAT YOU'RE AT THE PARTY, YOU HAVE TO DANCE!
?
WHEN YOU STEP ON THE TOES OF SOMEONE POWERFUL, YOU'D BETTER BE READY TO FACE THE CONSEQUENCES!
IS THAT A WARNING OR A THREAT?!
CRUNCH
WHATEVER THE REPLY IS, THAT LOOK ON VANILLA'S FACE PROMISES NOTHING GOOD FOR THE FUTURE!
BRAVO!
CLAP CLAP
THEA'S ARRIVED!
GIRLS!
YOU'RE FINALLY HERE!
?
WE HAVE A HEAP OF NEWS TO TELL YOU!
THEA!
COLETTE! NICKY! PAMELA! HOW BEAUTIFUL YOU ARE!
AN INCREDIBLE THING HAPPENED, THEA!
RIGHT HERE! TWO STEPS AWAY FROM WHALE ISLAND!
NOW THE PARTY IS REALLY COMPLETE!
I PROMISED YOU I'D MAKE IT!
IT'S THEA STILTON, SISTER OF GERONIMO STILTON! THE SPECIAL CORRESPONDENT TO THE RODENT'S GAZETTE!

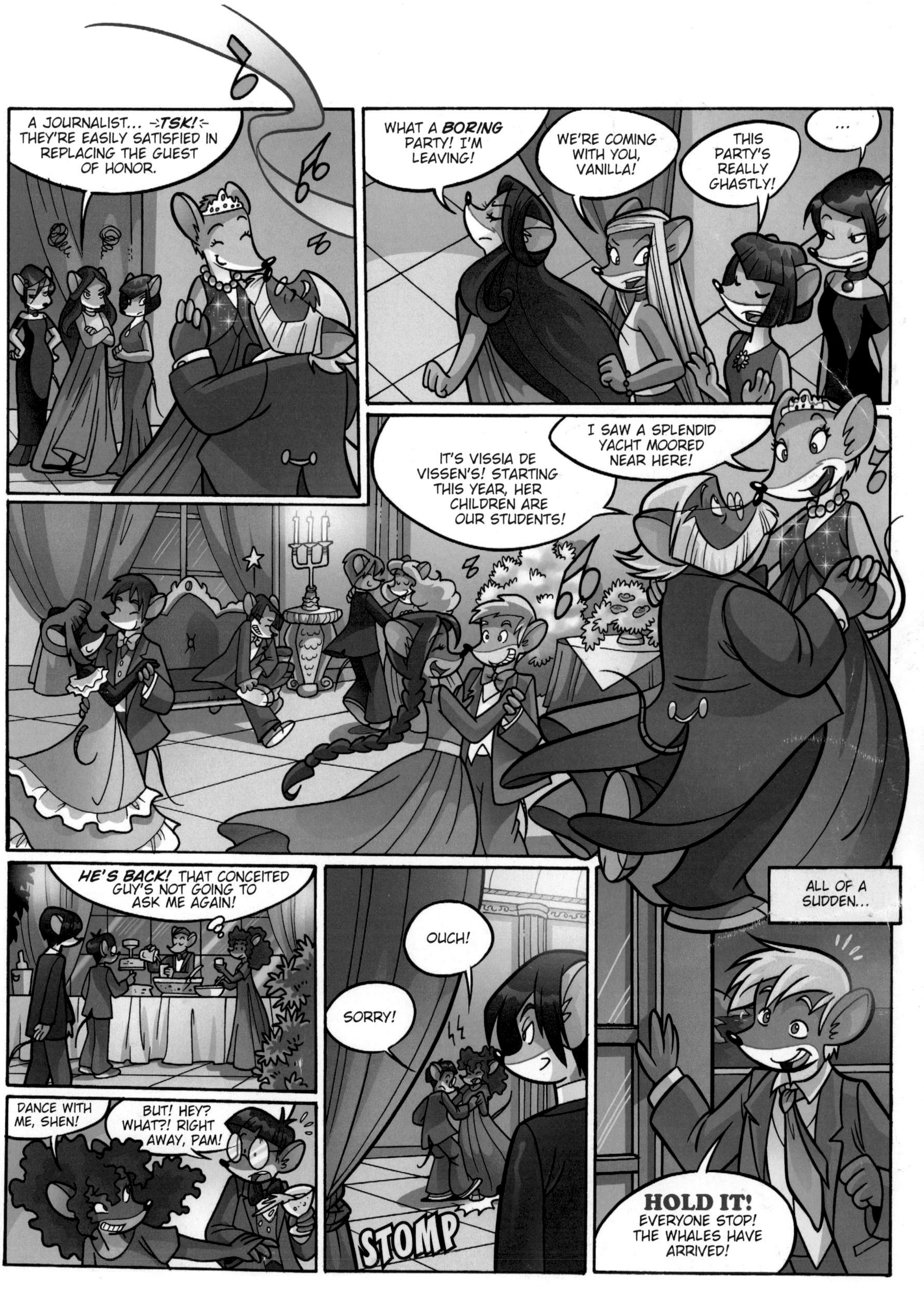
A JOURNALIST... -TSK!- THEY'RE EASILY SATISFIED IN REPLACING THE GUEST OF HONOR.
WHAT A BORING PARTY! I'M LEAVING!
WE'RE COMING WITH YOU, VANILLA!
THIS PARTY'S REALLY GHASTLY!
...
I SAW A SPLENDID YACHT MOORED NEAR HERE!
IT'S VISSIA DE VISSEN'S! STARTING THIS YEAR, HER CHILDREN ARE OUR STUDENTS!
HE'S BACK! THAT CONCEITED GUY'S NOT GOING TO ASK ME AGAIN!
DANCE WITH ME, SHEN!
BUT! HEY? WHAT?! RIGHT AWAY, PAM!
OUCH!
SORRY!
STOMP
ALL OF A SUDDEN...
HOLD IT! EVERYONE STOP! THE WHALES HAVE ARRIVED!

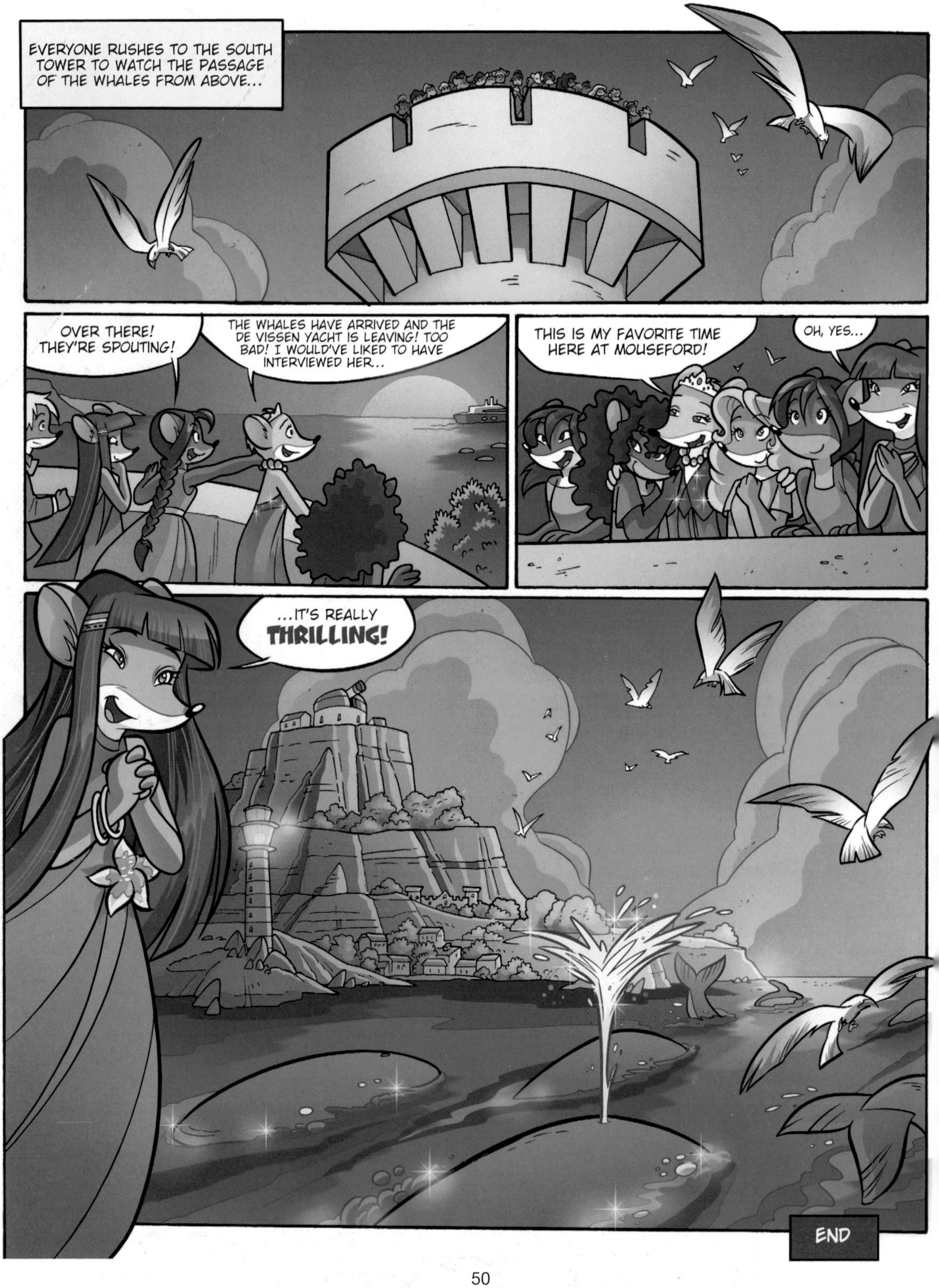

EVERYONE RUSHES TO THE SOUTH TOWER TO WATCH THE PASSAGE OF THE WHALES FROM ABOVE...
OVER THERE! THEY'RE SPOUTING!
THE WHALES HAVE ARRIVED AND THE DE VISSEN YACHT IS LEAVING! TOO BAD! I WOULD'VE LIKED TO HAVE INTERVIEWED HER...
THIS IS MY FAVORITE TIME HERE AT MOUSEFORD!
OH, YES...
...IT'S REALLY THRILLING!
END

REVENGE OF THE LIZARD CLUB

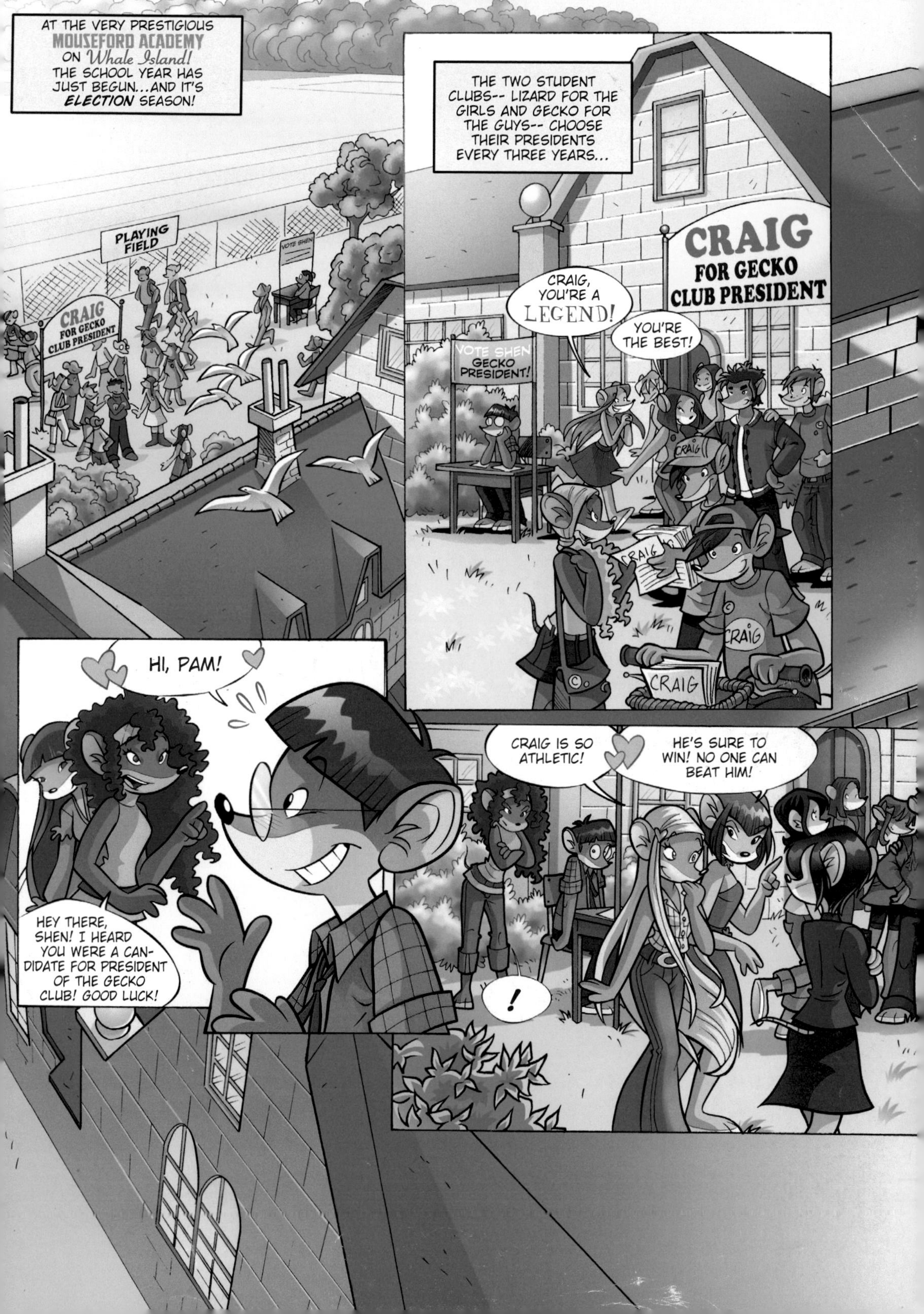

AT THE VERY PRESTIGIOUS MOUSEFORD ACADEMY ON Whale Island! THE SCHOOL YEAR HAS JUST BEGUN...AND IT'S ELECTION SEASON!
PLAYING FIELD
VOTE SHEN
CRAIG FOR GECKO CLUB PRESIDENT
THE TWO STUDENT CLUBS-- LIZARD FOR THE GIRLS AND GECKO FOR THE GUYS-- CHOOSE THEIR PRESIDENTS EVERY THREE YEARS...
CRAIG FOR GECKO CLUB PRESIDENT
VOTE SHEN GECKO PRESIDENT!
CRAIG, YOU'RE A LEGEND!
YOU'RE THE BEST!
CRAIG
CRAIG
CRAIG
CRAIG
HI, PAM!
HEY THERE, SHEN! I HEARD YOU WERE A CANDIDATE FOR PRESIDENT OF THE GECKO CLUB! GOOD LUCK!
CRAIG IS SO ATHLETIC!
HE'S SURE TO WIN! NO ONE CAN BEAT HIM!
!

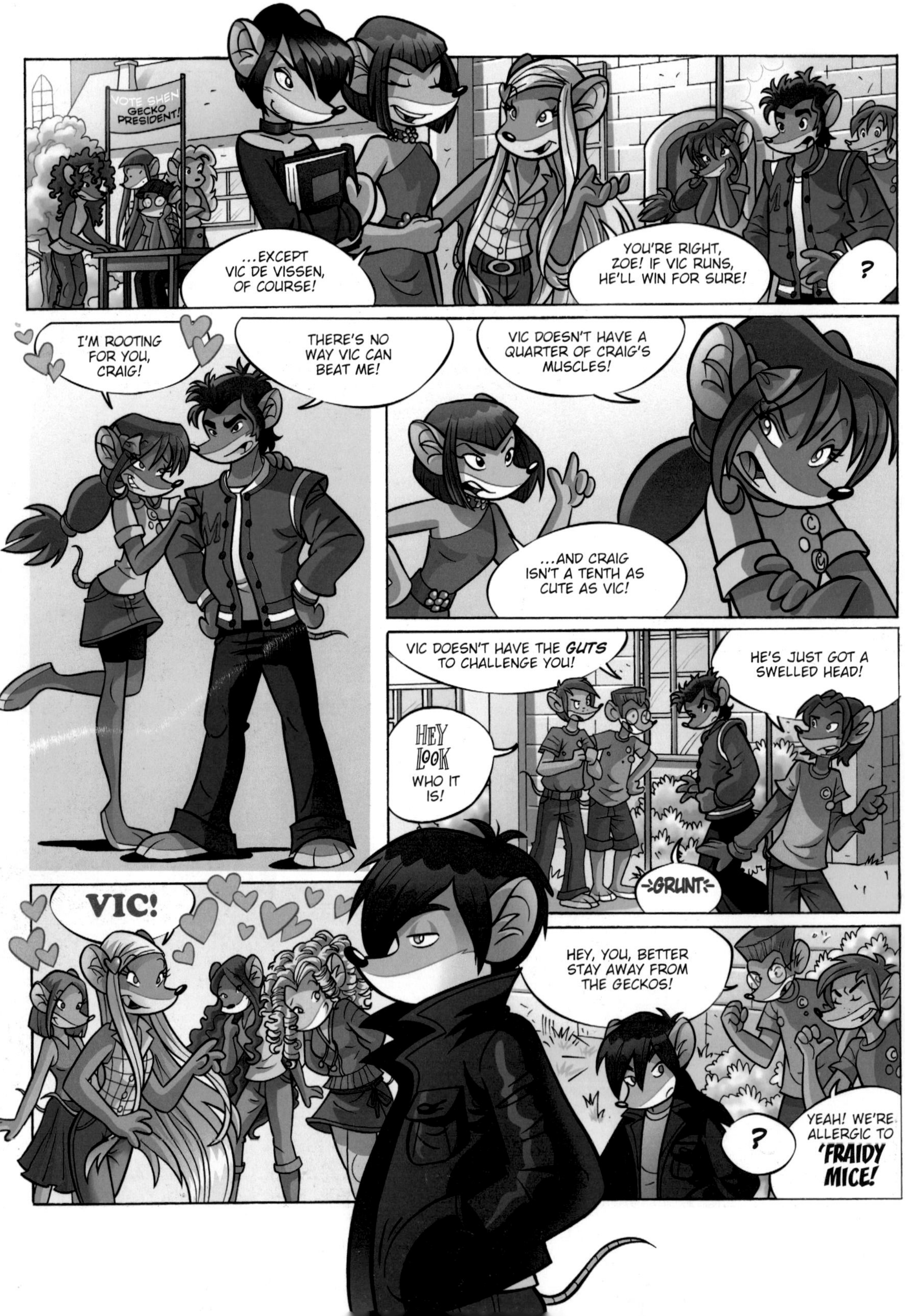

VOTE SHEN GECKO PRESIDENT!
...EXCEPT VIC DE VISSEN, OF COURSE!
YOU'RE RIGHT, ZOE! IF VIC RUNS, HE'LL WIN FOR SURE!
?
I'M ROOTING FOR YOU, CRAIG!
THERE'S NO WAY VIC CAN BEAT ME!
VIC DOESN'T HAVE A QUARTER OF CRAIG'S MUSCLES!
...AND CRAIG ISN'T A TENTH AS CUTE AS VIC!
VIC DOESN'T HAVE THE GUTS TO CHALLENGE YOU!
HE'S JUST GOT A SWELLED HEAD!
HEY LOOK WHO IT IS!
GRUNT
VIC!
HEY, YOU, BETTER STAY AWAY FROM THE GECKOS!
?
YEAH! WE'RE ALLERGIC TO 'FRAIDY MICE!

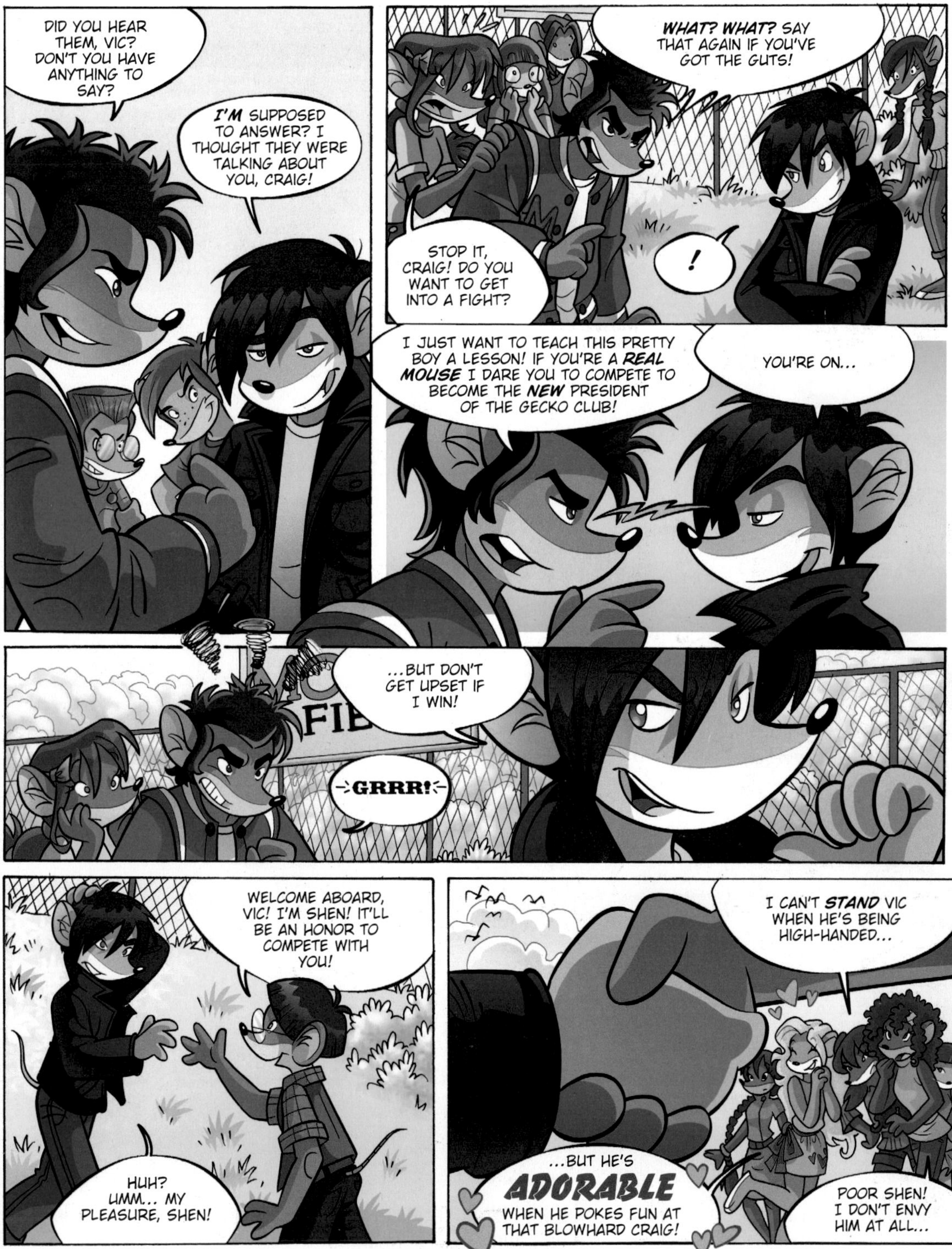

DID YOU HEAR THEM, VIC? DON'T YOU HAVE ANYTHING TO SAY?
I'M SUPPOSED TO ANSWER? I THOUGHT THEY WERE TALKING ABOUT YOU, CRAIG!
WHAT? WHAT? SAY THAT AGAIN IF YOU'VE GOT THE GUTS!
STOP IT, CRAIG! DO YOU WANT TO GET INTO A FIGHT?
!
I JUST WANT TO TEACH THIS PRETTY BOY A LESSON! IF YOU'RE A REAL MOUSE I DARE YOU TO COMPETE TO BECOME THE NEW PRESIDENT OF THE GECKO CLUB!
YOU'RE ON...
...BUT DON'T GET UPSET IF I WIN!
GRRR!
WELCOME ABOARD, VIC! I'M SHEN! IT'LL BE AN HONOR TO COMPETE WITH YOU!
HUH? UMM... MY PLEASURE, SHEN!
I CAN'T STAND VIC WHEN HE'S BEING HIGH-HANDED...
...BUT HE'S ADORABLE WHEN HE POKES FUN AT THAT BLOWHARD CRAIG!
POOR SHEN! I DON'T ENVY HIM AT ALL...

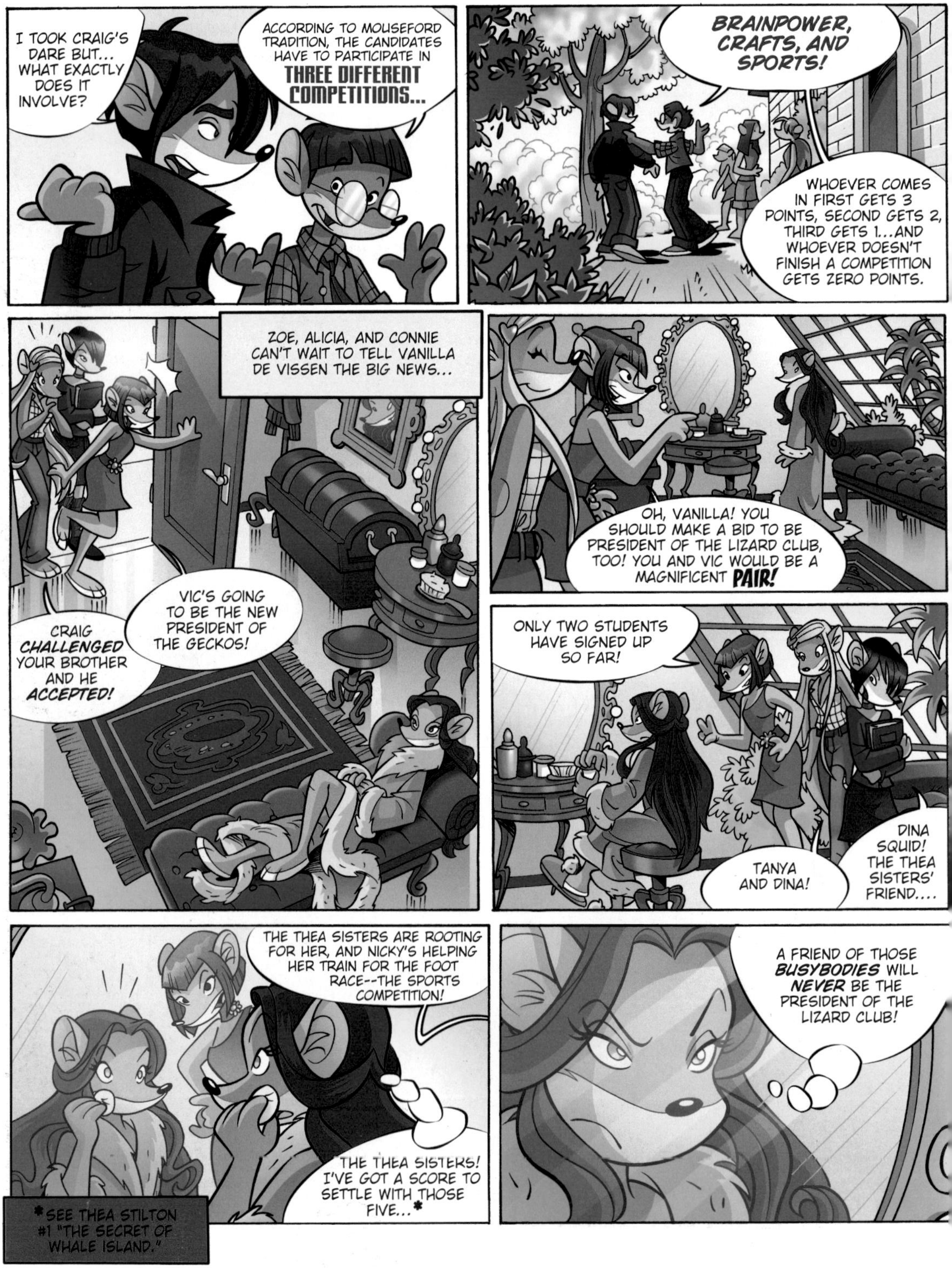
I TOOK CRAIG'S DARE BUT... WHAT EXACTLY DOES IT INVOLVE?
ACCORDING TO MOUSEFORD TRADITION, THE CANDIDATES HAVE TO PARTICIPATE IN THREE DIFFERENT COMPETITIONS...
BRAINPOWER, CRAFTS, AND SPORTS!
WHOEVER COMES IN FIRST GETS 3 POINTS, SECOND GETS 2, THIRD GETS 1...AND WHOEVER DOESN'T FINISH A COMPETITION GETS ZERO POINTS.
ZOE, ALICIA, AND CONNIE CAN'T WAIT TO TELL VANILLA DE VISSEN THE BIG NEWS...
VIC'S GOING TO BE THE NEW PRESIDENT OF THE GECKOS!
CRAIG CHALLENGED YOUR BROTHER AND HE ACCEPTED!
OH, VANILLA! YOU SHOULD MAKE A BID TO BE PRESIDENT OF THE LIZARD CLUB, TOO! YOU AND VIC WOULD BE A MAGNIFICENT PAIR!
ONLY TWO STUDENTS HAVE SIGNED UP SO FAR!
TANYA AND DINA!
DINA SQUID! THE THEA SISTERS' FRIEND....
THE THEA SISTERS ARE ROOTING FOR HER, AND NICKY'S HELPING HER TRAIN FOR THE FOOT RACE--THE SPORTS COMPETITION!
THE THEA SISTERS! I'VE GOT A SCORE TO SETTLE WITH THOSE FIVE...*
A FRIEND OF THOSE BUSYBODIES WILL NEVER BE THE PRESIDENT OF THE LIZARD CLUB!
*SEE THEA STILTON #1 "THE SECRET OF WHALE ISLAND."

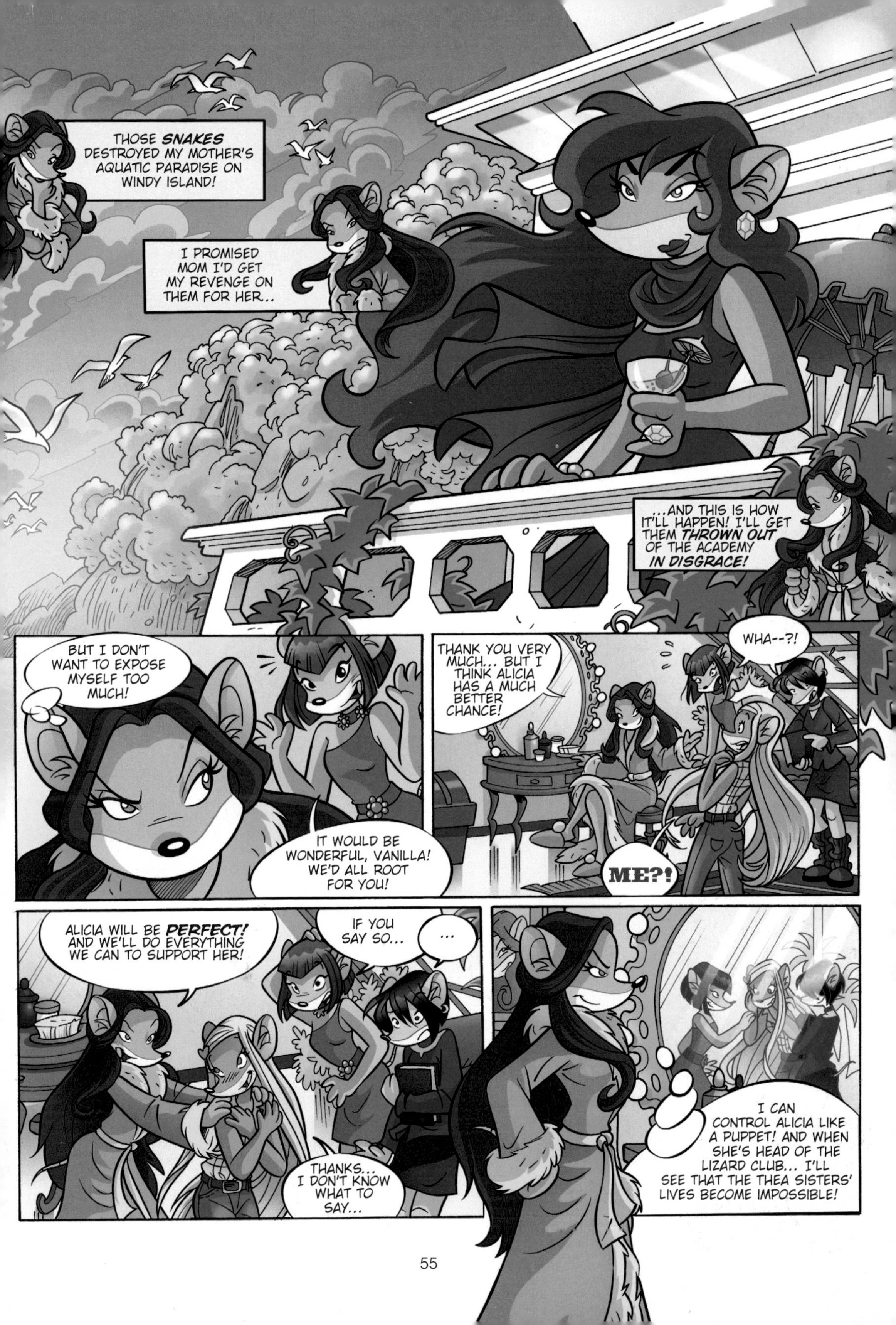
THOSE SNAKES DESTROYED MY MOTHER'S AQUATIC PARADISE ON WINDY ISLAND!
I PROMISED MOM I'D GET MY REVENGE ON THEM FOR HER...
...AND THIS IS HOW IT'LL HAPPEN! I'LL GET THEM THROWN OUT OF THE ACADEMY IN DISGRACE!
BUT I DON'T WANT TO EXPOSE MYSELF TOO MUCH!
IT WOULD BE WONDERFUL, VANILLA! WE'D ALL ROOT FOR YOU!
THANK YOU VERY MUCH... BUT I THINK ALICIA HAS A MUCH BETTER CHANCE!
WHA--?!
ME?!
ALICIA WILL BE PERFECT! AND WE'LL DO EVERYTHING WE CAN TO SUPPORT HER!
IF YOU SAY SO...
...
THANKS... I DON'T KNOW WHAT TO SAY...
I CAN CONTROL ALICIA LIKE A PUPPET! AND WHEN SHE'S HEAD OF THE LIZARD CLUB... I'LL SEE THAT THE THEA SISTERS' LIVES BECOME IMPOSSIBLE!

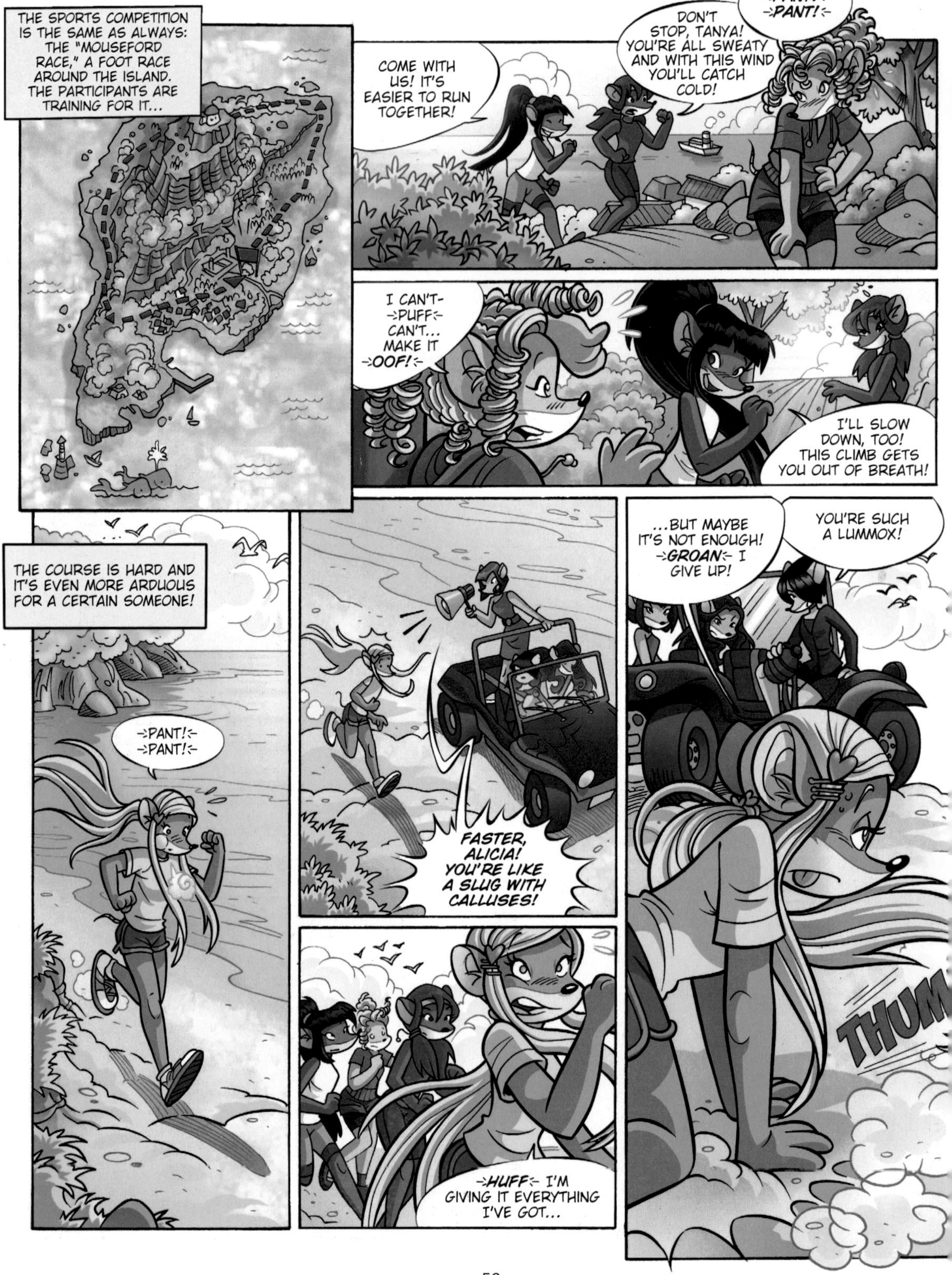
THE SPORTS COMPETITION IS THE SAME AS ALWAYS: THE "MOUSEFORD RACE," A FOOT RACE AROUND THE ISLAND. THE PARTICIPANTS ARE TRAINING FOR IT...
COME WITH US! IT'S EASIER TO RUN TOGETHER!
DON'T STOP, TANYA! YOU'RE ALL SWEATY AND WITH THIS WIND YOU'LL CATCH COLD!
-PANT!- -PANT!-
I CAN'T- -PUFF- CAN'T... MAKE IT -OOF!-
I'LL SLOW DOWN, TOO! THIS CLIMB GETS YOU OUT OF BREATH!
THE COURSE IS HARD AND IT'S EVEN MORE ARDUOUS FOR A CERTAIN SOMEONE!
-PANT!- -PANT!-
FASTER, ALICIA! YOU'RE LIKE A SLUG WITH CALLUSES!
-HUFF- I'M GIVING IT EVERYTHING I'VE GOT...
...BUT MAYBE IT'S NOT ENOUGH! -GROAN- I GIVE UP!
YOU'RE SUCH A LUMMOX!
THUM

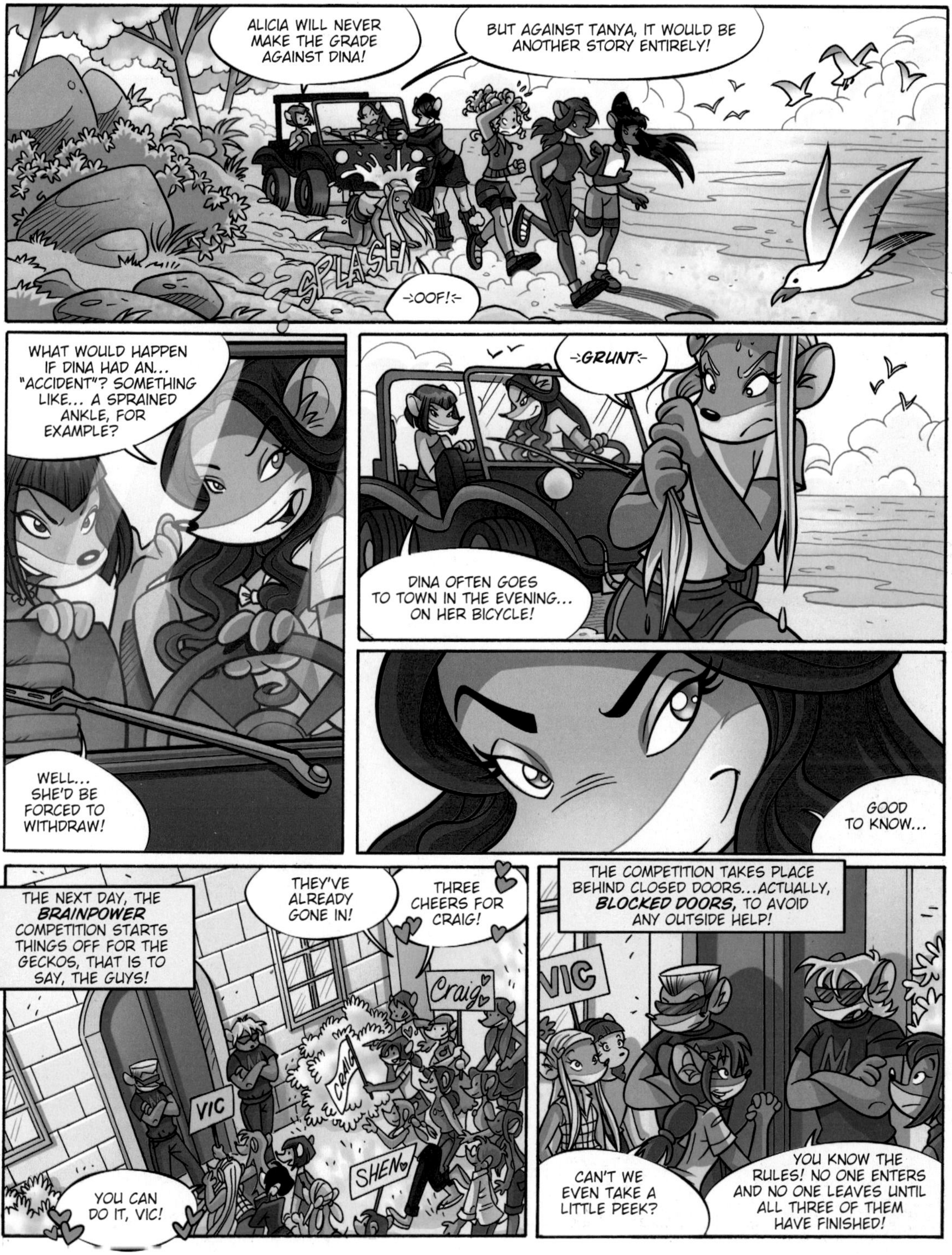
ALICIA WILL NEVER MAKE THE GRADE AGAINST DINA!
BUT AGAINST TANYA, IT WOULD BE ANOTHER STORY ENTIRELY!
SPLASH
OOF!
WHAT WOULD HAPPEN IF DINA HAD AN... "ACCIDENT"? SOMETHING LIKE... A SPRAINED ANKLE, FOR EXAMPLE?
WELL... SHE'D BE FORCED TO WITHDRAW!
GRUNT
DINA OFTEN GOES TO TOWN IN THE EVENING... ON HER BICYCLE!
GOOD TO KNOW...
THE NEXT DAY, THE BRAINPOWER COMPETITION STARTS THINGS OFF FOR THE GECKOS, THAT IS TO SAY, THE GUYS!
THEY'VE ALREADY GONE IN!
THREE CHEERS FOR CRAIG!
Craig
CRAIG
VIC
SHEN
YOU CAN DO IT, VIC!
THE COMPETITION TAKES PLACE BEHIND CLOSED DOORS...ACTUALLY, BLOCKED DOORS, TO AVOID ANY OUTSIDE HELP!
VIC
CAN'T WE EVEN TAKE A LITTLE PEEK?
YOU KNOW THE RULES! NO ONE ENTERS AND NO ONE LEAVES UNTIL ALL THREE OF THEM HAVE FINISHED!

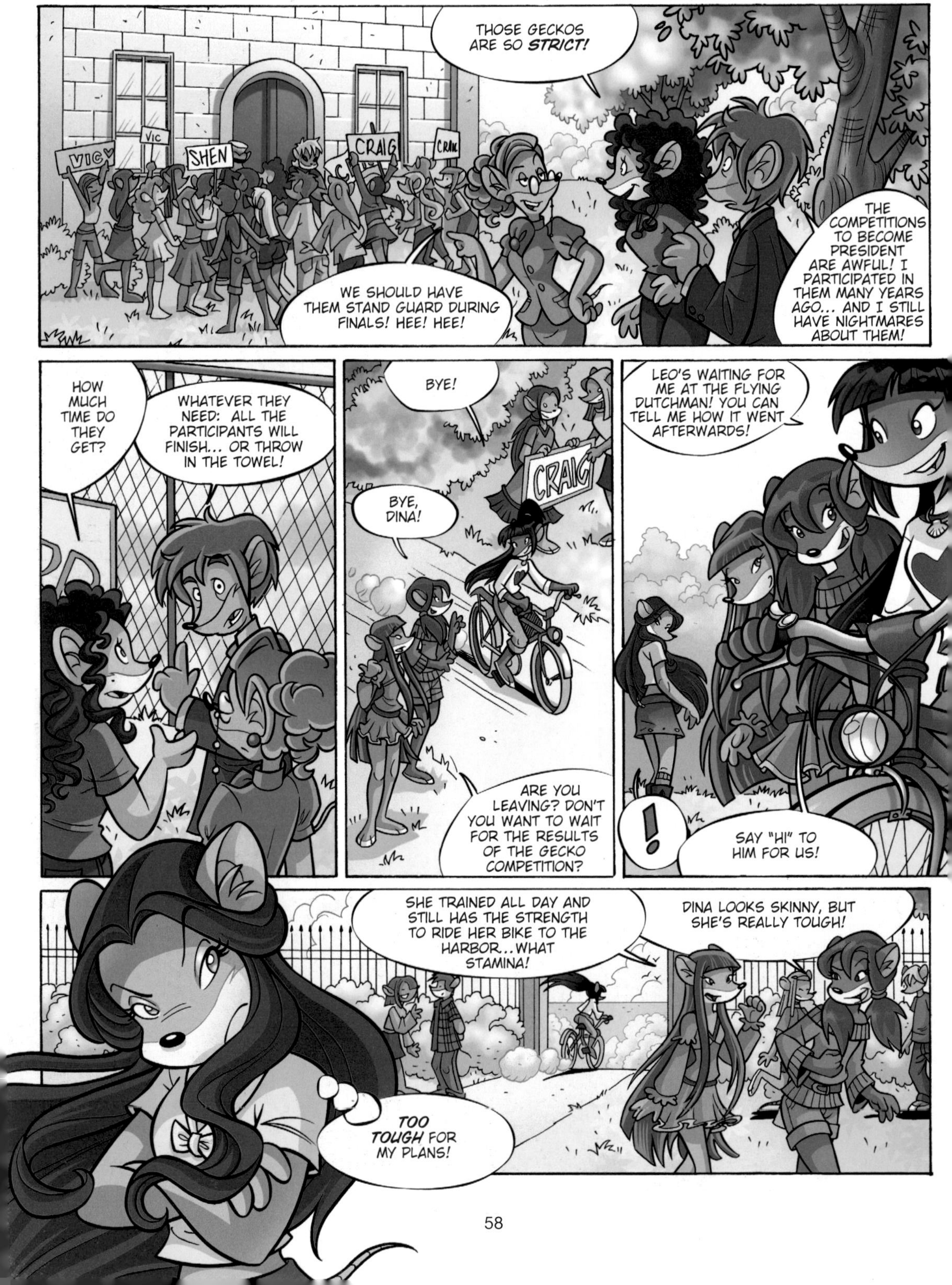
VIC
VIC
SHEN
CRAIG
CRAIG
THOSE GECKOS ARE SO *STRICT!*
WE SHOULD HAVE THEM STAND GUARD DURING FINALS! HEE! HEE!
THE COMPETITIONS TO BECOME PRESIDENT ARE AWFUL! I PARTICIPATED IN THEM MANY YEARS AGO... AND I STILL HAVE NIGHTMARES ABOUT THEM!
HOW MUCH TIME DO THEY GET?
WHATEVER THEY NEED: ALL THE PARTICIPANTS WILL FINISH... OR THROW IN THE TOWEL!
BYE!
CRAIG
BYE, DINA!
ARE YOU LEAVING? DON'T YOU WANT TO WAIT FOR THE RESULTS OF THE GECKO COMPETITION?
LEO'S WAITING FOR ME AT THE FLYING DUTCHMAN! YOU CAN TELL ME HOW IT WENT AFTERWARDS!
!
SAY "HI" TO HIM FOR US!
SHE TRAINED ALL DAY AND STILL HAS THE STRENGTH TO RIDE HER BIKE TO THE HARBOR...WHAT STAMINA!
DINA LOOKS SKINNY, BUT SHE'S REALLY TOUGH!
TOO TOUGH FOR MY PLANS!

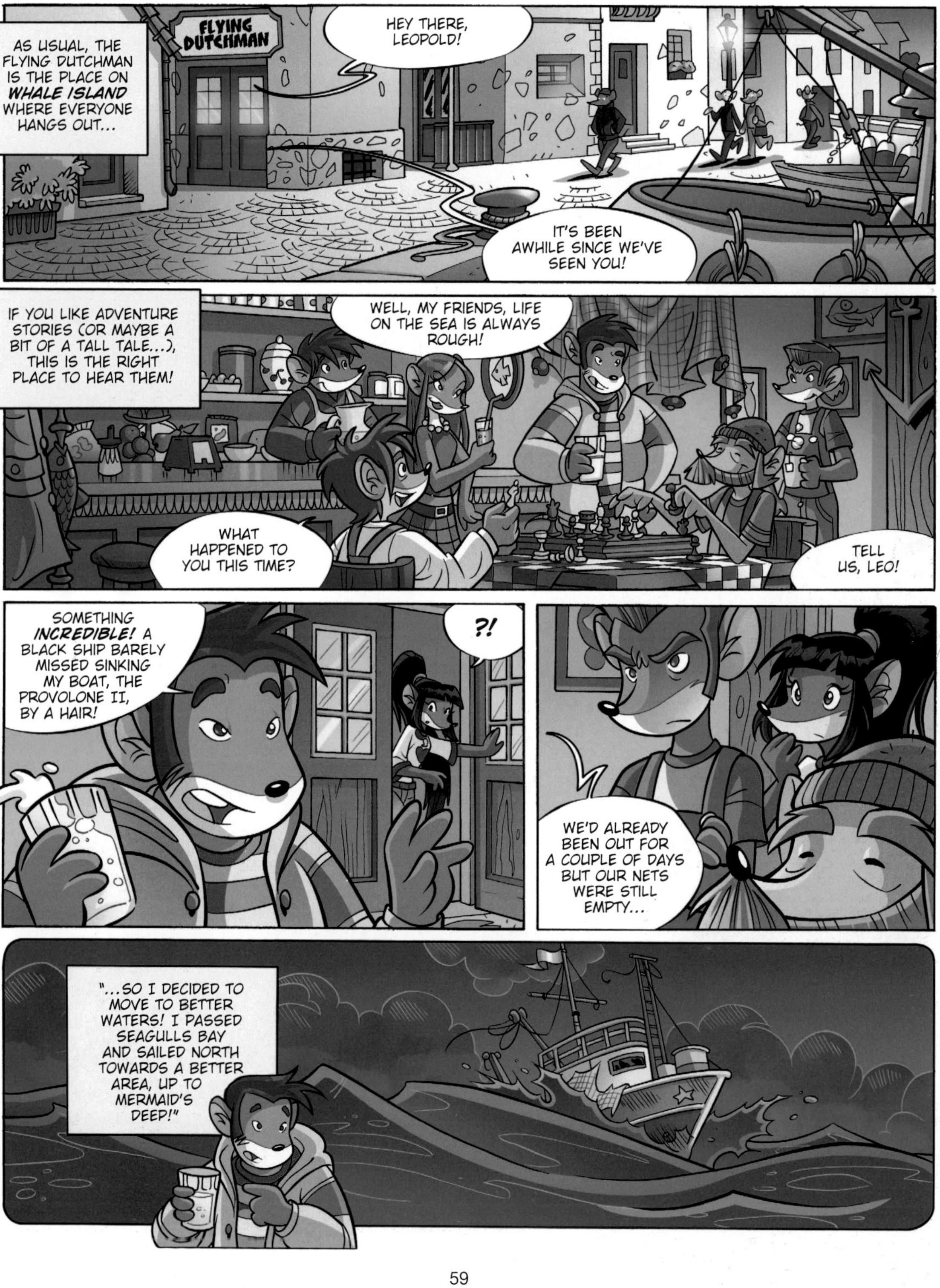
AS USUAL, THE FLYING DUTCHMAN IS THE PLACE ON ***WHALE ISLAND*** WHERE EVERYONE HANGS OUT...
FLYING DUTCHMAN
HEY THERE, LEOPOLD!
IT'S BEEN AWHILE SINCE WE'VE SEEN YOU!
IF YOU LIKE ADVENTURE STORIES (OR MAYBE A BIT OF A TALL TALE...), THIS IS THE RIGHT PLACE TO HEAR THEM!
WELL, MY FRIENDS, LIFE ON THE SEA IS ALWAYS ROUGH!
WHAT HAPPENED TO YOU THIS TIME?
TELL US, LEO!
SOMETHING ***INCREDIBLE!*** A BLACK SHIP BARELY MISSED SINKING MY BOAT, THE PROVOLONE II, BY A HAIR!
?!
WE'D ALREADY BEEN OUT FOR A COUPLE OF DAYS BUT OUR NETS WERE STILL EMPTY...
"...SO I DECIDED TO MOVE TO BETTER WATERS! I PASSED SEAGULLS BAY AND SAILED NORTH TOWARDS A BETTER AREA, UP TO MERMAID'S DEEP!"

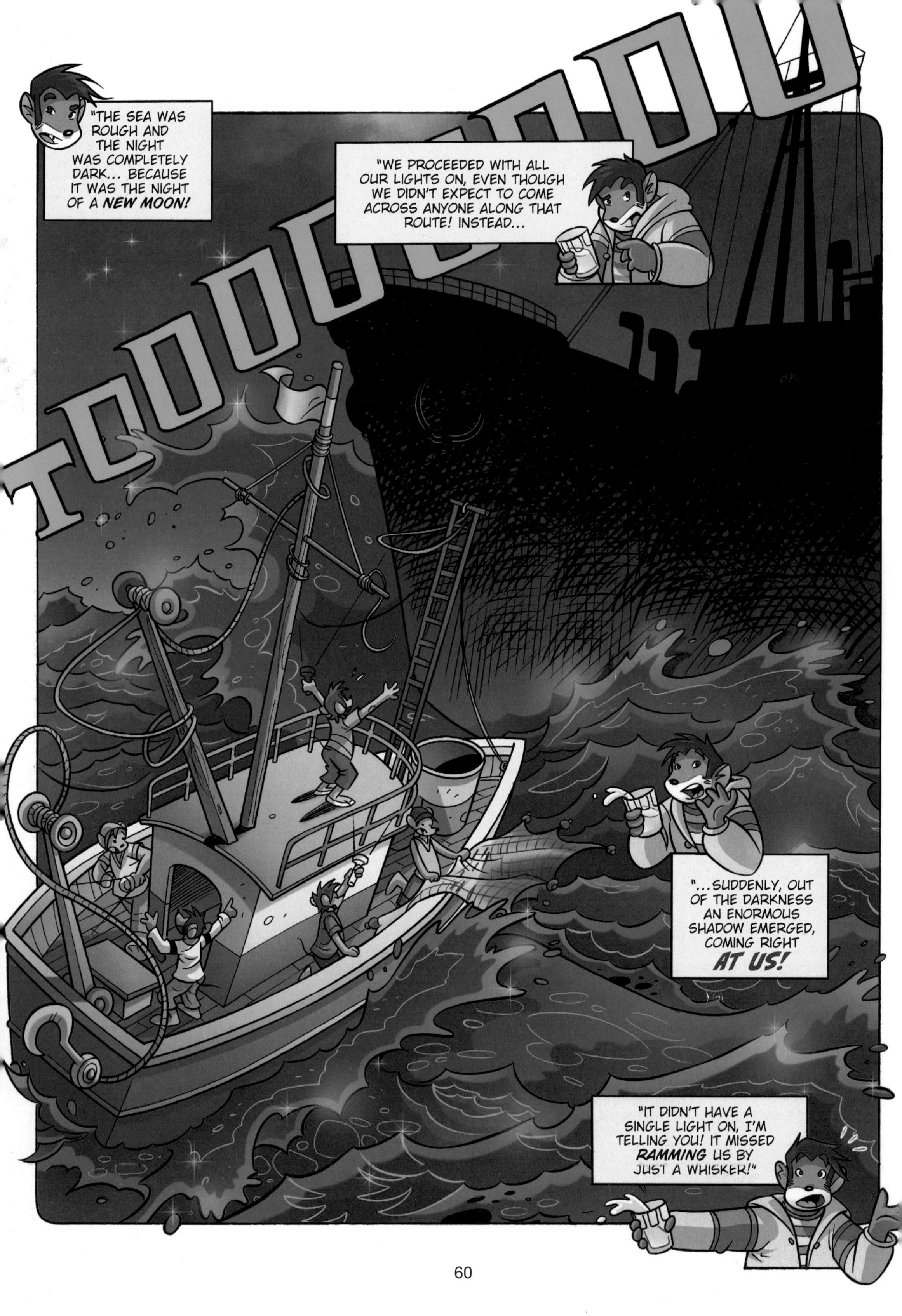
"THE SEA WAS ROUGH AND THE NIGHT WAS COMPLETELY DARK... BECAUSE IT WAS THE NIGHT OF A NEW MOON!
"WE PROCEEDED WITH ALL OUR LIGHTS ON, EVEN THOUGH WE DIDN'T EXPECT TO COME ACROSS ANYONE ALONG THAT ROUTE! INSTEAD...
TOOOOOOOU
"...SUDDENLY, OUT OF THE DARKNESS AN ENORMOUS SHADOW EMERGED, COMING RIGHT AT US!
"IT DIDN'T HAVE A SINGLE LIGHT ON, I'M TELLING YOU! IT MISSED RAMMING US BY JUST A WHISKER!"

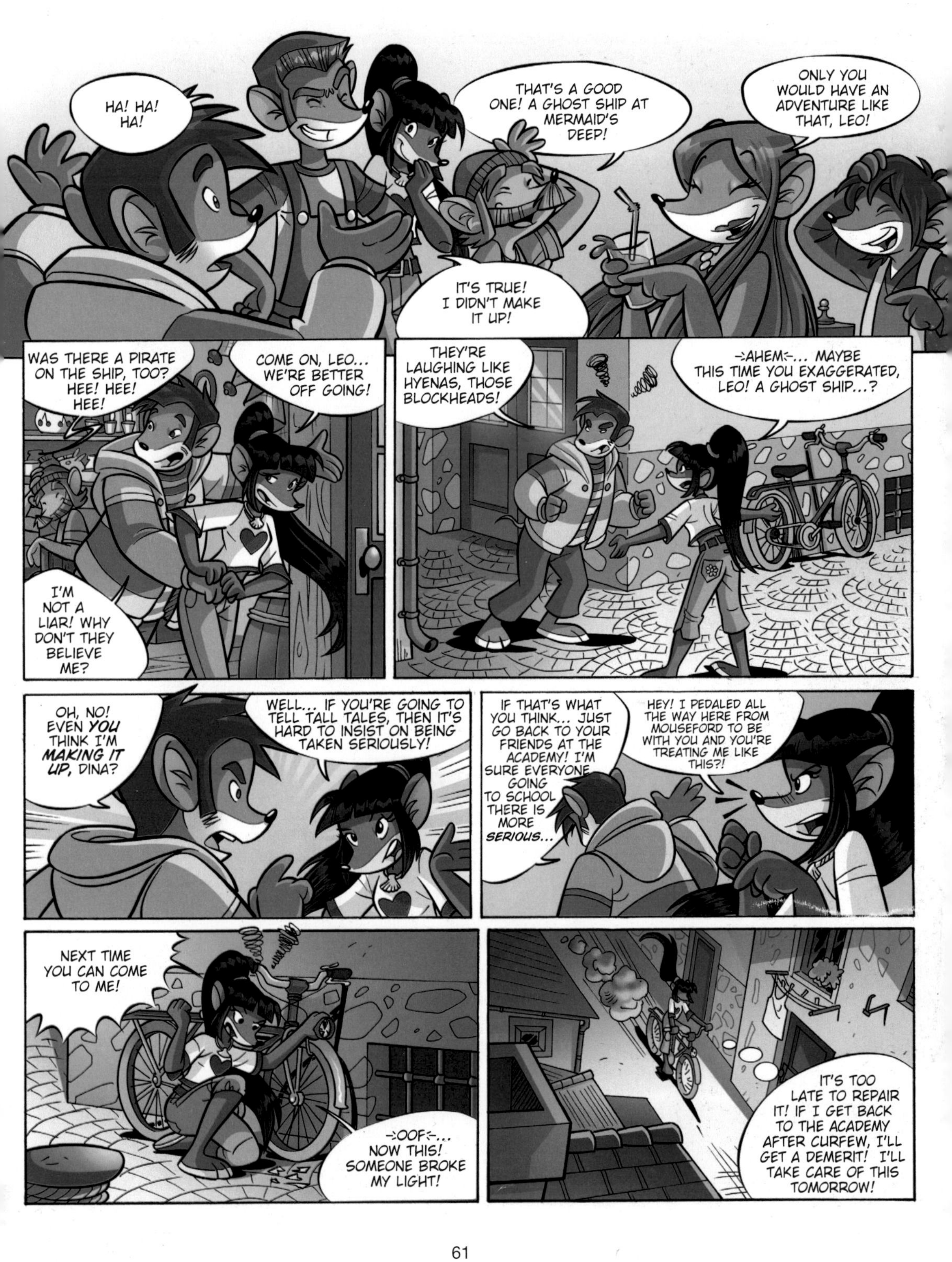
HA! HA! HA!
THAT'S A GOOD ONE! A GHOST SHIP AT MERMAID'S DEEP!
ONLY YOU WOULD HAVE AN ADVENTURE LIKE THAT, LEO!
IT'S TRUE! I DIDN'T MAKE IT UP!
WAS THERE A PIRATE ON THE SHIP, TOO? HEE! HEE! HEE!
COME ON, LEO... WE'RE BETTER OFF GOING!
I'M NOT A LIAR! WHY DON'T THEY BELIEVE ME?
THEY'RE LAUGHING LIKE HYENAS, THOSE BLOCKHEADS!
-AHEM-... MAYBE THIS TIME YOU EXAGGERATED, LEO! A GHOST SHIP...?
OH, NO! EVEN YOU THINK I'M MAKING IT UP, DINA?
WELL... IF YOU'RE GOING TO TELL TALL TALES, THEN IT'S HARD TO INSIST ON BEING TAKEN SERIOUSLY!
IF THAT'S WHAT YOU THINK... JUST GO BACK TO YOUR FRIENDS AT THE ACADEMY! I'M SURE EVERYONE GOING TO SCHOOL THERE IS MORE SERIOUS...
HEY! I PEDALED ALL THE WAY HERE FROM MOUSEFORD TO BE WITH YOU AND YOU'RE TREATING ME LIKE THIS?!
NEXT TIME YOU CAN COME TO ME!
-OOF-... NOW THIS! SOMEONE BROKE MY LIGHT!
IT'S TOO LATE TO REPAIR IT! IF I GET BACK TO THE ACADEMY AFTER CURFEW, I'LL GET A DEMERIT! I'LL TAKE CARE OF THIS TOMORROW!

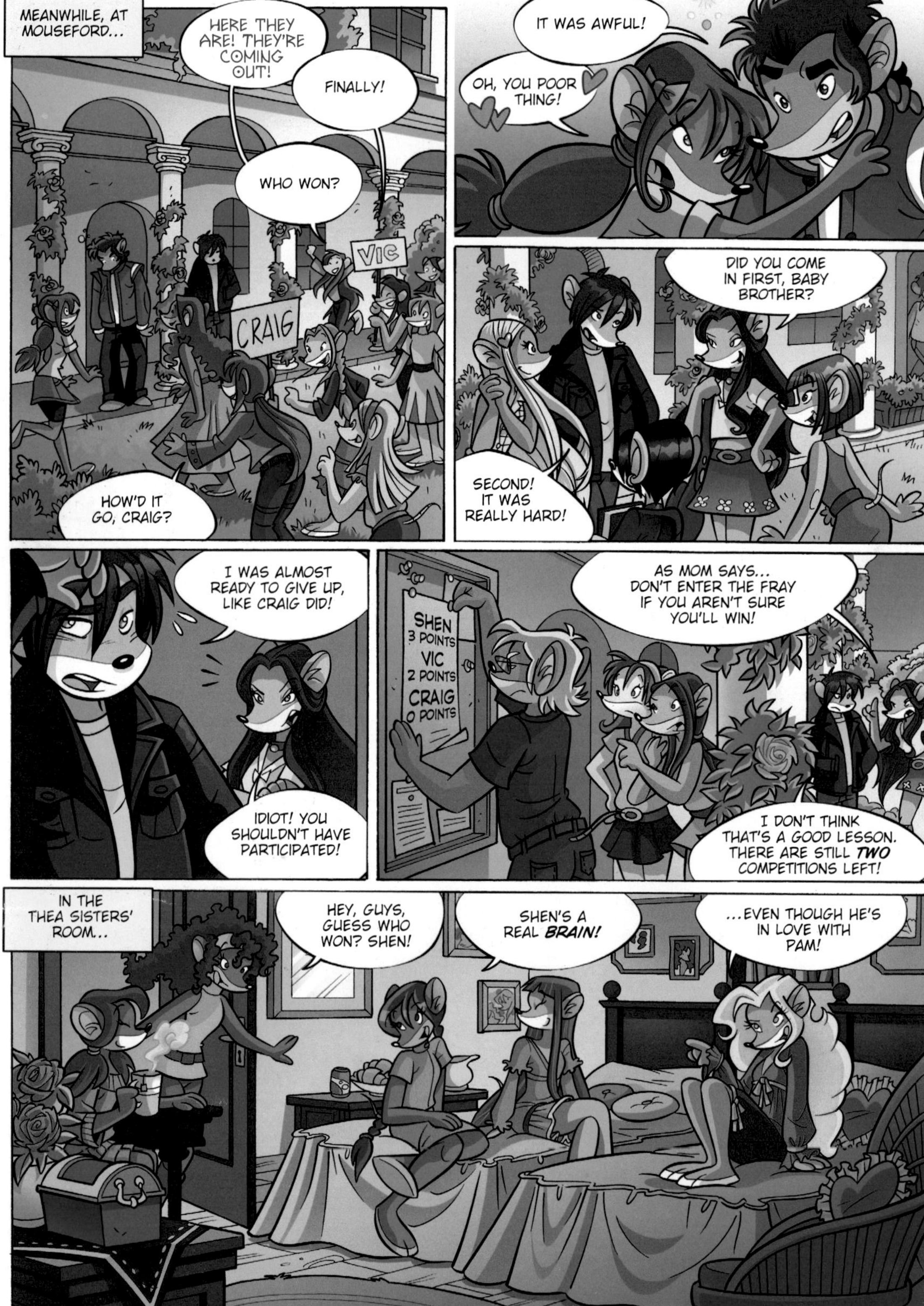

MEANWHILE, AT MOUSEFORD...
HERE THEY ARE! THEY'RE COMING OUT!
FINALLY!
WHO WON?
VIC
CRAIG
HOW'D IT GO, CRAIG?
IT WAS AWFUL!
OH, YOU POOR THING!
DID YOU COME IN FIRST, BABY BROTHER?
SECOND! IT WAS REALLY HARD!
I WAS ALMOST READY TO GIVE UP, LIKE CRAIG DID!
IDIOT! YOU SHOULDN'T HAVE PARTICIPATED!
SHEN 3 POINTS
VIC 2 POINTS
CRAIG 0 POINTS
AS MOM SAYS... DON'T ENTER THE FRAY IF YOU AREN'T SURE YOU'LL WIN!
I DON'T THINK THAT'S A GOOD LESSON. THERE ARE STILL *TWO* COMPETITIONS LEFT!
IN THE THEA SISTERS' ROOM...
HEY, GUYS, GUESS WHO WON? SHEN!
SHEN'S A REAL ***BRAIN!***
...EVEN THOUGH HE'S IN LOVE WITH PAM!

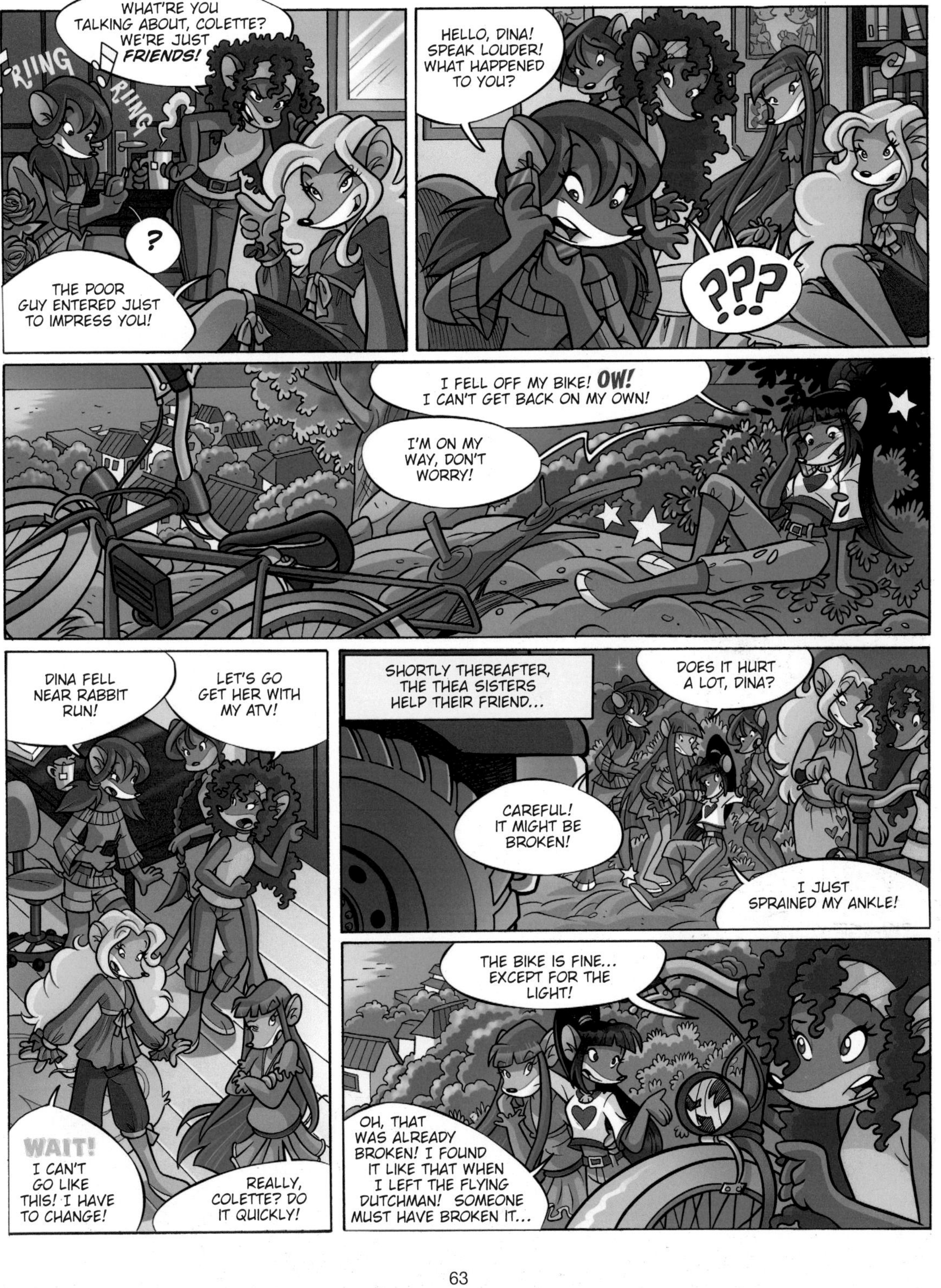

RIING
RIING
WHAT'RE YOU TALKING ABOUT, COLETTE? WE'RE JUST FRIENDS!
?
THE POOR GUY ENTERED JUST TO IMPRESS YOU!
HELLO, DINA! SPEAK LOUDER! WHAT HAPPENED TO YOU?
???
I FELL OFF MY BIKE! OW! I CAN'T GET BACK ON MY OWN!
I'M ON MY WAY, DON'T WORRY!
DINA FELL NEAR RABBIT RUN!
LET'S GO GET HER WITH MY ATV!
WAIT! I CAN'T GO LIKE THIS! I HAVE TO CHANGE!
REALLY, COLETTE? DO IT QUICKLY!
SHORTLY THEREAFTER, THE THEA SISTERS HELP THEIR FRIEND...
DOES IT HURT A LOT, DINA?
CAREFUL! IT MIGHT BE BROKEN!
I JUST SPRAINED MY ANKLE!
THE BIKE IS FINE... EXCEPT FOR THE LIGHT!
OH, THAT WAS ALREADY BROKEN! I FOUND IT LIKE THAT WHEN I LEFT THE FLYING DUTCHMAN! SOMEONE MUST HAVE BROKEN IT...

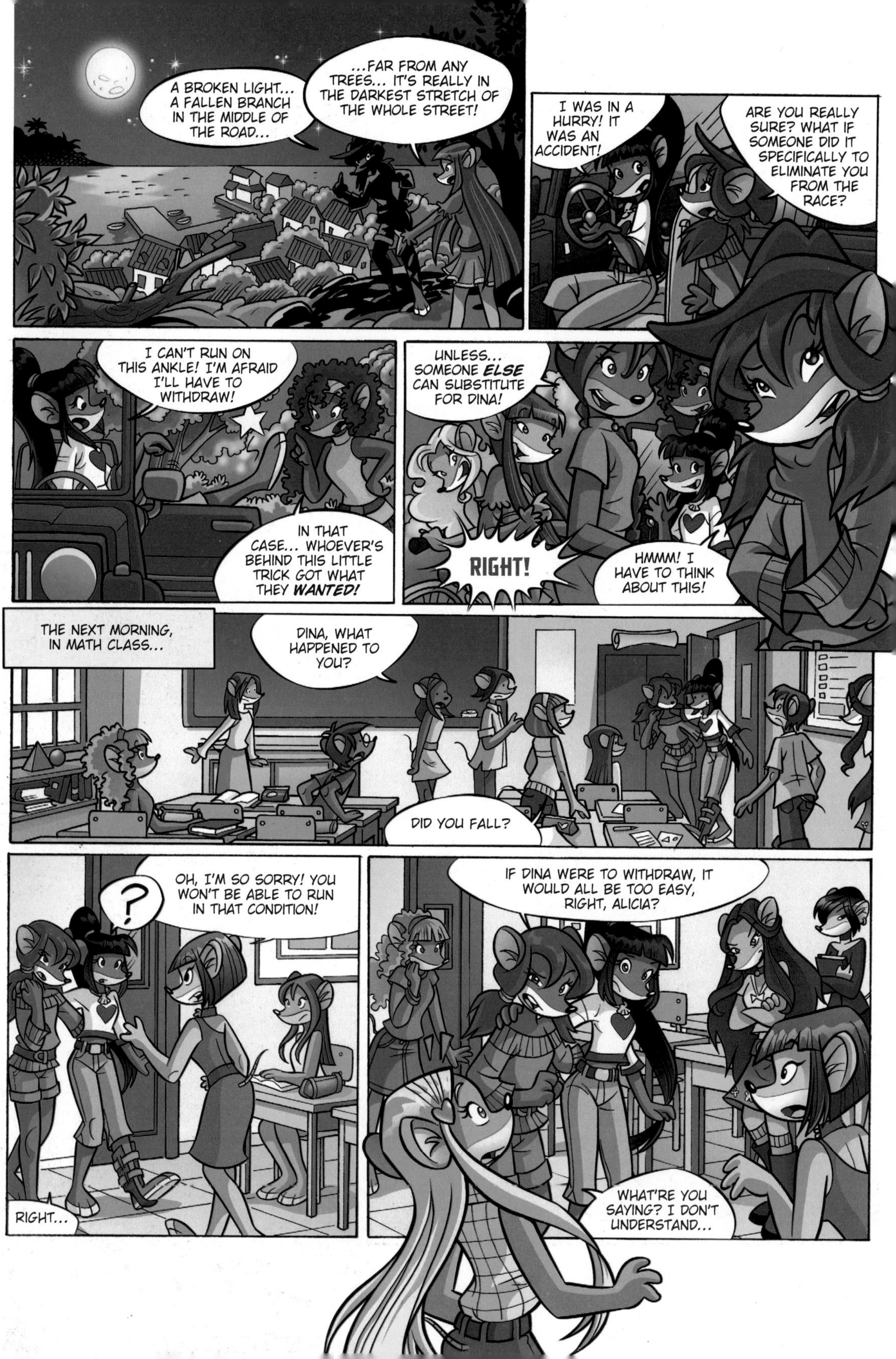
A BROKEN LIGHT... A FALLEN BRANCH IN THE MIDDLE OF THE ROAD...
...FAR FROM ANY TREES... IT'S REALLY IN THE DARKEST STRETCH OF THE WHOLE STREET!
I WAS IN A HURRY! IT WAS AN ACCIDENT!
ARE YOU REALLY SURE? WHAT IF SOMEONE DID IT SPECIFICALLY TO ELIMINATE YOU FROM THE RACE?
I CAN'T RUN ON THIS ANKLE! I'M AFRAID I'LL HAVE TO WITHDRAW!
IN THAT CASE... WHOEVER'S BEHIND THIS LITTLE TRICK GOT WHAT THEY WANTED!
UNLESS... SOMEONE ELSE CAN SUBSTITUTE FOR DINA!
RIGHT!
HMMM! I HAVE TO THINK ABOUT THIS!
THE NEXT MORNING, IN MATH CLASS...
DINA, WHAT HAPPENED TO YOU?
DID YOU FALL?
?
OH, I'M SO SORRY! YOU WON'T BE ABLE TO RUN IN THAT CONDITION!
RIGHT...
IF DINA WERE TO WITHDRAW, IT WOULD ALL BE TOO EASY, RIGHT, ALICIA?
WHAT'RE YOU SAYING? I DON'T UNDERSTAND...

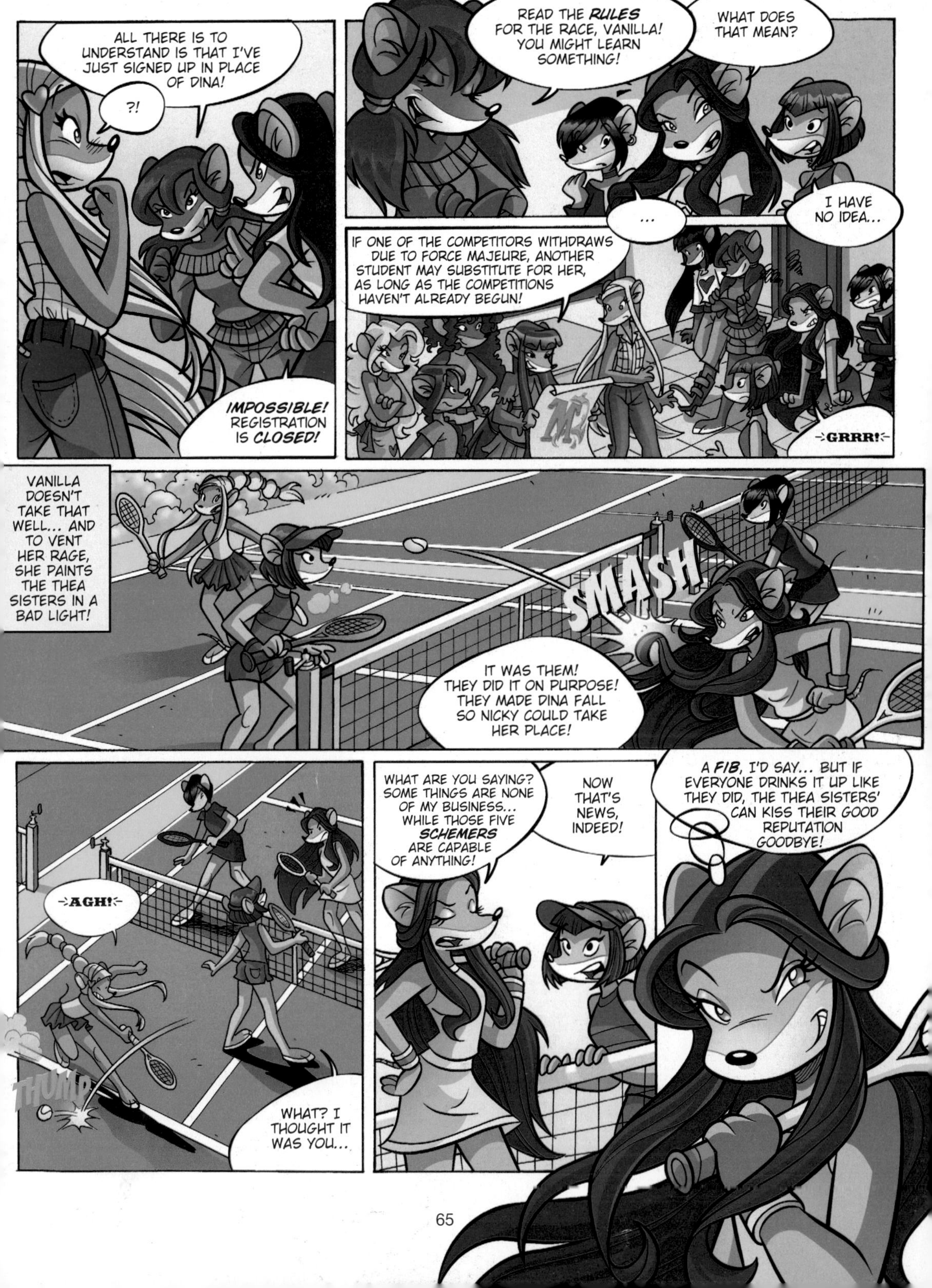

ALL THERE IS TO UNDERSTAND IS THAT I'VE JUST SIGNED UP IN PLACE OF DINA!
?!
IMPOSSIBLE! REGISTRATION IS CLOSED!
READ THE RULES FOR THE RACE, VANILLA! YOU MIGHT LEARN SOMETHING!
WHAT DOES THAT MEAN?
...
I HAVE NO IDEA...
IF ONE OF THE COMPETITORS WITHDRAWS DUE TO FORCE MAJEURE, ANOTHER STUDENT MAY SUBSTITUTE FOR HER, AS LONG AS THE COMPETITIONS HAVEN'T ALREADY BEGUN!
GRRR!
VANILLA DOESN'T TAKE THAT WELL... AND TO VENT HER RAGE, SHE PAINTS THE THEA SISTERS IN A BAD LIGHT!
SMASH
IT WAS THEM! THEY DID IT ON PURPOSE! THEY MADE DINA FALL SO NICKY COULD TAKE HER PLACE!
AGH!
THUMP
WHAT? I THOUGHT IT WAS YOU...
WHAT ARE YOU SAYING? SOME THINGS ARE NONE OF MY BUSINESS... WHILE THOSE FIVE SCHEMERS ARE CAPABLE OF ANYTHING!
NOW THAT'S NEWS, INDEED!
A FIB, I'D SAY... BUT IF EVERYONE DRINKS IT UP LIKE THEY DID, THE THEA SISTERS' CAN KISS THEIR GOOD REPUTATION GOODBYE!

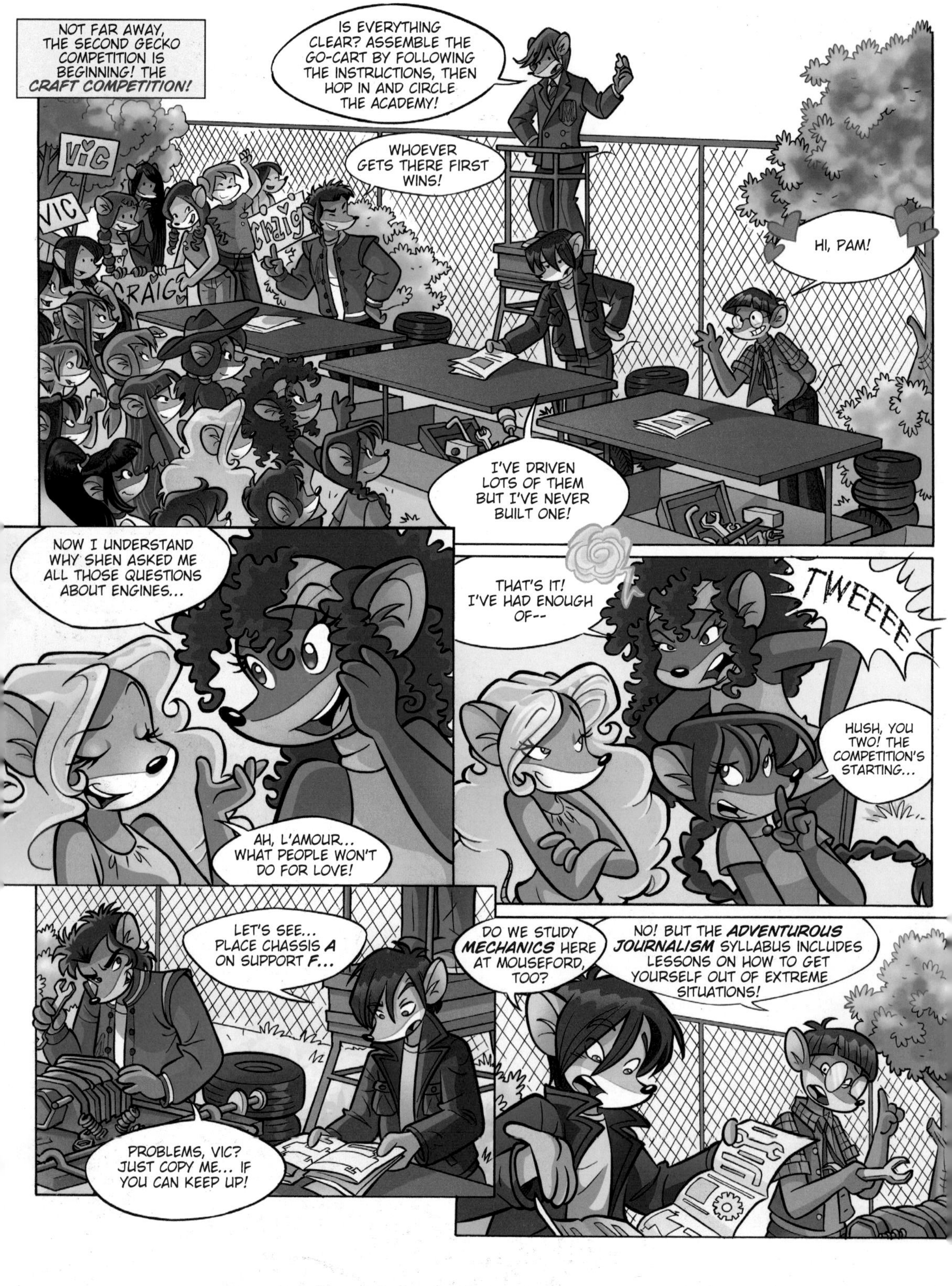
NOT FAR AWAY, THE SECOND GECKO COMPETITION IS BEGINNING! THE *CRAFT COMPETITION!*
IS EVERYTHING CLEAR? ASSEMBLE THE GO-CART BY FOLLOWING THE INSTRUCTIONS, THEN HOP IN AND CIRCLE THE ACADEMY!
WHOEVER GETS THERE FIRST WINS!
VIC
VIC
CRAIG
CRAIG
HI, PAM!
I'VE DRIVEN LOTS OF THEM BUT I'VE NEVER BUILT ONE!
NOW I UNDERSTAND WHY SHEN ASKED ME ALL THOSE QUESTIONS ABOUT ENGINES...
AH, L'AMOUR... WHAT PEOPLE WON'T DO FOR LOVE!
THAT'S IT! I'VE HAD ENOUGH OF--
TWEEEEE
HUSH, YOU TWO! THE COMPETITION'S STARTING...
LET'S SEE... PLACE CHASSIS **A** ON SUPPORT **F...**
PROBLEMS, VIC? JUST COPY ME... IF YOU CAN KEEP UP!
DO WE STUDY **MECHANICS** HERE AT MOUSEFORD, TOO?
NO! BUT THE ***ADVENTUROUS JOURNALISM*** SYLLABUS INCLUDES LESSONS ON HOW TO GET YOURSELF OUT OF EXTREME SITUATIONS!

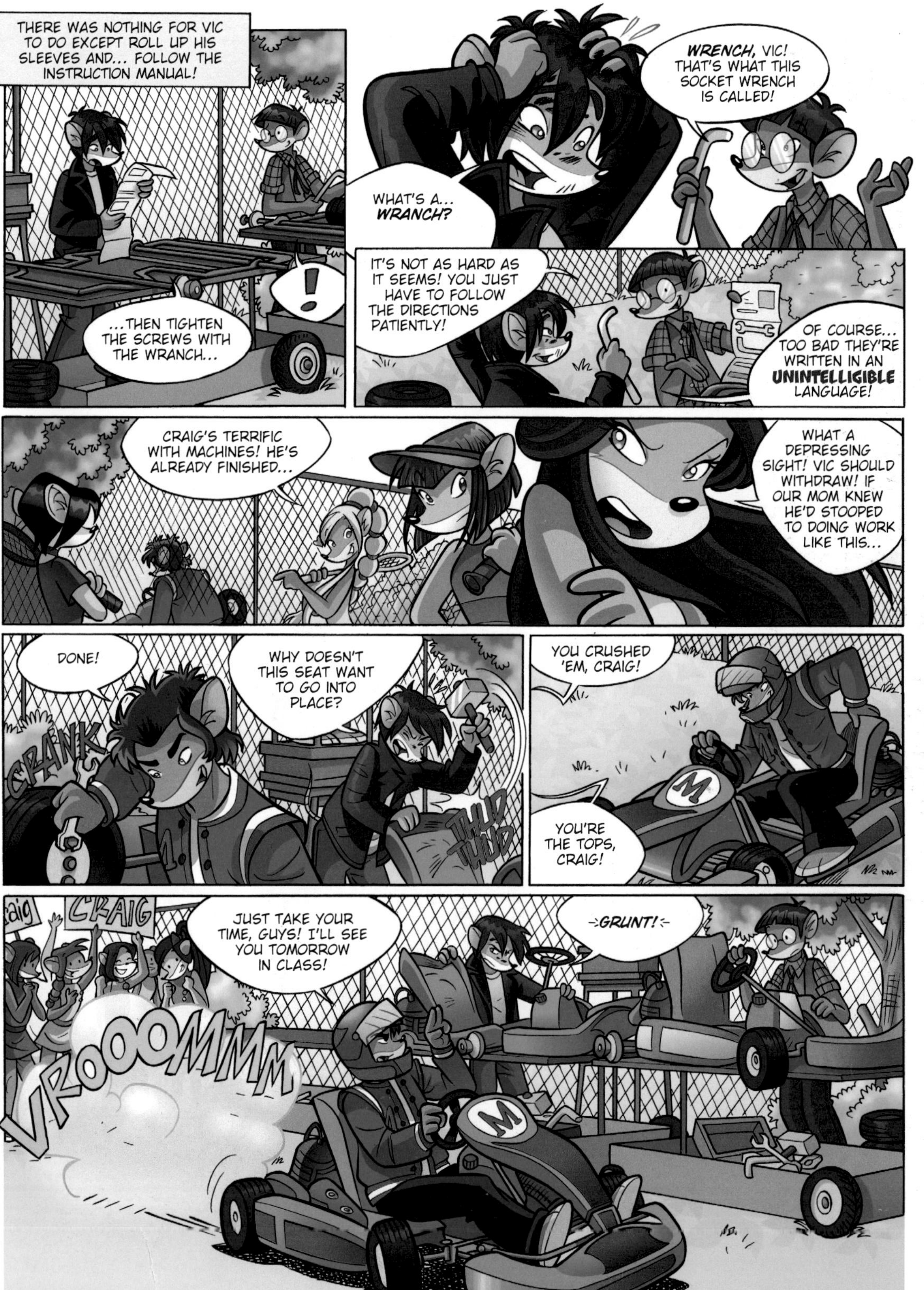
THERE WAS NOTHING FOR VIC TO DO EXCEPT ROLL UP HIS SLEEVES AND... FOLLOW THE INSTRUCTION MANUAL!
WRENCH, VIC! THAT'S WHAT THIS SOCKET WRENCH IS CALLED!
WHAT'S A... WRANCH?
...THEN TIGHTEN THE SCREWS WITH THE WRANCH...
!
IT'S NOT AS HARD AS IT SEEMS! YOU JUST HAVE TO FOLLOW THE DIRECTIONS PATIENTLY!
OF COURSE... TOO BAD THEY'RE WRITTEN IN AN UNINTELLIGIBLE LANGUAGE!
CRAIG'S TERRIFIC WITH MACHINES! HE'S ALREADY FINISHED...
WHAT A DEPRESSING SIGHT! VIC SHOULD WITHDRAW! IF OUR MOM KNEW HE'D STOOPED TO DOING WORK LIKE THIS...
DONE!
CRANK
WHY DOESN'T THIS SEAT WANT TO GO INTO PLACE?
THUD THUD
YOU CRUSHED 'EM, CRAIG!
YOU'RE THE TOPS, CRAIG!
CRAIG
JUST TAKE YOUR TIME, GUYS! I'LL SEE YOU TOMORROW IN CLASS!
GRUNT!
VROOOMMMM

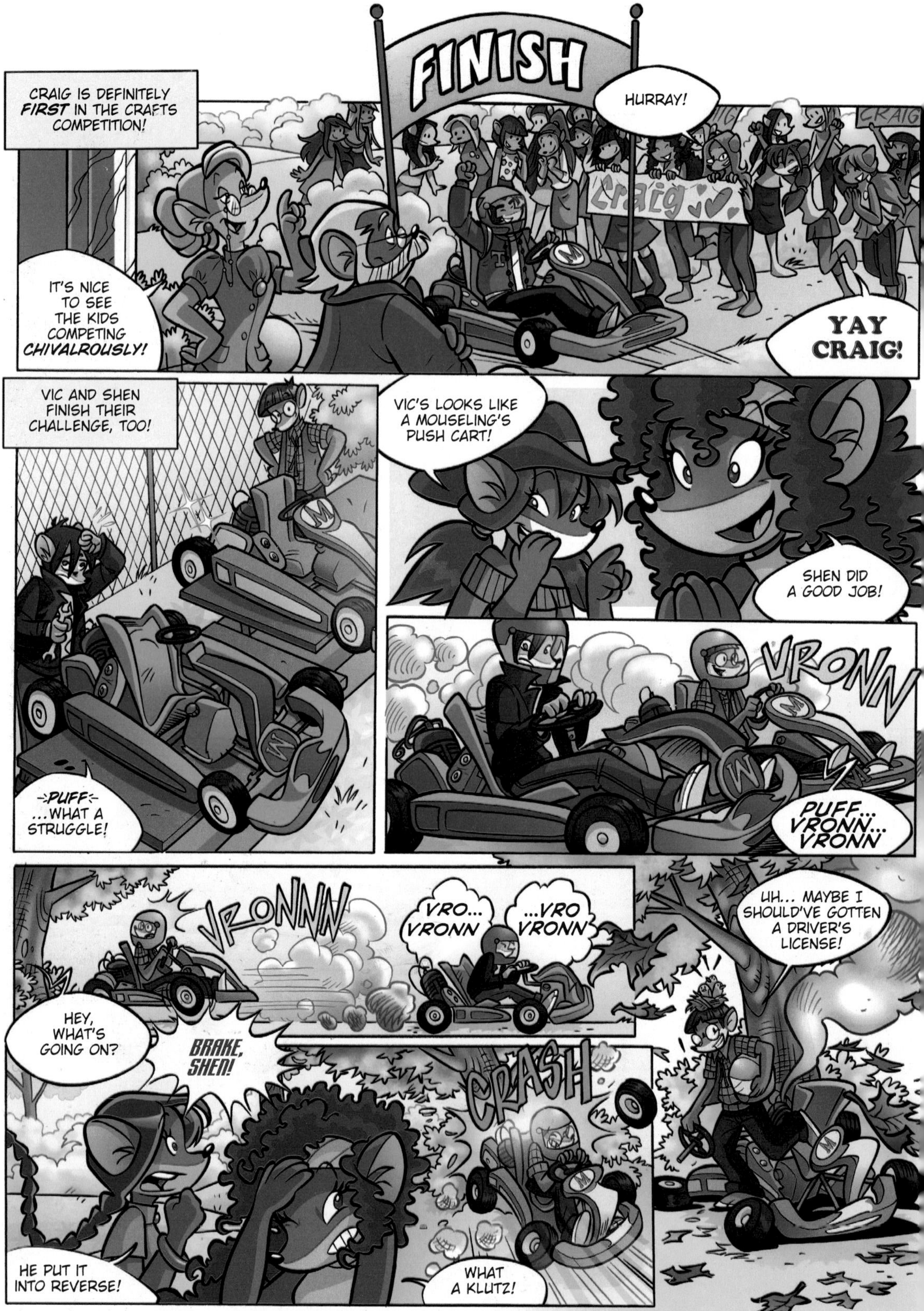
FINISH
CRAIG IS DEFINITELY FIRST IN THE CRAFTS COMPETITION!
HURRAY!
Craig
CRAIG
IT'S NICE TO SEE THE KIDS COMPETING CHIVALROUSLY!
YAY CRAIG!
VIC AND SHEN FINISH THEIR CHALLENGE, TOO!
VIC'S LOOKS LIKE A MOUSELING'S PUSH CART!
SHEN DID A GOOD JOB!
-PUFF- ...WHAT A STRUGGLE!
VRONN
PUFF... VRONN... VRONN
VRONNN
VRO... VRONN
...VRO VRONN
UH... MAYBE I SHOULD'VE GOTTEN A DRIVER'S LICENSE!
HEY, WHAT'S GOING ON?
BRAKE, SHEN!
CRASH
HE PUT IT INTO REVERSE!
WHAT A KLUTZ!

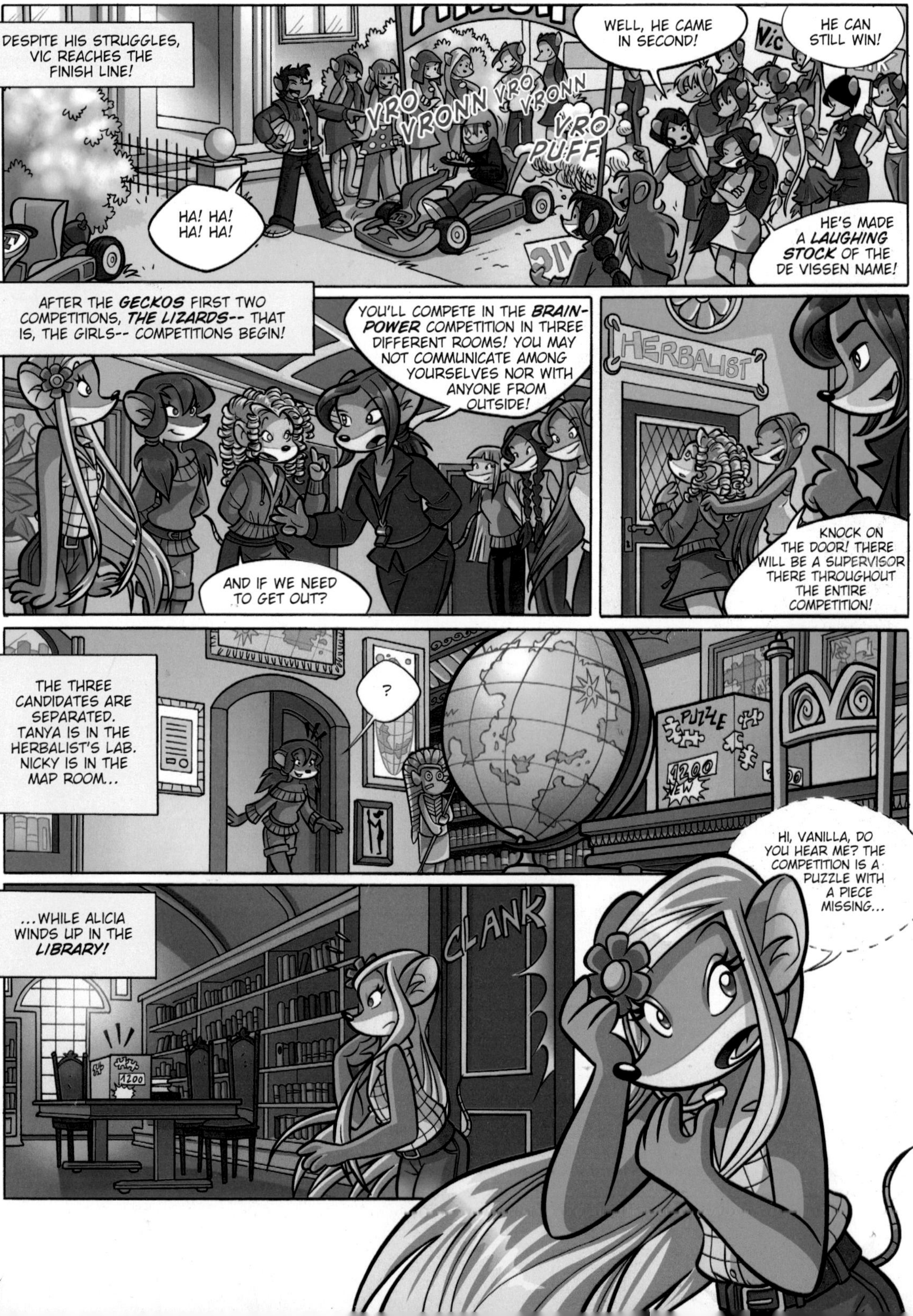
DESPITE HIS STRUGGLES, VIC REACHES THE FINISH LINE!
WELL, HE CAME IN SECOND!
HE CAN STILL WIN!
VRO VRONN VRO VRONN VRO PUFF
HA! HA! HA! HA!
HE'S MADE A ***LAUGHING STOCK*** OF THE DE VISSEN NAME!
AFTER THE ***GECKOS*** FIRST TWO COMPETITIONS, ***THE LIZARDS--*** THAT IS, THE GIRLS-- COMPETITIONS BEGIN!
YOU'LL COMPETE IN THE ***BRAIN-POWER*** COMPETITION IN THREE DIFFERENT ROOMS! YOU MAY NOT COMMUNICATE AMONG YOURSELVES NOR WITH ANYONE FROM OUTSIDE!
AND IF WE NEED TO GET OUT?
HERBALIST
KNOCK ON THE DOOR! THERE WILL BE A SUPERVISOR THERE THROUGHOUT THE ENTIRE COMPETITION!
THE THREE CANDIDATES ARE SEPARATED. TANYA IS IN THE HERBALIST'S LAB. NICKY IS IN THE MAP ROOM...
?
PUZZLE
1200
NEW
HI, VANILLA, DO YOU HEAR ME? THE COMPETITION IS A PUZZLE WITH A PIECE MISSING...
...WHILE ALICIA WINDS UP IN THE ***LIBRARY!***
CLANK
1200

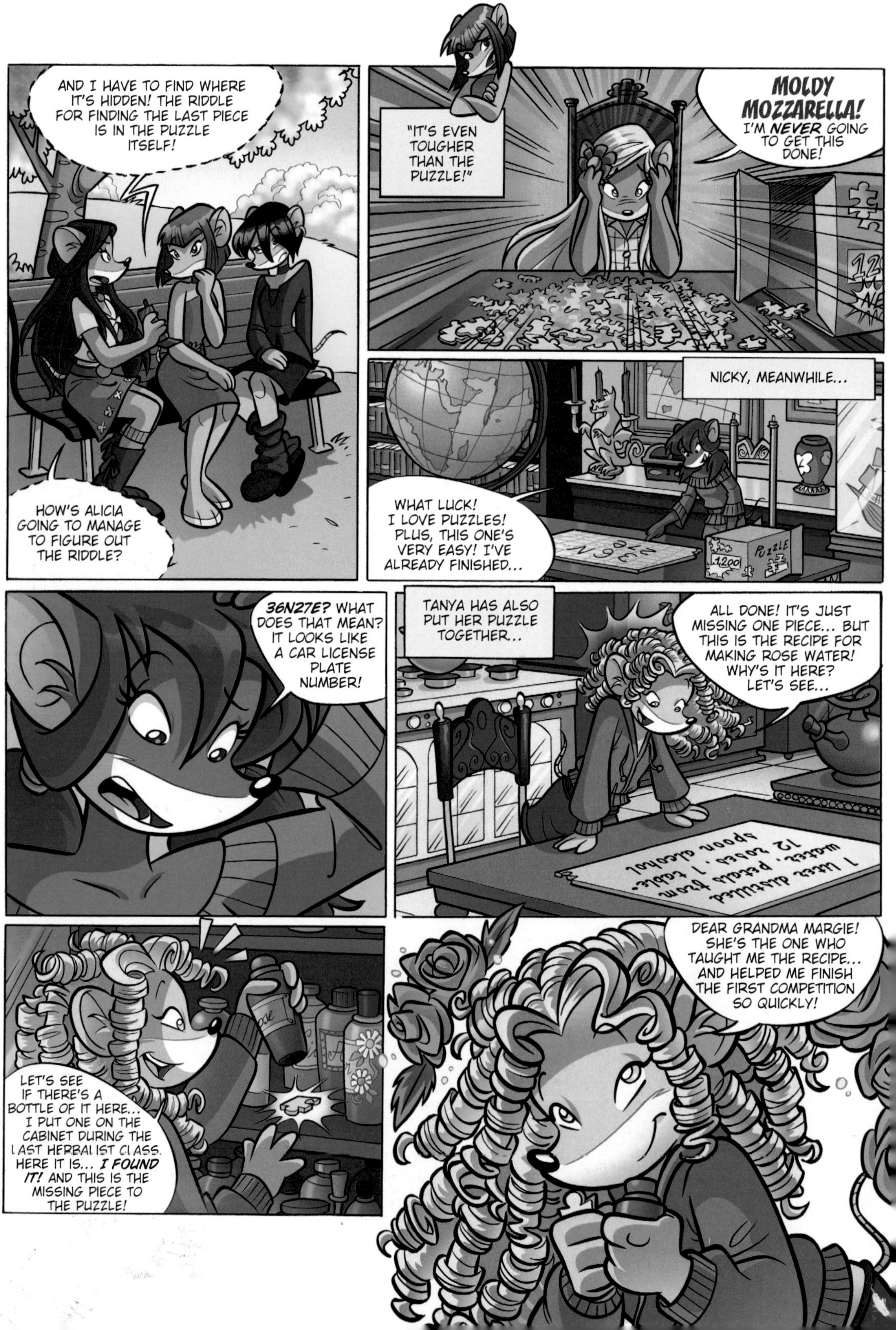
AND I HAVE TO FIND WHERE IT'S HIDDEN! THE RIDDLE FOR FINDING THE LAST PIECE IS IN THE PUZZLE ITSELF!
HOW'S ALICIA GOING TO MANAGE TO FIGURE OUT THE RIDDLE?
"IT'S EVEN TOUGHER THAN THE PUZZLE!"
MOLDY MOZZARELLA! I'M NEVER GOING TO GET THIS DONE!
NICKY, MEANWHILE...
WHAT LUCK! I LOVE PUZZLES! PLUS, THIS ONE'S VERY EASY! I'VE ALREADY FINISHED...
36N27E? WHAT DOES THAT MEAN? IT LOOKS LIKE A CAR LICENSE PLATE NUMBER!
TANYA HAS ALSO PUT HER PUZZLE TOGETHER...
ALL DONE! IT'S JUST MISSING ONE PIECE... BUT THIS IS THE RECIPE FOR MAKING ROSE WATER! WHY'S IT HERE? LET'S SEE...
1 liter distilled water, petals from 12 roses, 1 table-spoon alcohol.
LET'S SEE IF THERE'S A BOTTLE OF IT HERE... I PUT ONE ON THE CABINET DURING THE LAST HERBALIST CLASS. HERE IT IS... I FOUND IT! AND THIS IS THE MISSING PIECE TO THE PUZZLE!
DEAR GRANDMA MARGIE! SHE'S THE ONE WHO TAUGHT ME THE RECIPE... AND HELPED ME FINISH THE FIRST COMPETITION SO QUICKLY!

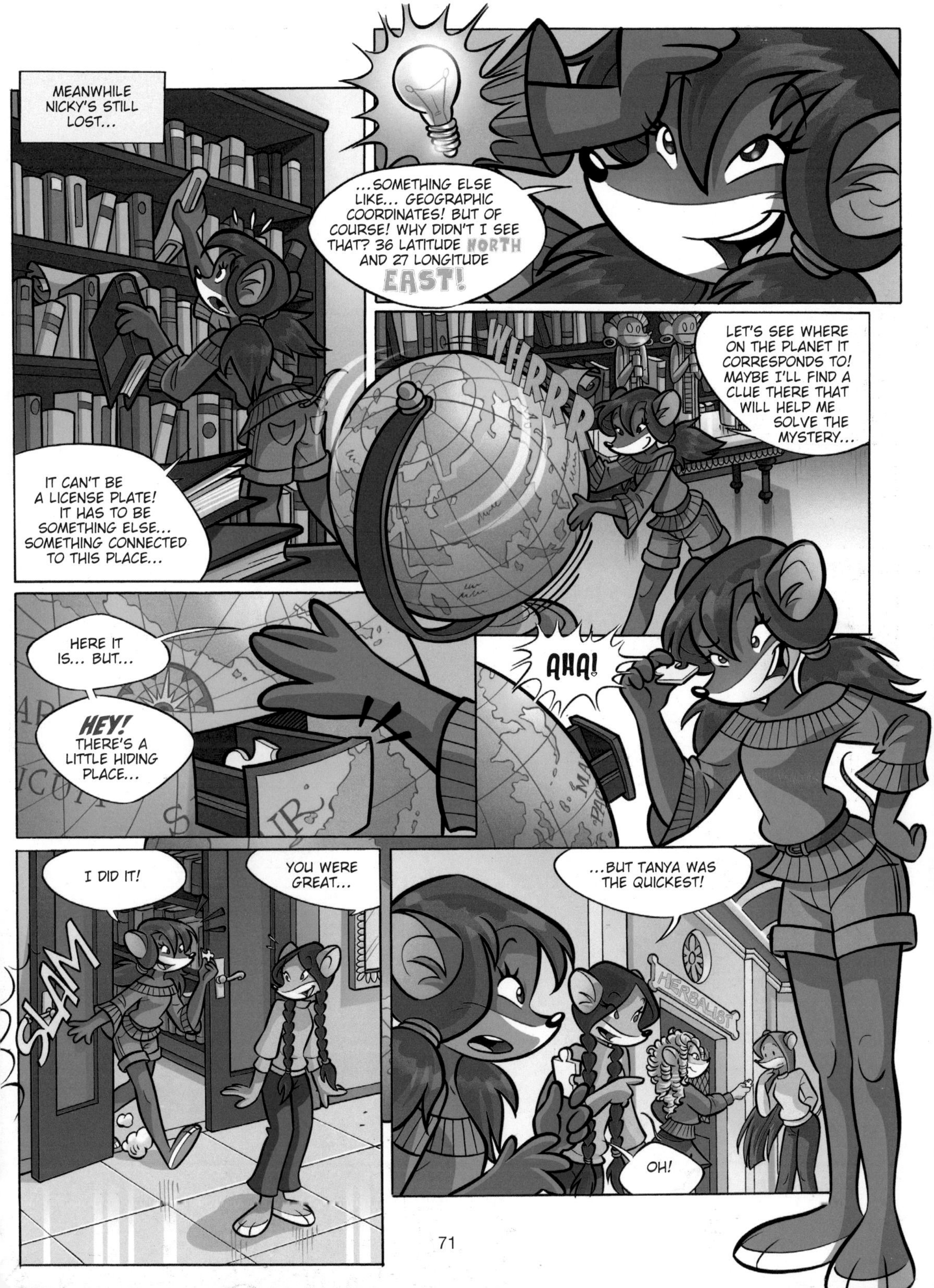
MEANWHILE NICKY'S STILL LOST...
IT CAN'T BE A LICENSE PLATE! IT HAS TO BE SOMETHING ELSE... SOMETHING CONNECTED TO THIS PLACE...
...SOMETHING ELSE LIKE... GEOGRAPHIC COORDINATES! BUT OF COURSE! WHY DIDN'T I SEE THAT? 36 LATITUDE NORTH AND 27 LONGITUDE EAST!
WHRRRR
LET'S SEE WHERE ON THE PLANET IT CORRESPONDS TO! MAYBE I'LL FIND A CLUE THERE THAT WILL HELP ME SOLVE THE MYSTERY...
HERE IT IS... BUT...
HEY! THERE'S A LITTLE HIDING PLACE...
AHA!
SLAM
I DID IT!
YOU WERE GREAT...
...BUT TANYA WAS THE QUICKEST!
HERBALIST
OH!

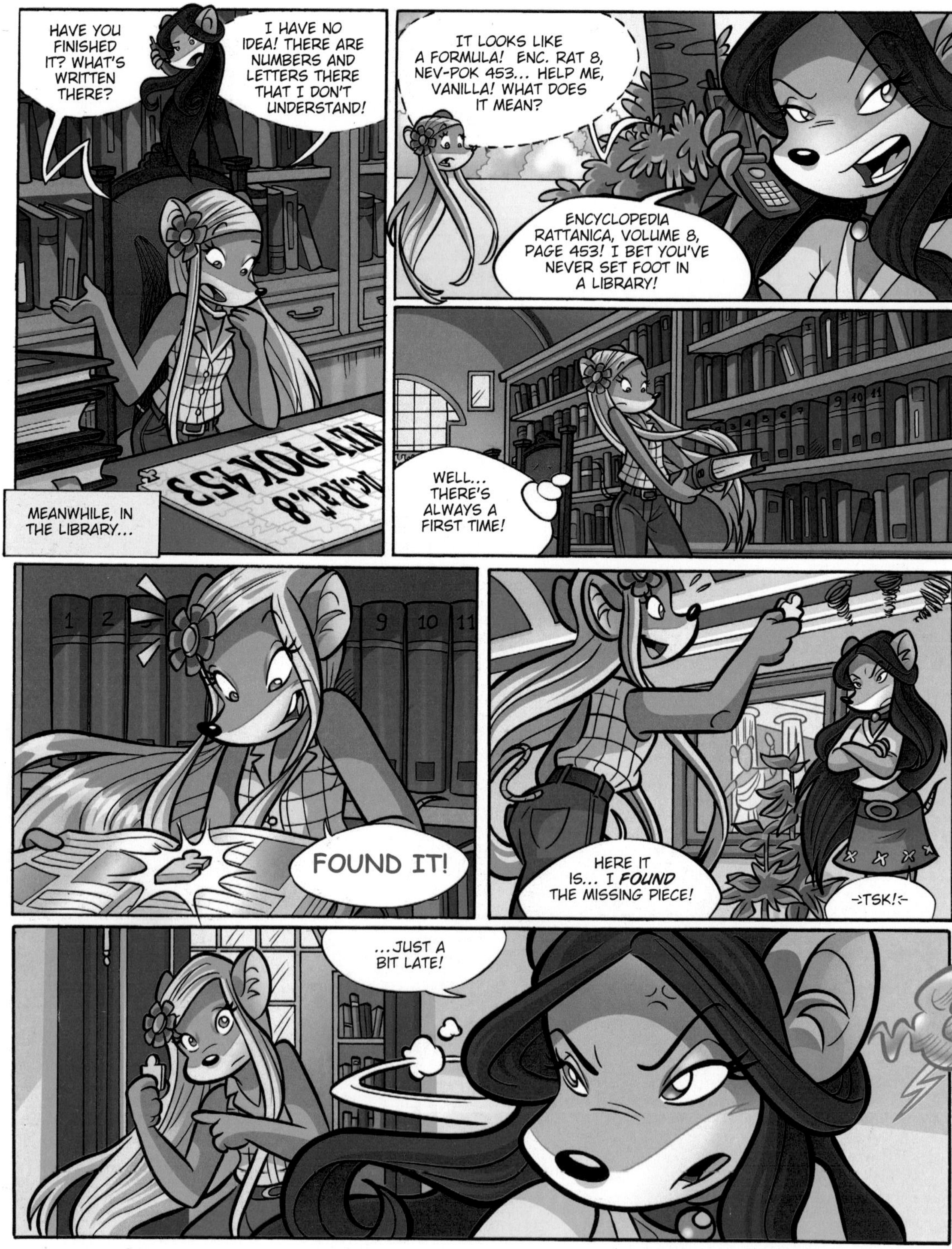
HAVE YOU FINISHED IT? WHAT'S WRITTEN THERE?
I HAVE NO IDEA! THERE ARE NUMBERS AND LETTERS THERE THAT I DON'T UNDERSTAND!
MEANWHILE, IN THE LIBRARY...
IT LOOKS LIKE A FORMULA! ENC. RAT 8, NEV-POK 453... HELP ME, VANILLA! WHAT DOES IT MEAN?
ENCYCLOPEDIA RATTANICA, VOLUME 8, PAGE 453! I BET YOU'VE NEVER SET FOOT IN A LIBRARY!
WELL... THERE'S ALWAYS A FIRST TIME!
FOUND IT!
HERE IT IS... I *FOUND* THE MISSING PIECE!
TSK!
...JUST A BIT LATE!

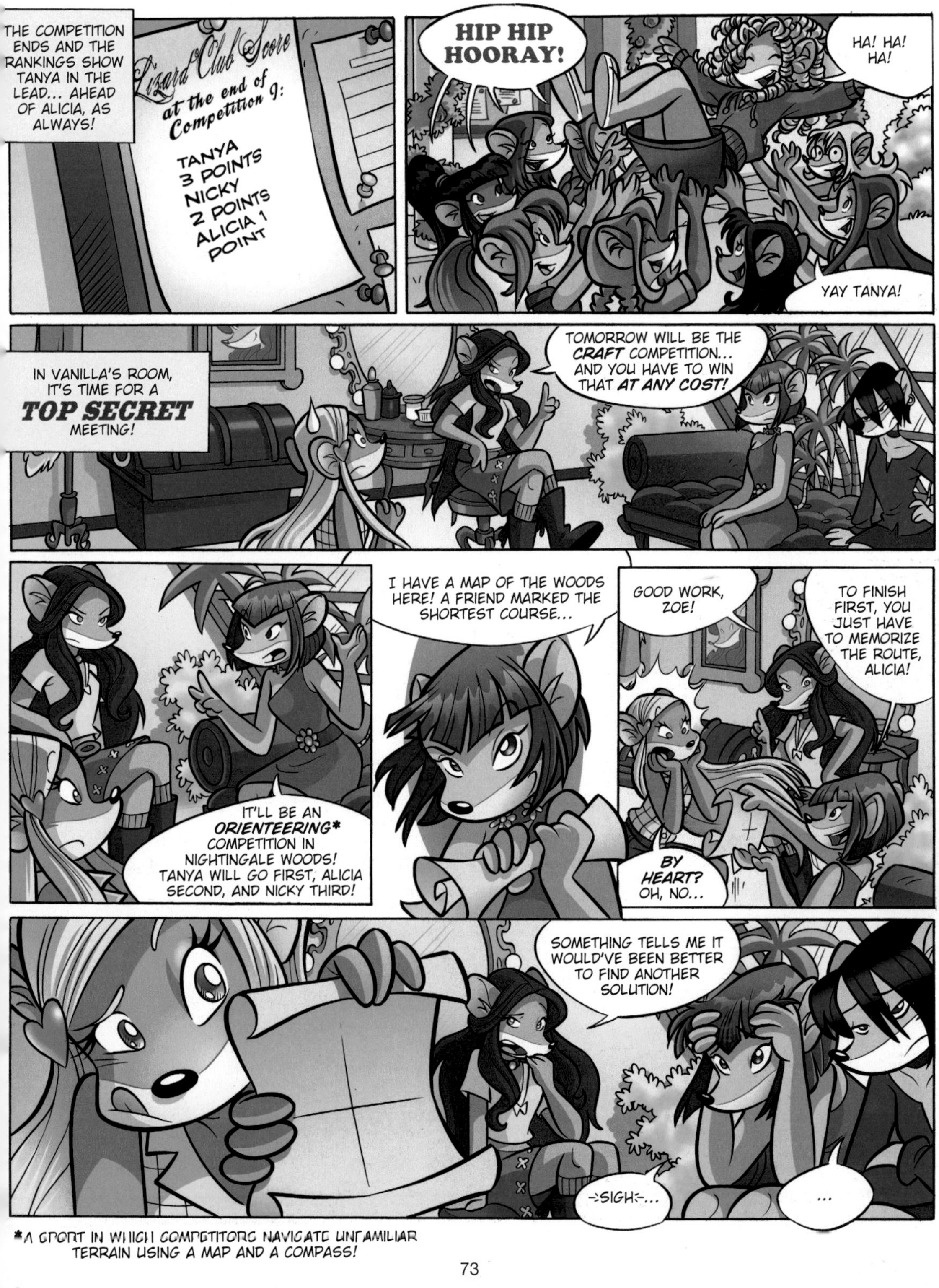
THE COMPETITION ENDS AND THE RANKINGS SHOW TANYA IN THE LEAD... AHEAD OF ALICIA, AS ALWAYS!
Lizard Club Score at the end of Competition 1:
TANYA 3 POINTS NICKY 2 POINTS ALICIA 1 POINT
HIP HIP HOORAY!
HA! HA! HA!
YAY TANYA!
IN VANILLA'S ROOM, IT'S TIME FOR A TOP SECRET MEETING!
TOMORROW WILL BE THE CRAFT COMPETITION... AND YOU HAVE TO WIN THAT AT ANY COST!
IT'LL BE AN ORIENTEERING* COMPETITION IN NIGHTINGALE WOODS! TANYA WILL GO FIRST, ALICIA SECOND, AND NICKY THIRD!
I HAVE A MAP OF THE WOODS HERE! A FRIEND MARKED THE SHORTEST COURSE...
GOOD WORK, ZOE!
TO FINISH FIRST, YOU JUST HAVE TO MEMORIZE THE ROUTE, ALICIA!
BY HEART? OH, NO...
SOMETHING TELLS ME IT WOULD'VE BEEN BETTER TO FIND ANOTHER SOLUTION!
-SIGH-...
...

*A SPORT IN WHICH COMPETITORS NAVIGATE UNFAMILIAR TERRAIN USING A MAP AND A COMPASS!

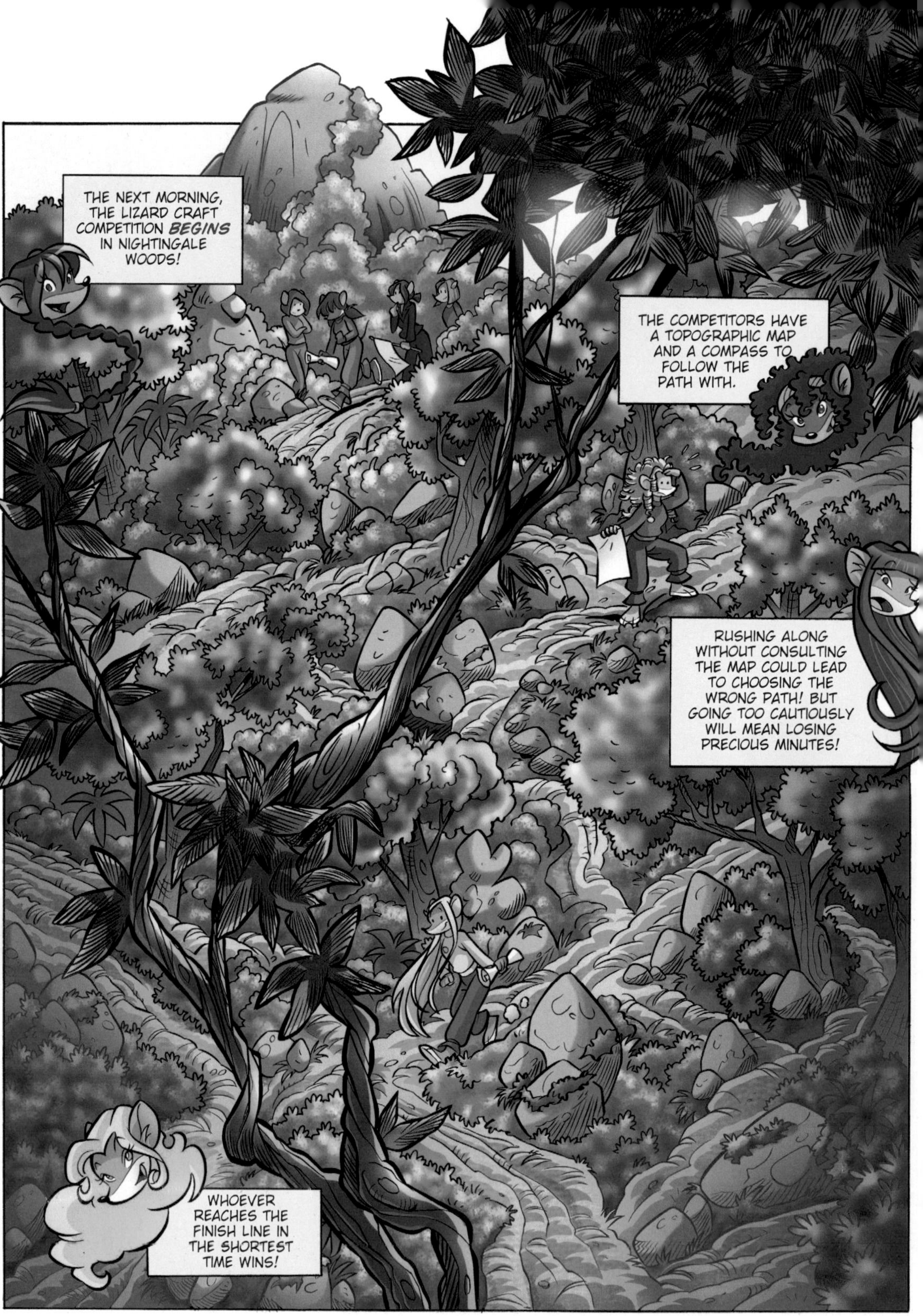
THE NEXT MORNING, THE LIZARD CRAFT COMPETITION BEGINS IN NIGHTINGALE WOODS!
THE COMPETITORS HAVE A TOPOGRAPHIC MAP AND A COMPASS TO FOLLOW THE PATH WITH.
RUSHING ALONG WITHOUT CONSULTING THE MAP COULD LEAD TO CHOOSING THE WRONG PATH! BUT GOING TOO CAUTIOUSLY WILL MEAN LOSING PRECIOUS MINUTES!
WHOEVER REACHES THE FINISH LINE IN THE SHORTEST TIME WINS!

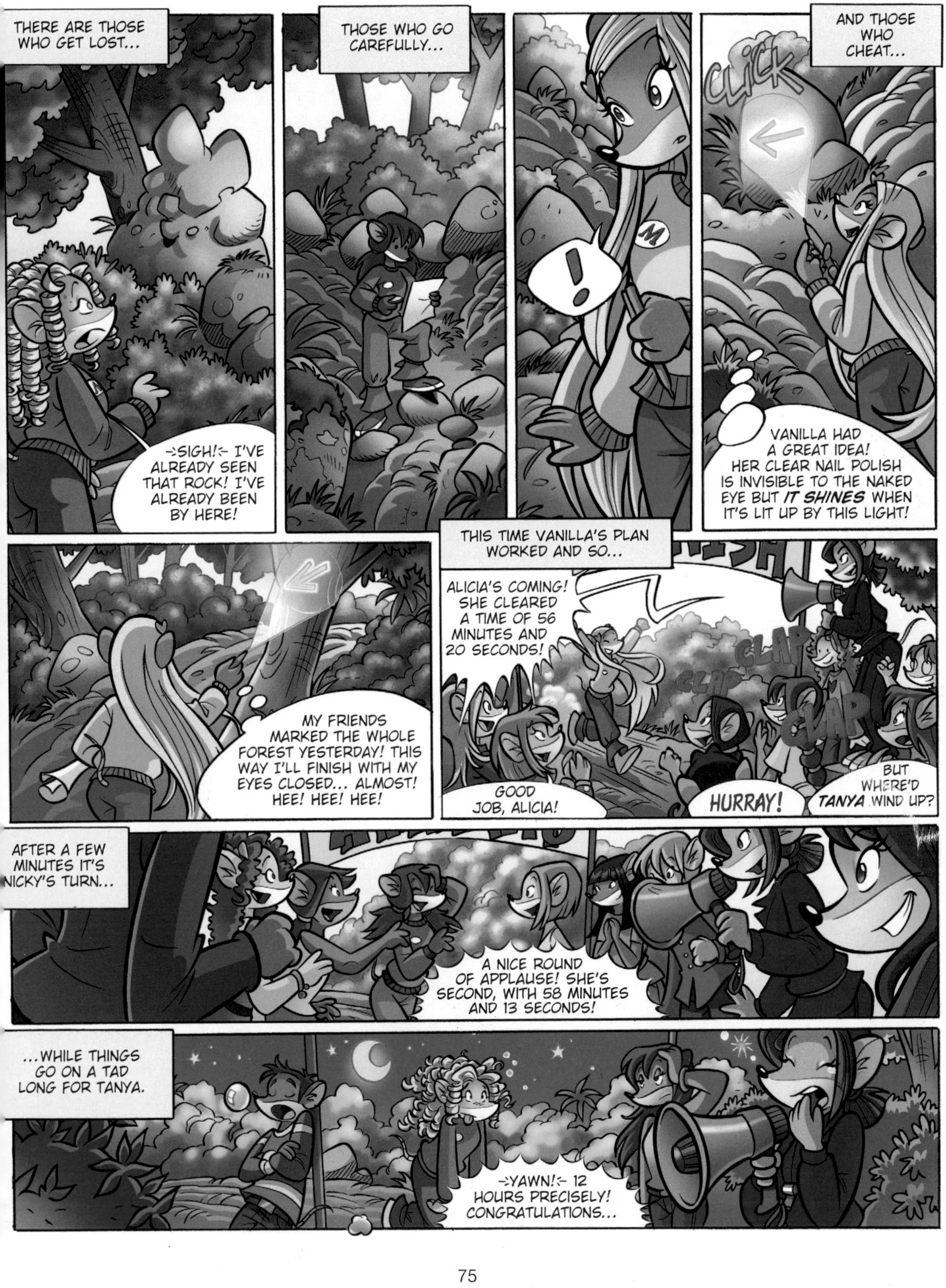

THERE ARE THOSE WHO GET LOST...
⇒SIGH!⇐ I'VE ALREADY SEEN THAT ROCK! I'VE ALREADY BEEN BY HERE!
THOSE WHO GO CAREFULLY...
!
AND THOSE WHO CHEAT...
CLICK
VANILLA HAD A GREAT IDEA! HER CLEAR NAIL POLISH IS INVISIBLE TO THE NAKED EYE BUT IT SHINES WHEN IT'S LIT UP BY THIS LIGHT!
MY FRIENDS MARKED THE WHOLE FOREST YESTERDAY! THIS WAY I'LL FINISH WITH MY EYES CLOSED... ALMOST! HEE! HEE! HEE!
THIS TIME VANILLA'S PLAN WORKED AND SO...
ALICIA'S COMING! SHE CLEARED A TIME OF 56 MINUTES AND 20 SECONDS!
CLAP CLAP CLAP
GOOD JOB, ALICIA!
HURRAY!
BUT WHERE'D TANYA WIND UP?
AFTER A FEW MINUTES IT'S NICKY'S TURN...
A NICE ROUND OF APPLAUSE! SHE'S SECOND, WITH 58 MINUTES AND 13 SECONDS!
...WHILE THINGS GO ON A TAD LONG FOR TANYA.
⇒YAWN!⇐ 12 HOURS PRECISELY! CONGRATULATIONS...

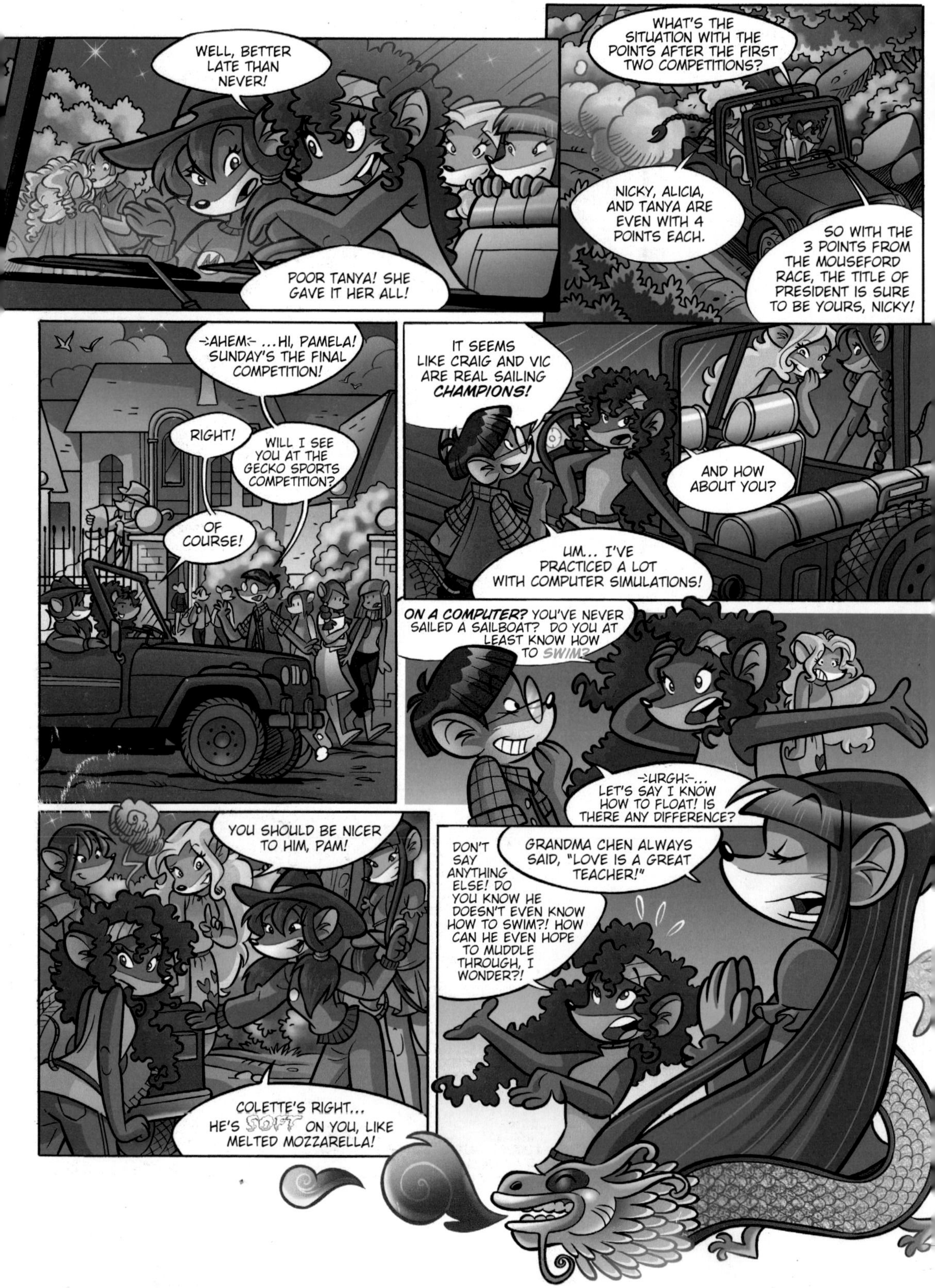
WELL, BETTER LATE THAN NEVER!
POOR TANYA! SHE GAVE IT HER ALL!
WHAT'S THE SITUATION WITH THE POINTS AFTER THE FIRST TWO COMPETITIONS?
NICKY, ALICIA, AND TANYA ARE EVEN WITH 4 POINTS EACH.
SO WITH THE 3 POINTS FROM THE MOUSEFORD RACE, THE TITLE OF PRESIDENT IS SURE TO BE YOURS, NICKY!
-AHEM- ...HI, PAMELA! SUNDAY'S THE FINAL COMPETITION!
RIGHT!
WILL I SEE YOU AT THE GECKO SPORTS COMPETITION?
OF COURSE!
IT SEEMS LIKE CRAIG AND VIC ARE REAL SAILING CHAMPIONS!
AND HOW ABOUT YOU?
UM... I'VE PRACTICED A LOT WITH COMPUTER SIMULATIONS!
ON A COMPUTER? YOU'VE NEVER SAILED A SAILBOAT? DO YOU AT LEAST KNOW HOW TO SWIM?
-URGH-... LET'S SAY I KNOW HOW TO FLOAT! IS THERE ANY DIFFERENCE?
YOU SHOULD BE NICER TO HIM, PAM!
COLETTE'S RIGHT... HE'S SOFT ON YOU, LIKE MELTED MOZZARELLA!
DON'T SAY ANYTHING ELSE! DO YOU KNOW HE DOESN'T EVEN KNOW HOW TO SWIM?! HOW CAN HE EVEN HOPE TO MUDDLE THROUGH, I WONDER?!
GRANDMA CHEN ALWAYS SAID, "LOVE IS A GREAT TEACHER!"

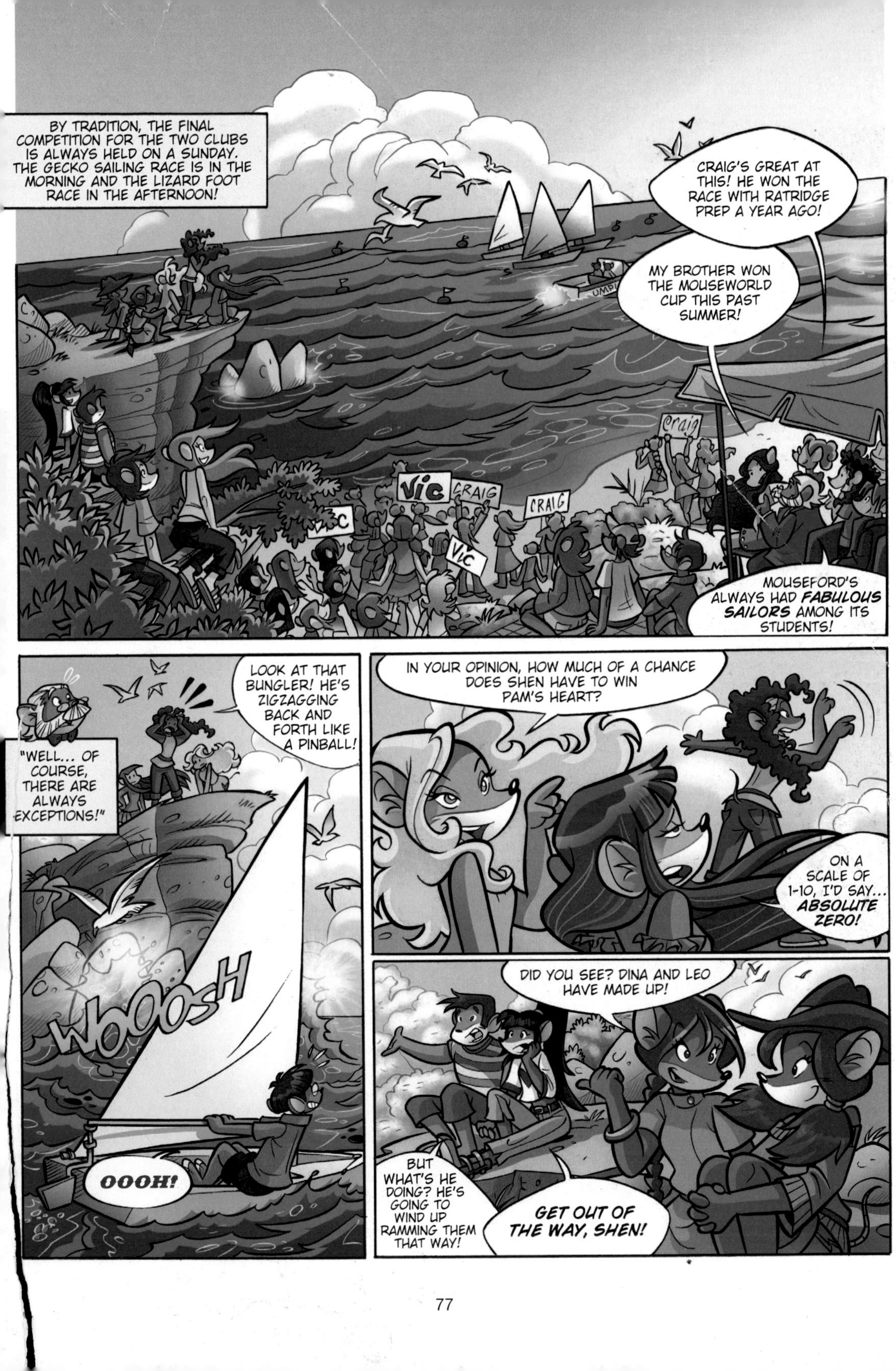

BY TRADITION, THE FINAL COMPETITION FOR THE TWO CLUBS IS ALWAYS HELD ON A SUNDAY. THE GECKO SAILING RACE IS IN THE MORNING AND THE LIZARD FOOT RACE IN THE AFTERNOON!
CRAIG'S GREAT AT THIS! HE WON THE RACE WITH RATRIDGE PREP A YEAR AGO!
MY BROTHER WON THE MOUSEWORLD CUP THIS PAST SUMMER!
Craig
VIC
CRAIG
CRAIG
VIC
MOUSEFORD'S ALWAYS HAD **FABULOUS SAILORS** AMONG ITS STUDENTS!
LOOK AT THAT BUNGLER! HE'S ZIGZAGGING BACK AND FORTH LIKE A PINBALL!
"WELL... OF COURSE, THERE ARE ALWAYS EXCEPTIONS!"
WOOOSH
OOOH!
IN YOUR OPINION, HOW MUCH OF A CHANCE DOES SHEN HAVE TO WIN PAM'S HEART?
ON A SCALE OF 1-10, I'D SAY... **ABSOLUTE ZERO!**
DID YOU SEE? DINA AND LEO HAVE MADE UP!
BUT WHAT'S HE DOING? HE'S GOING TO WIND UP RAMMING THEM THAT WAY!
GET OUT OF THE WAY, SHEN!

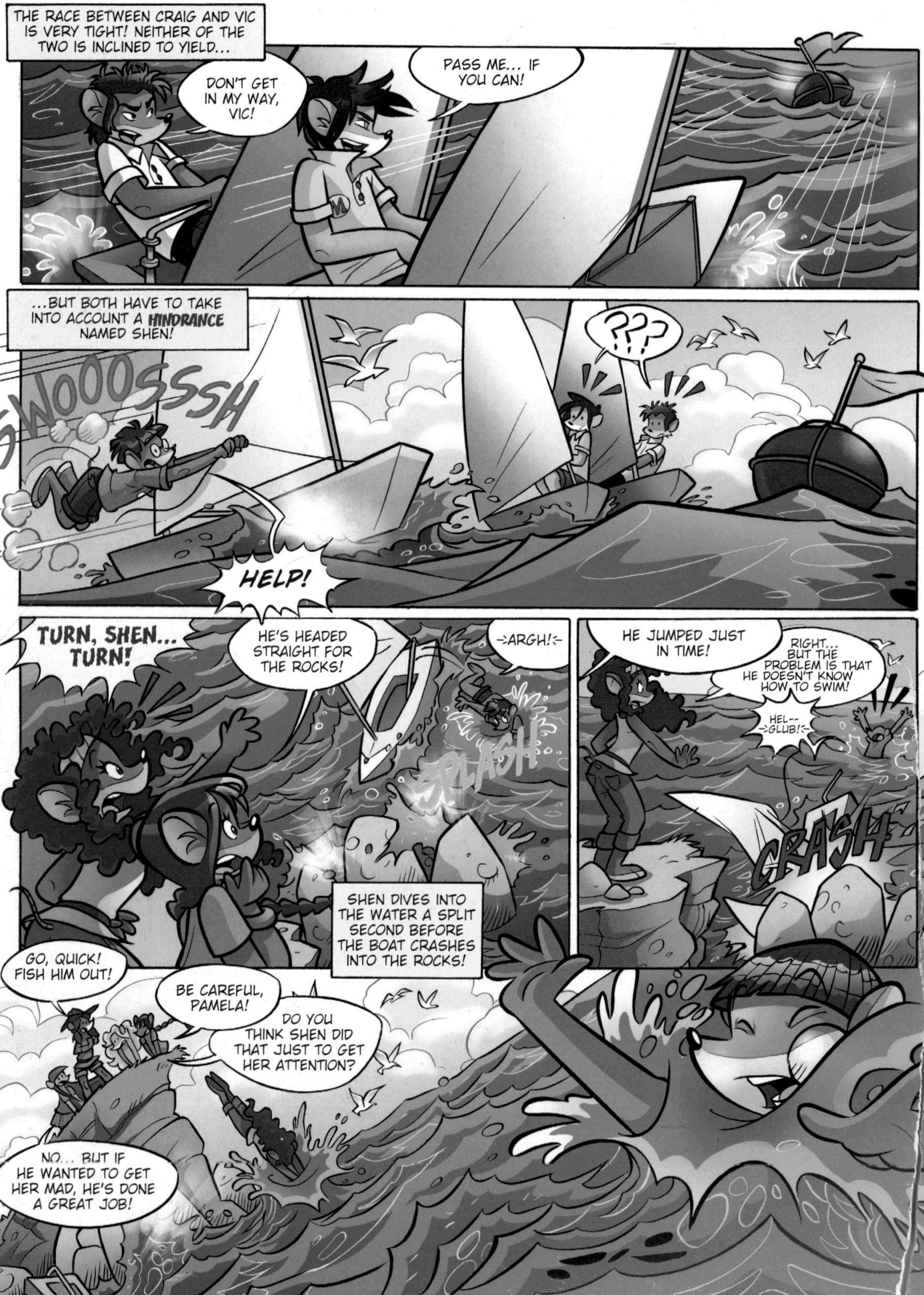
THE RACE BETWEEN CRAIG AND VIC IS VERY TIGHT! NEITHER OF THE TWO IS INCLINED TO YIELD...
DON'T GET IN MY WAY, VIC!
PASS ME... IF YOU CAN!
...BUT BOTH HAVE TO TAKE INTO ACCOUNT A HINDRANCE NAMED SHEN!
???
SWOOOSSSH
HELP!
TURN, SHEN... TURN!
HE'S HEADED STRAIGHT FOR THE ROCKS!
ARGH!
SPLASH
SHEN DIVES INTO THE WATER A SPLIT SECOND BEFORE THE BOAT CRASHES INTO THE ROCKS!
HE JUMPED JUST IN TIME!
RIGHT... BUT THE PROBLEM IS THAT HE DOESN'T KNOW HOW TO SWIM!
HEL-- GLUB!
CRASH
GO, QUICK! FISH HIM OUT!
BE CAREFUL, PAMELA!
DO YOU THINK SHEN DID THAT JUST TO GET HER ATTENTION?
NO... BUT IF HE WANTED TO GET HER MAD, HE'S DONE A GREAT JOB!

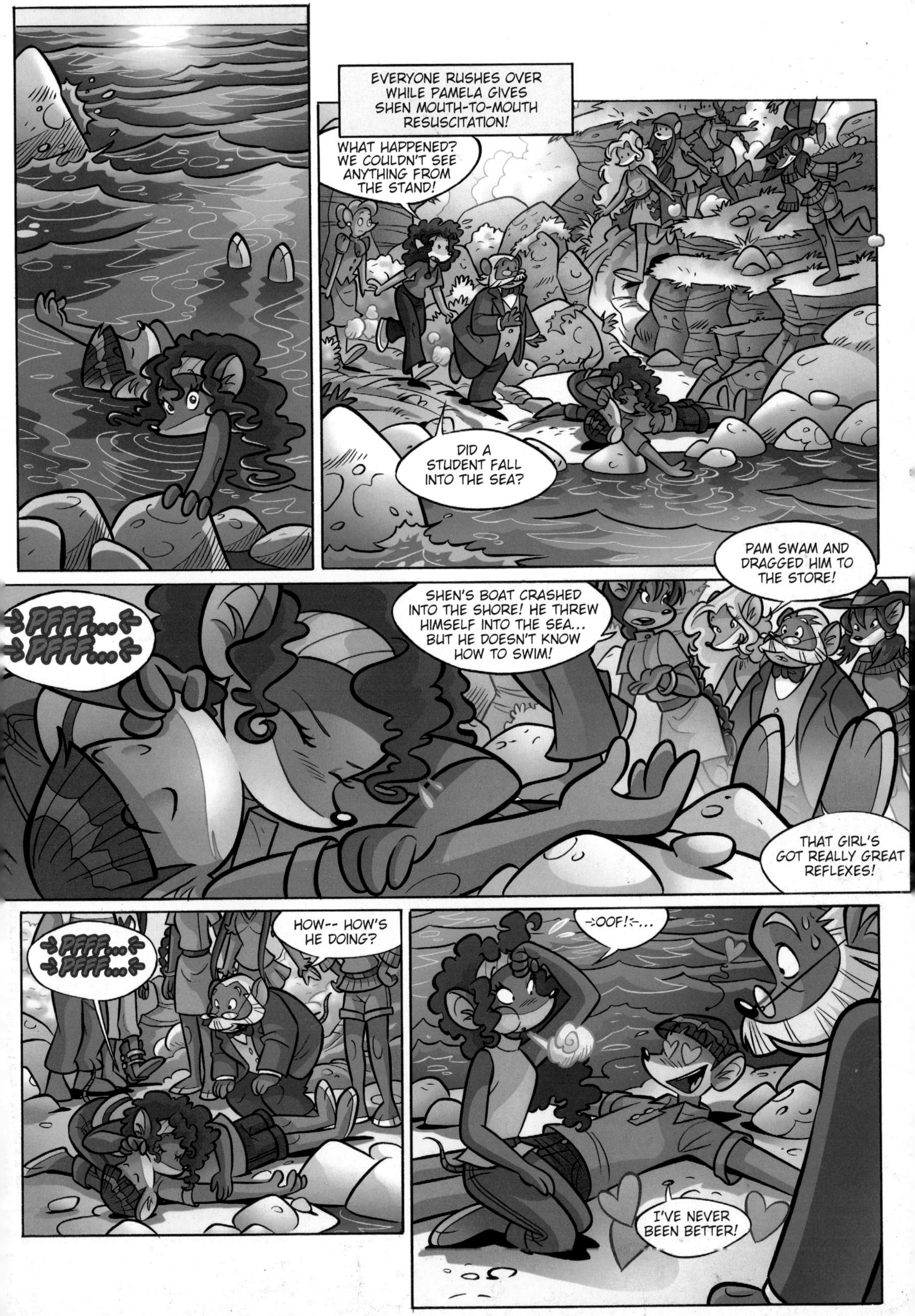
EVERYONE RUSHES OVER WHILE PAMELA GIVES SHEN MOUTH-TO-MOUTH RESUSCITATION!
WHAT HAPPENED? WE COULDN'T SEE ANYTHING FROM THE STAND!
DID A STUDENT FALL INTO THE SEA?
PFFF... PFFF...
SHEN'S BOAT CRASHED INTO THE SHORE! HE THREW HIMSELF INTO THE SEA... BUT HE DOESN'T KNOW HOW TO SWIM!
PAM SWAM AND DRAGGED HIM TO THE STORE!
THAT GIRL'S GOT REALLY GREAT REFLEXES!
PFFF... PFFF...
HOW-- HOW'S HE DOING?
OOF!...
I'VE NEVER BEEN BETTER!

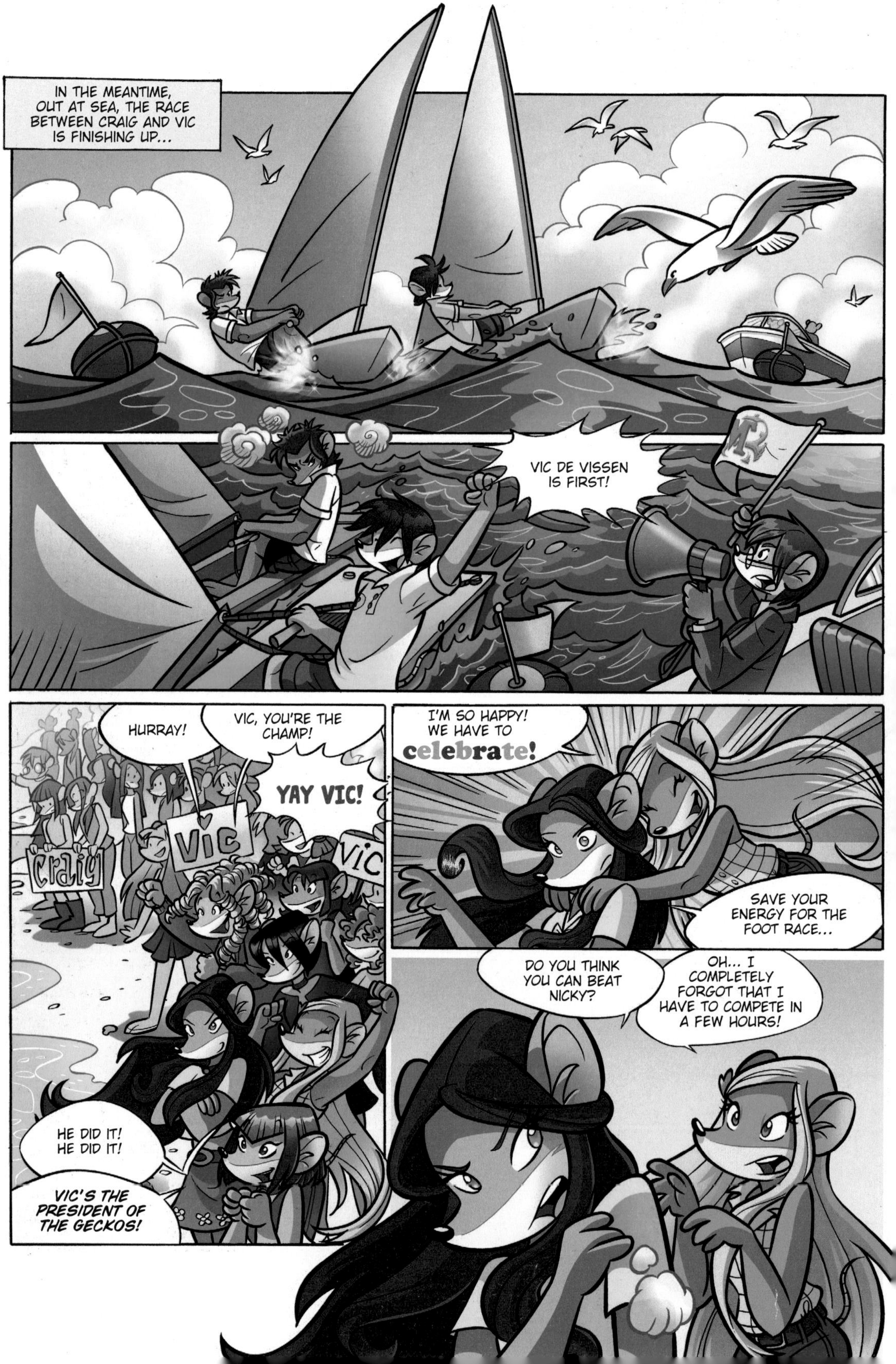
IN THE MEANTIME, OUT AT SEA, THE RACE BETWEEN CRAIG AND VIC IS FINISHING UP...
VIC DE VISSEN IS FIRST!
HURRAY!
VIC, YOU'RE THE CHAMP!
YAY VIC!
craig
Vic
Vic
HE DID IT! HE DID IT!
VIC'S THE PRESIDENT OF THE GECKOS!
I'M SO HAPPY! WE HAVE TO celebrate!
SAVE YOUR ENERGY FOR THE FOOT RACE...
DO YOU THINK YOU CAN BEAT NICKY?
OH... I COMPLETELY FORGOT THAT I HAVE TO COMPETE IN A FEW HOURS!

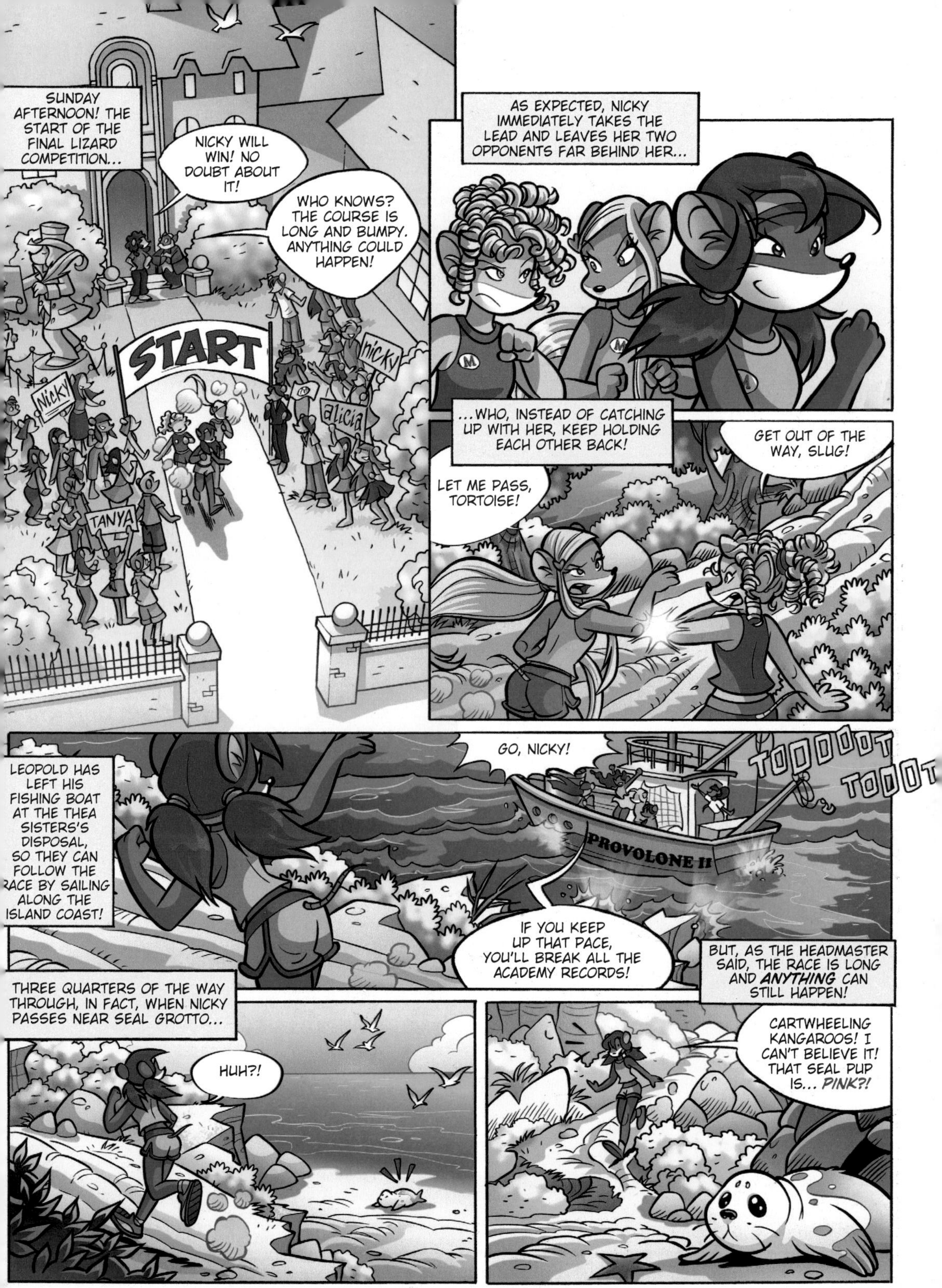
SUNDAY AFTERNOON! THE START OF THE FINAL LIZARD COMPETITION...
NICKY WILL WIN! NO DOUBT ABOUT IT!
WHO KNOWS? THE COURSE IS LONG AND BUMPY. ANYTHING COULD HAPPEN!
START
NICKY
NICKY
ALICIA
TANYA
AS EXPECTED, NICKY IMMEDIATELY TAKES THE LEAD AND LEAVES HER TWO OPPONENTS FAR BEHIND HER...
...WHO, INSTEAD OF CATCHING UP WITH HER, KEEP HOLDING EACH OTHER BACK!
GET OUT OF THE WAY, SLUG!
LET ME PASS, TORTOISE!
LEOPOLD HAS LEFT HIS FISHING BOAT AT THE THEA SISTERS'S DISPOSAL, SO THEY CAN FOLLOW THE RACE BY SAILING ALONG THE ISLAND COAST!
GO, NICKY!
TOOOOOT
TOOOT
PROVOLONE II
IF YOU KEEP UP THAT PACE, YOU'LL BREAK ALL THE ACADEMY RECORDS!
BUT, AS THE HEADMASTER SAID, THE RACE IS LONG AND *ANYTHING* CAN STILL HAPPEN!
THREE QUARTERS OF THE WAY THROUGH, IN FACT, WHEN NICKY PASSES NEAR SEAL GROTTO...
HUH?!
CARTWHEELING KANGAROOS! I CAN'T BELIEVE IT! THAT SEAL PUP IS... *PINK?!*

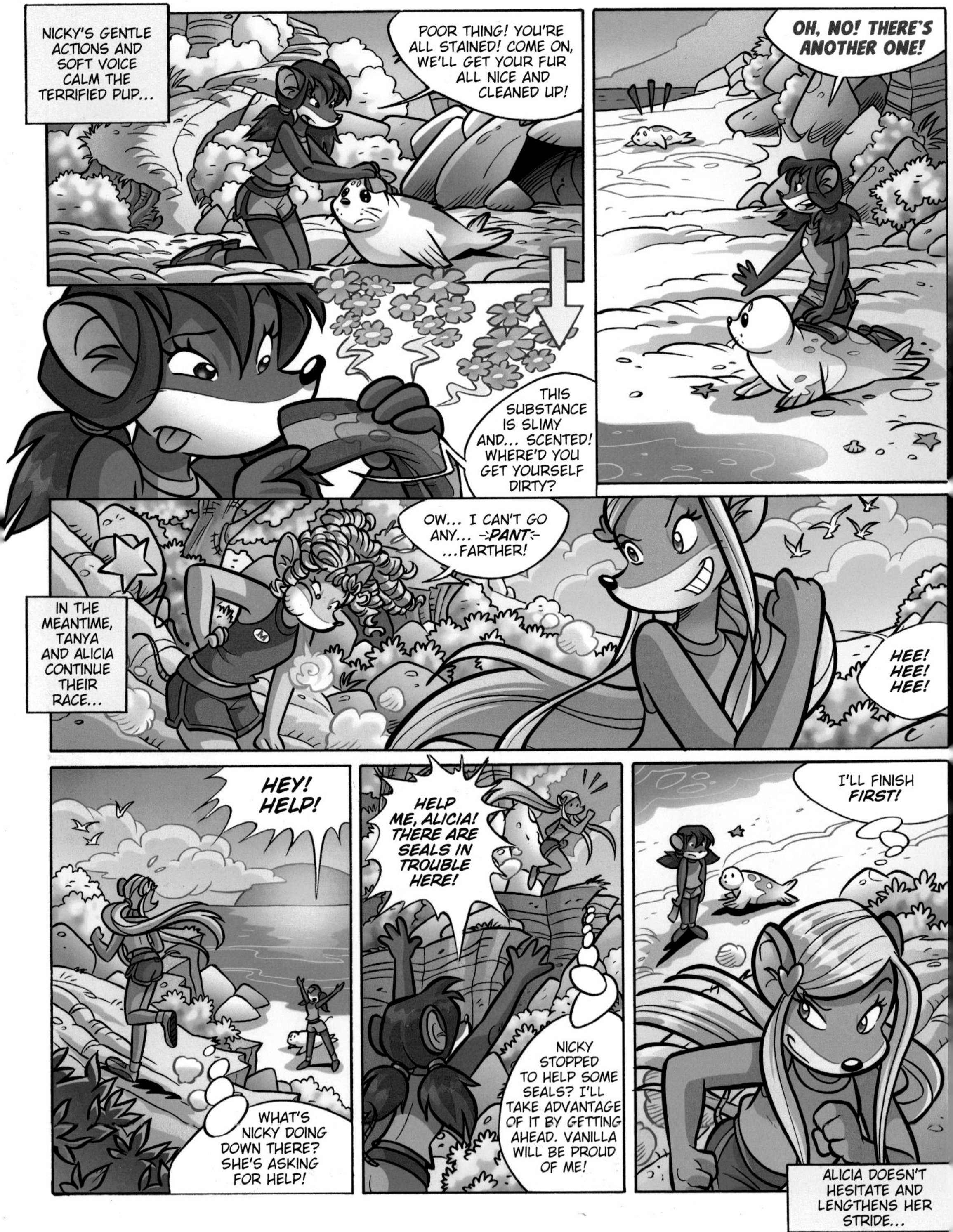
NICKY'S GENTLE ACTIONS AND SOFT VOICE CALM THE TERRIFIED PUP...
POOR THING! YOU'RE ALL STAINED! COME ON, WE'LL GET YOUR FUR ALL NICE AND CLEANED UP!
THIS SUBSTANCE IS SLIMY AND... SCENTED! WHERE'D YOU GET YOURSELF DIRTY?
OH, NO! THERE'S ANOTHER ONE!
IN THE MEANTIME, TANYA AND ALICIA CONTINUE THEIR RACE...
OW... I CAN'T GO ANY... -PANT- ...FARTHER!
HEE! HEE! HEE!
HEY! HELP!
WHAT'S NICKY DOING DOWN THERE? SHE'S ASKING FOR HELP!
HELP ME, ALICIA! THERE ARE SEALS IN TROUBLE HERE!
NICKY STOPPED TO HELP SOME SEALS? I'LL TAKE ADVANTAGE OF IT BY GETTING AHEAD. VANILLA WILL BE PROUD OF ME!
I'LL FINISH FIRST!
ALICIA DOESN'T HESITATE AND LENGTHENS HER STRIDE...

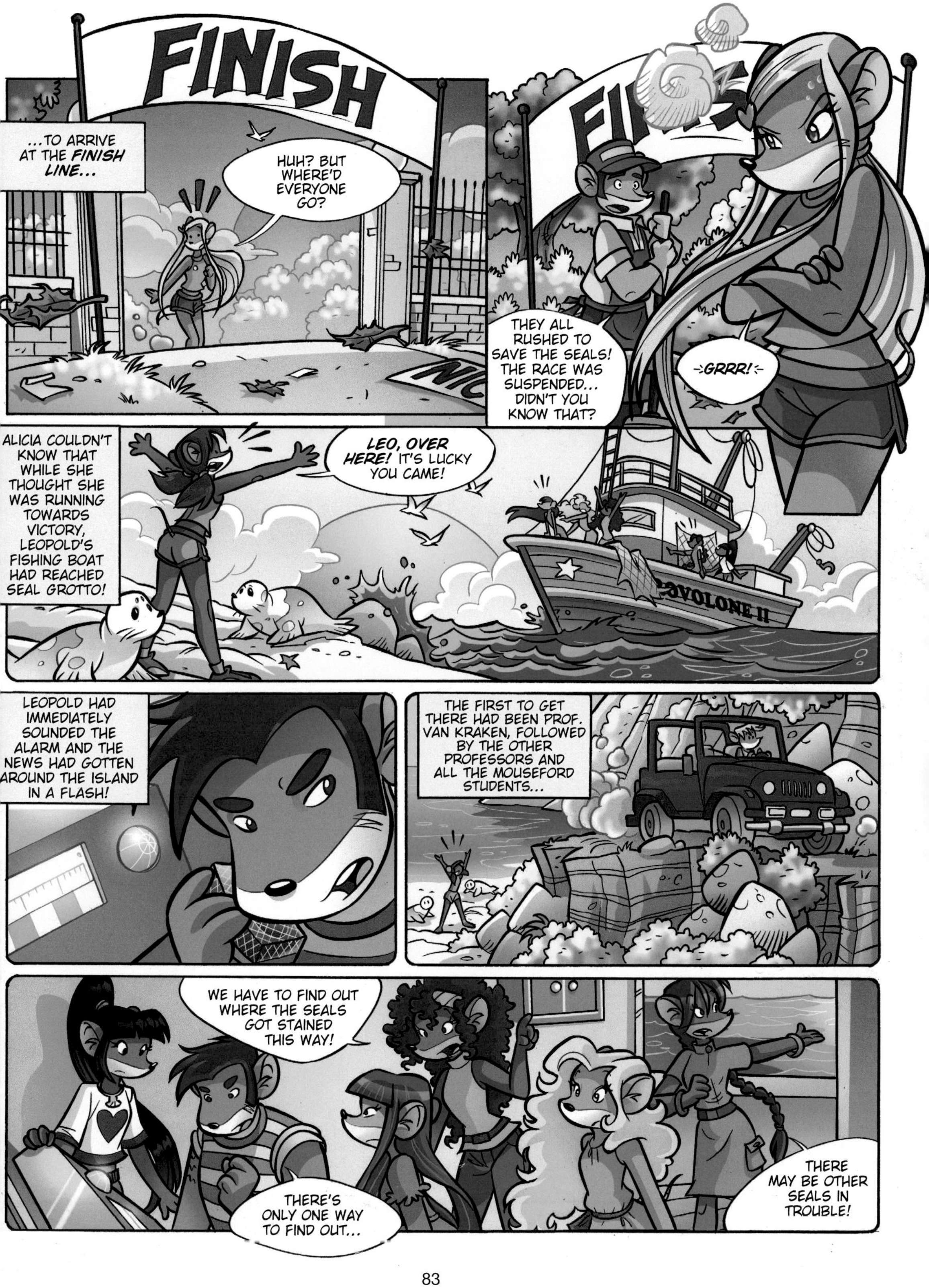
FINISH
...TO ARRIVE AT THE FINISH LINE...
HUH? BUT WHERE'D EVERYONE GO?
THEY ALL RUSHED TO SAVE THE SEALS! THE RACE WAS SUSPENDED... DIDN'T YOU KNOW THAT?
GRRR!
ALICIA COULDN'T KNOW THAT WHILE SHE THOUGHT SHE WAS RUNNING TOWARDS VICTORY, LEOPOLD'S FISHING BOAT HAD REACHED SEAL GROTTO!
LEO, OVER HERE! IT'S LUCKY YOU CAME!
LEOPOLD HAD IMMEDIATELY SOUNDED THE ALARM AND THE NEWS HAD GOTTEN AROUND THE ISLAND IN A FLASH!
THE FIRST TO GET THERE HAD BEEN PROF. VAN KRAKEN, FOLLOWED BY THE OTHER PROFESSORS AND ALL THE MOUSEFORD STUDENTS...
WE HAVE TO FIND OUT WHERE THE SEALS GOT STAINED THIS WAY!
THERE'S ONLY ONE WAY TO FIND OUT...
THERE MAY BE OTHER SEALS IN TROUBLE!

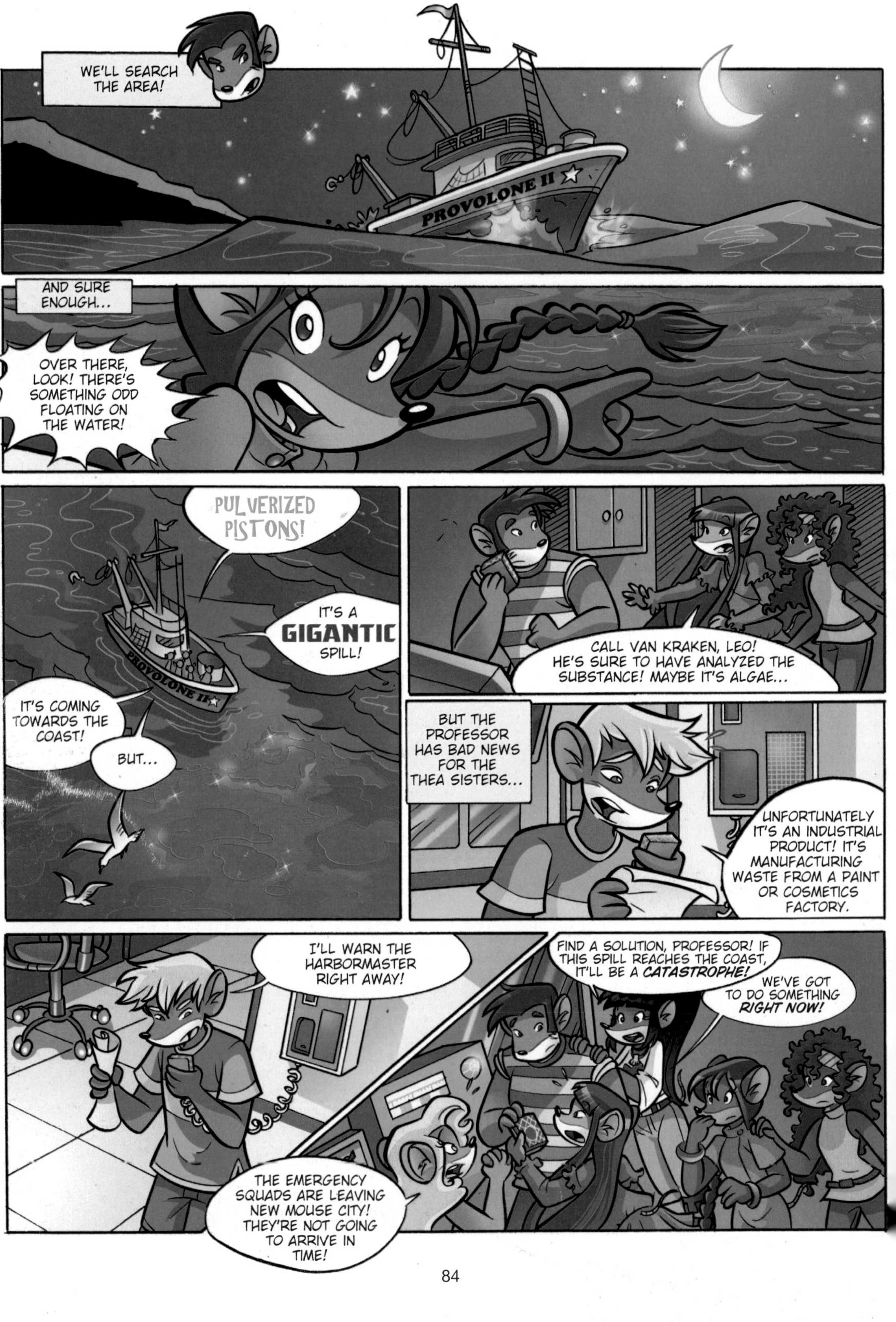
WE'LL SEARCH THE AREA!
PROVOLONE II
AND SURE ENOUGH...
OVER THERE, LOOK! THERE'S SOMETHING ODD FLOATING ON THE WATER!
PULVERIZED PISTONS!
IT'S A GIGANTIC SPILL!
IT'S COMING TOWARDS THE COAST!
BUT...
CALL VAN KRAKEN, LEO! HE'S SURE TO HAVE ANALYZED THE SUBSTANCE! MAYBE IT'S ALGAE...
BUT THE PROFESSOR HAS BAD NEWS FOR THE THEA SISTERS...
UNFORTUNATELY IT'S AN INDUSTRIAL PRODUCT! IT'S MANUFACTURING WASTE FROM A PAINT OR COSMETICS FACTORY.
I'LL WARN THE HARBORMASTER RIGHT AWAY!
FIND A SOLUTION, PROFESSOR! IF THIS SPILL REACHES THE COAST, IT'LL BE A CATASTROPHE!
WE'VE GOT TO DO SOMETHING RIGHT NOW!
THE EMERGENCY SQUADS ARE LEAVING NEW MOUSE CITY! THEY'RE NOT GOING TO ARRIVE IN TIME!

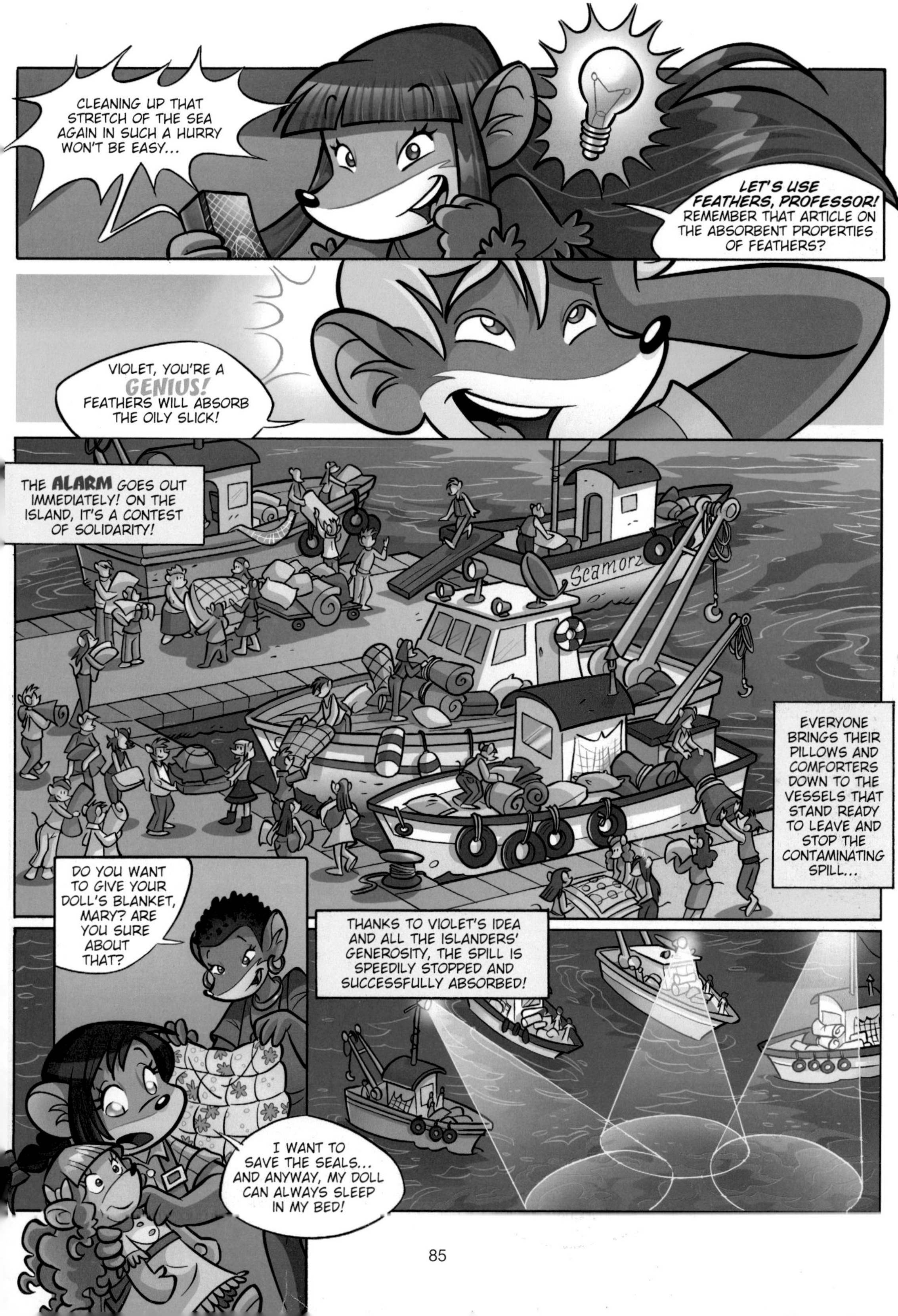
CLEANING UP THAT STRETCH OF THE SEA AGAIN IN SUCH A HURRY WON'T BE EASY...
LET'S USE FEATHERS, PROFESSOR! REMEMBER THAT ARTICLE ON THE ABSORBENT PROPERTIES OF FEATHERS?
VIOLET, YOU'RE A GENIUS! FEATHERS WILL ABSORB THE OILY SLICK!
THE ALARM GOES OUT IMMEDIATELY! ON THE ISLAND, IT'S A CONTEST OF SOLIDARITY!
Seamorz
EVERYONE BRINGS THEIR PILLOWS AND COMFORTERS DOWN TO THE VESSELS THAT STAND READY TO LEAVE AND STOP THE CONTAMINATING SPILL...
DO YOU WANT TO GIVE YOUR DOLL'S BLANKET, MARY? ARE YOU SURE ABOUT THAT?
I WANT TO SAVE THE SEALS... AND ANYWAY, MY DOLL CAN ALWAYS SLEEP IN MY BED!
THANKS TO VIOLET'S IDEA AND ALL THE ISLANDERS' GENEROSITY, THE SPILL IS SPEEDILY STOPPED AND SUCCESSFULLY ABSORBED!

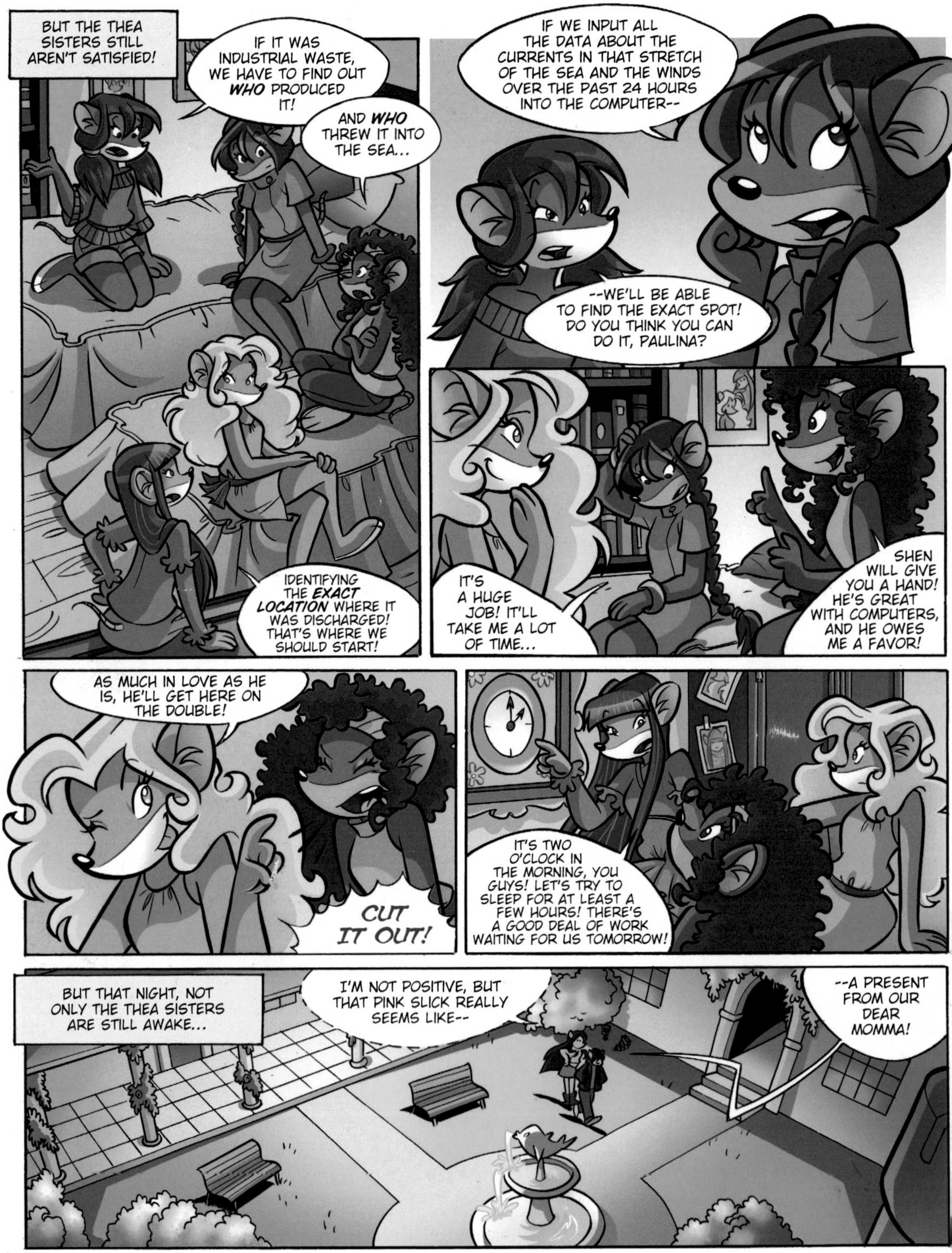

BUT THE THEA SISTERS STILL AREN'T SATISFIED!
IF IT WAS INDUSTRIAL WASTE, WE HAVE TO FIND OUT **WHO** PRODUCED IT!
AND **WHO** THREW IT INTO THE SEA...
IDENTIFYING THE **EXACT LOCATION** WHERE IT WAS DISCHARGED! THAT'S WHERE WE SHOULD START!
IF WE INPUT ALL THE DATA ABOUT THE CURRENTS IN THAT STRETCH OF THE SEA AND THE WINDS OVER THE PAST 24 HOURS INTO THE COMPUTER--
--WE'LL BE ABLE TO FIND THE EXACT SPOT! DO YOU THINK YOU CAN DO IT, PAULINA?
IT'S A HUGE JOB! IT'LL TAKE ME A LOT OF TIME...
SHEN WILL GIVE YOU A HAND! HE'S GREAT WITH COMPUTERS, AND HE OWES ME A FAVOR!
AS MUCH IN LOVE AS HE IS, HE'LL GET HERE ON THE DOUBLE!
CUT IT OUT!
IT'S TWO O'CLOCK IN THE MORNING, YOU GUYS! LET'S TRY TO SLEEP FOR AT LEAST A FEW HOURS! THERE'S A GOOD DEAL OF WORK WAITING FOR US TOMORROW!
BUT THAT NIGHT, NOT ONLY THE THEA SISTERS ARE STILL AWAKE...
I'M NOT POSITIVE, BUT THAT PINK SLICK REALLY SEEMS LIKE--
--A PRESENT FROM OUR DEAR MOMMA!

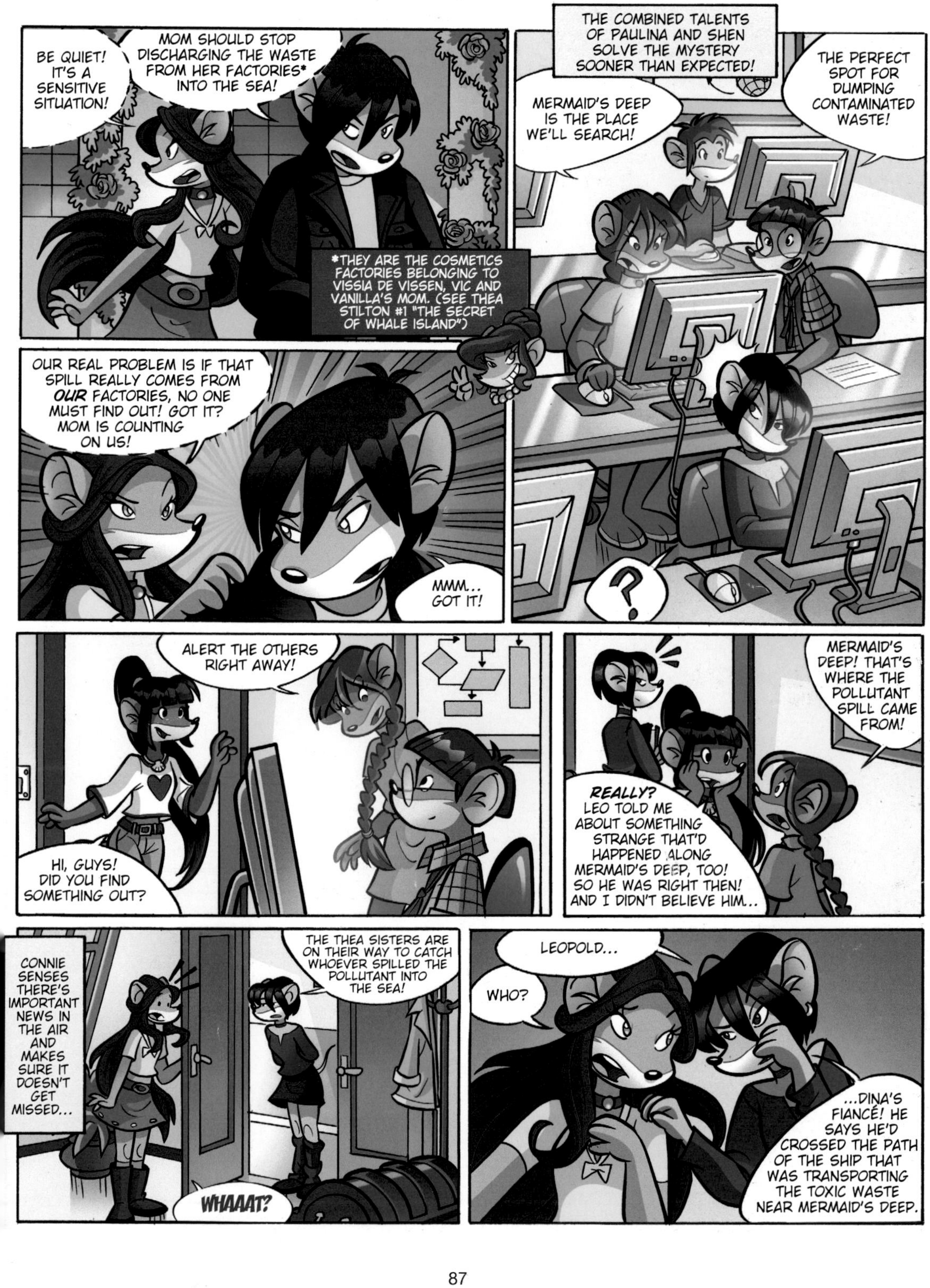
BE QUIET! IT'S A SENSITIVE SITUATION!
MOM SHOULD STOP DISCHARGING THE WASTE FROM HER FACTORIES* INTO THE SEA!
*THEY ARE THE COSMETICS FACTORIES BELONGING TO VISSIA DE VISSEN, VIC AND VANILLA'S MOM. (SEE THEA STILTON #1 "THE SECRET OF WHALE ISLAND")
THE COMBINED TALENTS OF PAULINA AND SHEN SOLVE THE MYSTERY SOONER THAN EXPECTED!
MERMAID'S DEEP IS THE PLACE WE'LL SEARCH!
THE PERFECT SPOT FOR DUMPING CONTAMINATED WASTE!
OUR REAL PROBLEM IS IF THAT SPILL REALLY COMES FROM ***OUR*** FACTORIES, NO ONE MUST FIND OUT! GOT IT? MOM IS COUNTING ON US!
MMM.. GOT IT!
?
ALERT THE OTHERS RIGHT AWAY!
HI, GUYS! DID YOU FIND SOMETHING OUT?
MERMAID'S DEEP! THAT'S WHERE THE POLLUTANT SPILL CAME FROM!
REALLY? LEO TOLD ME ABOUT SOMETHING STRANGE THAT'D HAPPENED ALONG MERMAID'S DEEP, TOO! SO HE WAS RIGHT THEN! AND I DIDN'T BELIEVE HIM..
CONNIE SENSES THERE'S IMPORTANT NEWS IN THE AIR AND MAKES SURE IT DOESN'T GET MISSED...
THE THEA SISTERS ARE ON THEIR WAY TO CATCH WHOEVER SPILLED THE POLLUTANT INTO THE SEA!
WHAAAT?
LEOPOLD...
WHO?
...DINA'S FIANCÉ! HE SAYS HE'D CROSSED THE PATH OF THE SHIP THAT WAS TRANSPORTING THE TOXIC WASTE NEAR MERMAID'S DEEP.

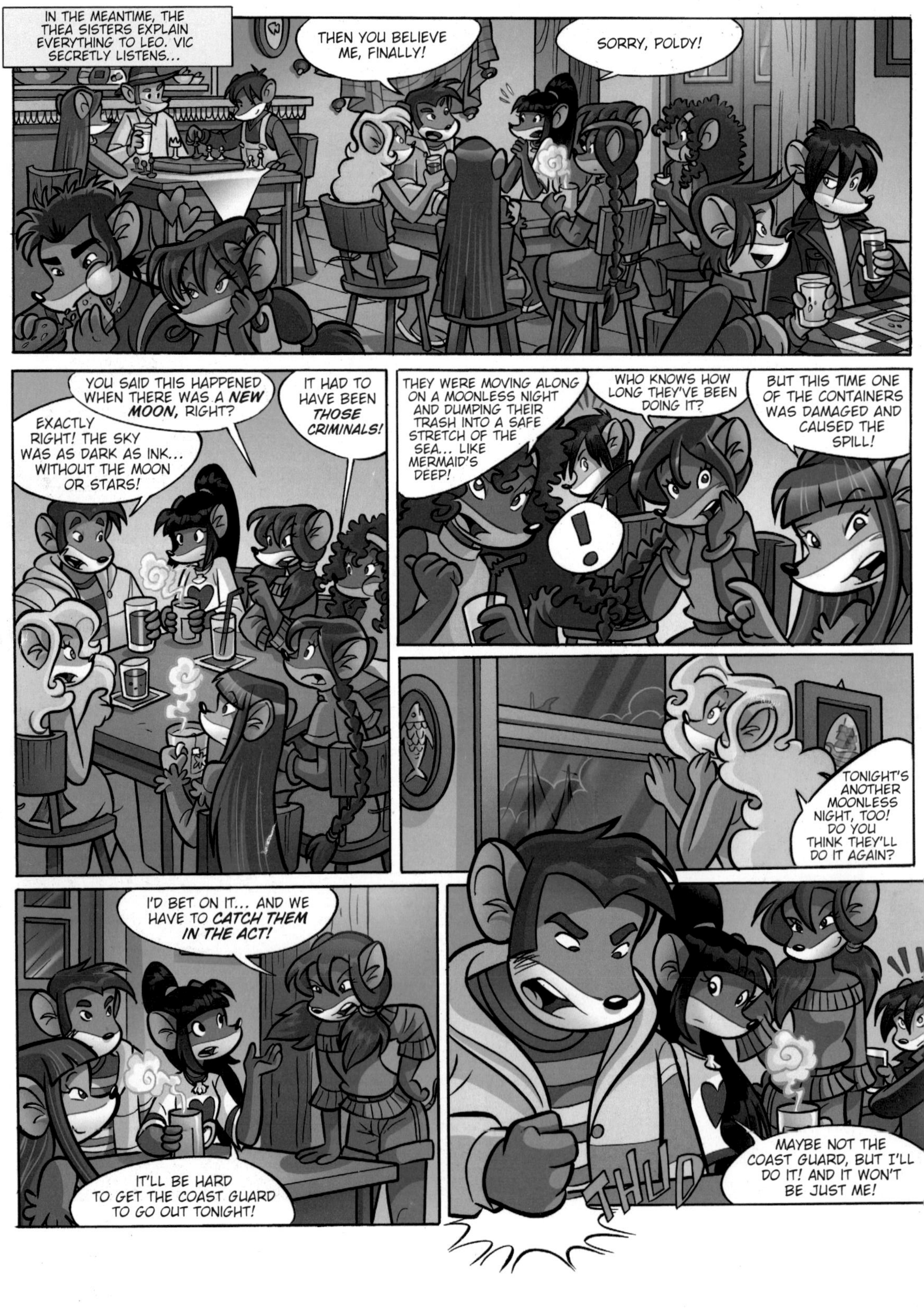
IN THE MEANTIME, THE THEA SISTERS EXPLAIN EVERYTHING TO LEO. VIC SECRETLY LISTENS...
THEN YOU BELIEVE ME, FINALLY!
SORRY, POLDY!
YOU SAID THIS HAPPENED WHEN THERE WAS A NEW MOON, RIGHT?
EXACTLY RIGHT! THE SKY WAS AS DARK AS INK... WITHOUT THE MOON OR STARS!
IT HAD TO HAVE BEEN THOSE CRIMINALS!
THEY WERE MOVING ALONG ON A MOONLESS NIGHT AND DUMPING THEIR TRASH INTO A SAFE STRETCH OF THE SEA... LIKE MERMAID'S DEEP!
WHO KNOWS HOW LONG THEY'VE BEEN DOING IT?
BUT THIS TIME ONE OF THE CONTAINERS WAS DAMAGED AND CAUSED THE SPILL!
!
TONIGHT'S ANOTHER MOONLESS NIGHT, TOO! DO YOU THINK THEY'LL DO IT AGAIN?
I'D BET ON IT... AND WE HAVE TO CATCH THEM IN THE ACT!
IT'LL BE HARD TO GET THE COAST GUARD TO GO OUT TONIGHT!
THUD
MAYBE NOT THE COAST GUARD, BUT I'LL DO IT! AND IT WON'T BE JUST ME!

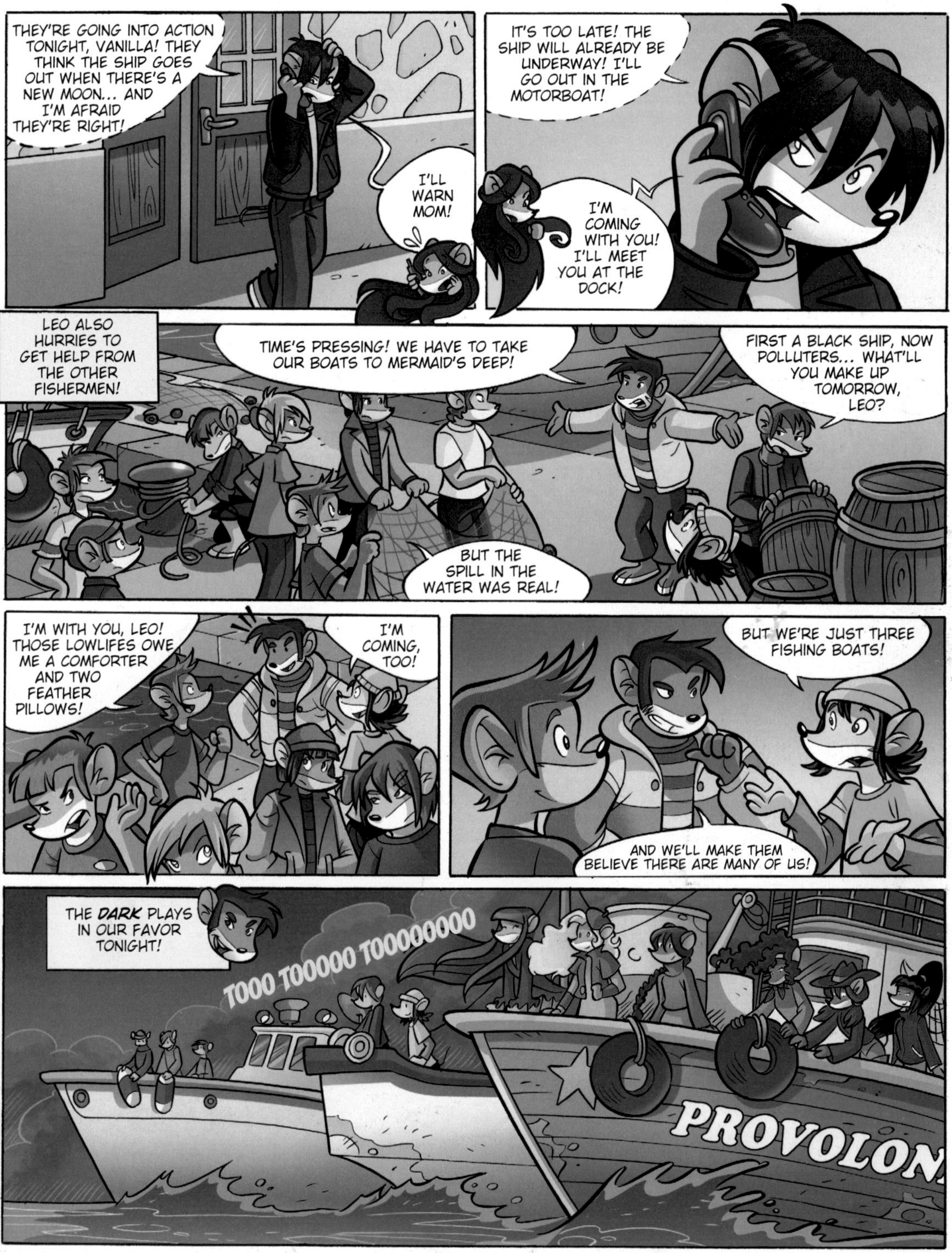
THEY'RE GOING INTO ACTION TONIGHT, VANILLA! THEY THINK THE SHIP GOES OUT WHEN THERE'S A NEW MOON... AND I'M AFRAID THEY'RE RIGHT!
I'LL WARN MOM!
IT'S TOO LATE! THE SHIP WILL ALREADY BE UNDERWAY! I'LL GO OUT IN THE MOTORBOAT!
I'M COMING WITH YOU! I'LL MEET YOU AT THE DOCK!
LEO ALSO HURRIES TO GET HELP FROM THE OTHER FISHERMEN!
TIME'S PRESSING! WE HAVE TO TAKE OUR BOATS TO MERMAID'S DEEP!
FIRST A BLACK SHIP, NOW POLLUTERS... WHAT'LL YOU MAKE UP TOMORROW, LEO?
BUT THE SPILL IN THE WATER WAS REAL!
I'M WITH YOU, LEO! THOSE LOWLIFES OWE ME A COMFORTER AND TWO FEATHER PILLOWS!
I'M COMING, TOO!
BUT WE'RE JUST THREE FISHING BOATS!
AND WE'LL MAKE THEM BELIEVE THERE ARE MANY OF US!
THE DARK PLAYS IN OUR FAVOR TONIGHT!
TOOO TOOOOO TOOOOOOOO
PROVOLON

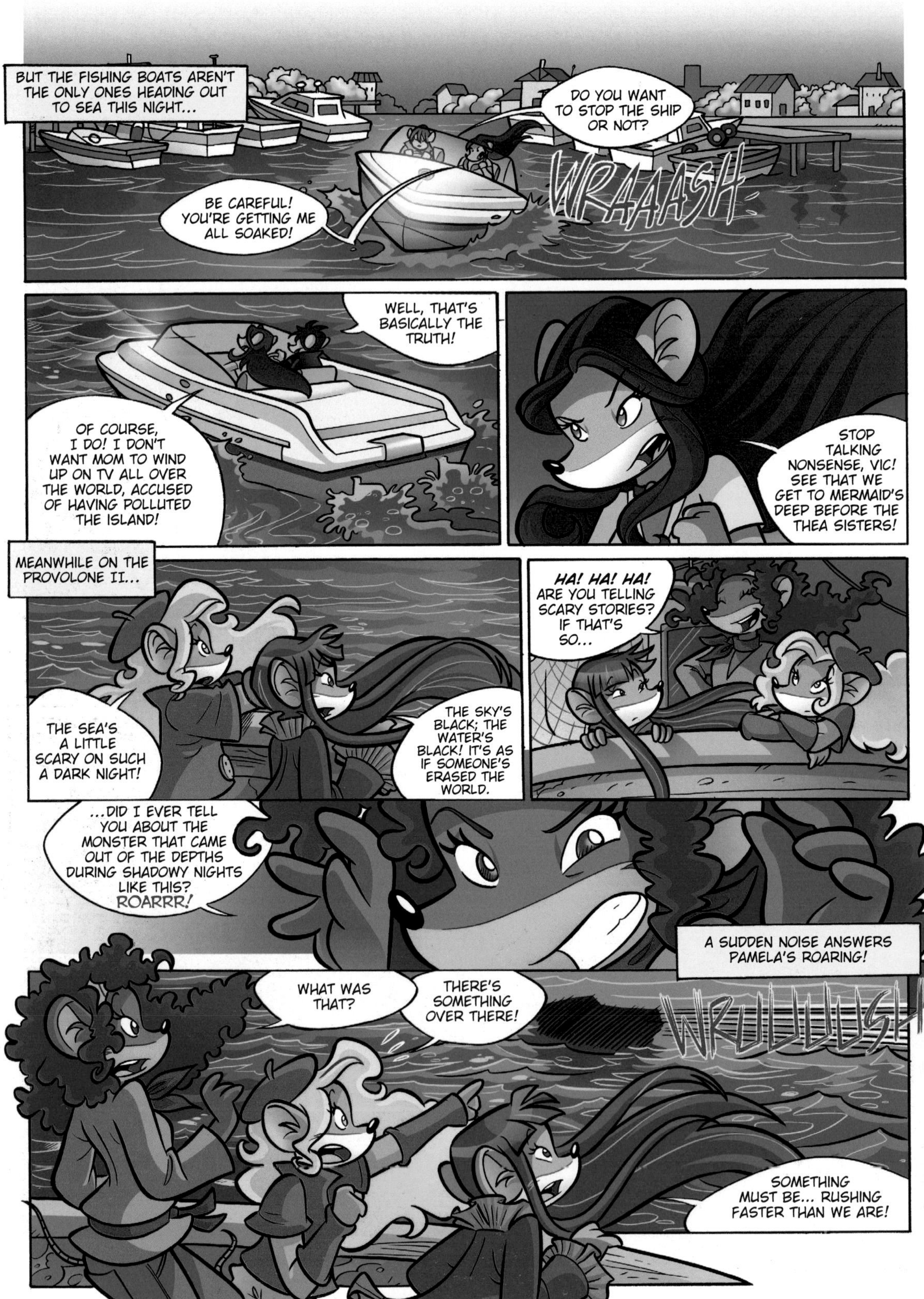

BUT THE FISHING BOATS AREN'T THE ONLY ONES HEADING OUT TO SEA THIS NIGHT...
DO YOU WANT TO STOP THE SHIP OR NOT?
WRAAASH
BE CAREFUL! YOU'RE GETTING ME ALL SOAKED!
WELL, THAT'S BASICALLY THE TRUTH!
OF COURSE, I DO! I DON'T WANT MOM TO WIND UP ON TV ALL OVER THE WORLD, ACCUSED OF HAVING POLLUTED THE ISLAND!
STOP TALKING NONSENSE, VIC! SEE THAT WE GET TO MERMAID'S DEEP BEFORE THE THEA SISTERS!
MEANWHILE ON THE PROVOLONE II...
THE SEA'S A LITTLE SCARY ON SUCH A DARK NIGHT!
THE SKY'S BLACK; THE WATER'S BLACK! IT'S AS IF SOMEONE'S ERASED THE WORLD.
HA! HA! HA! ARE YOU TELLING SCARY STORIES? IF THAT'S SO...
...DID I EVER TELL YOU ABOUT THE MONSTER THAT CAME OUT OF THE DEPTHS DURING SHADOWY NIGHTS LIKE THIS? ROARRR!
A SUDDEN NOISE ANSWERS PAMELA'S ROARING!
WHAT WAS THAT?
THERE'S SOMETHING OVER THERE!
WRUUUUSH
SOMETHING MUST BE... RUSHING FASTER THAN WE ARE!

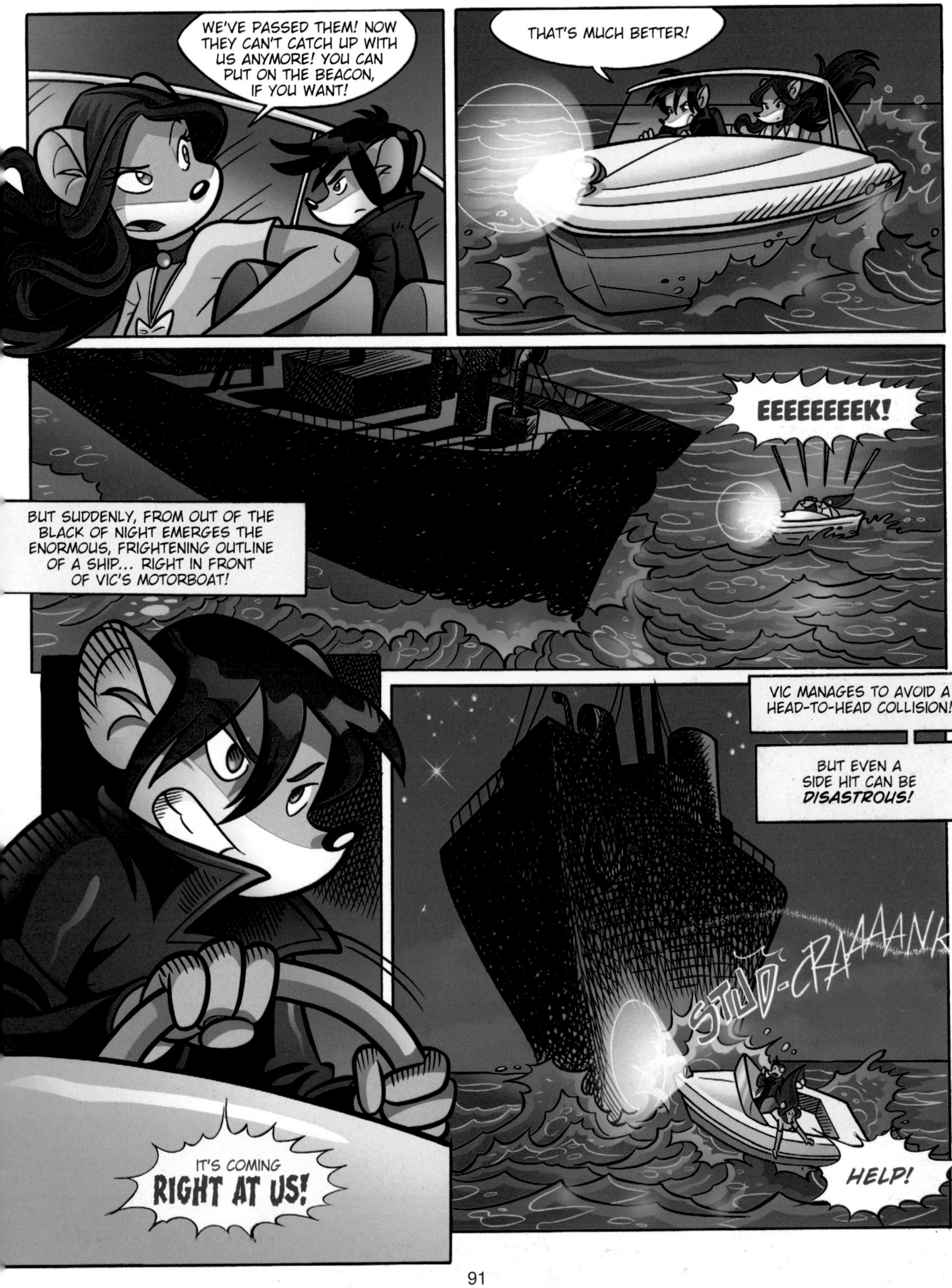
WE'VE PASSED THEM! NOW THEY CAN'T CATCH UP WITH US ANYMORE! YOU CAN PUT ON THE BEACON, IF YOU WANT!
THAT'S MUCH BETTER!
EEEEEEEEK!
BUT SUDDENLY, FROM OUT OF THE BLACK OF NIGHT EMERGES THE ENORMOUS, FRIGHTENING OUTLINE OF A SHIP... RIGHT IN FRONT OF VIC'S MOTORBOAT!
IT'S COMING RIGHT AT US!
VIC MANAGES TO AVOID A HEAD-TO-HEAD COLLISION!
BUT EVEN A SIDE HIT CAN BE DISASTROUS!
STUD-CRAAAANK
HELP!

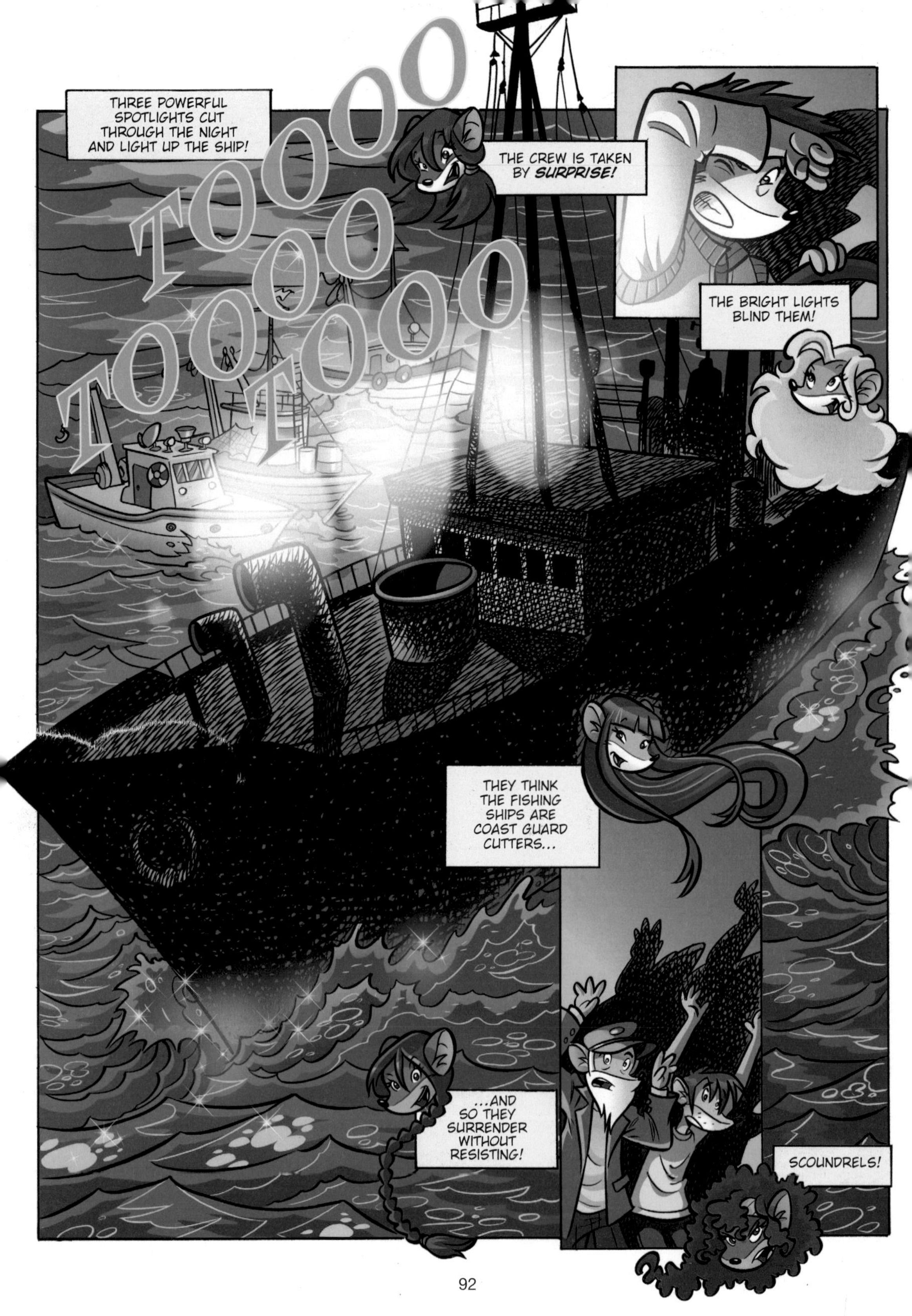
THREE POWERFUL SPOTLIGHTS CUT THROUGH THE NIGHT AND LIGHT UP THE SHIP!
TOOOOO TOOOO TOOOOO
THE CREW IS TAKEN BY SURPRISE!
THE BRIGHT LIGHTS BLIND THEM!
THEY THINK THE FISHING SHIPS ARE COAST GUARD CUTTERS...
...AND SO THEY SURRENDER WITHOUT RESISTING!
SCOUNDRELS!

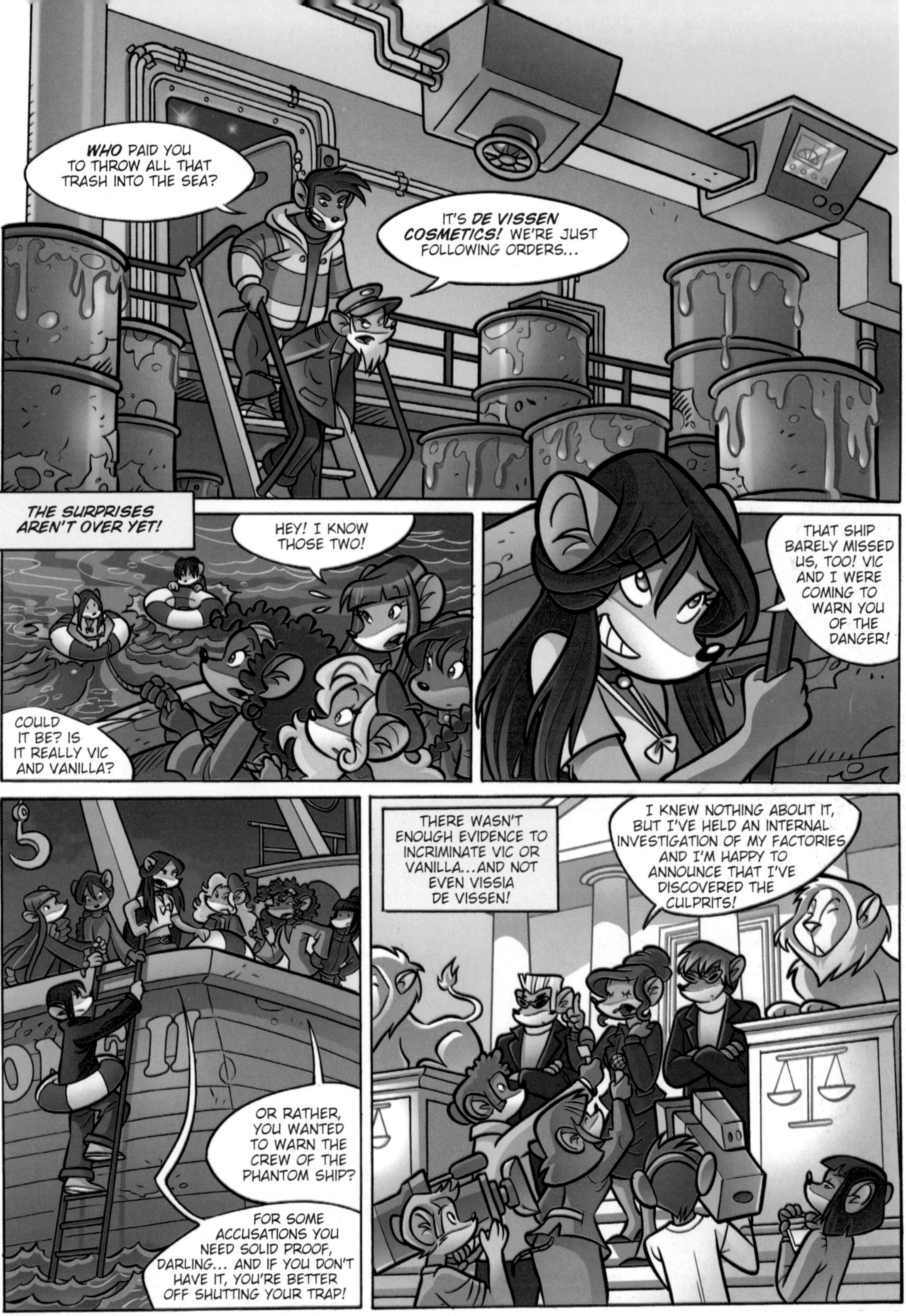
WHO PAID YOU TO THROW ALL THAT TRASH INTO THE SEA?
IT'S DE VISSEN COSMETICS! WE'RE JUST FOLLOWING ORDERS...
THE SURPRISES AREN'T OVER YET!
HEY! I KNOW THOSE TWO!
COULD IT BE? IS IT REALLY VIC AND VANILLA?
THAT SHIP BARELY MISSED US, TOO! VIC AND I WERE COMING TO WARN YOU OF THE DANGER!
OR RATHER, YOU WANTED TO WARN THE CREW OF THE PHANTOM SHIP?
FOR SOME ACCUSATIONS YOU NEED SOLID PROOF, DARLING... AND IF YOU DON'T HAVE IT, YOU'RE BETTER OFF SHUTTING YOUR TRAP!
THERE WASN'T ENOUGH EVIDENCE TO INCRIMINATE VIC OR VANILLA...AND NOT EVEN VISSIA DE VISSEN!
I KNEW NOTHING ABOUT IT, BUT I'VE HELD AN INTERNAL INVESTIGATION OF MY FACTORIES AND I'M HAPPY TO ANNOUNCE THAT I'VE DISCOVERED THE CULPRITS!

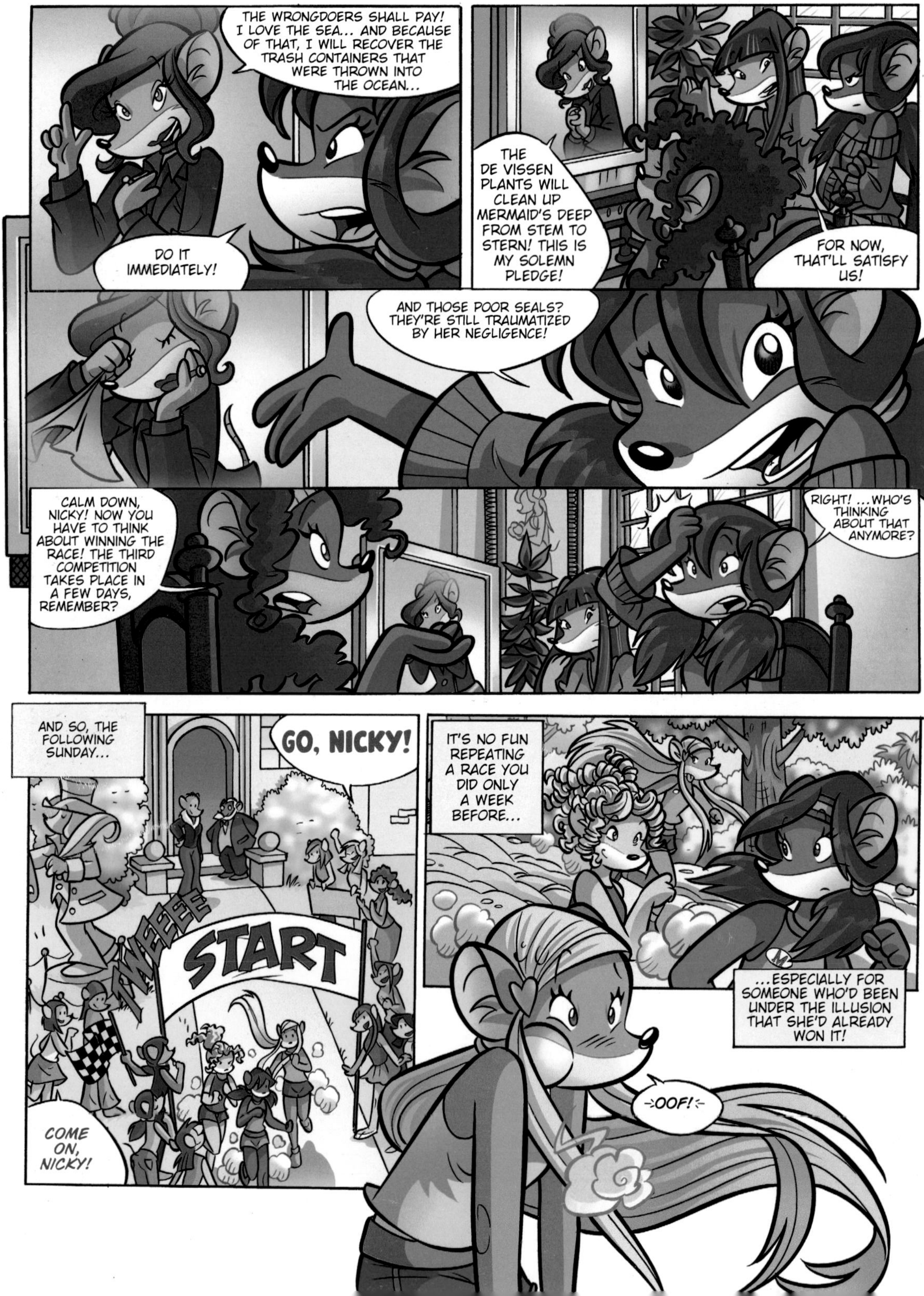
THE WRONGDOERS SHALL PAY! I LOVE THE SEA... AND BECAUSE OF THAT, I WILL RECOVER THE TRASH CONTAINERS THAT WERE THROWN INTO THE OCEAN...
DO IT IMMEDIATELY!
THE DE VISSEN PLANTS WILL CLEAN UP MERMAID'S DEEP FROM STEM TO STERN! THIS IS MY SOLEMN PLEDGE!
FOR NOW, THAT'LL SATISFY US!
AND THOSE POOR SEALS? THEY'RE STILL TRAUMATIZED BY HER NEGLIGENCE!
CALM DOWN, NICKY! NOW YOU HAVE TO THINK ABOUT WINNING THE RACE! THE THIRD COMPETITION TAKES PLACE IN A FEW DAYS, REMEMBER?
RIGHT! ...WHO'S THINKING ABOUT THAT ANYMORE?
AND SO, THE FOLLOWING SUNDAY...
GO, NICKY!
TWEEEE
START
COME ON, NICKY!
IT'S NO FUN REPEATING A RACE YOU DID ONLY A WEEK BEFORE...
...ESPECIALLY FOR SOMEONE WHO'D BEEN UNDER THE ILLUSION THAT SHE'D ALREADY WON IT!
OOF!

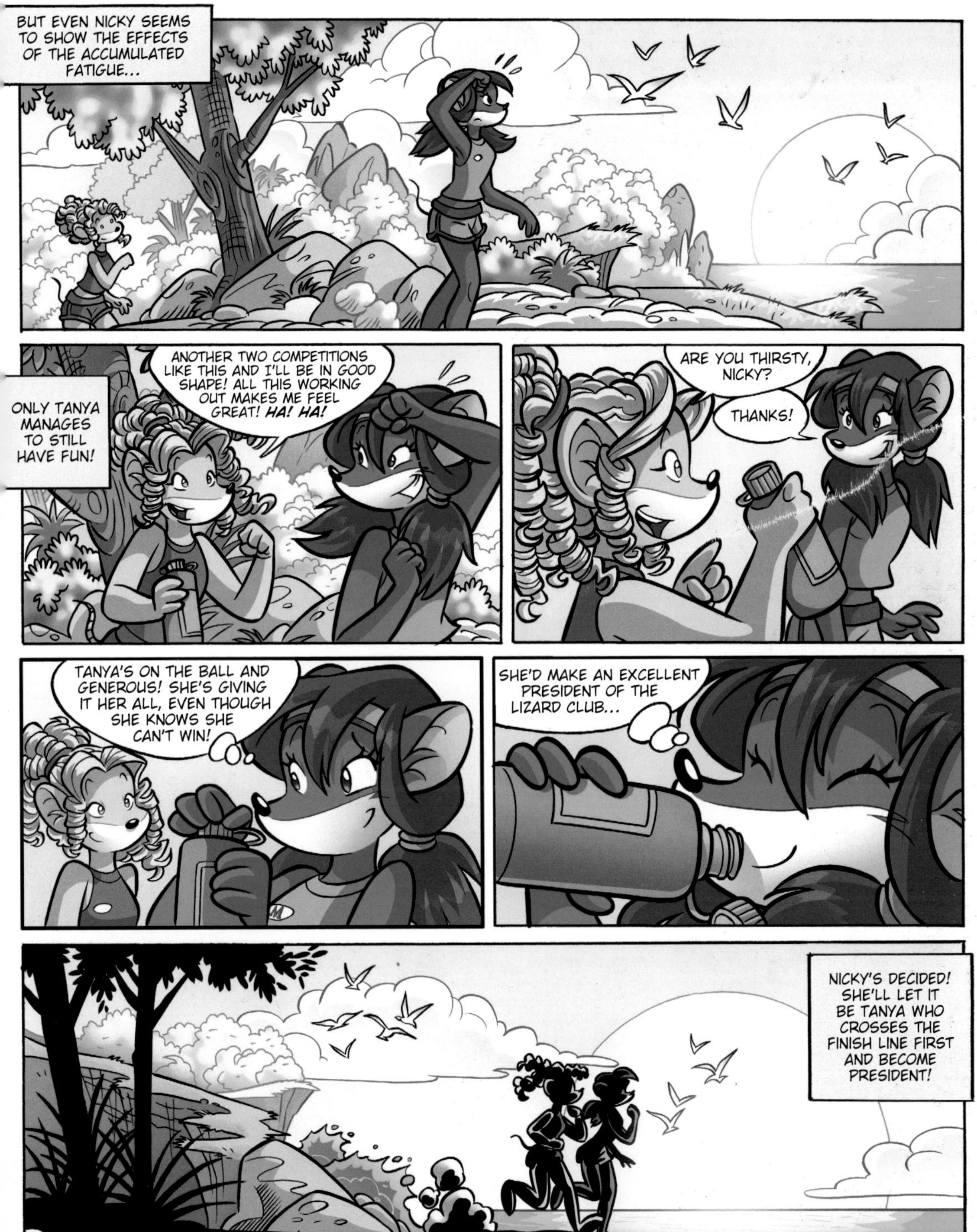
BUT EVEN NICKY SEEMS TO SHOW THE EFFECTS OF THE ACCUMULATED FATIGUE...
ONLY TANYA MANAGES TO STILL HAVE FUN!
ANOTHER TWO COMPETITIONS LIKE THIS AND I'LL BE IN GOOD SHAPE! ALL THIS WORKING OUT MAKES ME FEEL GREAT! HA! HA!
ARE YOU THIRSTY, NICKY?
THANKS!
TANYA'S ON THE BALL AND GENEROUS! SHE'S GIVING IT HER ALL, EVEN THOUGH SHE KNOWS SHE CAN'T WIN!
SHE'D MAKE AN EXCELLENT PRESIDENT OF THE LIZARD CLUB...
NICKY'S DECIDED! SHE'LL LET IT BE TANYA WHO CROSSES THE FINISH LINE FIRST AND BECOME PRESIDENT!

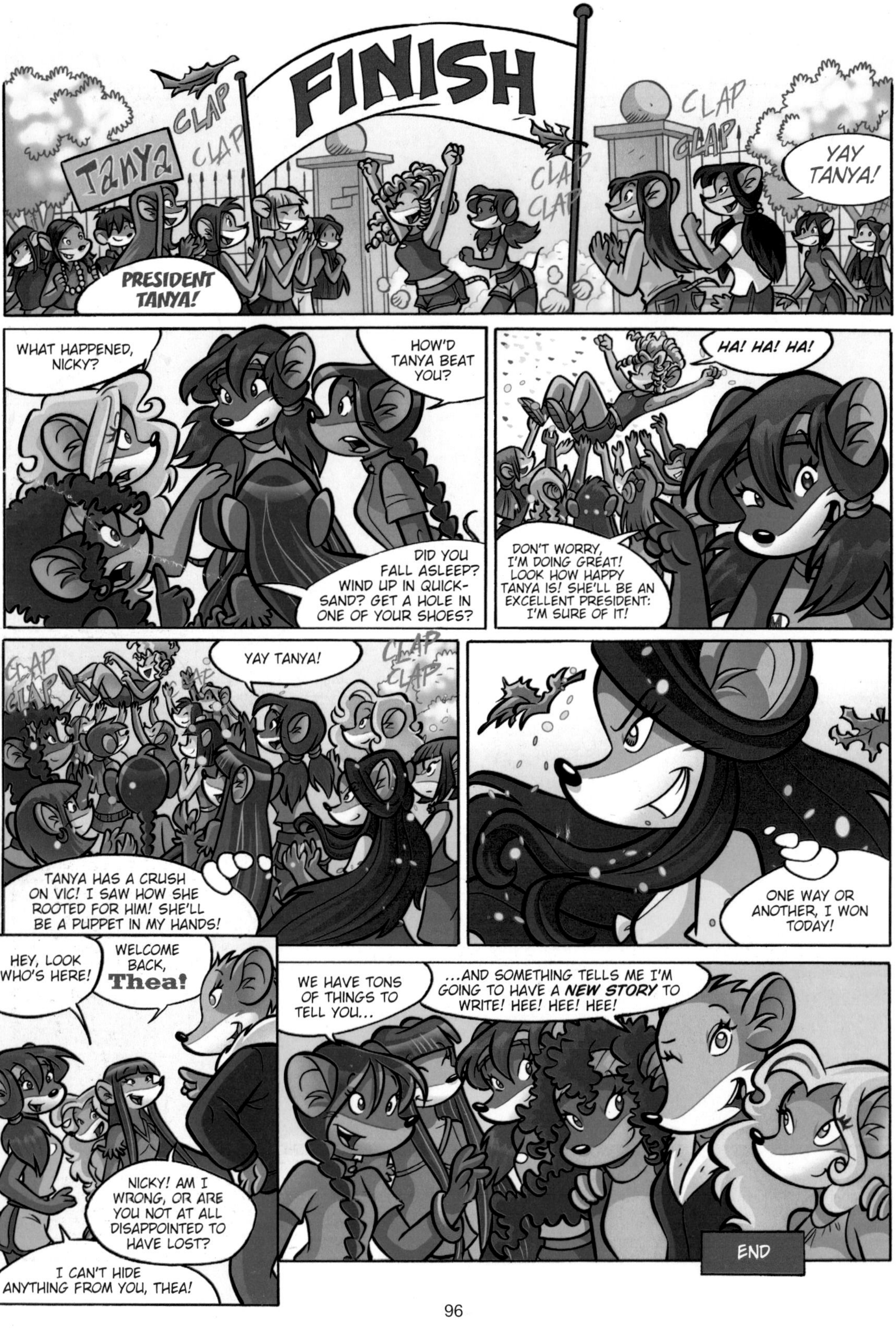
FINISH
TANYA
CLAP CLAP
CLAP CLAP
CLAP CLAP
CLAP CLAP
YAY TANYA!
PRESIDENT TANYA!
WHAT HAPPENED, NICKY?
HOW'D TANYA BEAT YOU?
DID YOU FALL ASLEEP? WIND UP IN QUICK-SAND? GET A HOLE IN ONE OF YOUR SHOES?
HA! HA! HA!
DON'T WORRY, I'M DOING GREAT! LOOK HOW HAPPY TANYA IS! SHE'LL BE AN EXCELLENT PRESIDENT: I'M SURE OF IT!
YAY TANYA!
CLAP CLAP
CLAP CLAP
TANYA HAS A CRUSH ON VIC! I SAW HOW SHE ROOTED FOR HIM! SHE'LL BE A PUPPET IN MY HANDS!
ONE WAY OR ANOTHER, I WON TODAY!
HEY, LOOK WHO'S HERE!
WELCOME BACK, Thea!
NICKY! AM I WRONG, OR ARE YOU NOT AT ALL DISAPPOINTED TO HAVE LOST?
I CAN'T HIDE ANYTHING FROM YOU, THEA!
WE HAVE TONS OF THINGS TO TELL YOU...
...AND SOMETHING TELLS ME I'M GOING TO HAVE A NEW STORY TO WRITE! HEE! HEE! HEE!
END

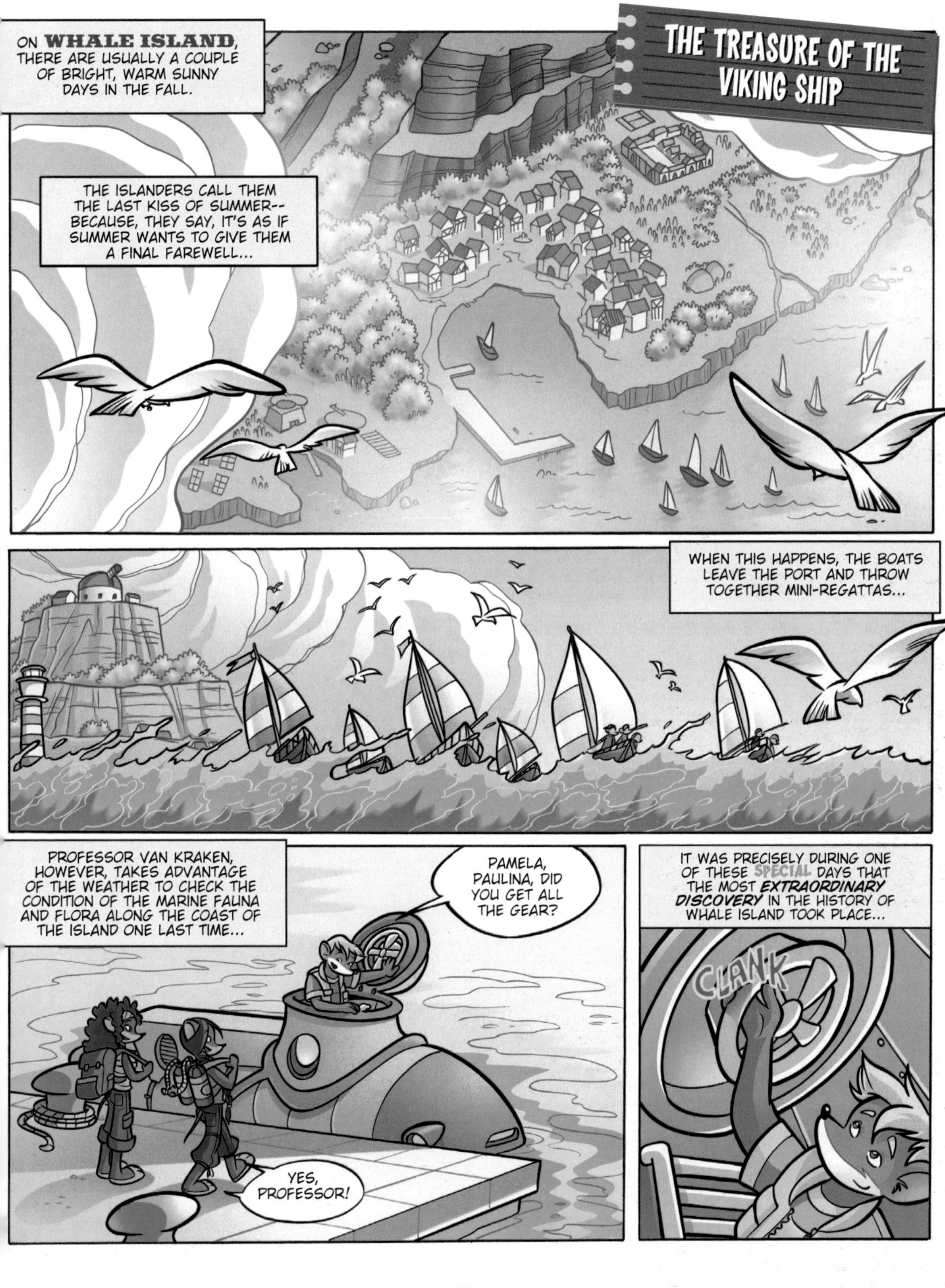

THE TREASURE OF THE VIKING SHIP
ON WHALE ISLAND, THERE ARE USUALLY A COUPLE OF BRIGHT, WARM SUNNY DAYS IN THE FALL.
THE ISLANDERS CALL THEM THE LAST KISS OF SUMMER-- BECAUSE, THEY SAY, IT'S AS IF SUMMER WANTS TO GIVE THEM A FINAL FAREWELL...
WHEN THIS HAPPENS, THE BOATS LEAVE THE PORT AND THROW TOGETHER MINI-REGATTAS...
PROFESSOR VAN KRAKEN, HOWEVER, TAKES ADVANTAGE OF THE WEATHER TO CHECK THE CONDITION OF THE MARINE FAUNA AND FLORA ALONG THE COAST OF THE ISLAND ONE LAST TIME...
PAMELA, PAULINA, DID YOU GET ALL THE GEAR?
YES, PROFESSOR!
IT WAS PRECISELY DURING ONE OF THESE SPECIAL DAYS THAT THE MOST EXTRAORDINARY DISCOVERY IN THE HISTORY OF WHALE ISLAND TOOK PLACE...
CLANK

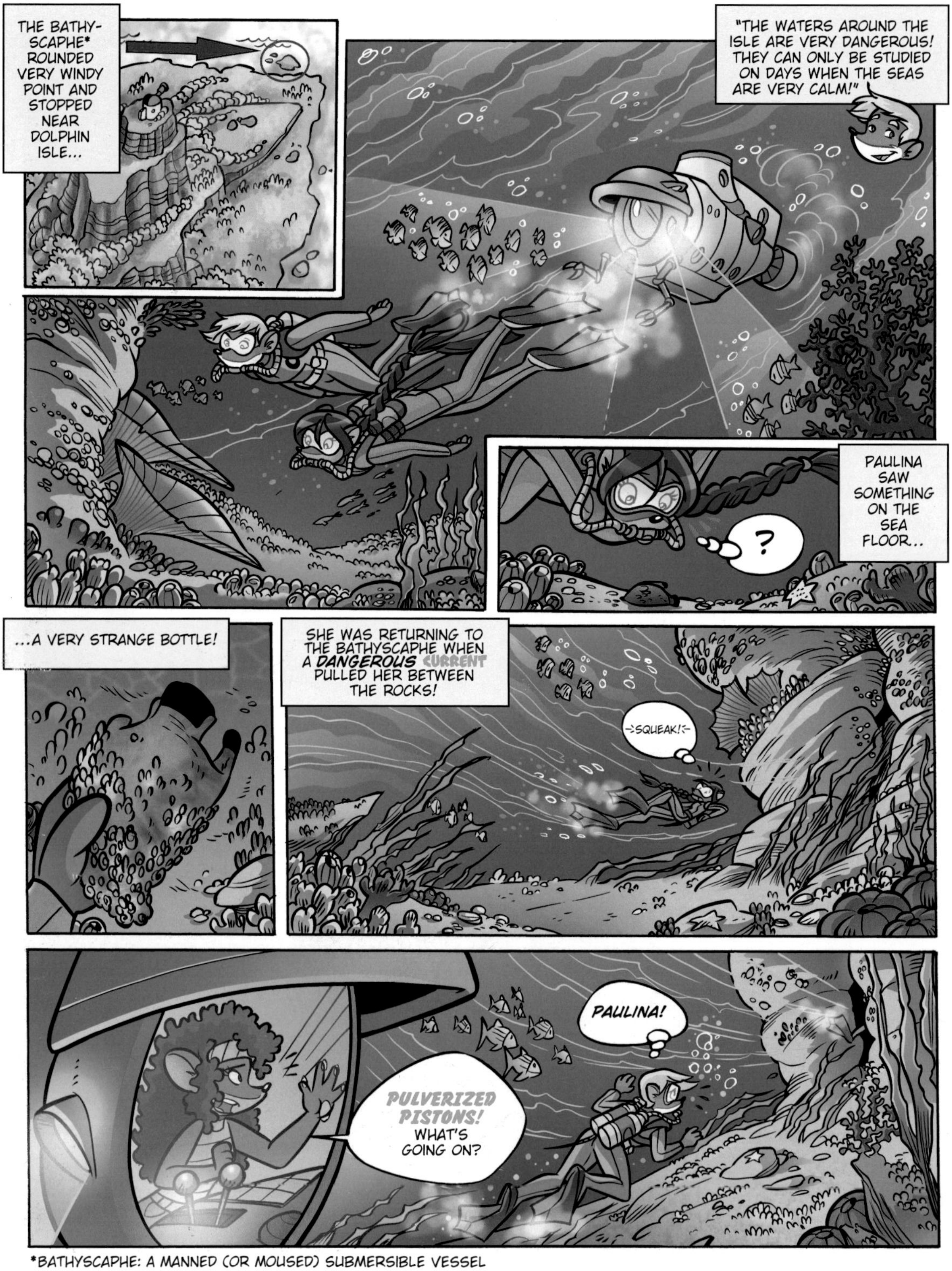
THE BATHY-SCAPHE* ROUNDED VERY WINDY POINT AND STOPPED NEAR DOLPHIN ISLE...
"THE WATERS AROUND THE ISLE ARE VERY DANGEROUS! THEY CAN ONLY BE STUDIED ON DAYS WHEN THE SEAS ARE VERY CALM!"
PAULINA SAW SOMETHING ON THE SEA FLOOR...
?
...A VERY STRANGE BOTTLE!
SHE WAS RETURNING TO THE BATHYSCAPHE WHEN A DANGEROUS CURRENT PULLED HER BETWEEN THE ROCKS!
SQUEAK!
PAULINA!
PULVERIZED PISTONS! WHAT'S GOING ON?

*BATHYSCAPHE: A MANNED (OR MOUSED) SUBMERSIBLE VESSEL

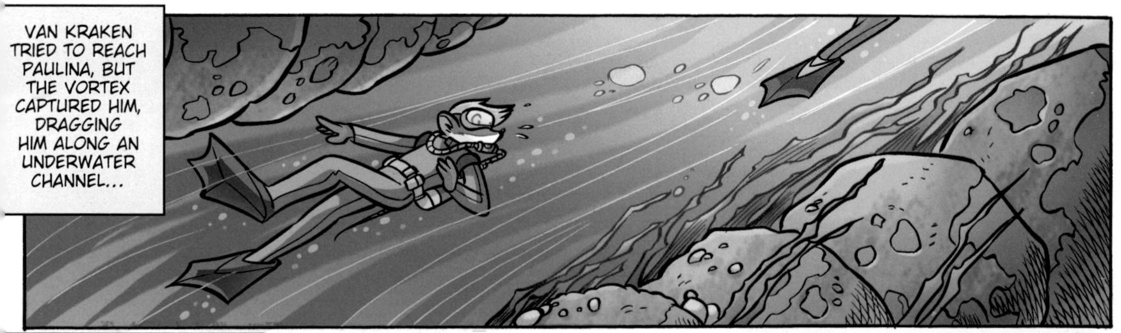
VAN KRAKEN TRIED TO REACH PAULINA, BUT THE VORTEX CAPTURED HIM, DRAGGING HIM ALONG AN UNDERWATER CHANNEL...

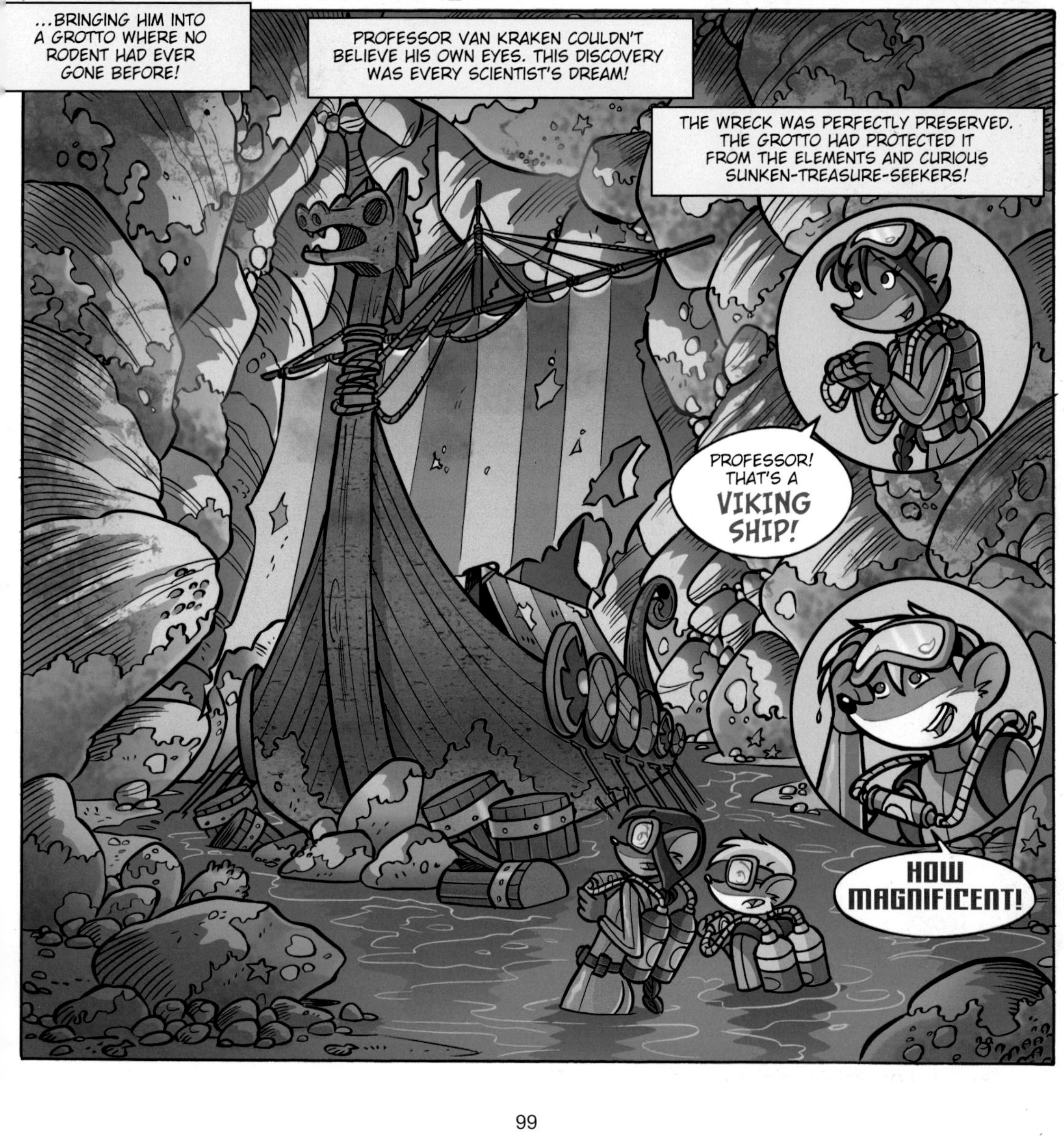
...BRINGING HIM INTO A GROTTO WHERE NO RODENT HAD EVER GONE BEFORE!
PROFESSOR VAN KRAKEN COULDN'T BELIEVE HIS OWN EYES. THIS DISCOVERY WAS EVERY SCIENTIST'S DREAM!
THE WRECK WAS PERFECTLY PRESERVED. THE GROTTO HAD PROTECTED IT FROM THE ELEMENTS AND CURIOUS SUNKEN-TREASURE-SEEKERS!
PROFESSOR! THAT'S A VIKING SHIP!
HOW MAGNIFICENT!

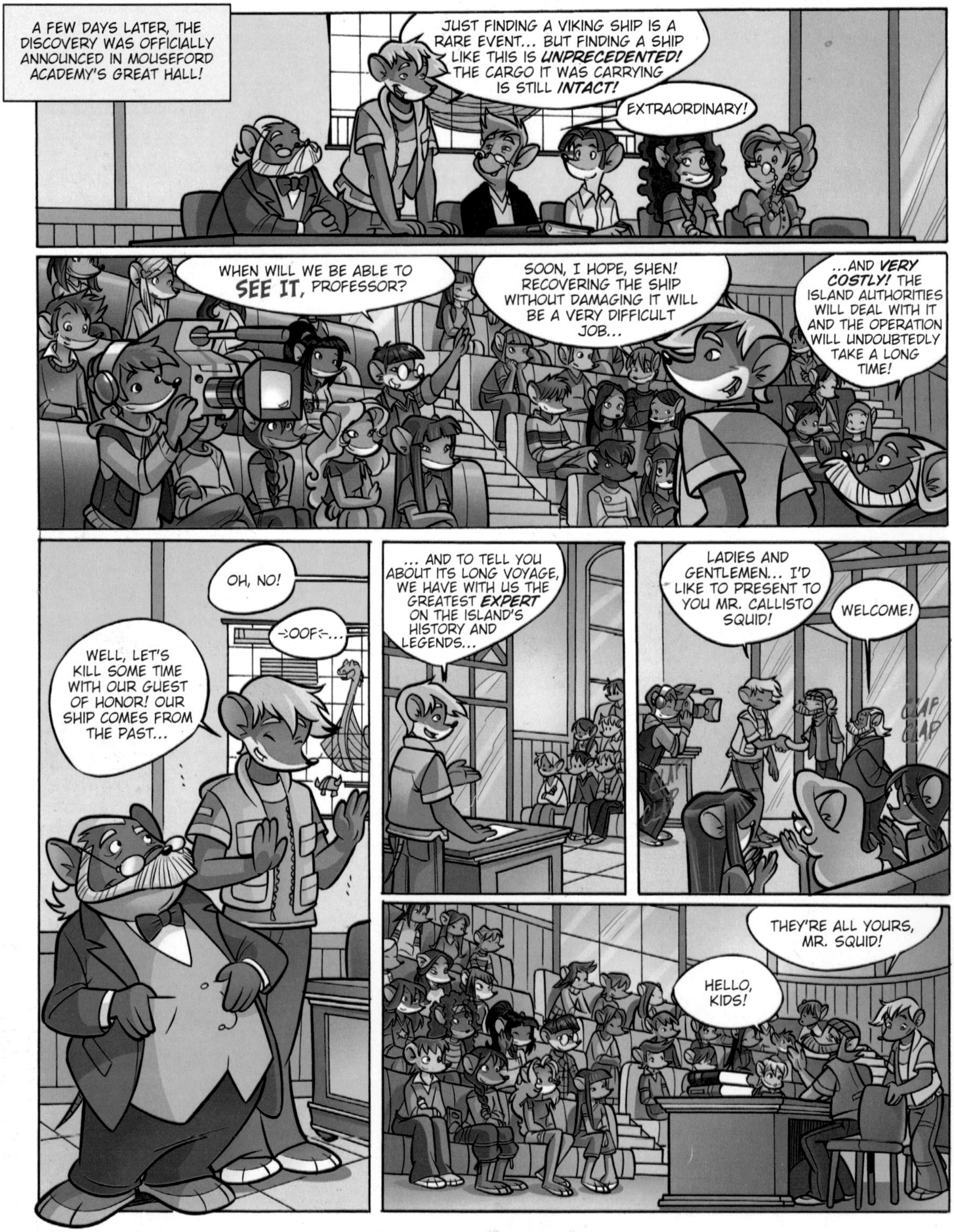
A FEW DAYS LATER, THE DISCOVERY WAS OFFICIALLY ANNOUNCED IN MOUSEFORD ACADEMY'S GREAT HALL!
JUST FINDING A VIKING SHIP IS A RARE EVENT... BUT FINDING A SHIP LIKE THIS IS UNPRECEDENTED! THE CARGO IT WAS CARRYING IS STILL INTACT!
EXTRAORDINARY!
WHEN WILL WE BE ABLE TO SEE IT, PROFESSOR?
SOON, I HOPE, SHEN! RECOVERING THE SHIP WITHOUT DAMAGING IT WILL BE A VERY DIFFICULT JOB...
...AND VERY COSTLY! THE ISLAND AUTHORITIES WILL DEAL WITH IT AND THE OPERATION WILL UNDOUBTEDLY TAKE A LONG TIME!
WELL, LET'S KILL SOME TIME WITH OUR GUEST OF HONOR! OUR SHIP COMES FROM THE PAST...
OH, NO!
>OOF<...
... AND TO TELL YOU ABOUT ITS LONG VOYAGE, WE HAVE WITH US THE GREATEST EXPERT ON THE ISLAND'S HISTORY AND LEGENDS...
LADIES AND GENTLEMEN... I'D LIKE TO PRESENT TO YOU MR. CALLISTO SQUID!
WELCOME!
CLAP CLAP
THEY'RE ALL YOURS, MR. SQUID!
HELLO, KIDS!

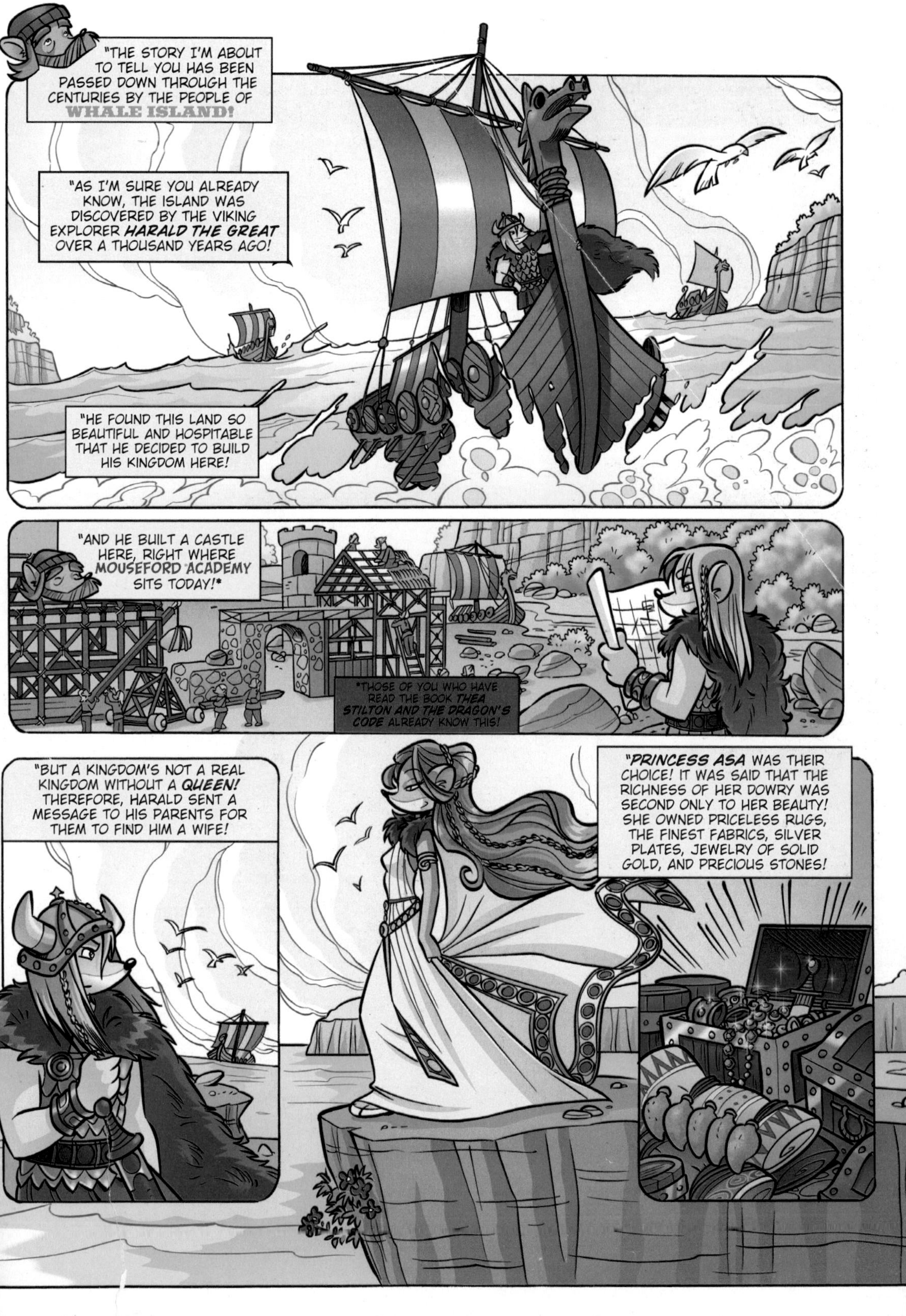
"THE STORY I'M ABOUT TO TELL YOU HAS BEEN PASSED DOWN THROUGH THE CENTURIES BY THE PEOPLE OF WHALE ISLAND!
"AS I'M SURE YOU ALREADY KNOW, THE ISLAND WAS DISCOVERED BY THE VIKING EXPLORER HARALD THE GREAT OVER A THOUSAND YEARS AGO!
"HE FOUND THIS LAND SO BEAUTIFUL AND HOSPITABLE THAT HE DECIDED TO BUILD HIS KINGDOM HERE!
"AND HE BUILT A CASTLE HERE, RIGHT WHERE MOUSEFORD ACADEMY SITS TODAY!*
*THOSE OF YOU WHO HAVE READ THE BOOK THEA STILTON AND THE DRAGON'S CODE ALREADY KNOW THIS!
"BUT A KINGDOM'S NOT A REAL KINGDOM WITHOUT A QUEEN! THEREFORE, HARALD SENT A MESSAGE TO HIS PARENTS FOR THEM TO FIND HIM A WIFE!
"PRINCESS ASA WAS THEIR CHOICE! IT WAS SAID THAT THE RICHNESS OF HER DOWRY WAS SECOND ONLY TO HER BEAUTY! SHE OWNED PRICELESS RUGS, THE FINEST FABRICS, SILVER PLATES, JEWELRY OF SOLID GOLD, AND PRECIOUS STONES!

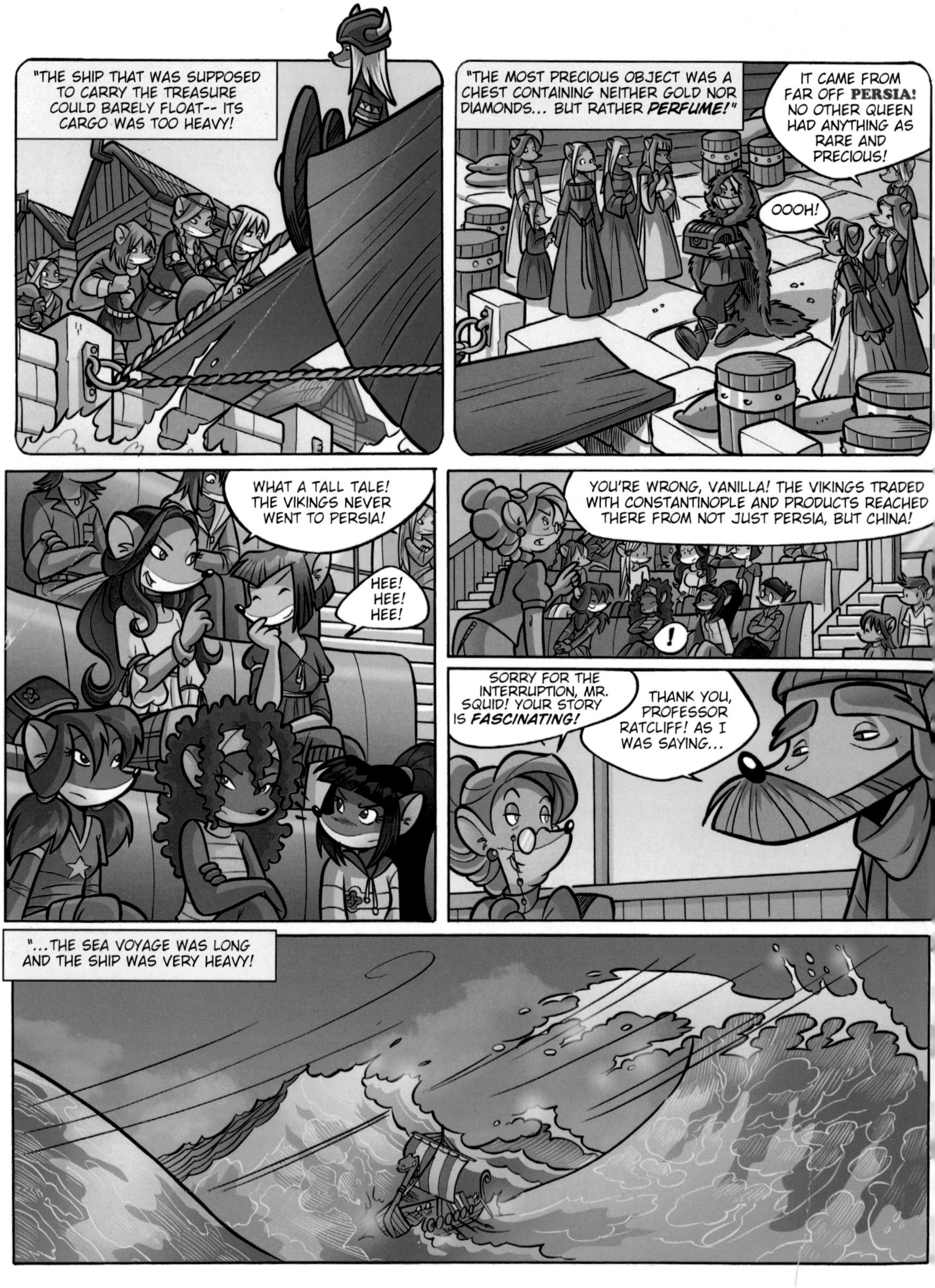
"THE SHIP THAT WAS SUPPOSED TO CARRY THE TREASURE COULD BARELY FLOAT-- ITS CARGO WAS TOO HEAVY!
"THE MOST PRECIOUS OBJECT WAS A CHEST CONTAINING NEITHER GOLD NOR DIAMONDS... BUT RATHER PERFUME!"
IT CAME FROM FAR OFF PERSIA! NO OTHER QUEEN HAD ANYTHING AS RARE AND PRECIOUS!
OOOH!
WHAT A TALL TALE! THE VIKINGS NEVER WENT TO PERSIA!
HEE! HEE! HEE!
YOU'RE WRONG, VANILLA! THE VIKINGS TRADED WITH CONSTANTINOPLE AND PRODUCTS REACHED THERE FROM NOT JUST PERSIA, BUT CHINA!
!
SORRY FOR THE INTERRUPTION, MR. SQUID! YOUR STORY IS FASCINATING!
THANK YOU, PROFESSOR RATCLIFF! AS I WAS SAYING...
"...THE SEA VOYAGE WAS LONG AND THE SHIP WAS VERY HEAVY!

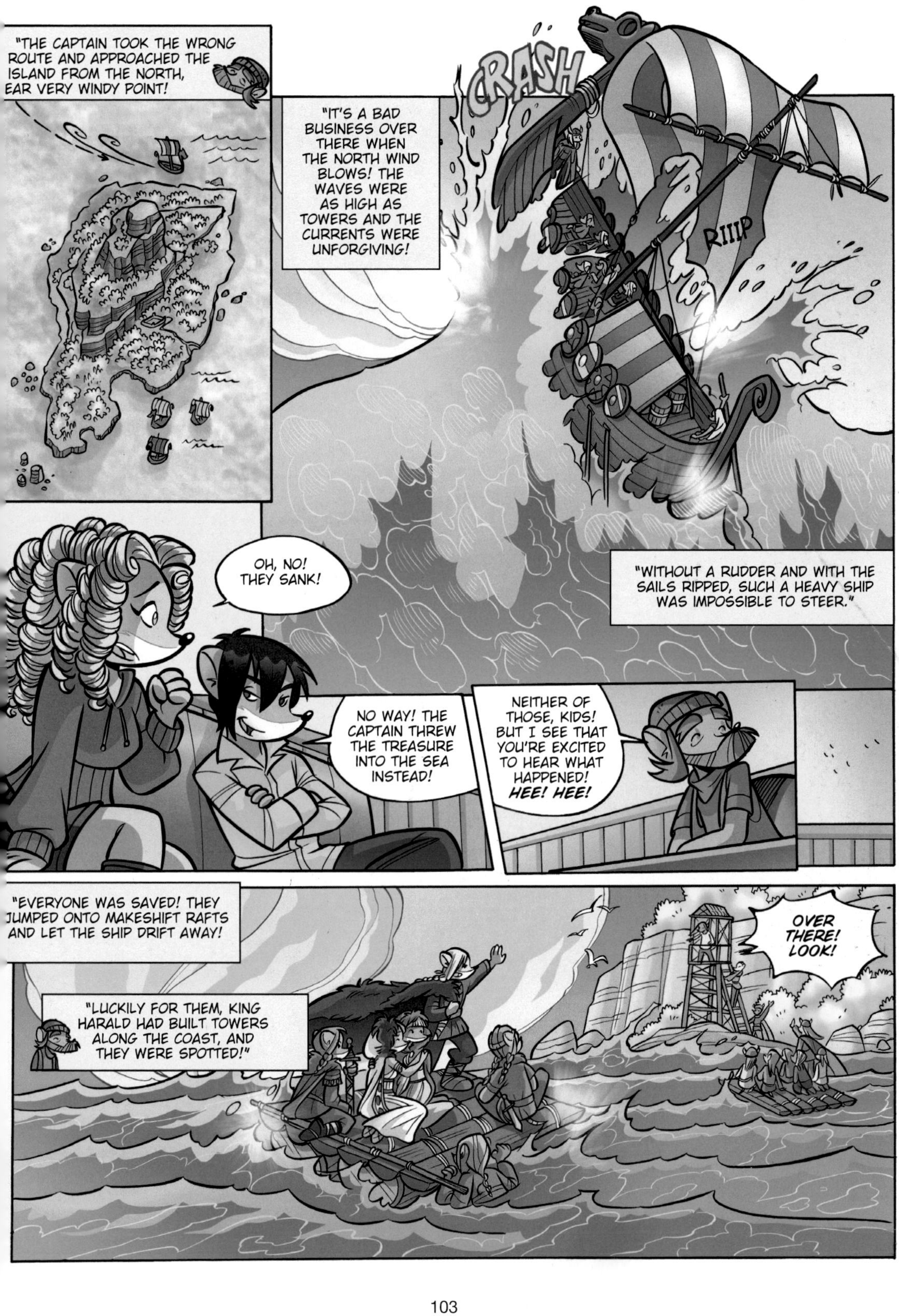
"THE CAPTAIN TOOK THE WRONG ROUTE AND APPROACHED THE ISLAND FROM THE NORTH, EAR VERY WINDY POINT!
"IT'S A BAD BUSINESS OVER THERE WHEN THE NORTH WIND BLOWS! THE WAVES WERE AS HIGH AS TOWERS AND THE CURRENTS WERE UNFORGIVING!
CRASH
RIIIP
"WITHOUT A RUDDER AND WITH THE SAILS RIPPED, SUCH A HEAVY SHIP WAS IMPOSSIBLE TO STEER."
OH, NO! THEY SANK!
NO WAY! THE CAPTAIN THREW THE TREASURE INTO THE SEA INSTEAD!
NEITHER OF THOSE, KIDS! BUT I SEE THAT YOU'RE EXCITED TO HEAR WHAT HAPPENED! HEE! HEE!
"EVERYONE WAS SAVED! THEY JUMPED ONTO MAKESHIFT RAFTS AND LET THE SHIP DRIFT AWAY!
OVER THERE! LOOK!
"LUCKILY FOR THEM, KING HARALD HAD BUILT TOWERS ALONG THE COAST, AND THEY WERE SPOTTED!"

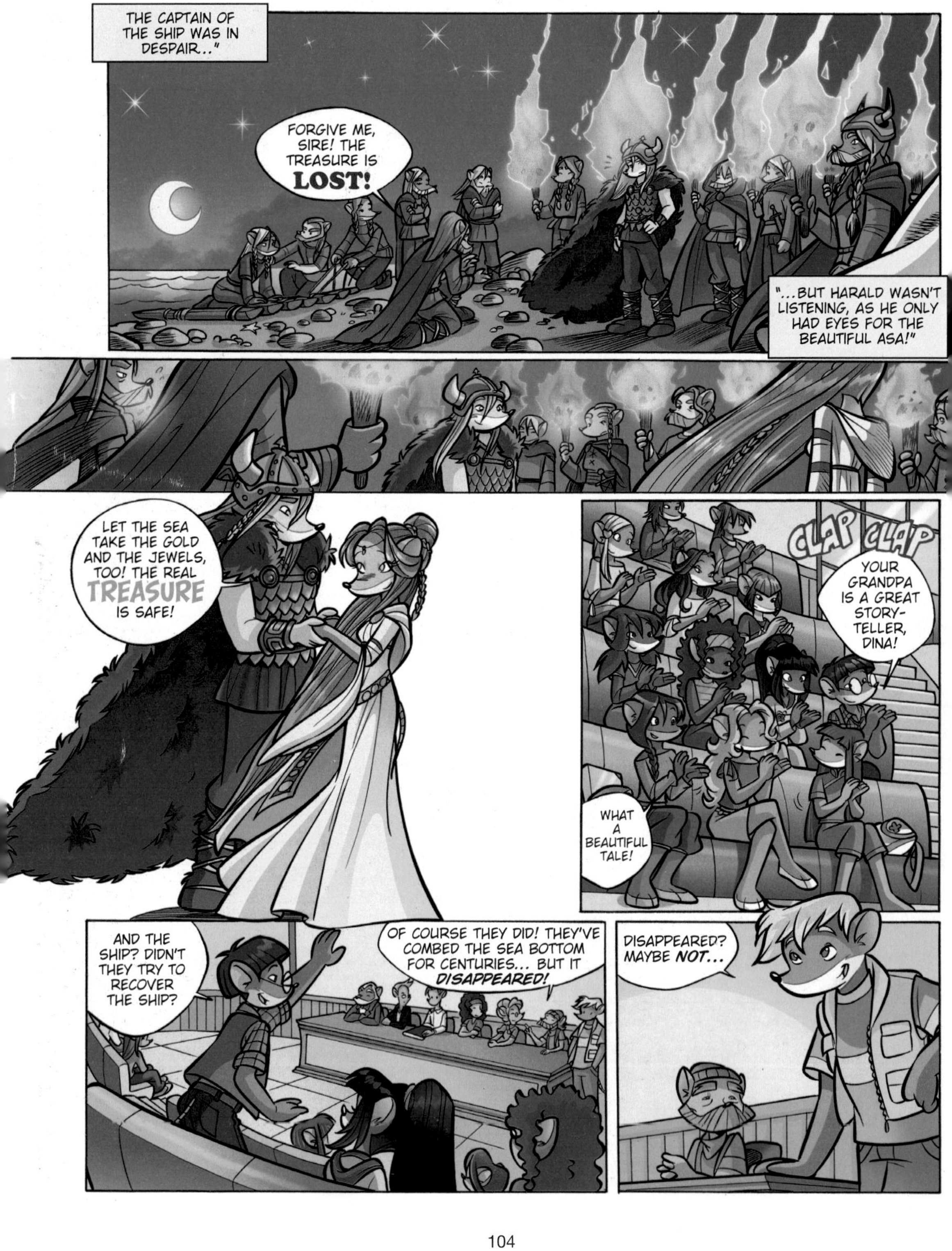

THE CAPTAIN OF THE SHIP WAS IN DESPAIR..."
FORGIVE ME, SIRE! THE TREASURE IS LOST!
"...BUT HARALD WASN'T LISTENING, AS HE ONLY HAD EYES FOR THE BEAUTIFUL ASA!"
LET THE SEA TAKE THE GOLD AND THE JEWELS, TOO! THE REAL TREASURE IS SAFE!
CLAP CLAP
YOUR GRANDPA IS A GREAT STORY-TELLER, DINA!
WHAT A BEAUTIFUL TALE!
AND THE SHIP? DIDN'T THEY TRY TO RECOVER THE SHIP?
OF COURSE THEY DID! THEY'VE COMBED THE SEA BOTTOM FOR CENTURIES... BUT IT DISAPPEARED!
DISAPPEARED? MAYBE NOT...

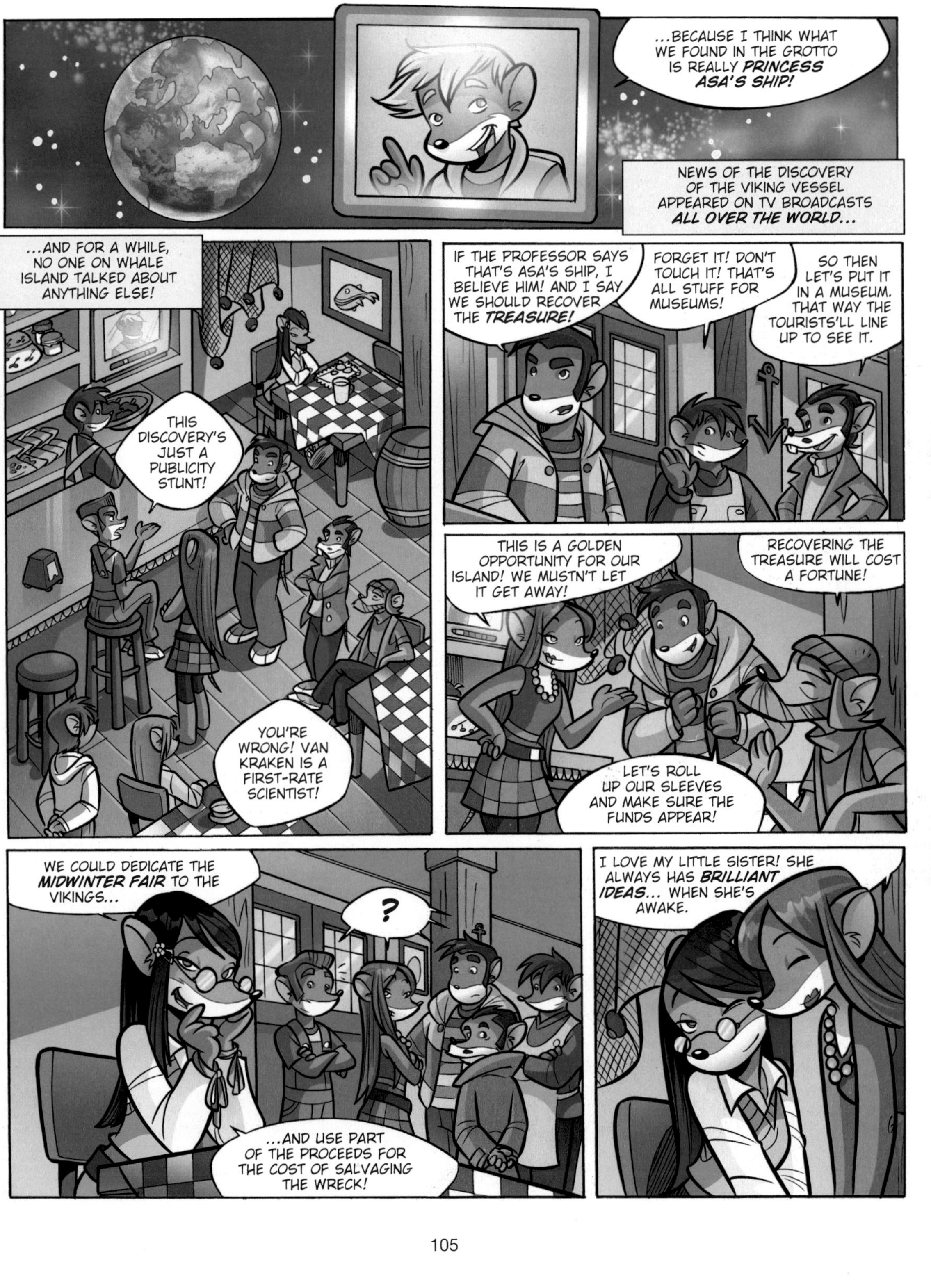
...BECAUSE I THINK WHAT WE FOUND IN THE GROTTO IS REALLY PRINCESS ASA'S SHIP!
NEWS OF THE DISCOVERY OF THE VIKING VESSEL APPEARED ON TV BROADCASTS ALL OVER THE WORLD...
...AND FOR A WHILE, NO ONE ON WHALE ISLAND TALKED ABOUT ANYTHING ELSE!
THIS DISCOVERY'S JUST A PUBLICITY STUNT!
YOU'RE WRONG! VAN KRAKEN IS A FIRST-RATE SCIENTIST!
IF THE PROFESSOR SAYS THAT'S ASA'S SHIP, I BELIEVE HIM! AND I SAY WE SHOULD RECOVER THE TREASURE!
FORGET IT! DON'T TOUCH IT! THAT'S ALL STUFF FOR MUSEUMS!
SO THEN LET'S PUT IT IN A MUSEUM. THAT WAY THE TOURISTS'LL LINE UP TO SEE IT.
THIS IS A GOLDEN OPPORTUNITY FOR OUR ISLAND! WE MUSTN'T LET IT GET AWAY!
RECOVERING THE TREASURE WILL COST A FORTUNE!
LET'S ROLL UP OUR SLEEVES AND MAKE SURE THE FUNDS APPEAR!
WE COULD DEDICATE THE MIDWINTER FAIR TO THE VIKINGS...
?
...AND USE PART OF THE PROCEEDS FOR THE COST OF SALVAGING THE WRECK!
I LOVE MY LITTLE SISTER! SHE ALWAYS HAS BRILLIANT IDEAS... WHEN SHE'S AWAKE.

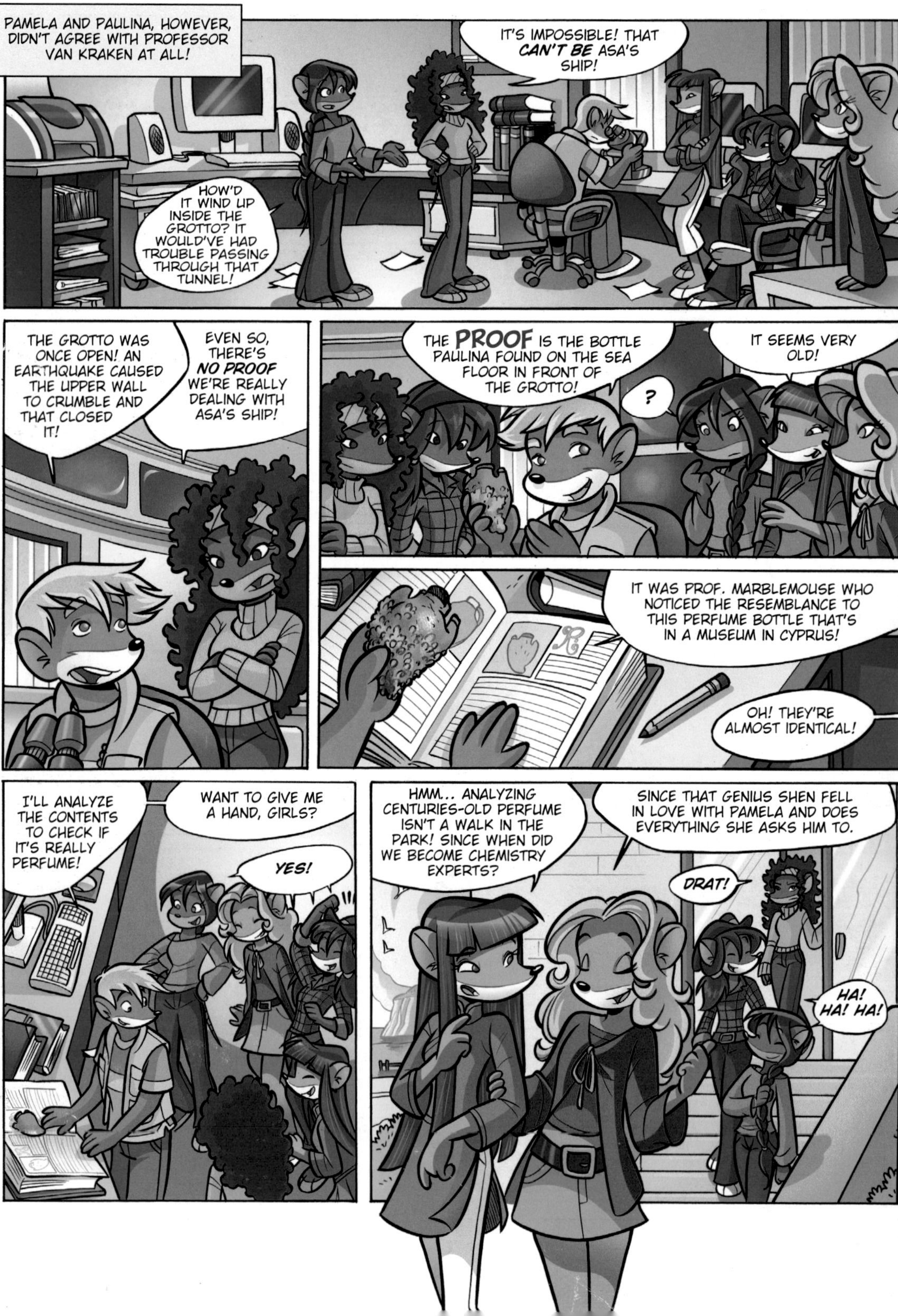
PAMELA AND PAULINA, HOWEVER, DIDN'T AGREE WITH PROFESSOR VAN KRAKEN AT ALL!
IT'S IMPOSSIBLE! THAT CAN'T BE ASA'S SHIP!
HOW'D IT WIND UP INSIDE THE GROTTO? IT WOULD'VE HAD TROUBLE PASSING THROUGH THAT TUNNEL!
THE GROTTO WAS ONCE OPEN! AN EARTHQUAKE CAUSED THE UPPER WALL TO CRUMBLE AND THAT CLOSED IT!
EVEN SO, THERE'S NO PROOF WE'RE REALLY DEALING WITH ASA'S SHIP!
THE PROOF IS THE BOTTLE PAULINA FOUND ON THE SEA FLOOR IN FRONT OF THE GROTTO!
?
IT SEEMS VERY OLD!
IT WAS PROF. MARBLEMOUSE WHO NOTICED THE RESEMBLANCE TO THIS PERFUME BOTTLE THAT'S IN A MUSEUM IN CYPRUS!
OH! THEY'RE ALMOST IDENTICAL!
I'LL ANALYZE THE CONTENTS TO CHECK IF IT'S REALLY PERFUME!
WANT TO GIVE ME A HAND, GIRLS?
YES!
!!
HMM... ANALYZING CENTURIES-OLD PERFUME ISN'T A WALK IN THE PARK! SINCE WHEN DID WE BECOME CHEMISTRY EXPERTS?
SINCE THAT GENIUS SHEN FELL IN LOVE WITH PAMELA AND DOES EVERYTHING SHE ASKS HIM TO.
DRAT!
HA! HA! HA!

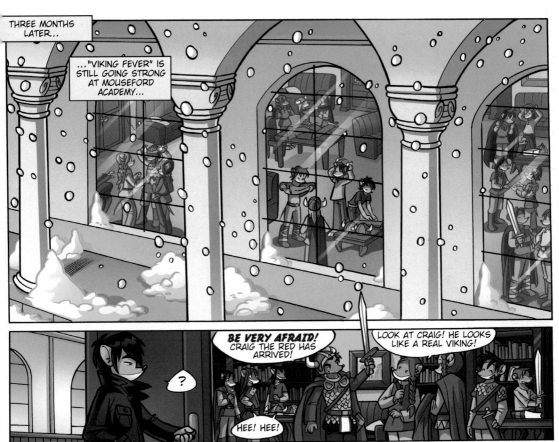

..."VIKING FEVER" IS STILL GOING STRONG AT MOUSEFORD ACADEMY...

?

BE VERY AFRAID! CRAIG THE RED HAS ARRIVED!

LOOK AT CRAIG! HE LOOKS LIKE A REAL VIKING!

HEE! HEE!

YOU'RE LATE, VIC! THE WARRIOR COSTUMES ARE ALREADY ALL TAKEN... ONLY A *FISHERMAN'S* LEFT!

I DON'T DRESS UP IN COSTUMES. AT THE FAIR, I'LL BE THE SUPERVISOR-- CERTAINLY NOT A CHEESE VENDOR!

!

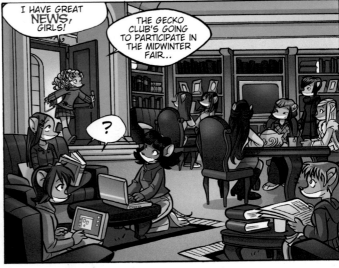

I HAVE GREAT NEWS, GIRLS!

THE GECKO CLUB'S GOING TO PARTICIPATE IN THE MIDWINTER FAIR...

?

107

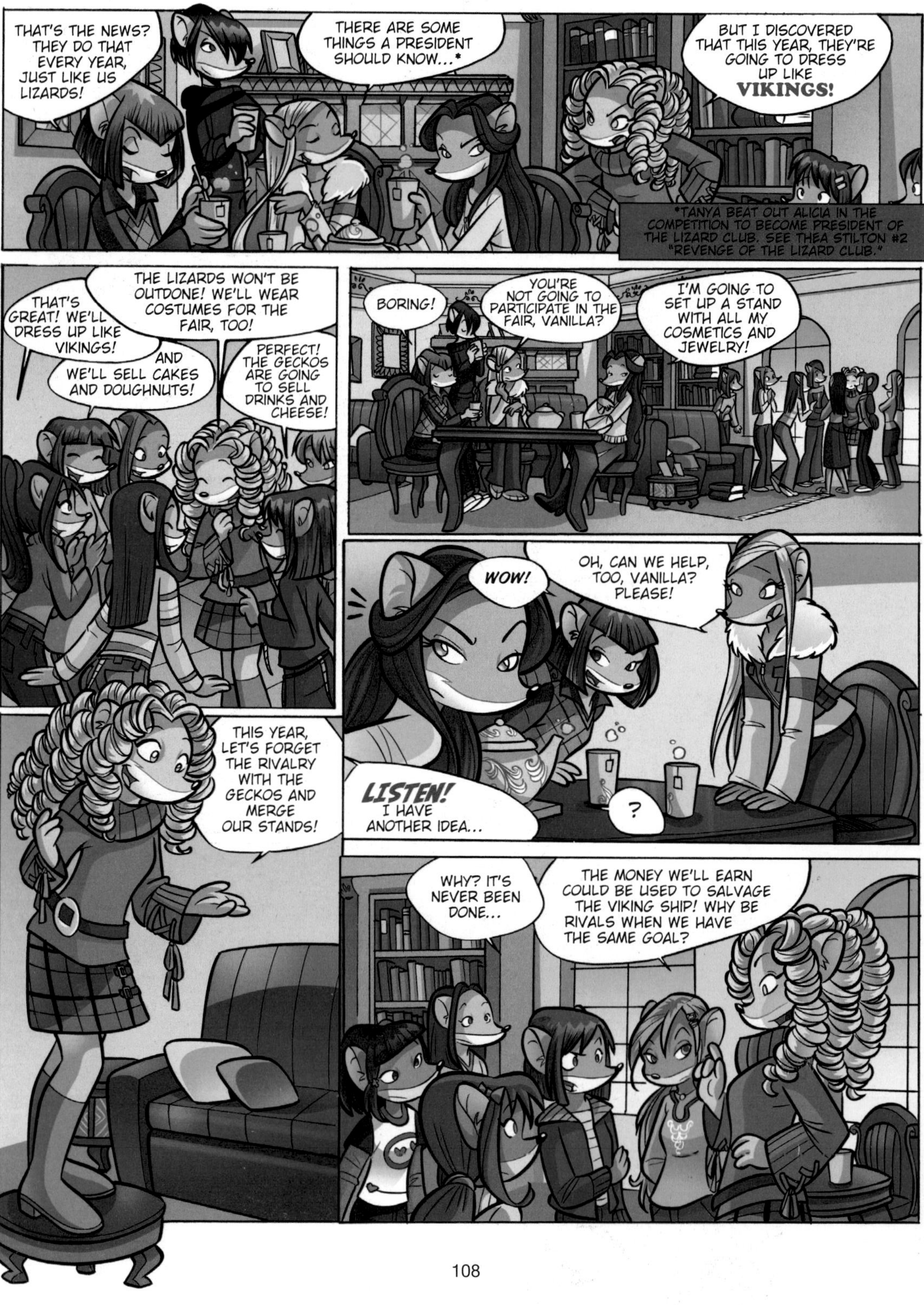

THAT'S THE NEWS? THEY DO THAT EVERY YEAR, JUST LIKE US LIZARDS!
THERE ARE SOME THINGS A PRESIDENT SHOULD KNOW...*
BUT I DISCOVERED THAT THIS YEAR, THEY'RE GOING TO DRESS UP LIKE VIKINGS!
*TANYA BEAT OUT ALICIA IN THE COMPETITION TO BECOME PRESIDENT OF THE LIZARD CLUB. SEE THEA STILTON #2 "REVENGE OF THE LIZARD CLUB."
THAT'S GREAT! WE'LL DRESS UP LIKE VIKINGS!
THE LIZARDS WON'T BE OUTDONE! WE'LL WEAR COSTUMES FOR THE FAIR, TOO!
AND WE'LL SELL CAKES AND DOUGHNUTS!
PERFECT! THE GECKOS ARE GOING TO SELL DRINKS AND CHEESE!
BORING!
YOU'RE NOT GOING TO PARTICIPATE IN THE FAIR, VANILLA?
I'M GOING TO SET UP A STAND WITH ALL MY COSMETICS AND JEWELRY!
WOW!
OH, CAN WE HELP, TOO, VANILLA? PLEASE!
LISTEN! I HAVE ANOTHER IDEA...
?
THIS YEAR, LET'S FORGET THE RIVALRY WITH THE GECKOS AND MERGE OUR STANDS!
WHY? IT'S NEVER BEEN DONE...
THE MONEY WE'LL EARN COULD BE USED TO SALVAGE THE VIKING SHIP! WHY BE RIVALS WHEN WE HAVE THE SAME GOAL?

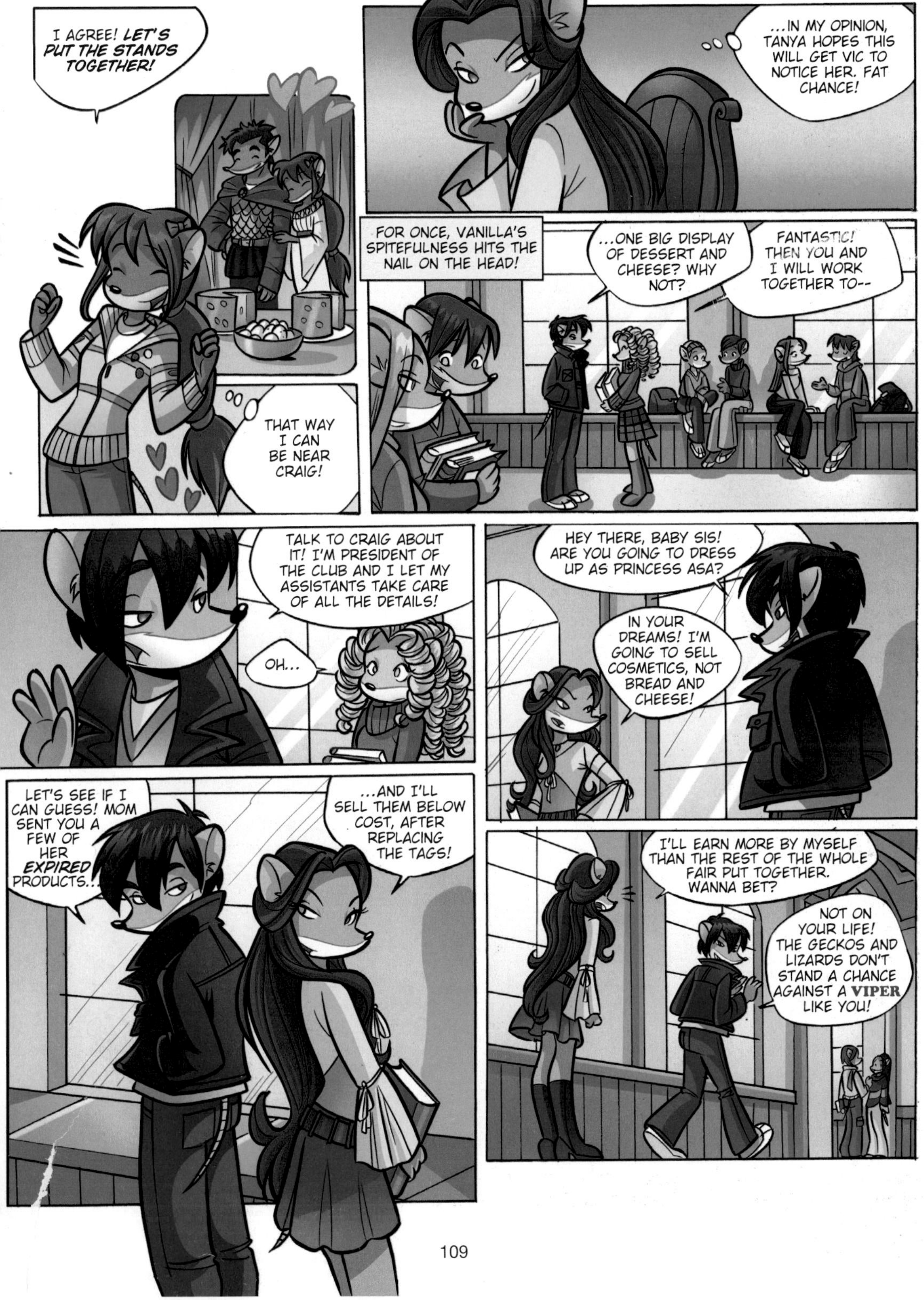
I AGREE! LET'S PUT THE STANDS TOGETHER!
THAT WAY I CAN BE NEAR CRAIG!
...IN MY OPINION, TANYA HOPES THIS WILL GET VIC TO NOTICE HER. FAT CHANCE!
FOR ONCE, VANILLA'S SPITEFULNESS HITS THE NAIL ON THE HEAD!
...ONE BIG DISPLAY OF DESSERT AND CHEESE? WHY NOT?
FANTASTIC! THEN YOU AND I WILL WORK TOGETHER TO--
TALK TO CRAIG ABOUT IT! I'M PRESIDENT OF THE CLUB AND I LET MY ASSISTANTS TAKE CARE OF ALL THE DETAILS!
OH...
HEY THERE, BABY SIS! ARE YOU GOING TO DRESS UP AS PRINCESS ASA?
IN YOUR DREAMS! I'M GOING TO SELL COSMETICS, NOT BREAD AND CHEESE!
LET'S SEE IF I CAN GUESS! MOM SENT YOU A FEW OF HER EXPIRED PRODUCTS...
...AND I'LL SELL THEM BELOW COST, AFTER REPLACING THE TAGS!
I'LL EARN MORE BY MYSELF THAN THE REST OF THE WHOLE FAIR PUT TOGETHER. WANNA BET?
NOT ON YOUR LIFE! THE GECKOS AND LIZARDS DON'T STAND A CHANCE AGAINST A VIPER LIKE YOU!

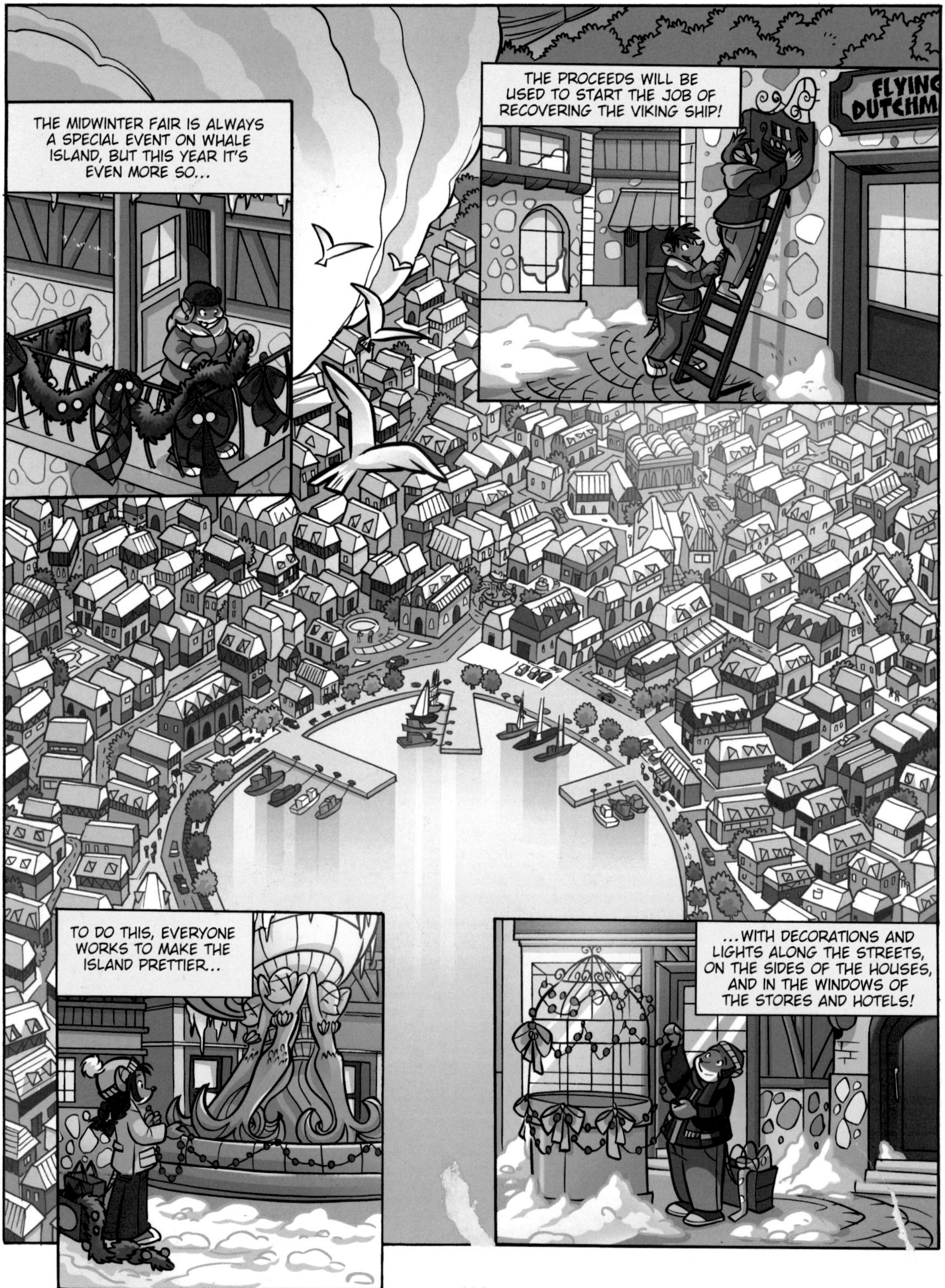
THE MIDWINTER FAIR IS ALWAYS A SPECIAL EVENT ON WHALE ISLAND, BUT THIS YEAR IT'S EVEN MORE SO...
THE PROCEEDS WILL BE USED TO START THE JOB OF RECOVERING THE VIKING SHIP!
FLYING DUTCHM
TO DO THIS, EVERYONE WORKS TO MAKE THE ISLAND PRETTIER...
...WITH DECORATIONS AND LIGHTS ALONG THE STREETS, ON THE SIDES OF THE HOUSES, AND IN THE WINDOWS OF THE STORES AND HOTELS!

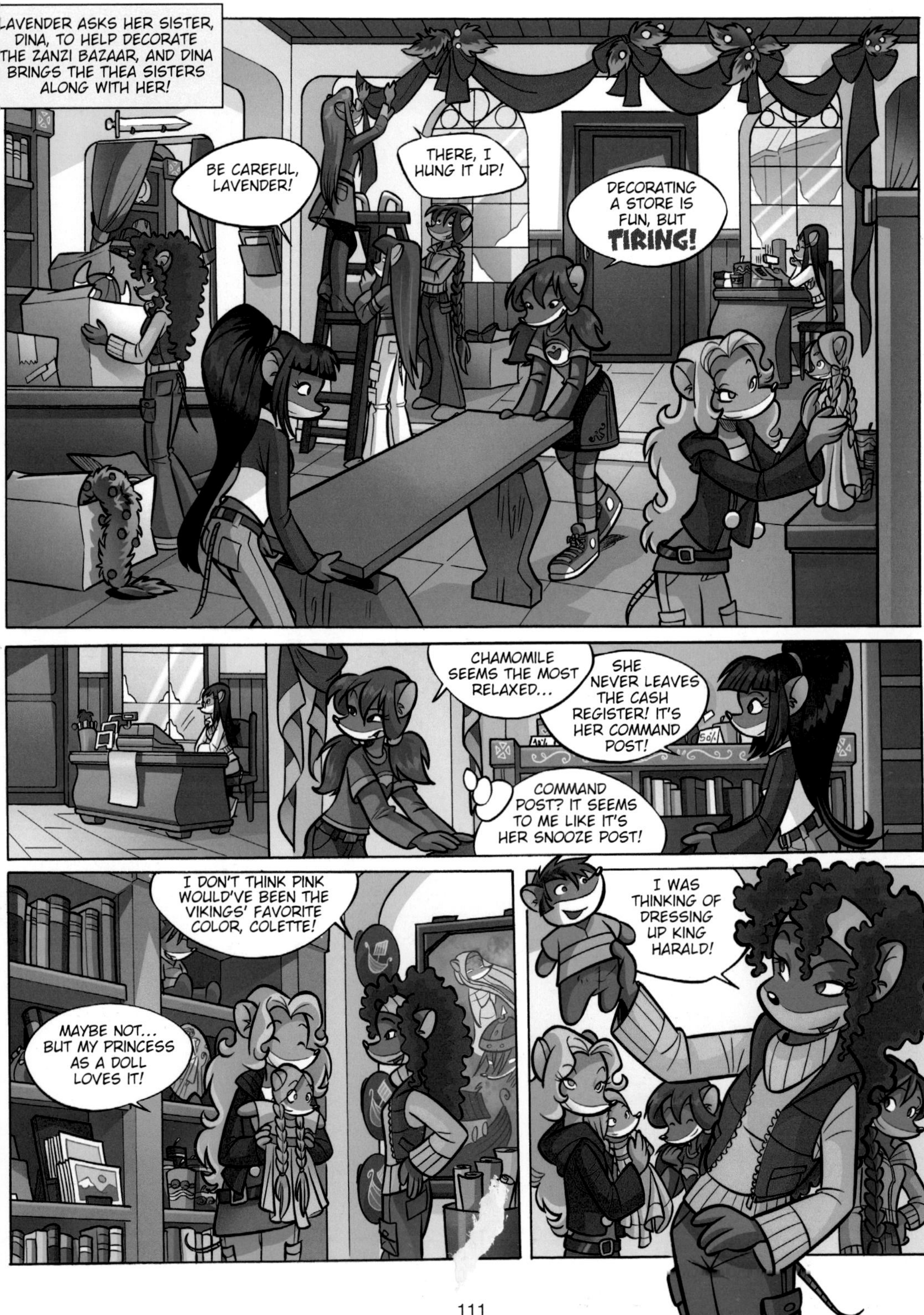
LAVENDER ASKS HER SISTER, DINA, TO HELP DECORATE THE ZANZI BAZAAR, AND DINA BRINGS THE THEA SISTERS ALONG WITH HER!
BE CAREFUL, LAVENDER!
THERE, I HUNG IT UP!
DECORATING A STORE IS FUN, BUT TIRING!
CHAMOMILE SEEMS THE MOST RELAXED...
SHE NEVER LEAVES THE CASH REGISTER! IT'S HER COMMAND POST!
COMMAND POST? IT SEEMS TO ME LIKE IT'S HER SNOOZE POST!
I DON'T THINK PINK WOULD'VE BEEN THE VIKINGS' FAVORITE COLOR, COLETTE!
MAYBE NOT... BUT MY PRINCESS AS A DOLL LOVES IT!
I WAS THINKING OF DRESSING UP KING HARALD!

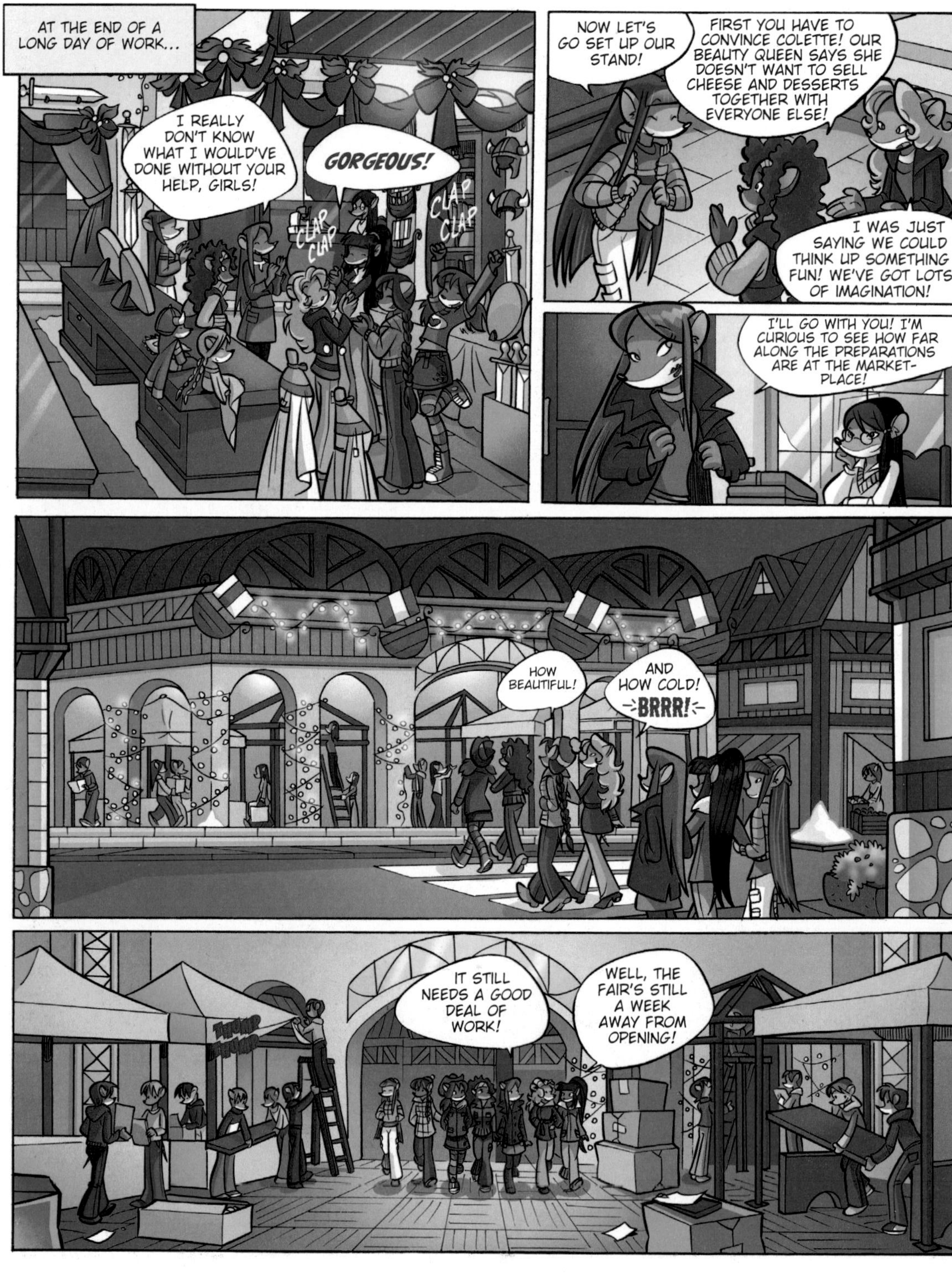
AT THE END OF A LONG DAY OF WORK...
I REALLY DON'T KNOW WHAT I WOULD'VE DONE WITHOUT YOUR HELP, GIRLS!
GORGEOUS!
CLAP CLAP
CLAP CLAP
NOW LET'S GO SET UP OUR STAND!
FIRST YOU HAVE TO CONVINCE COLETTE! OUR BEAUTY QUEEN SAYS SHE DOESN'T WANT TO SELL CHEESE AND DESSERTS TOGETHER WITH EVERYONE ELSE!
I WAS JUST SAYING WE COULD THINK UP SOMETHING FUN! WE'VE GOT LOTS OF IMAGINATION!
I'LL GO WITH YOU! I'M CURIOUS TO SEE HOW FAR ALONG THE PREPARATIONS ARE AT THE MARKET-PLACE!
HOW BEAUTIFUL!
AND HOW COLD! BRRR!
IT STILL NEEDS A GOOD DEAL OF WORK!
WELL, THE FAIR'S STILL A WEEK AWAY FROM OPENING!

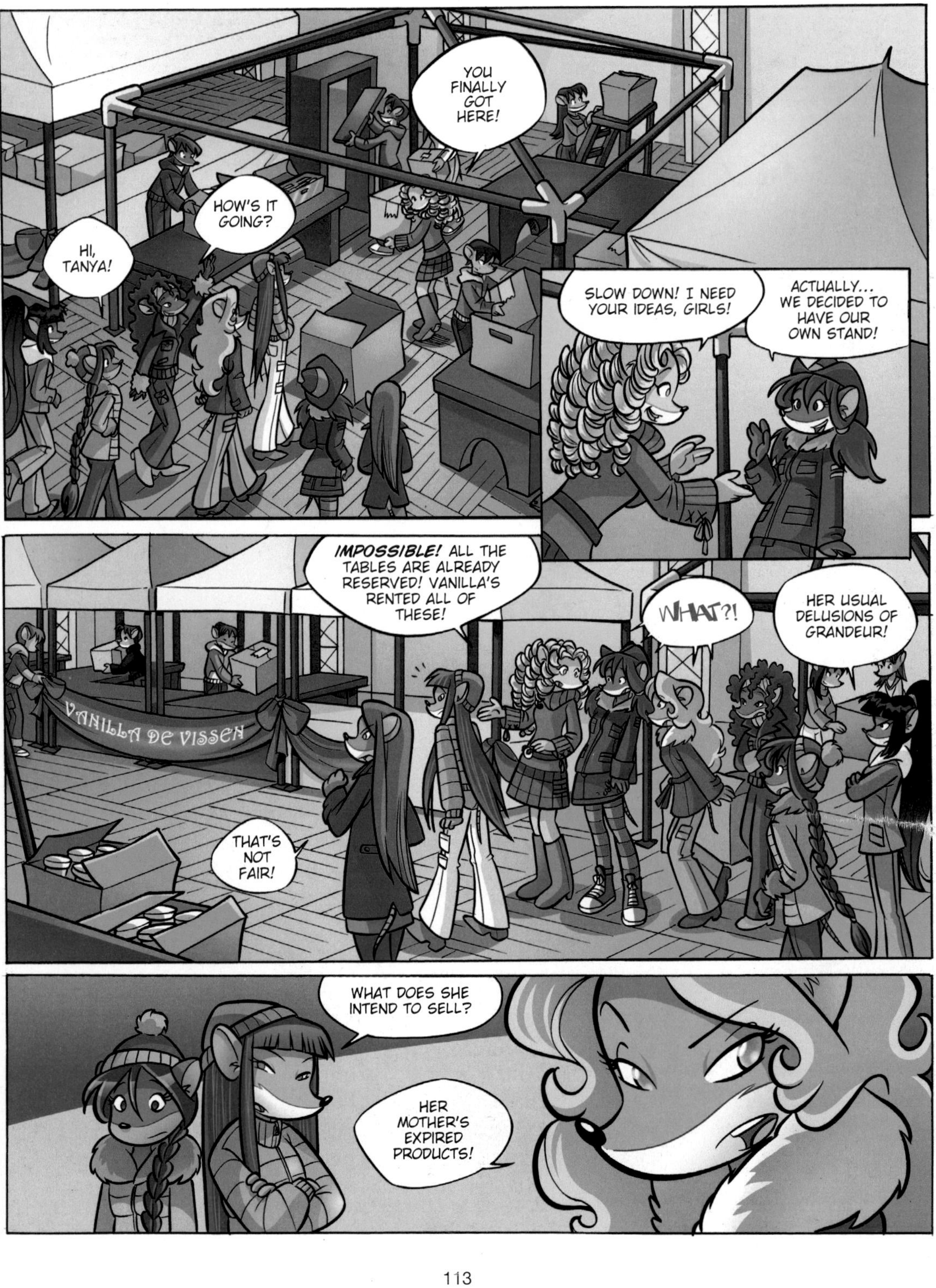
YOU FINALLY GOT HERE!
HOW'S IT GOING?
HI, TANYA!
SLOW DOWN! I NEED YOUR IDEAS, GIRLS!
ACTUALLY... WE DECIDED TO HAVE OUR OWN STAND!
VANILLA DE VISSEN
IMPOSSIBLE! ALL THE TABLES ARE ALREADY RESERVED! VANILLA'S RENTED ALL OF THESE!
WHAT?!
HER USUAL DELUSIONS OF GRANDEUR!
THAT'S NOT FAIR!
WHAT DOES SHE INTEND TO SELL?
HER MOTHER'S EXPIRED PRODUCTS!

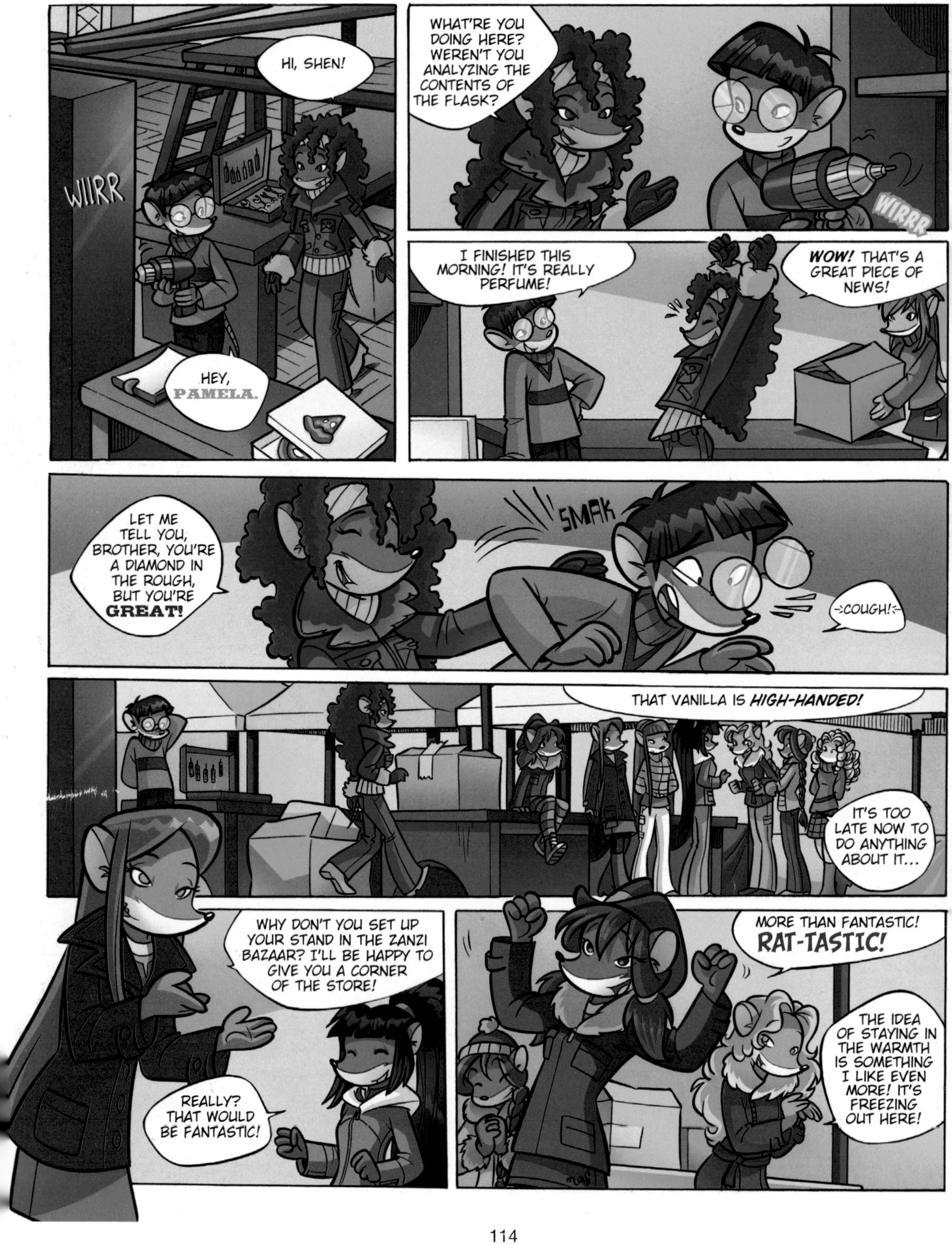
HI, SHEN!
WIIRR
HEY, PAMELA.
WHAT'RE YOU DOING HERE? WEREN'T YOU ANALYZING THE CONTENTS OF THE FLASK?
WIRRR
I FINISHED THIS MORNING! IT'S REALLY PERFUME!
WOW! THAT'S A GREAT PIECE OF NEWS!
LET ME TELL YOU, BROTHER, YOU'RE A DIAMOND IN THE ROUGH, BUT YOU'RE GREAT!
SMAK
COUGH!
THAT VANILLA IS HIGH-HANDED!
IT'S TOO LATE NOW TO DO ANYTHING ABOUT IT...
WHY DON'T YOU SET UP YOUR STAND IN THE ZANZI BAZAAR? I'LL BE HAPPY TO GIVE YOU A CORNER OF THE STORE!
REALLY? THAT WOULD BE FANTASTIC!
MORE THAN FANTASTIC! RAT-TASTIC!
THE IDEA OF STAYING IN THE WARMTH IS SOMETHING I LIKE EVEN MORE! IT'S FREEZING OUT HERE!

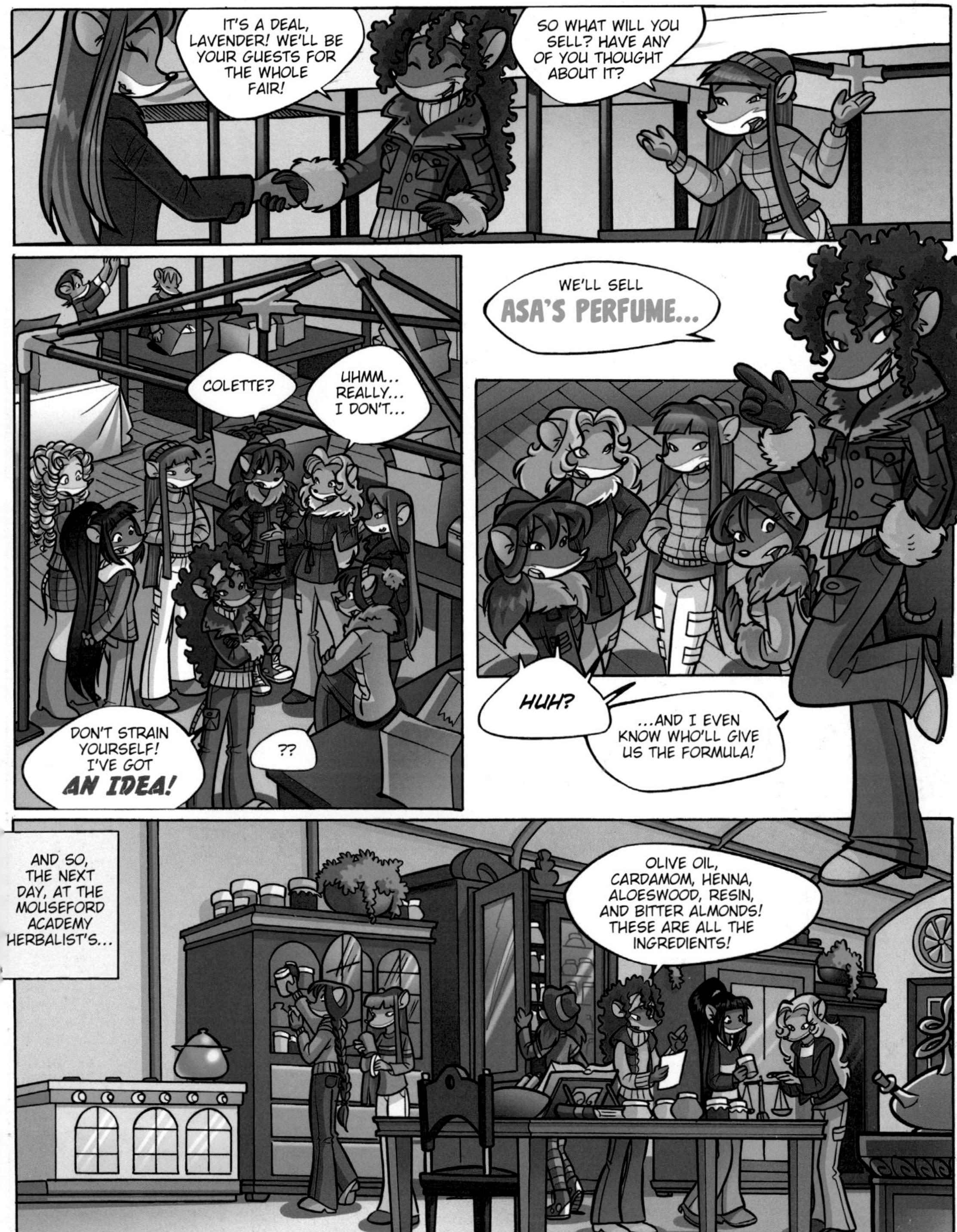
IT'S A DEAL, LAVENDER! WE'LL BE YOUR GUESTS FOR THE WHOLE FAIR!
SO WHAT WILL YOU SELL? HAVE ANY OF YOU THOUGHT ABOUT IT?
COLETTE?
UHMM... REALLY... I DON'T...
DON'T STRAIN YOURSELF! I'VE GOT AN IDEA!
??
WE'LL SELL ASA'S PERFUME...
HUH?
...AND I EVEN KNOW WHO'LL GIVE US THE FORMULA!
AND SO, THE NEXT DAY, AT THE MOUSEFORD ACADEMY HERBALIST'S...
OLIVE OIL, CARDAMOM, HENNA, ALOESWOOD, RESIN, AND BITTER ALMONDS! THESE ARE ALL THE INGREDIENTS!

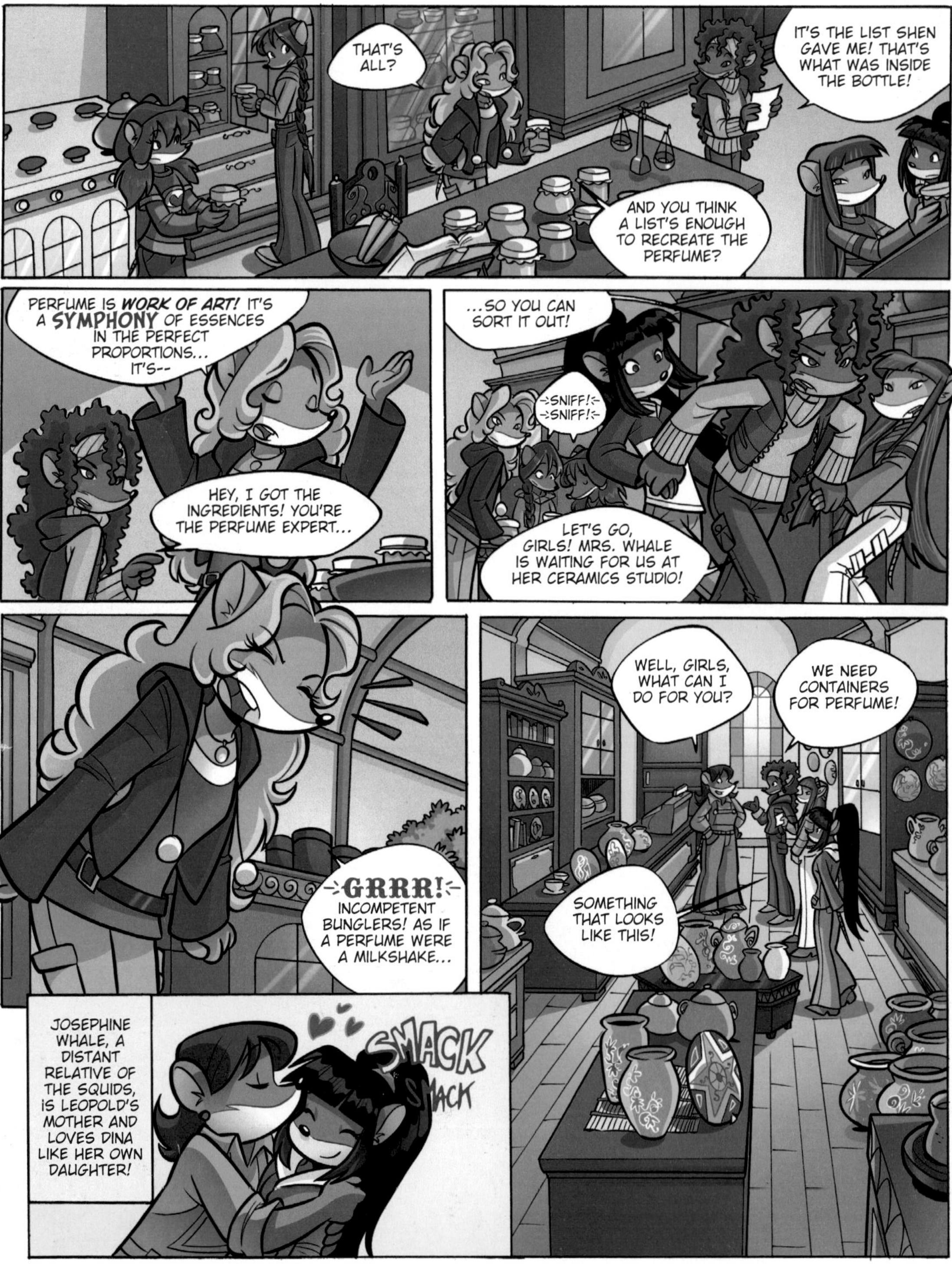

THAT'S ALL?
IT'S THE LIST SHEN GAVE ME! THAT'S WHAT WAS INSIDE THE BOTTLE!
AND YOU THINK A LIST'S ENOUGH TO RECREATE THE PERFUME?
PERFUME IS WORK OF ART! IT'S A SYMPHONY OF ESSENCES IN THE PERFECT PROPORTIONS... IT'S--
HEY, I GOT THE INGREDIENTS! YOU'RE THE PERFUME EXPERT...
...SO YOU CAN SORT IT OUT!
SNIFF! SNIFF!
LET'S GO, GIRLS! MRS. WHALE IS WAITING FOR US AT HER CERAMICS STUDIO!
GRRR! INCOMPETENT BUNGLERS! AS IF A PERFUME WERE A MILKSHAKE...
WELL, GIRLS, WHAT CAN I DO FOR YOU?
WE NEED CONTAINERS FOR PERFUME!
SOMETHING THAT LOOKS LIKE THIS!
JOSEPHINE WHALE, A DISTANT RELATIVE OF THE SQUIDS, IS LEOPOLD'S MOTHER AND LOVES DINA LIKE HER OWN DAUGHTER!
SMACK
SMACK

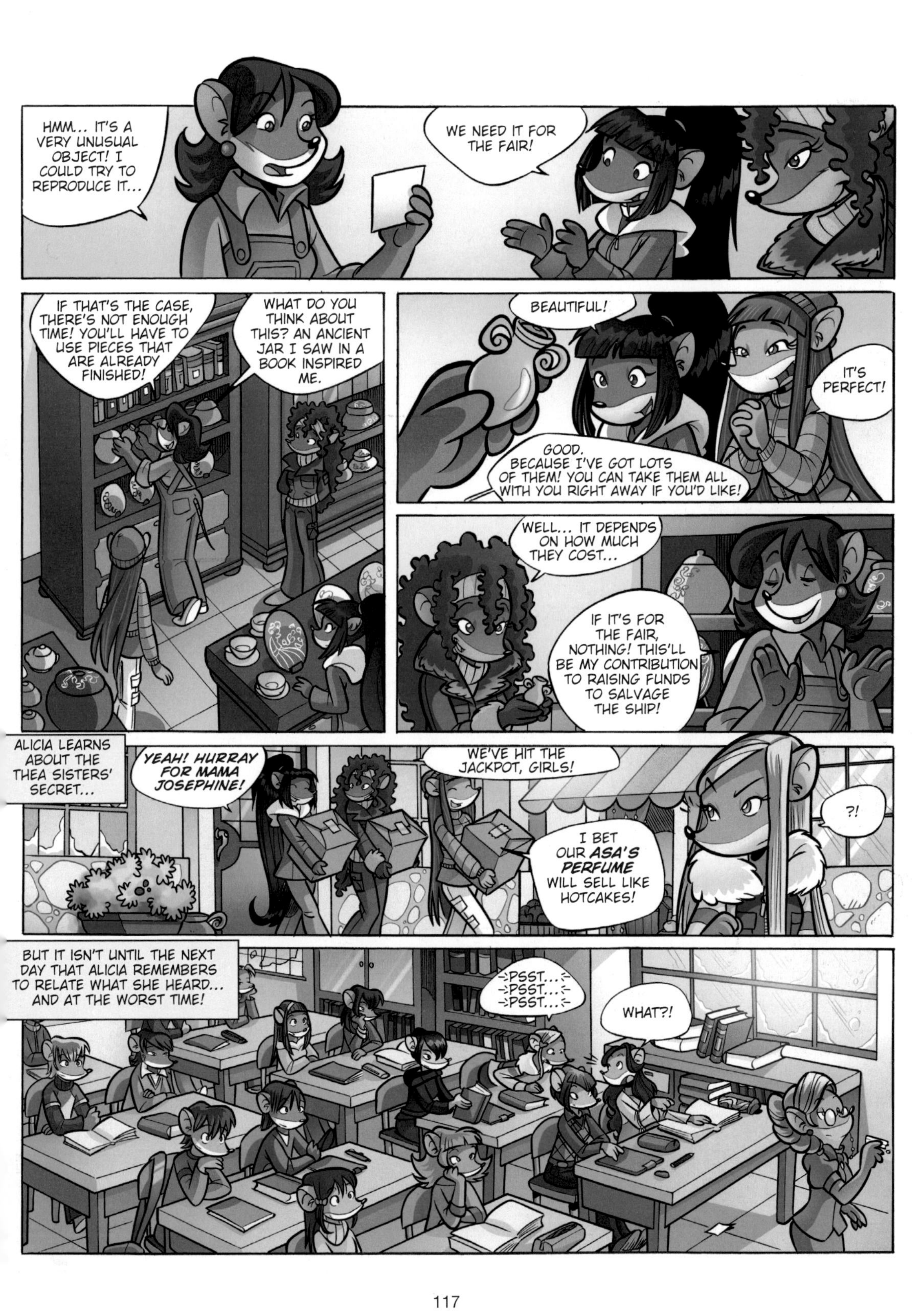
HMM... IT'S A VERY UNUSUAL OBJECT! I COULD TRY TO REPRODUCE IT...
WE NEED IT FOR THE FAIR!
IF THAT'S THE CASE, THERE'S NOT ENOUGH TIME! YOU'LL HAVE TO USE PIECES THAT ARE ALREADY FINISHED!
WHAT DO YOU THINK ABOUT THIS? AN ANCIENT JAR I SAW IN A BOOK INSPIRED ME.
BEAUTIFUL!
IT'S PERFECT!
GOOD. BECAUSE I'VE GOT LOTS OF THEM! YOU CAN TAKE THEM ALL WITH YOU RIGHT AWAY IF YOU'D LIKE!
WELL... IT DEPENDS ON HOW MUCH THEY COST...
IF IT'S FOR THE FAIR, NOTHING! THIS'LL BE MY CONTRIBUTION TO RAISING FUNDS TO SALVAGE THE SHIP!
ALICIA LEARNS ABOUT THE THEA SISTERS' SECRET...
YEAH! HURRAY FOR MAMA JOSEPHINE!
WE'VE HIT THE JACKPOT, GIRLS!
I BET OUR ASA'S PERFUME WILL SELL LIKE HOTCAKES!
?!
BUT IT ISN'T UNTIL THE NEXT DAY THAT ALICIA REMEMBERS TO RELATE WHAT SHE HEARD... AND AT THE WORST TIME!
PSST...
PSST...
PSST...
WHAT?!

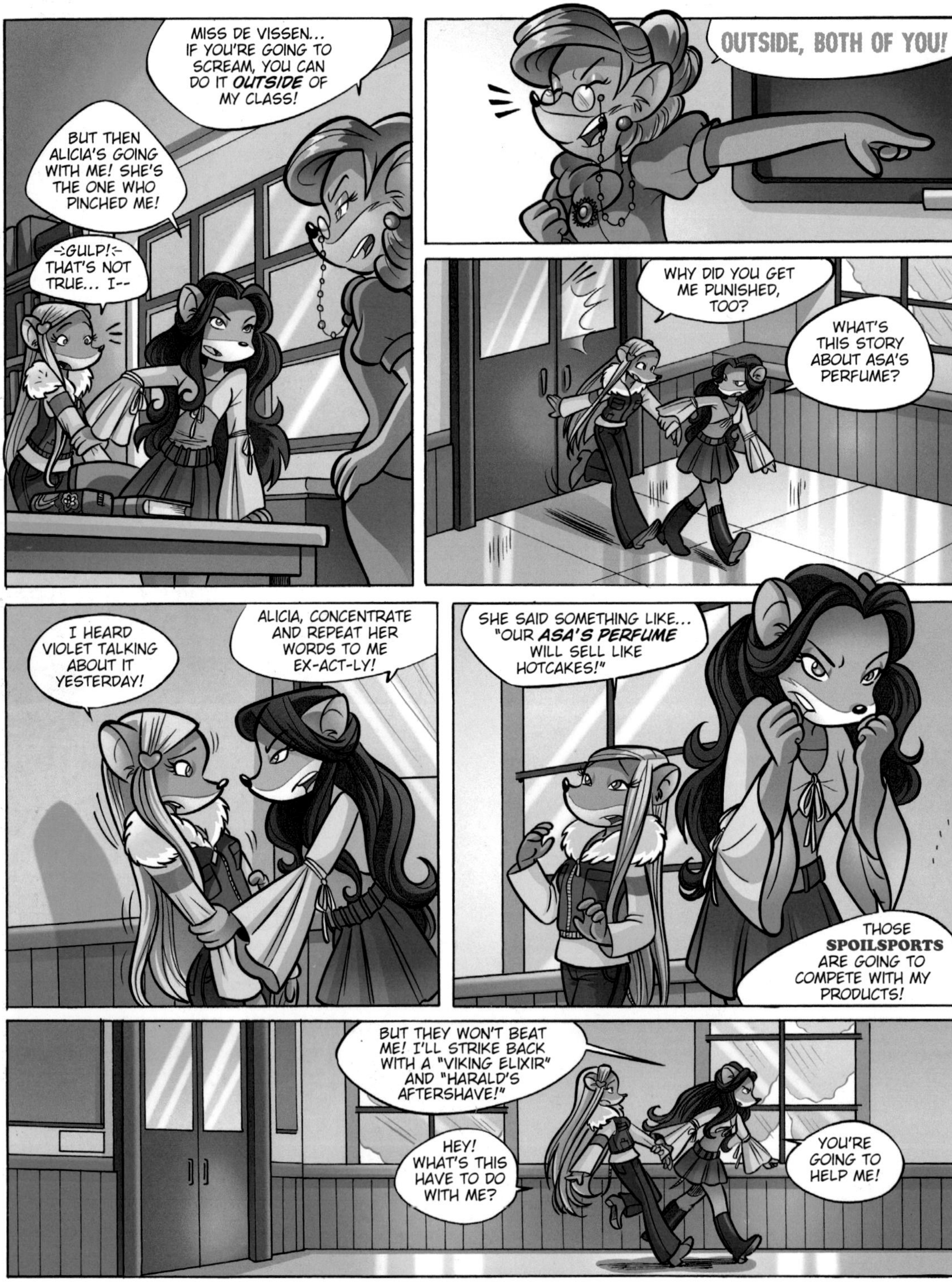

MISS DE VISSEN... IF YOU'RE GOING TO SCREAM, YOU CAN DO IT OUTSIDE OF MY CLASS!
BUT THEN ALICIA'S GOING WITH ME! SHE'S THE ONE WHO PINCHED ME!
GULP! THAT'S NOT TRUE... I--
OUTSIDE, BOTH OF YOU!
WHY DID YOU GET ME PUNISHED, TOO?
WHAT'S THIS STORY ABOUT ASA'S PERFUME?
I HEARD VIOLET TALKING ABOUT IT YESTERDAY!
ALICIA, CONCENTRATE AND REPEAT HER WORDS TO ME EX-ACT-LY!
SHE SAID SOMETHING LIKE... "OUR ASA'S PERFUME WILL SELL LIKE HOTCAKES!"
THOSE SPOILSPORTS ARE GOING TO COMPETE WITH MY PRODUCTS!
BUT THEY WON'T BEAT ME! I'LL STRIKE BACK WITH A "VIKING ELIXIR" AND "HARALD'S AFTERSHAVE!"
HEY! WHAT'S THIS HAVE TO DO WITH ME?
YOU'RE GOING TO HELP ME!

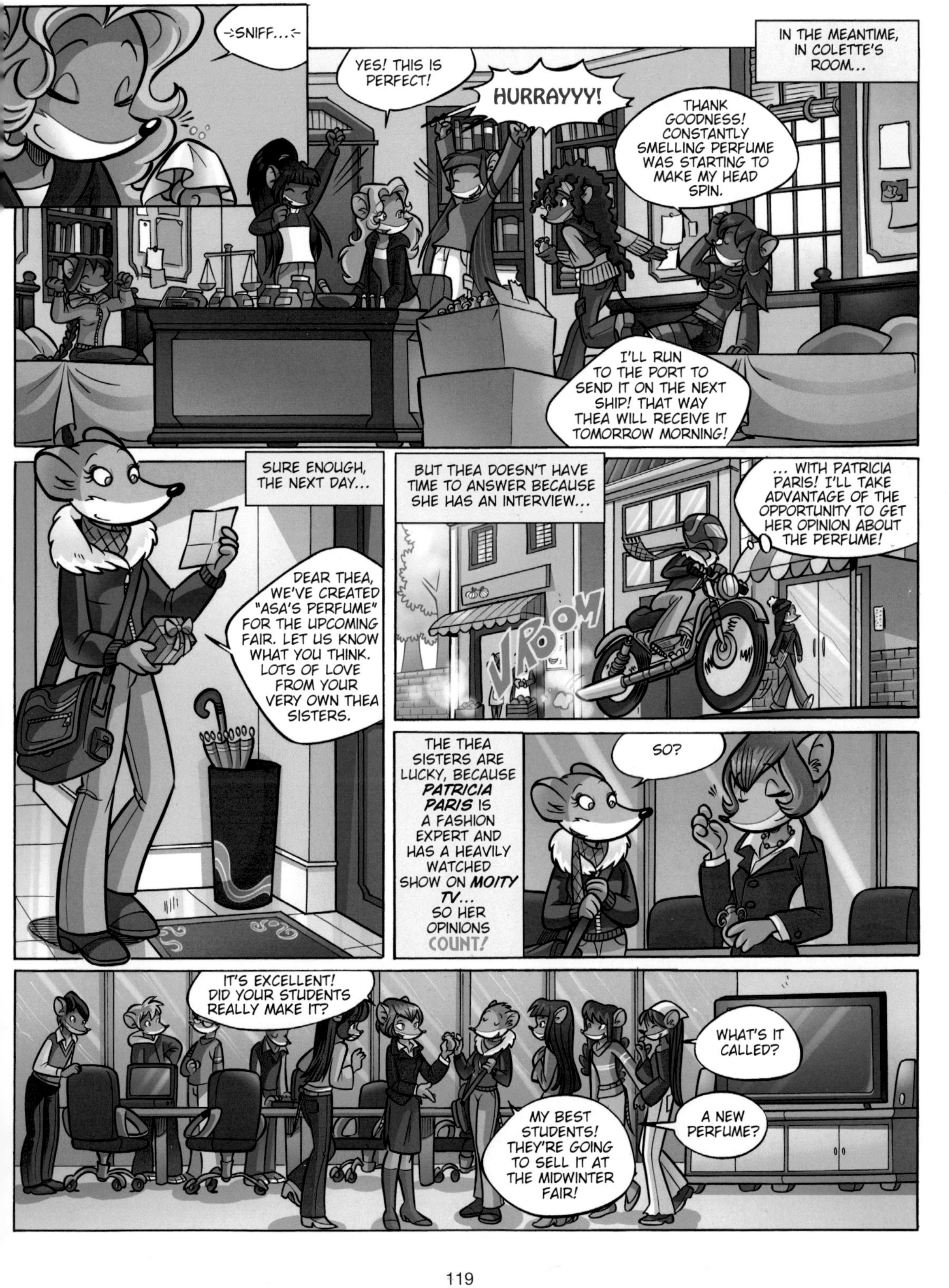

-SNIFF...-
IN THE MEANTIME, IN COLETTE'S ROOM...
YES! THIS IS PERFECT!
HURRAYYY!
THANK GOODNESS! CONSTANTLY SMELLING PERFUME WAS STARTING TO MAKE MY HEAD SPIN.
I'LL RUN TO THE PORT TO SEND IT ON THE NEXT SHIP! THAT WAY THEA WILL RECEIVE IT TOMORROW MORNING!
SURE ENOUGH, THE NEXT DAY...
DEAR THEA, WE'VE CREATED "ASA'S PERFUME" FOR THE UPCOMING FAIR. LET US KNOW WHAT YOU THINK. LOTS OF LOVE FROM YOUR VERY OWN THEA SISTERS.
BUT THEA DOESN'T HAVE TIME TO ANSWER BECAUSE SHE HAS AN INTERVIEW...
... WITH PATRICIA PARIS! I'LL TAKE ADVANTAGE OF THE OPPORTUNITY TO GET HER OPINION ABOUT THE PERFUME!
VROOM
THE THEA SISTERS ARE LUCKY, BECAUSE PATRICIA PARIS IS A FASHION EXPERT AND HAS A HEAVILY WATCHED SHOW ON MOITY TV... SO HER OPINIONS COUNT!
SO?
IT'S EXCELLENT! DID YOUR STUDENTS REALLY MAKE IT?
MY BEST STUDENTS! THEY'RE GOING TO SELL IT AT THE MIDWINTER FAIR!
A NEW PERFUME?
WHAT'S IT CALLED?

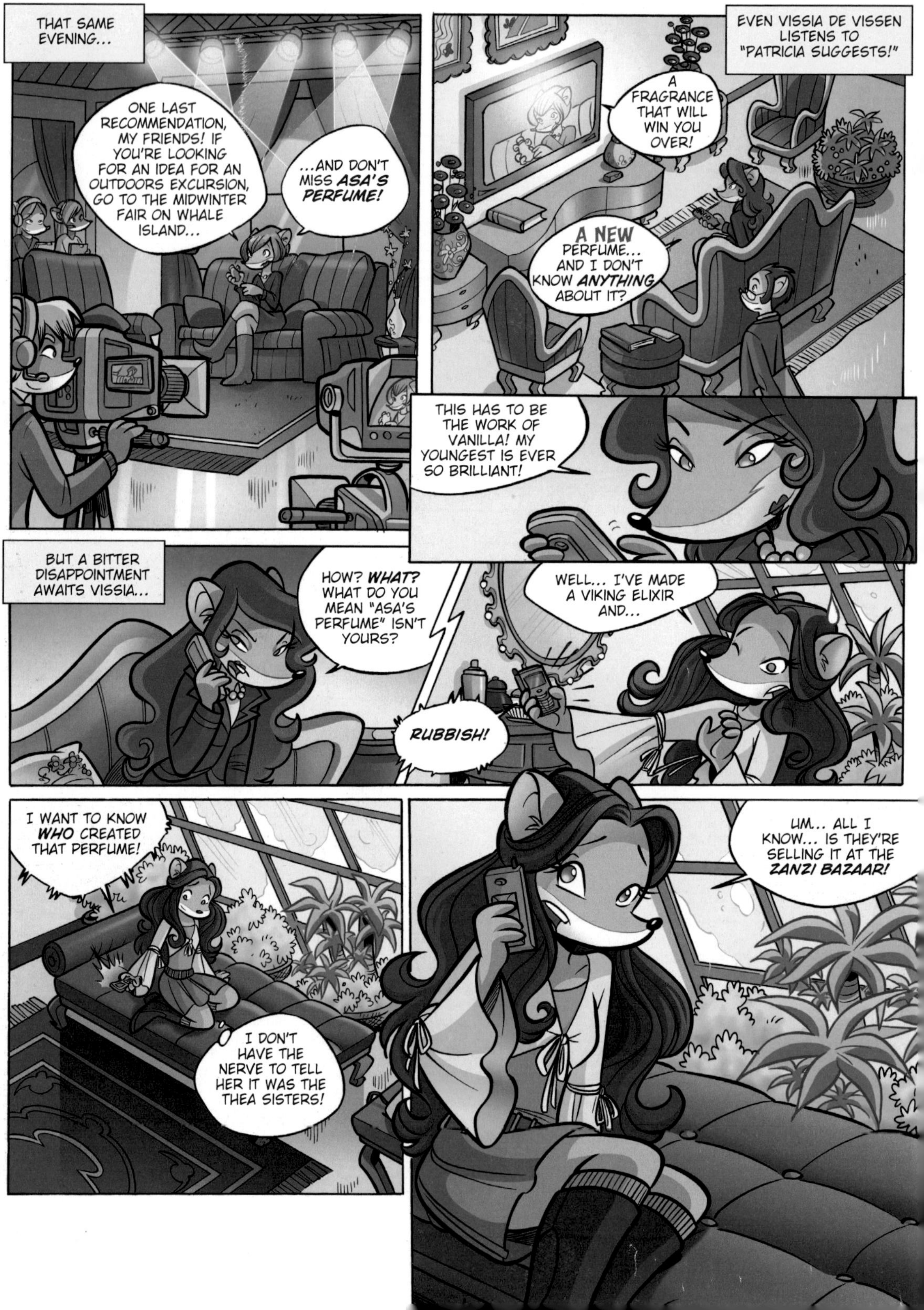
THAT SAME EVENING...
ONE LAST RECOMMENDATION, MY FRIENDS! IF YOU'RE LOOKING FOR AN IDEA FOR AN OUTDOORS EXCURSION, GO TO THE MIDWINTER FAIR ON WHALE ISLAND...
...AND DON'T MISS **ASA'S PERFUME!**
EVEN VISSIA DE VISSEN LISTENS TO "PATRICIA SUGGESTS!"
A FRAGRANCE THAT WILL WIN YOU OVER!
A NEW PERFUME... AND I DON'T KNOW **ANYTHING** ABOUT IT?
THIS HAS TO BE THE WORK OF VANILLA! MY YOUNGEST IS EVER SO BRILLIANT!
BUT A BITTER DISAPPOINTMENT AWAITS VISSIA...
HOW? **WHAT?** WHAT DO YOU MEAN "ASA'S PERFUME" ISN'T YOURS?
WELL... I'VE MADE A VIKING ELIXIR AND...
RUBBISH!
I WANT TO KNOW **WHO** CREATED THAT PERFUME!
I DON'T HAVE THE NERVE TO TELL HER IT WAS THE THEA SISTERS!
UM... ALL I KNOW... IS THEY'RE SELLING IT AT THE **ZANZI BAZAAR!**

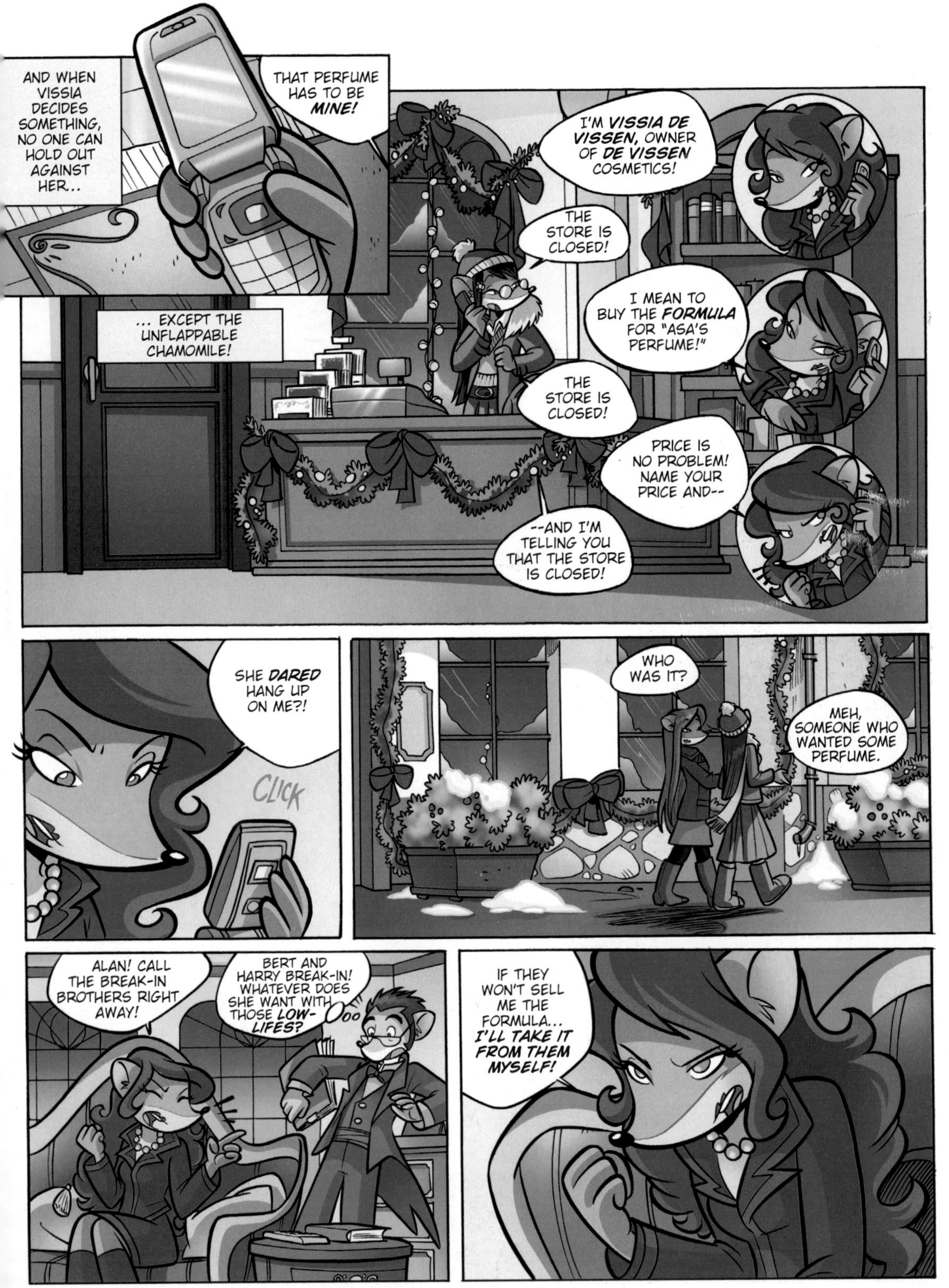

AND WHEN VISSIA DECIDES SOMETHING, NO ONE CAN HOLD OUT AGAINST HER...
THAT PERFUME HAS TO BE MINE!
I'M VISSIA DE VISSEN, OWNER OF DE VISSEN COSMETICS!
THE STORE IS CLOSED!
... EXCEPT THE UNFLAPPABLE CHAMOMILE!
I MEAN TO BUY THE FORMULA FOR "ASA'S PERFUME!"
THE STORE IS CLOSED!
PRICE IS NO PROBLEM! NAME YOUR PRICE AND--
--AND I'M TELLING YOU THAT THE STORE IS CLOSED!
SHE DARED HANG UP ON ME?!
CLICK
WHO WAS IT?
MEH, SOMEONE WHO WANTED SOME PERFUME.
ALAN! CALL THE BREAK-IN BROTHERS RIGHT AWAY!
BERT AND HARRY BREAK-IN! WHATEVER DOES SHE WANT WITH THOSE LOW-LIFES?
IF THEY WON'T SELL ME THE FORMULA... I'LL TAKE IT FROM THEM MYSELF!

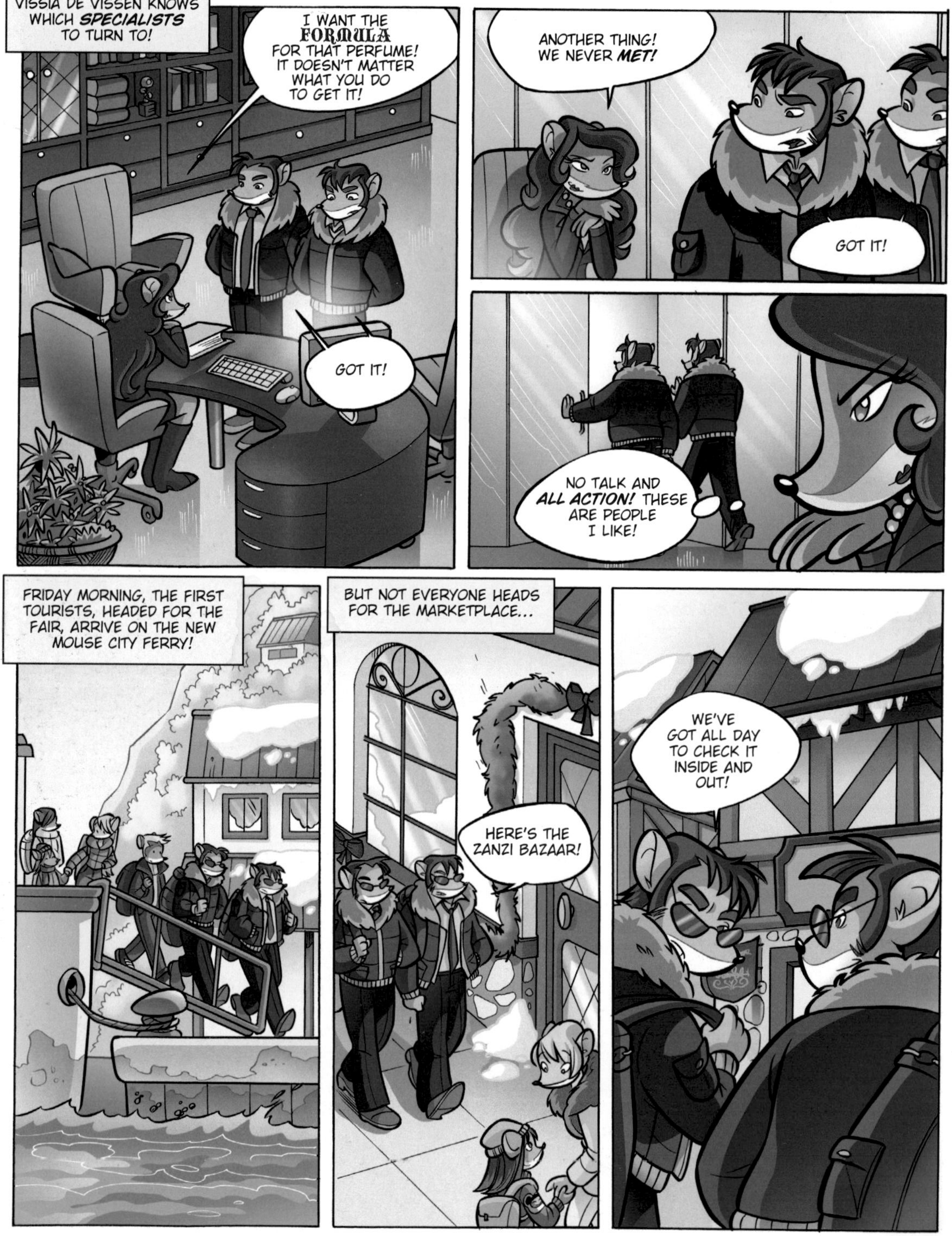
VISSIA DE VISSEN KNOWS WHICH SPECIALISTS TO TURN TO!
I WANT THE FORMULA FOR THAT PERFUME! IT DOESN'T MATTER WHAT YOU DO TO GET IT!
GOT IT!
ANOTHER THING! WE NEVER MET!
GOT IT!
NO TALK AND ALL ACTION! THESE ARE PEOPLE I LIKE!
FRIDAY MORNING, THE FIRST TOURISTS, HEADED FOR THE FAIR, ARRIVE ON THE NEW MOUSE CITY FERRY!
BUT NOT EVERYONE HEADS FOR THE MARKETPLACE...
HERE'S THE ZANZI BAZAAR!
WE'VE GOT ALL DAY TO CHECK IT INSIDE AND OUT!

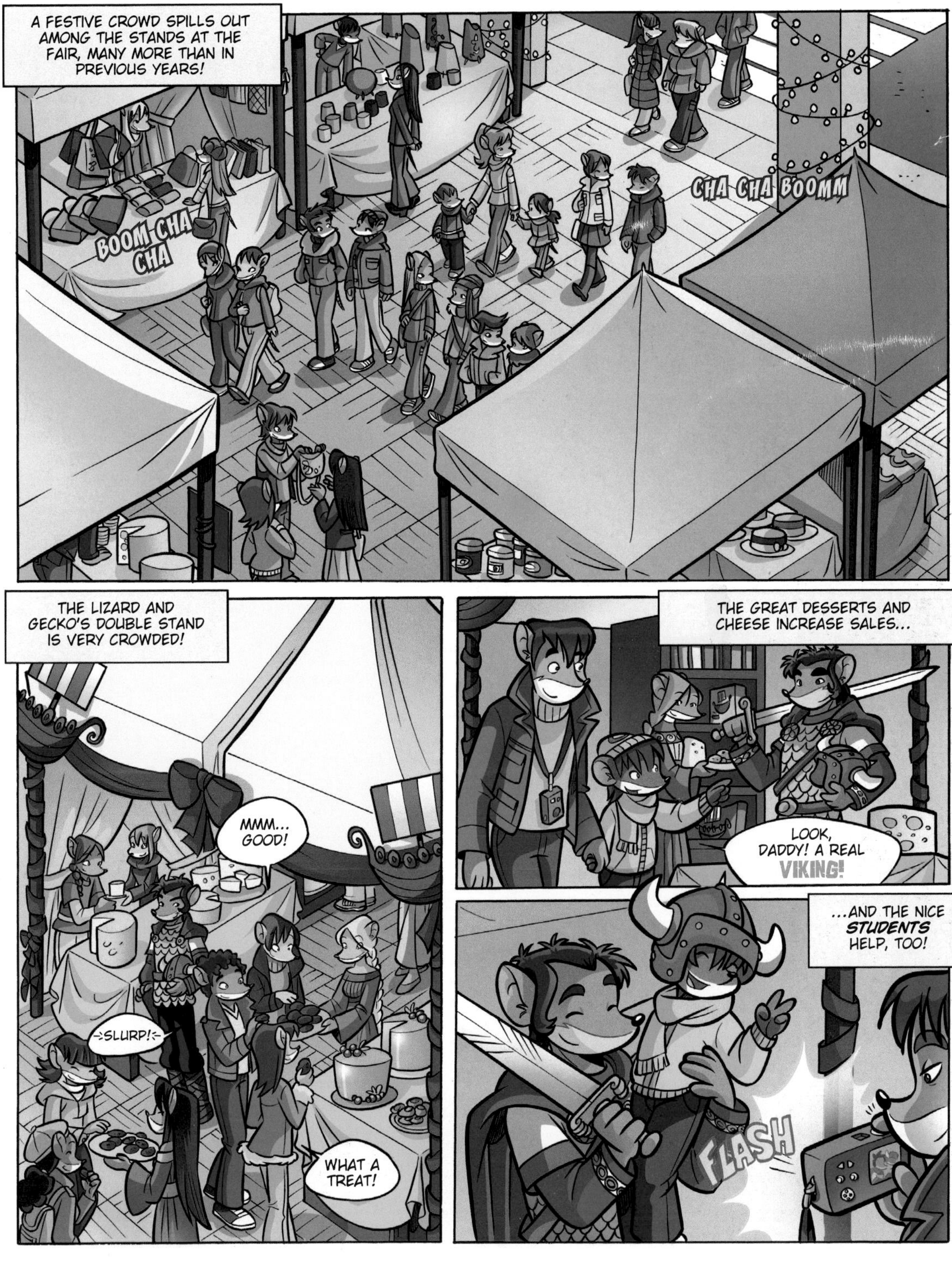
A FESTIVE CROWD SPILLS OUT AMONG THE STANDS AT THE FAIR, MANY MORE THAN IN PREVIOUS YEARS!
BOOM CHA CHA
CHA CHA BOOMM
THE LIZARD AND GECKO'S DOUBLE STAND IS VERY CROWDED!
MMM... GOOD!
-SLURP!-
WHAT A TREAT!
THE GREAT DESSERTS AND CHEESE INCREASE SALES...
LOOK, DADDY! A REAL VIKING!
...AND THE NICE STUDENTS HELP, TOO!
FLASH

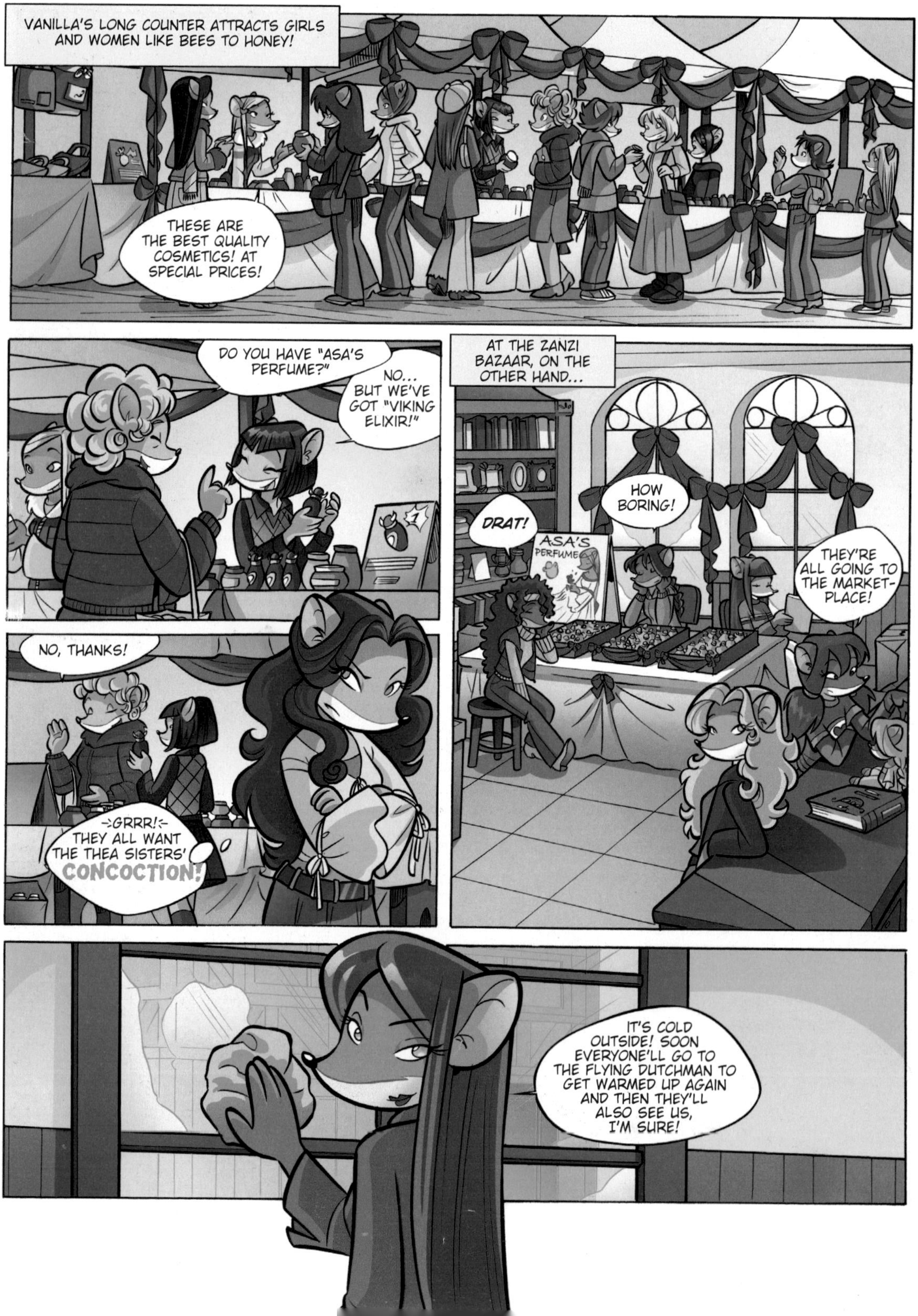
VANILLA'S LONG COUNTER ATTRACTS GIRLS AND WOMEN LIKE BEES TO HONEY!
THESE ARE THE BEST QUALITY COSMETICS! AT SPECIAL PRICES!
DO YOU HAVE "ASA'S PERFUME?"
NO... BUT WE'VE GOT "VIKING ELIXIR!"
NO, THANKS!
-GRRR!- THEY ALL WANT THE THEA SISTERS' CONCOCTION!
AT THE ZANZI BAZAAR, ON THE OTHER HAND...
HOW BORING!
DRAT!
ASA'S PERFUME
THEY'RE ALL GOING TO THE MARKET-PLACE!
IT'S COLD OUTSIDE! SOON EVERYONE'LL GO TO THE FLYING DUTCHMAN TO GET WARMED UP AGAIN AND THEN THEY'LL ALSO SEE US, I'M SURE!

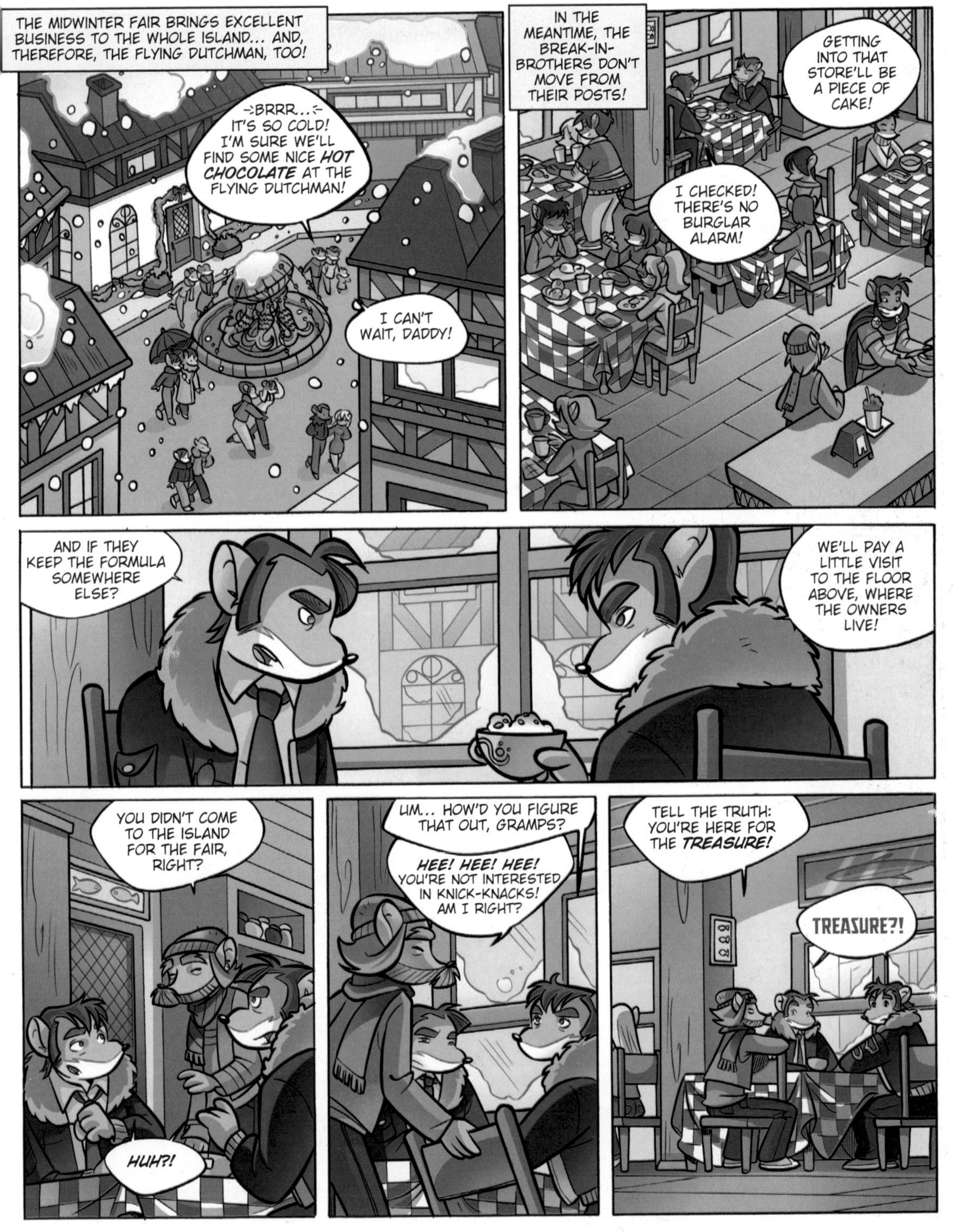
THE MIDWINTER FAIR BRINGS EXCELLENT BUSINESS TO THE WHOLE ISLAND... AND, THEREFORE, THE FLYING DUTCHMAN, TOO!
BRRR... IT'S SO COLD! I'M SURE WE'LL FIND SOME NICE HOT CHOCOLATE AT THE FLYING DUTCHMAN!
I CAN'T WAIT, DADDY!
IN THE MEANTIME, THE BREAK-IN-BROTHERS DON'T MOVE FROM THEIR POSTS!
GETTING INTO THAT STORE'LL BE A PIECE OF CAKE!
I CHECKED! THERE'S NO BURGLAR ALARM!
AND IF THEY KEEP THE FORMULA SOMEWHERE ELSE?
WE'LL PAY A LITTLE VISIT TO THE FLOOR ABOVE, WHERE THE OWNERS LIVE!
YOU DIDN'T COME TO THE ISLAND FOR THE FAIR, RIGHT?
HUH?!
UM... HOW'D YOU FIGURE THAT OUT, GRAMPS?
HEE! HEE! HEE! YOU'RE NOT INTERESTED IN KNICK-KNACKS! AM I RIGHT?
TELL THE TRUTH: YOU'RE HERE FOR THE TREASURE!
TREASURE?!

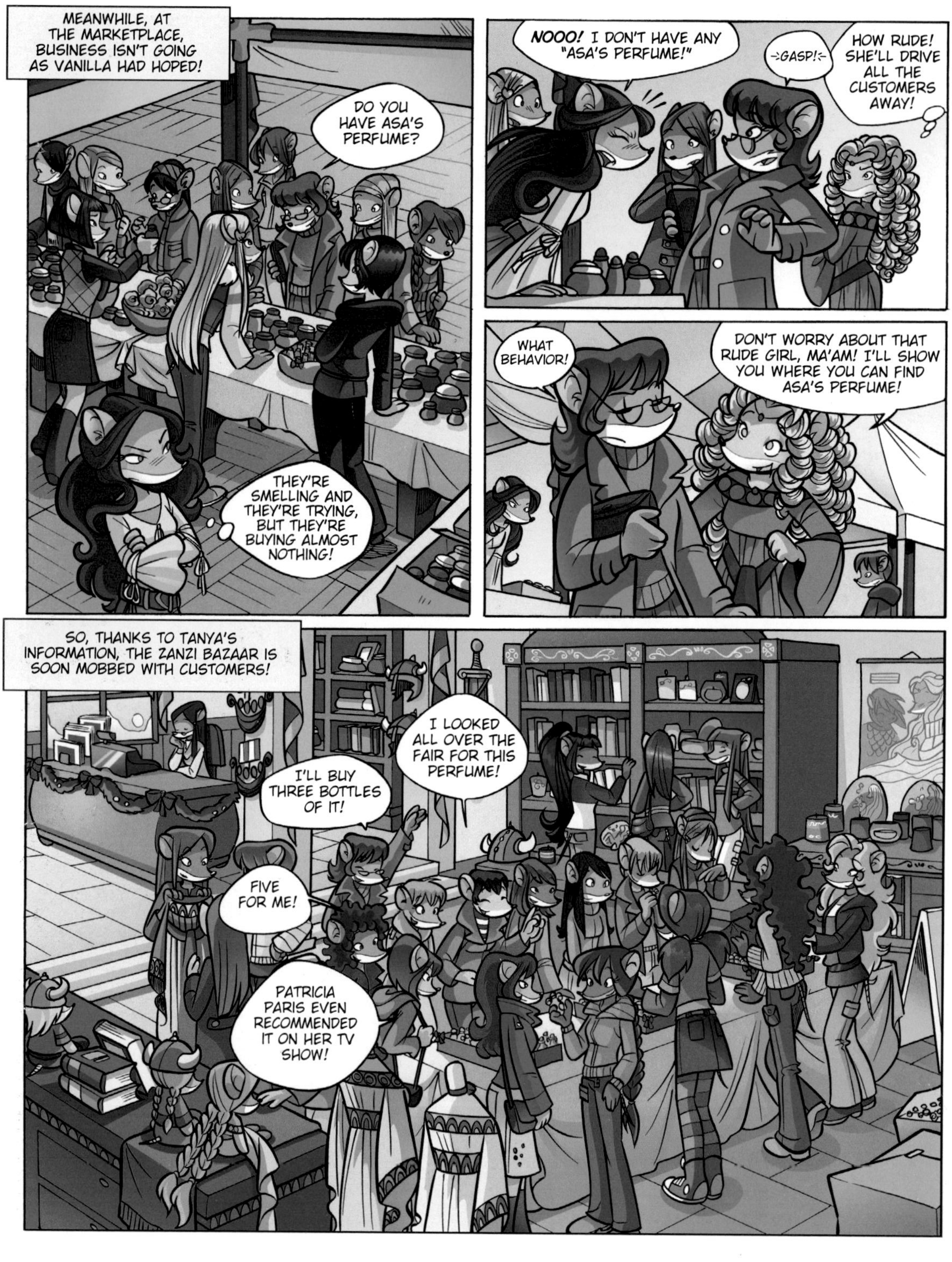
MEANWHILE, AT THE MARKETPLACE, BUSINESS ISN'T GOING AS VANILLA HAD HOPED!
DO YOU HAVE ASA'S PERFUME?
THEY'RE SMELLING AND THEY'RE TRYING, BUT THEY'RE BUYING ALMOST NOTHING!
NOOO! I DON'T HAVE ANY "ASA'S PERFUME!"
GASP!
HOW RUDE! SHE'LL DRIVE ALL THE CUSTOMERS AWAY!
WHAT BEHAVIOR!
DON'T WORRY ABOUT THAT RUDE GIRL, MA'AM! I'LL SHOW YOU WHERE YOU CAN FIND ASA'S PERFUME!
SO, THANKS TO TANYA'S INFORMATION, THE ZANZI BAZAAR IS SOON MOBBED WITH CUSTOMERS!
I LOOKED ALL OVER THE FAIR FOR THIS PERFUME!
I'LL BUY THREE BOTTLES OF IT!
FIVE FOR ME!
PATRICIA PARIS EVEN RECOMMENDED IT ON HER TV SHOW!

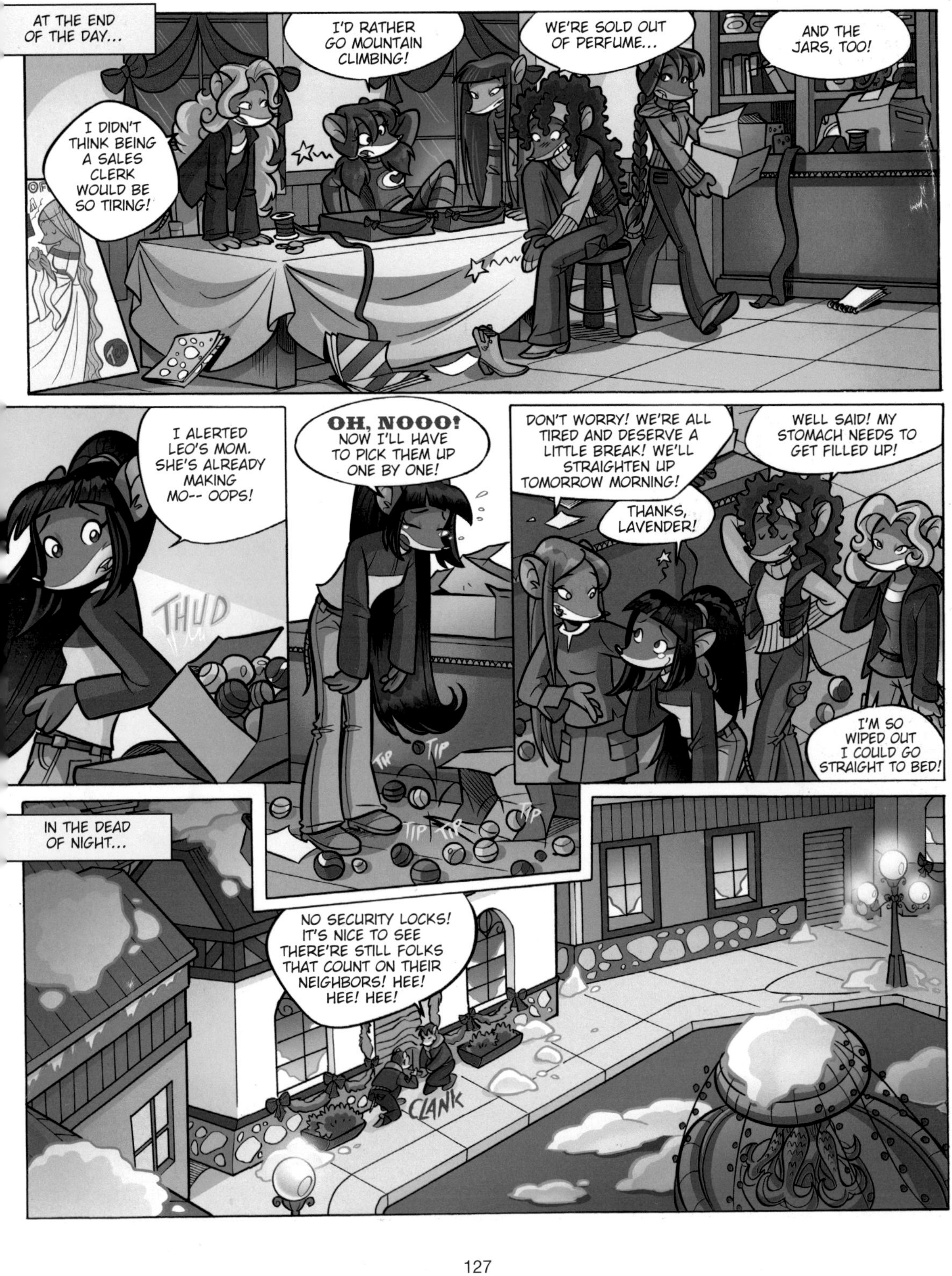
AT THE END OF THE DAY...
I DIDN'T THINK BEING A SALES CLERK WOULD BE SO TIRING!
I'D RATHER GO MOUNTAIN CLIMBING!
WE'RE SOLD OUT OF PERFUME...
AND THE JARS, TOO!
I ALERTED LEO'S MOM. SHE'S ALREADY MAKING MO-- OOPS!
THUD
OH, NOOO! NOW I'LL HAVE TO PICK THEM UP ONE BY ONE!
TIP TIP TIP TIP TIP
DON'T WORRY! WE'RE ALL TIRED AND DESERVE A LITTLE BREAK! WE'LL STRAIGHTEN UP TOMORROW MORNING!
THANKS, LAVENDER!
WELL SAID! MY STOMACH NEEDS TO GET FILLED UP!
I'M SO WIPED OUT I COULD GO STRAIGHT TO BED!
IN THE DEAD OF NIGHT...
NO SECURITY LOCKS! IT'S NICE TO SEE THERE'RE STILL FOLKS THAT COUNT ON THEIR NEIGHBORS! HEE! HEE! HEE!
CLANK

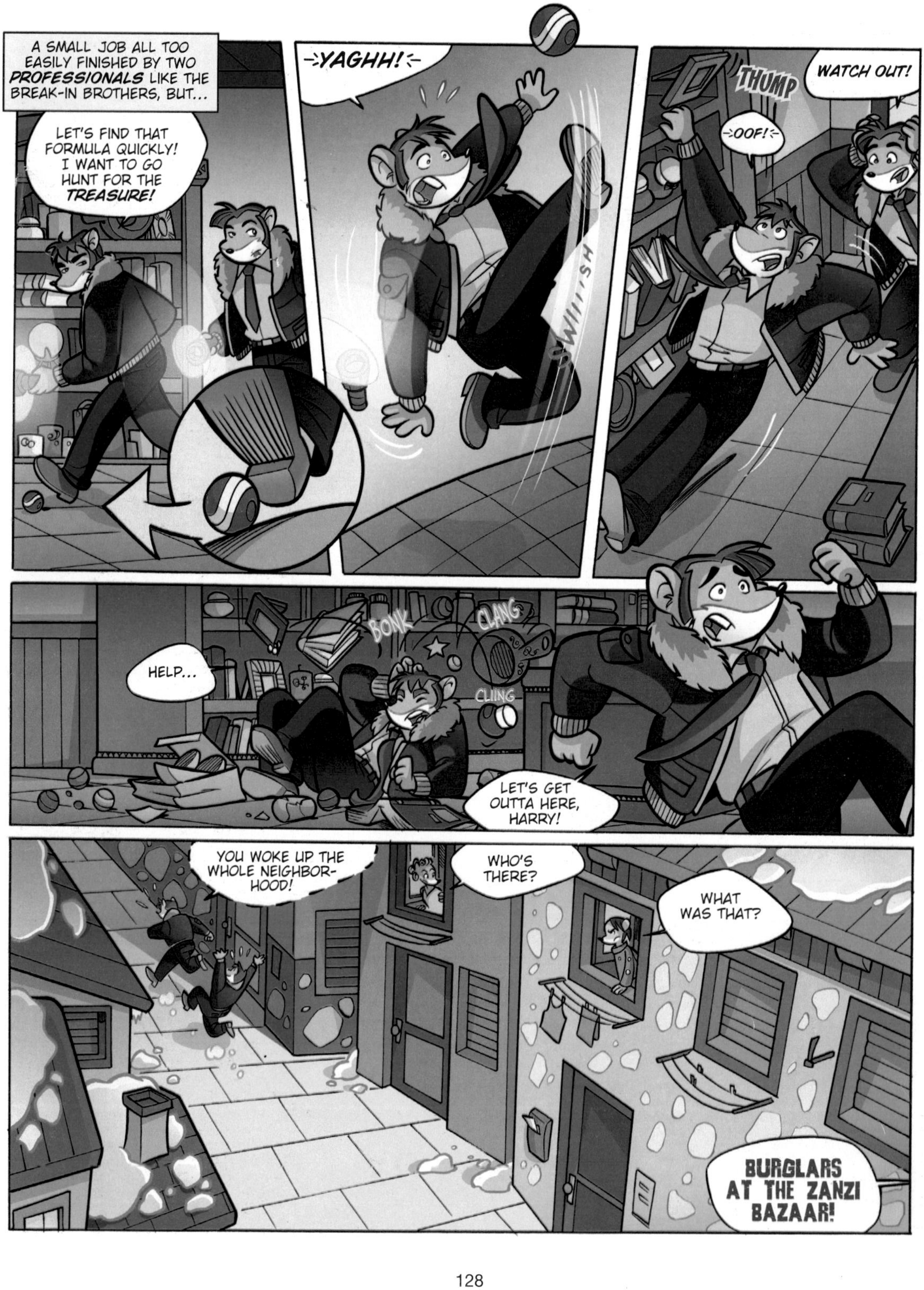
A SMALL JOB ALL TOO EASILY FINISHED BY TWO PROFESSIONALS LIKE THE BREAK-IN BROTHERS, BUT...
LET'S FIND THAT FORMULA QUICKLY! I WANT TO GO HUNT FOR THE TREASURE!
YAGHH!
SWIIISH
THUMP
WATCH OUT!
OOF!
BONK
CLANG
HELP...
CLIING
LET'S GET OUTTA HERE, HARRY!
YOU WOKE UP THE WHOLE NEIGHBOR-HOOD!
WHO'S THERE?
WHAT WAS THAT?
BURGLARS AT THE ZANZI BAZAAR!

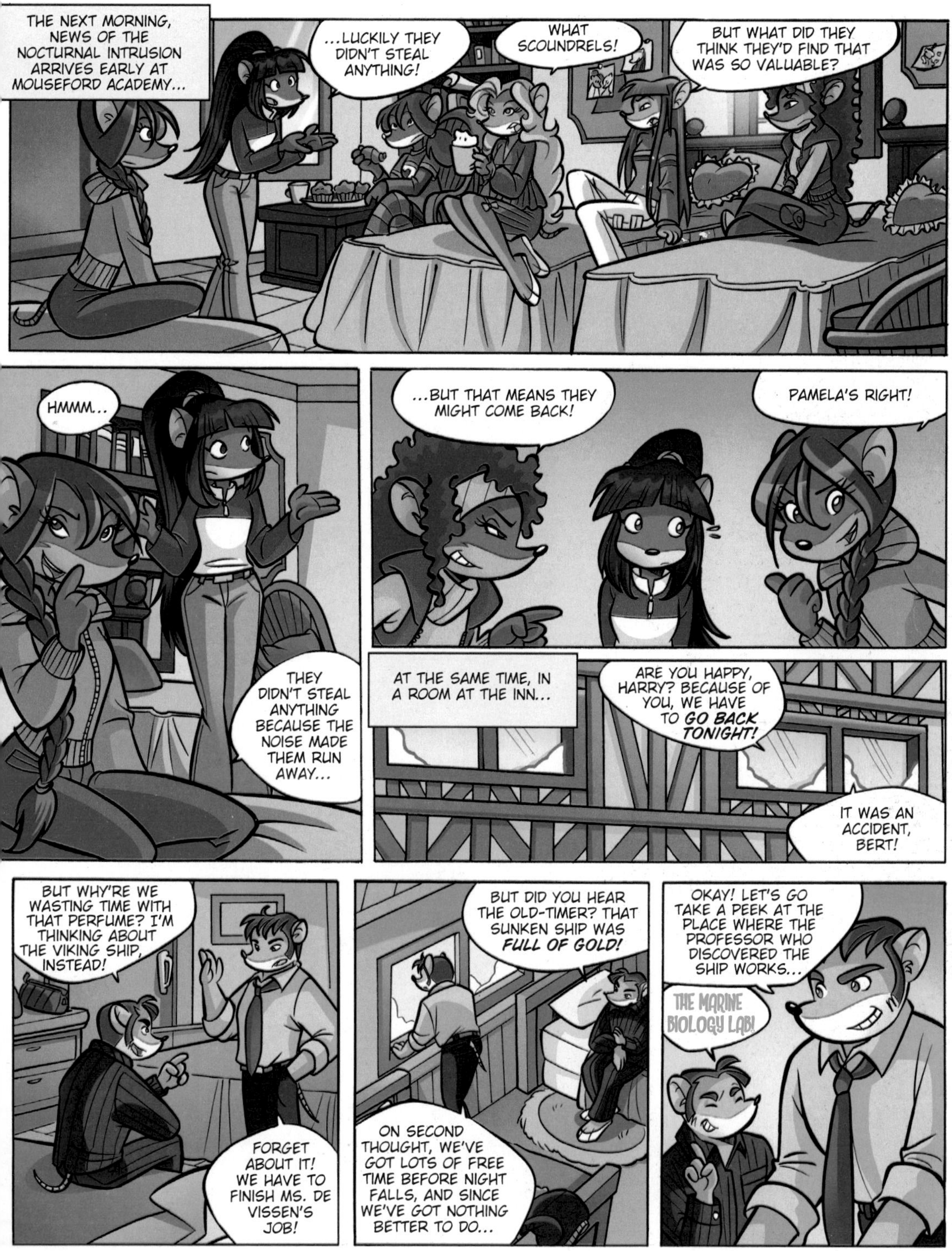
THE NEXT MORNING, NEWS OF THE NOCTURNAL INTRUSION ARRIVES EARLY AT MOUSEFORD ACADEMY...
...LUCKILY THEY DIDN'T STEAL ANYTHING!
WHAT SCOUNDRELS!
BUT WHAT DID THEY THINK THEY'D FIND THAT WAS SO VALUABLE?
HMMM...
THEY DIDN'T STEAL ANYTHING BECAUSE THE NOISE MADE THEM RUN AWAY...
...BUT THAT MEANS THEY MIGHT COME BACK!
PAMELA'S RIGHT!
AT THE SAME TIME, IN A ROOM AT THE INN...
ARE YOU HAPPY, HARRY? BECAUSE OF YOU, WE HAVE TO **GO BACK TONIGHT!**
IT WAS AN ACCIDENT, BERT!
BUT WHY'RE WE WASTING TIME WITH THAT PERFUME? I'M THINKING ABOUT THE VIKING SHIP, INSTEAD!
FORGET ABOUT IT! WE HAVE TO FINISH MS. DE VISSEN'S JOB!
BUT DID YOU HEAR THE OLD-TIMER? THAT SUNKEN SHIP WAS **FULL OF GOLD!**
ON SECOND THOUGHT, WE'VE GOT LOTS OF FREE TIME BEFORE NIGHT FALLS, AND SINCE WE'VE GOT NOTHING BETTER TO DO...
OKAY! LET'S GO TAKE A PEEK AT THE PLACE WHERE THE PROFESSOR WHO DISCOVERED THE SHIP WORKS...
THE MARINE BIOLOGY LAB!

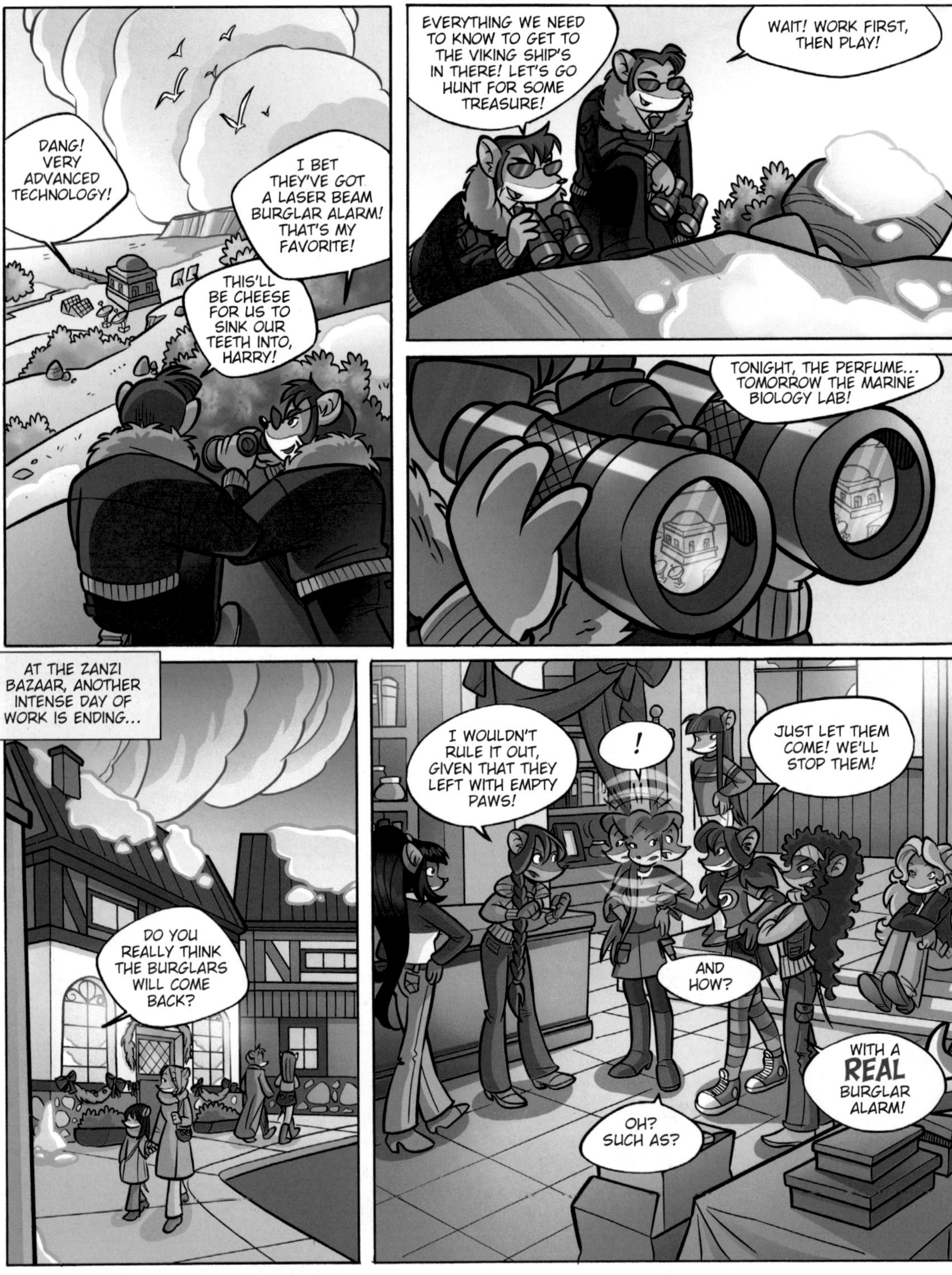
DANG! VERY ADVANCED TECHNOLOGY!
I BET THEY'VE GOT A LASER BEAM BURGLAR ALARM! THAT'S MY FAVORITE!
THIS'LL BE CHEESE FOR US TO SINK OUR TEETH INTO, HARRY!
EVERYTHING WE NEED TO KNOW TO GET TO THE VIKING SHIP'S IN THERE! LET'S GO HUNT FOR SOME TREASURE!
WAIT! WORK FIRST, THEN PLAY!
TONIGHT, THE PERFUME... TOMORROW THE MARINE BIOLOGY LAB!
AT THE ZANZI BAZAAR, ANOTHER INTENSE DAY OF WORK IS ENDING...
DO YOU REALLY THINK THE BURGLARS WILL COME BACK?
I WOULDN'T RULE IT OUT, GIVEN THAT THEY LEFT WITH EMPTY PAWS!
!
JUST LET THEM COME! WE'LL STOP THEM!
AND HOW?
OH? SUCH AS?
WITH A REAL BURGLAR ALARM!

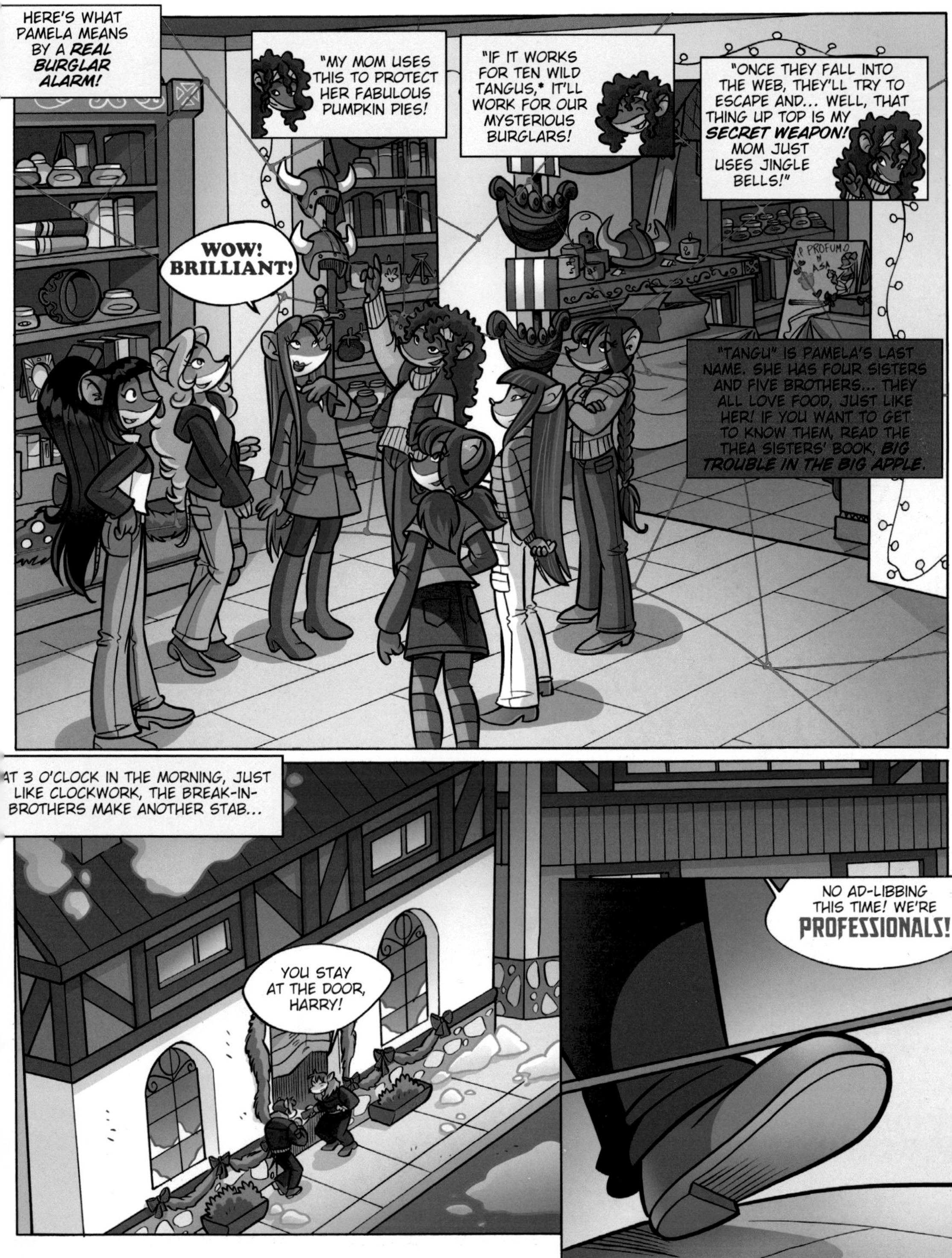
HERE'S WHAT PAMELA MEANS BY A ***REAL BURGLAR ALARM!***
"MY MOM USES THIS TO PROTECT HER FABULOUS PUMPKIN PIES!
"IF IT WORKS FOR TEN WILD TANGUS,* IT'LL WORK FOR OUR MYSTERIOUS BURGLARS!
"ONCE THEY FALL INTO THE WEB, THEY'LL TRY TO ESCAPE AND... WELL, THAT THING UP TOP IS MY ***SECRET WEAPON!*** MOM JUST USES JINGLE BELLS!"
WOW! BRILLIANT!
*"TANGU" IS PAMELA'S LAST NAME. SHE HAS FOUR SISTERS AND FIVE BROTHERS... THEY ALL LOVE FOOD, JUST LIKE HER! IF YOU WANT TO GET TO KNOW THEM, READ THE THEA SISTERS' BOOK, ***BIG TROUBLE IN THE BIG APPLE***.
AT 3 O'CLOCK IN THE MORNING, JUST LIKE CLOCKWORK, THE BREAK-IN-BROTHERS MAKE ANOTHER STAB...
YOU STAY AT THE DOOR, HARRY!
NO AD-LIBBING THIS TIME! WE'RE **PROFESSIONALS!**

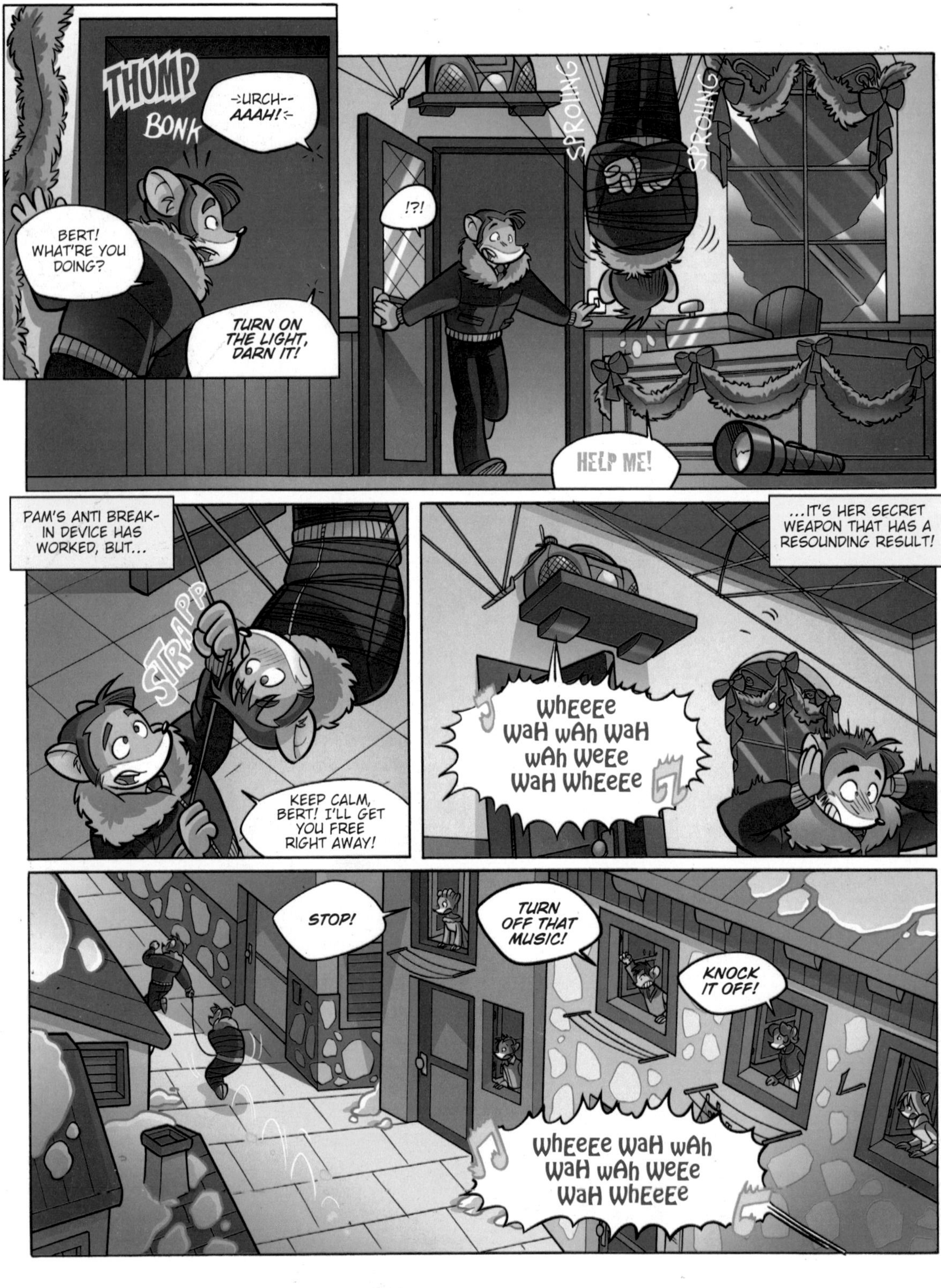
THUMP
BONK
-URCH-- AAAH!-
BERT! WHAT'RE YOU DOING?
TURN ON THE LIGHT, DARN IT!
!?!
SPROING
SPROING
HELP ME!
PAM'S ANTI BREAK-IN DEVICE HAS WORKED, BUT...
STRAPP
KEEP CALM, BERT! I'LL GET YOU FREE RIGHT AWAY!
...IT'S HER SECRET WEAPON THAT HAS A RESOUNDING RESULT!
WhEEEE WaH wAh WaH wAh WeEe WaH WhEeEe
STOP!
TURN OFF THAT MUSIC!
KNOCK IT OFF!
WhEEEe WaH wAh WaH wAh WeEe WaH WhEeEe

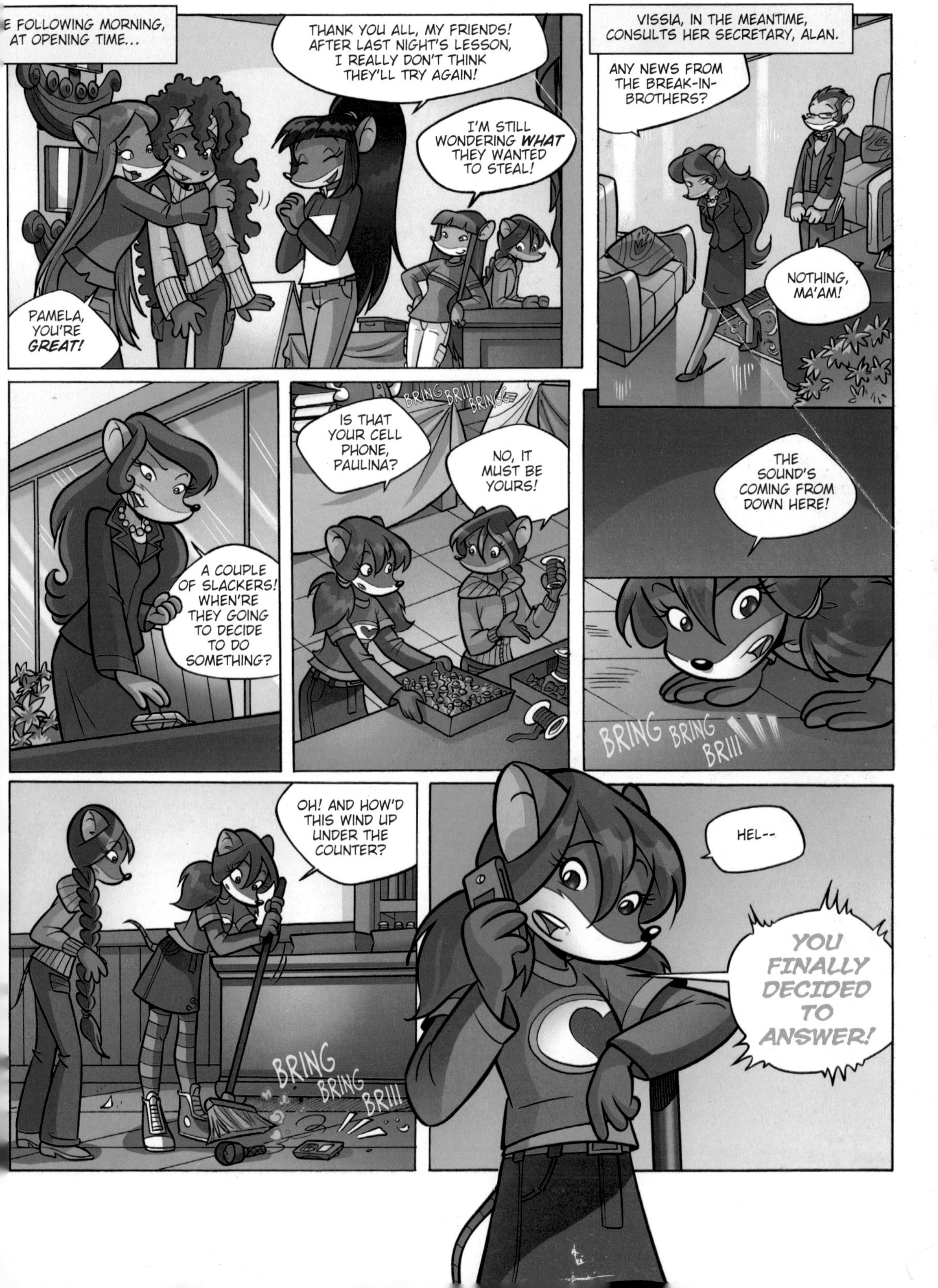
E FOLLOWING MORNING, AT OPENING TIME...
THANK YOU ALL, MY FRIENDS! AFTER LAST NIGHT'S LESSON, I REALLY DON'T THINK THEY'LL TRY AGAIN!
I'M STILL WONDERING **WHAT** THEY WANTED TO STEAL!
PAMELA, YOU'RE **GREAT!**
VISSIA, IN THE MEANTIME, CONSULTS HER SECRETARY, ALAN.
ANY NEWS FROM THE BREAK-IN-BROTHERS?
NOTHING, MA'AM!
A COUPLE OF SLACKERS! WHEN'RE THEY GOING TO DECIDE TO DO SOMETHING?
BRING BRIII BRINGG
IS THAT YOUR CELL PHONE, PAULINA?
NO, IT MUST BE YOURS!
THE SOUND'S COMING FROM DOWN HERE!
BRING BRING BRIII
OH! AND HOW'D THIS WIND UP UNDER THE COUNTER?
BRING BRING BRIII
HEL--
YOU FINALLY DECIDED TO ANSWER!

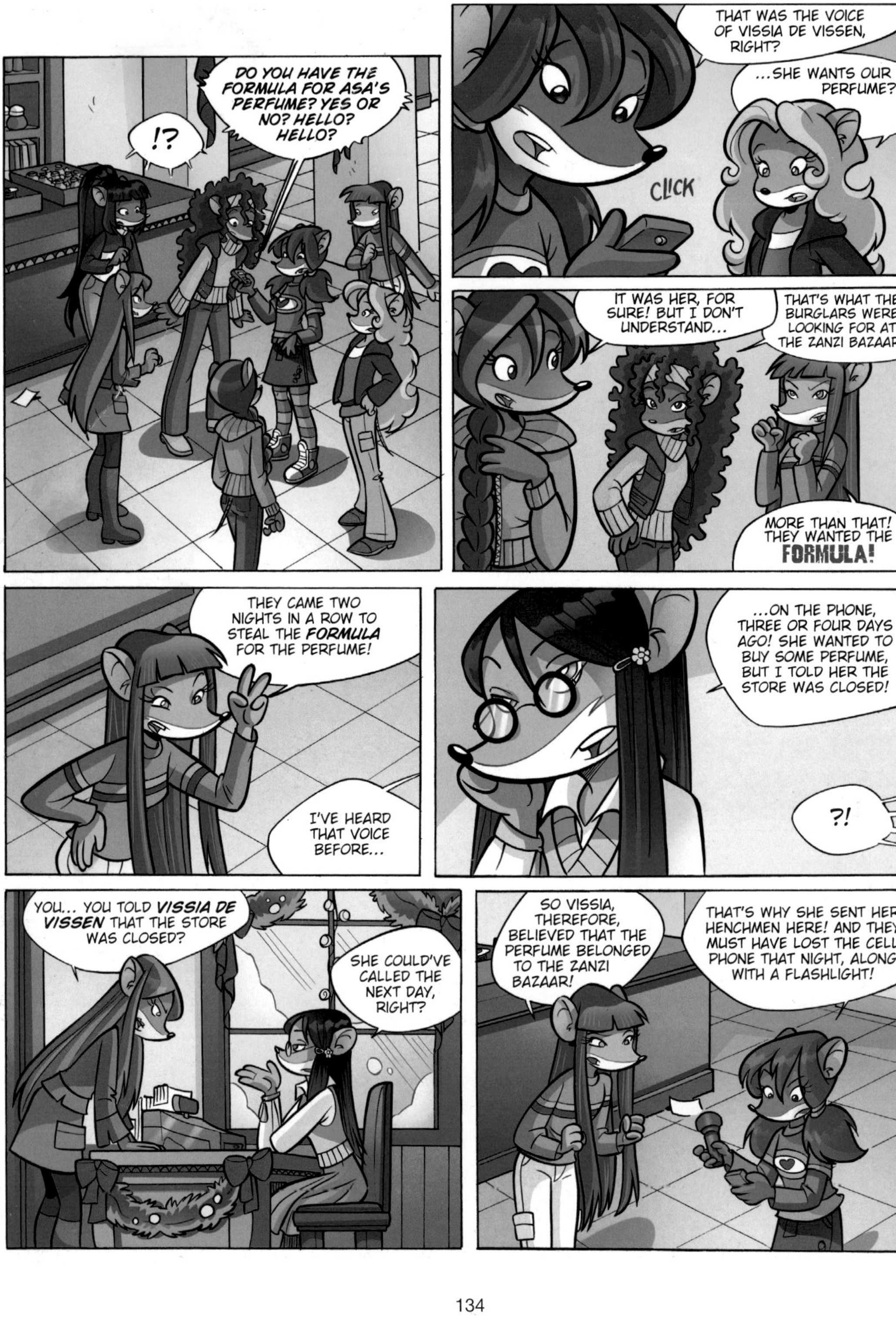

DO YOU HAVE THE FORMULA FOR ASA'S PERFUME? YES OR NO? HELLO? HELLO?
!?
THAT WAS THE VOICE OF VISSIA DE VISSEN, RIGHT?
...SHE WANTS OUR PERFUME?
CLICK
IT WAS HER, FOR SURE! BUT I DON'T UNDERSTAND...
THAT'S WHAT THE BURGLARS WERE LOOKING FOR AT THE ZANZI BAZAAR!
MORE THAN THAT! THEY WANTED THE FORMULA!
THEY CAME TWO NIGHTS IN A ROW TO STEAL THE FORMULA FOR THE PERFUME!
I'VE HEARD THAT VOICE BEFORE...
...ON THE PHONE, THREE OR FOUR DAYS AGO! SHE WANTED TO BUY SOME PERFUME, BUT I TOLD HER THE STORE WAS CLOSED!
?!
YOU... YOU TOLD VISSIA DE VISSEN THAT THE STORE WAS CLOSED?
SHE COULD'VE CALLED THE NEXT DAY, RIGHT?
SO VISSIA, THEREFORE, BELIEVED THAT THE PERFUME BELONGED TO THE ZANZI BAZAAR!
THAT'S WHY SHE SENT HER HENCHMEN HERE! AND THEY MUST HAVE LOST THE CELL PHONE THAT NIGHT, ALONG WITH A FLASHLIGHT!

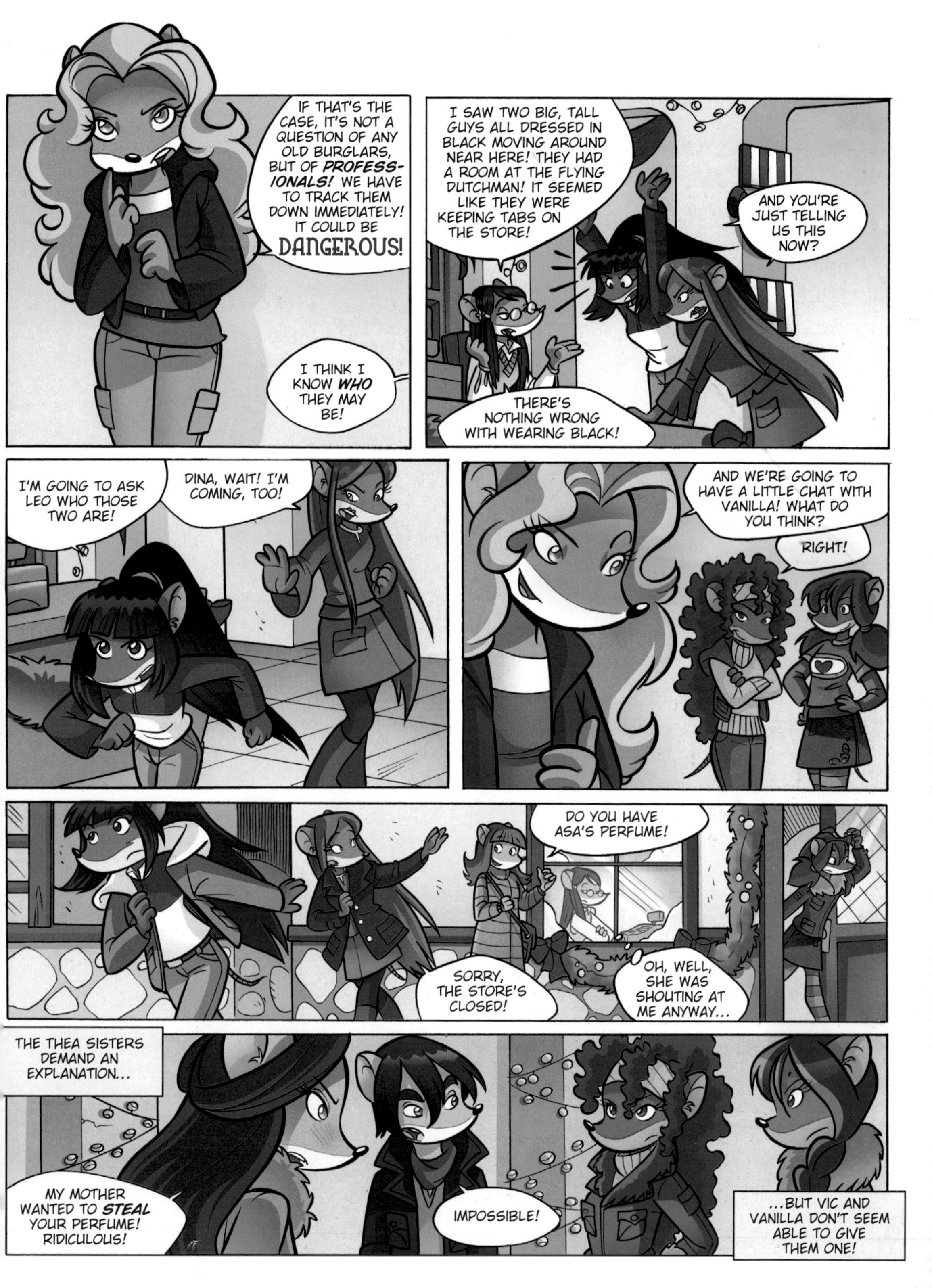

IF THAT'S THE CASE, IT'S NOT A QUESTION OF ANY OLD BURGLARS, BUT OF PROFESS-IONALS! WE HAVE TO TRACK THEM DOWN IMMEDIATELY! IT COULD BE DANGEROUS!
I THINK I KNOW WHO THEY MAY BE!
I SAW TWO BIG, TALL GUYS ALL DRESSED IN BLACK MOVING AROUND NEAR HERE! THEY HAD A ROOM AT THE FLYING DUTCHMAN! IT SEEMED LIKE THEY WERE KEEPING TABS ON THE STORE!
AND YOU'RE JUST TELLING US THIS NOW?
THERE'S NOTHING WRONG WITH WEARING BLACK!
I'M GOING TO ASK LEO WHO THOSE TWO ARE!
DINA, WAIT! I'M COMING, TOO!
AND WE'RE GOING TO HAVE A LITTLE CHAT WITH VANILLA! WHAT DO YOU THINK?
RIGHT!
DO YOU HAVE ASA'S PERFUME!
SORRY, THE STORE'S CLOSED!
OH, WELL, SHE WAS SHOUTING AT ME ANYWAY...
THE THEA SISTERS DEMAND AN EXPLANATION...
MY MOTHER WANTED TO STEAL YOUR PERFUME! RIDICULOUS!
IMPOSSIBLE!
...BUT VIC AND VANILLA DON'T SEEM ABLE TO GIVE THEM ONE!

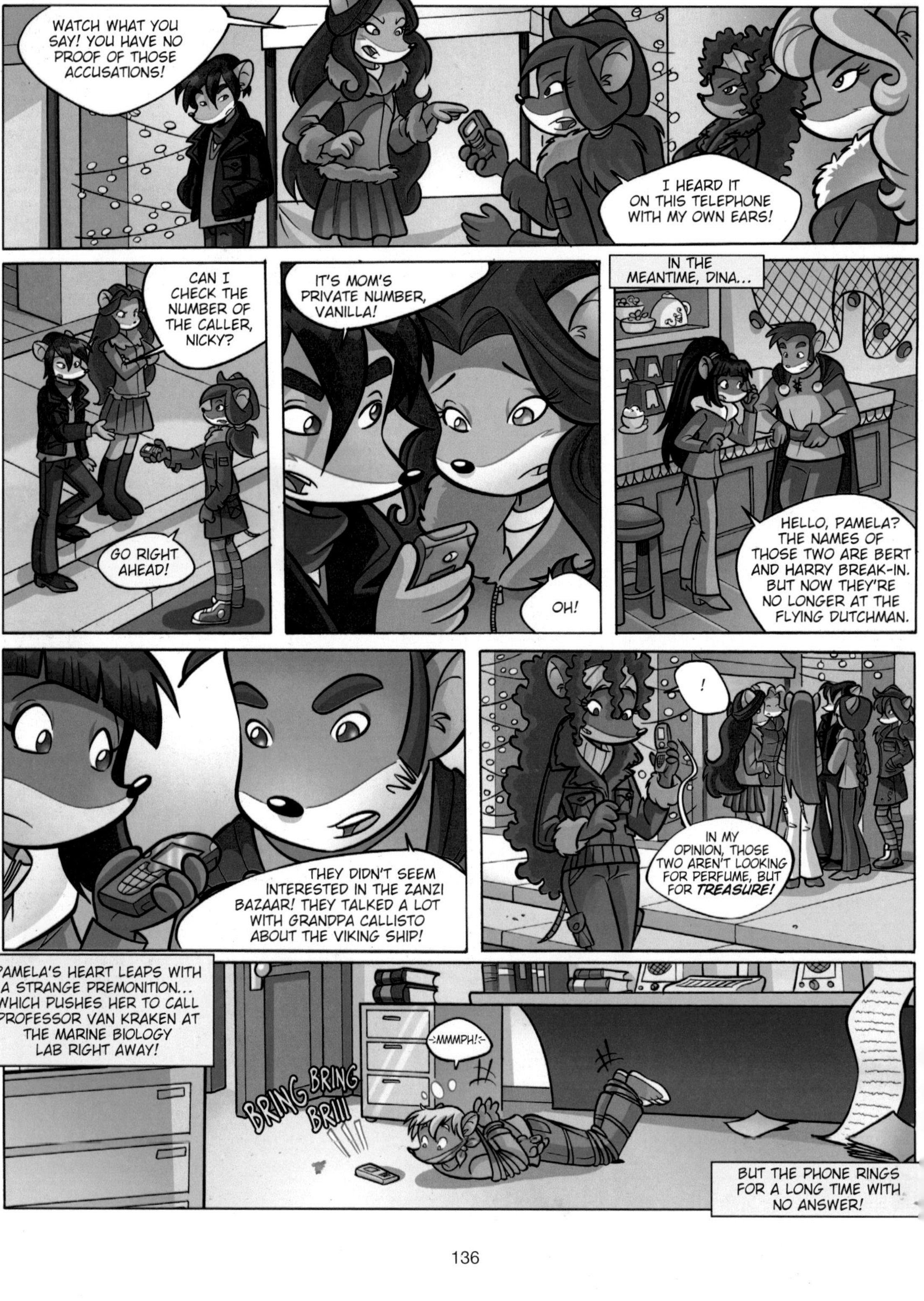
WATCH WHAT YOU SAY! YOU HAVE NO PROOF OF THOSE ACCUSATIONS!
I HEARD IT ON THIS TELEPHONE WITH MY OWN EARS!
CAN I CHECK THE NUMBER OF THE CALLER, NICKY?
GO RIGHT AHEAD!
IT'S MOM'S PRIVATE NUMBER, VANILLA!
OH!
IN THE MEANTIME, DINA...
HELLO, PAMELA? THE NAMES OF THOSE TWO ARE BERT AND HARRY BREAK-IN. BUT NOW THEY'RE NO LONGER AT THE FLYING DUTCHMAN.
THEY DIDN'T SEEM INTERESTED IN THE ZANZI BAZAAR! THEY TALKED A LOT WITH GRANDPA CALLISTO ABOUT THE VIKING SHIP!
!
IN MY OPINION, THOSE TWO AREN'T LOOKING FOR PERFUME, BUT FOR **TREASURE!**
PAMELA'S HEART LEAPS WITH A STRANGE PREMONITION... WHICH PUSHES HER TO CALL PROFESSOR VAN KRAKEN AT THE MARINE BIOLOGY LAB RIGHT AWAY!
MMMPH!
BRING BRING BRIII
BUT THE PHONE RINGS FOR A LONG TIME WITH NO ANSWER!

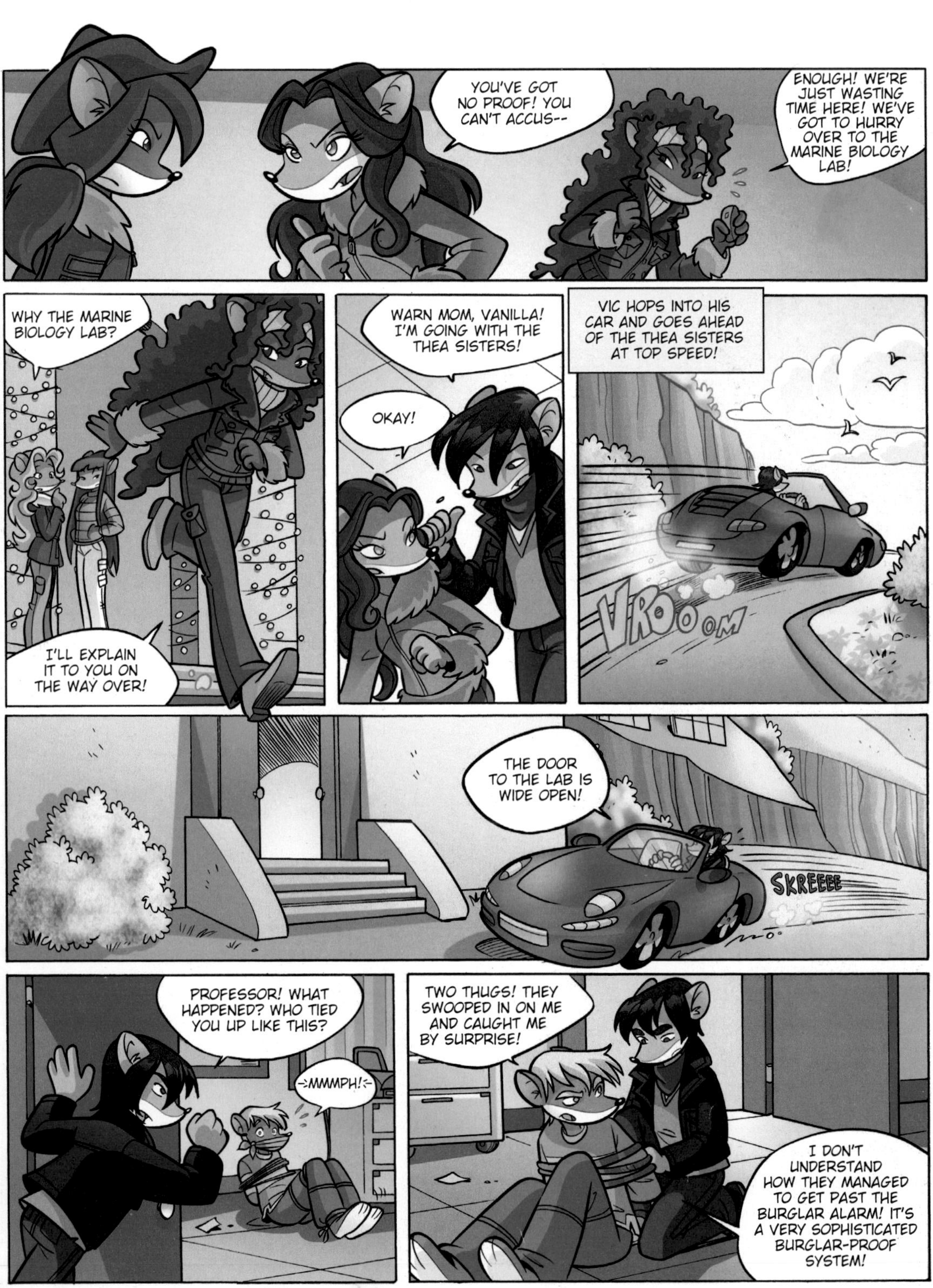
YOU'VE GOT NO PROOF! YOU CAN'T ACCUS--
ENOUGH! WE'RE JUST WASTING TIME HERE! WE'VE GOT TO HURRY OVER TO THE MARINE BIOLOGY LAB!
WHY THE MARINE BIOLOGY LAB?
I'LL EXPLAIN IT TO YOU ON THE WAY OVER!
WARN MOM, VANILLA! I'M GOING WITH THE THEA SISTERS!
OKAY!
VIC HOPS INTO HIS CAR AND GOES AHEAD OF THE THEA SISTERS AT TOP SPEED!
VROOOOM
THE DOOR TO THE LAB IS WIDE OPEN!
SKREEEEE
PROFESSOR! WHAT HAPPENED? WHO TIED YOU UP LIKE THIS?
MMMPH!
TWO THUGS! THEY SWOOPED IN ON ME AND CAUGHT ME BY SURPRISE!
I DON'T UNDERSTAND HOW THEY MANAGED TO GET PAST THE BURGLAR ALARM! IT'S A VERY SOPHISTICATED BURGLAR-PROOF SYSTEM!

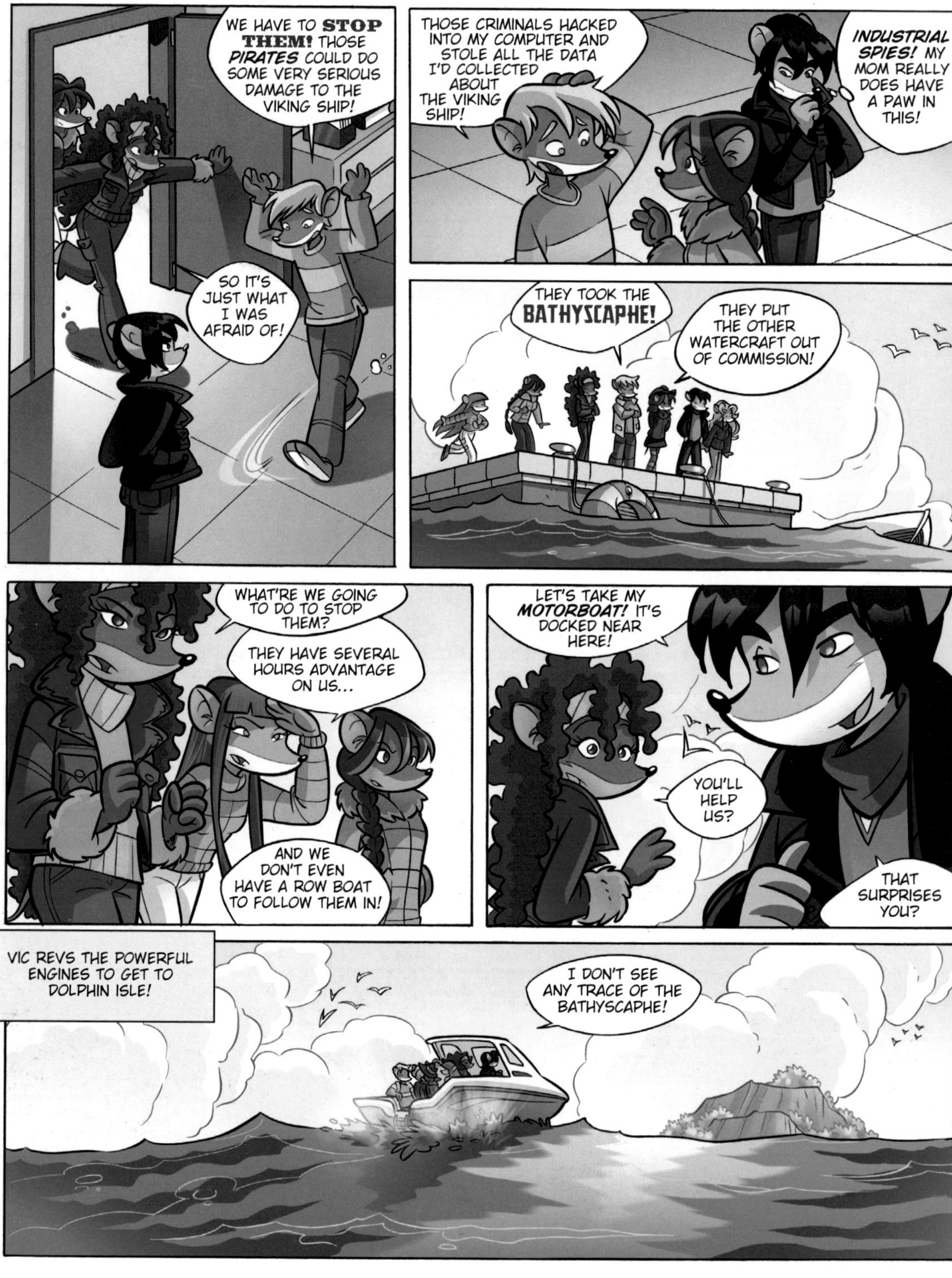

WE HAVE TO **STOP THEM!** THOSE ***PIRATES*** COULD DO SOME VERY SERIOUS DAMAGE TO THE VIKING SHIP!
SO IT'S JUST WHAT I WAS AFRAID OF!
THOSE CRIMINALS HACKED INTO MY COMPUTER AND STOLE ALL THE DATA I'D COLLECTED ABOUT THE VIKING SHIP!
INDUSTRIAL SPIES! MY MOM REALLY DOES HAVE A PAW IN THIS!
THEY TOOK THE **BATHYSCAPHE!**
THEY PUT THE OTHER WATERCRAFT OUT OF COMMISSION!
WHAT'RE WE GOING TO DO TO STOP THEM?
THEY HAVE SEVERAL HOURS ADVANTAGE ON US...
AND WE DON'T EVEN HAVE A ROW BOAT TO FOLLOW THEM IN!
LET'S TAKE MY ***MOTORBOAT!*** IT'S DOCKED NEAR HERE!
YOU'LL HELP US?
THAT SURPRISES YOU?
VIC REVS THE POWERFUL ENGINES TO GET TO DOLPHIN ISLE!
I DON'T SEE ANY TRACE OF THE BATHYSCAPHE!

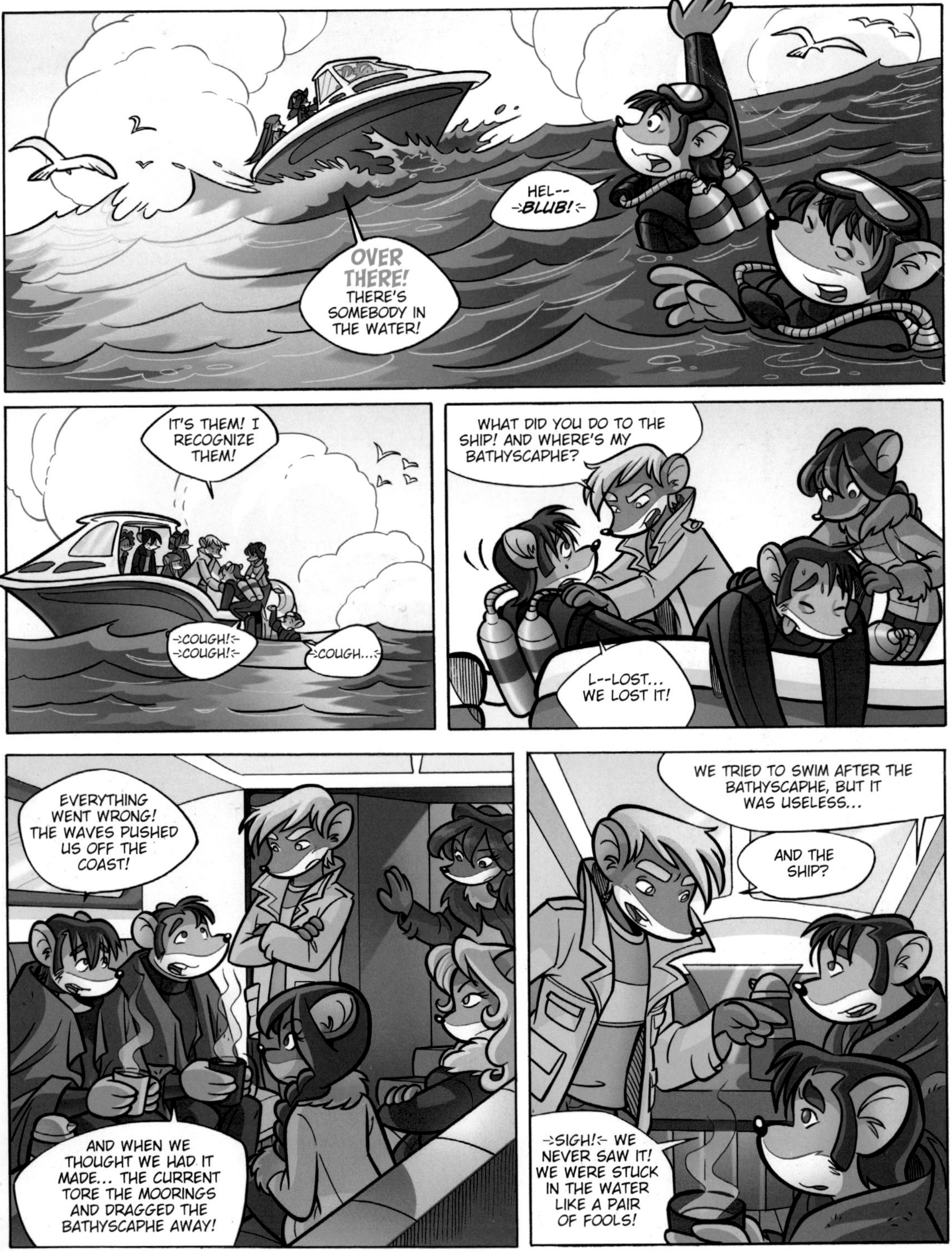
OVER THERE! THERE'S SOMEBODY IN THE WATER!
HEL-- -BLUB!-
IT'S THEM! I RECOGNIZE THEM!
-COUGH!- -COUGH!-
-COUGH...-
WHAT DID YOU DO TO THE SHIP! AND WHERE'S MY BATHYSCAPHE?
L--LOST... WE LOST IT!
EVERYTHING WENT WRONG! THE WAVES PUSHED US OFF THE COAST!
AND WHEN WE THOUGHT WE HAD IT MADE... THE CURRENT TORE THE MOORINGS AND DRAGGED THE BATHYSCAPHE AWAY!
WE TRIED TO SWIM AFTER THE BATHYSCAPHE, BUT IT WAS USELESS...
AND THE SHIP?
-SIGH!- WE NEVER SAW IT! WE WERE STUCK IN THE WATER LIKE A PAIR OF FOOLS!

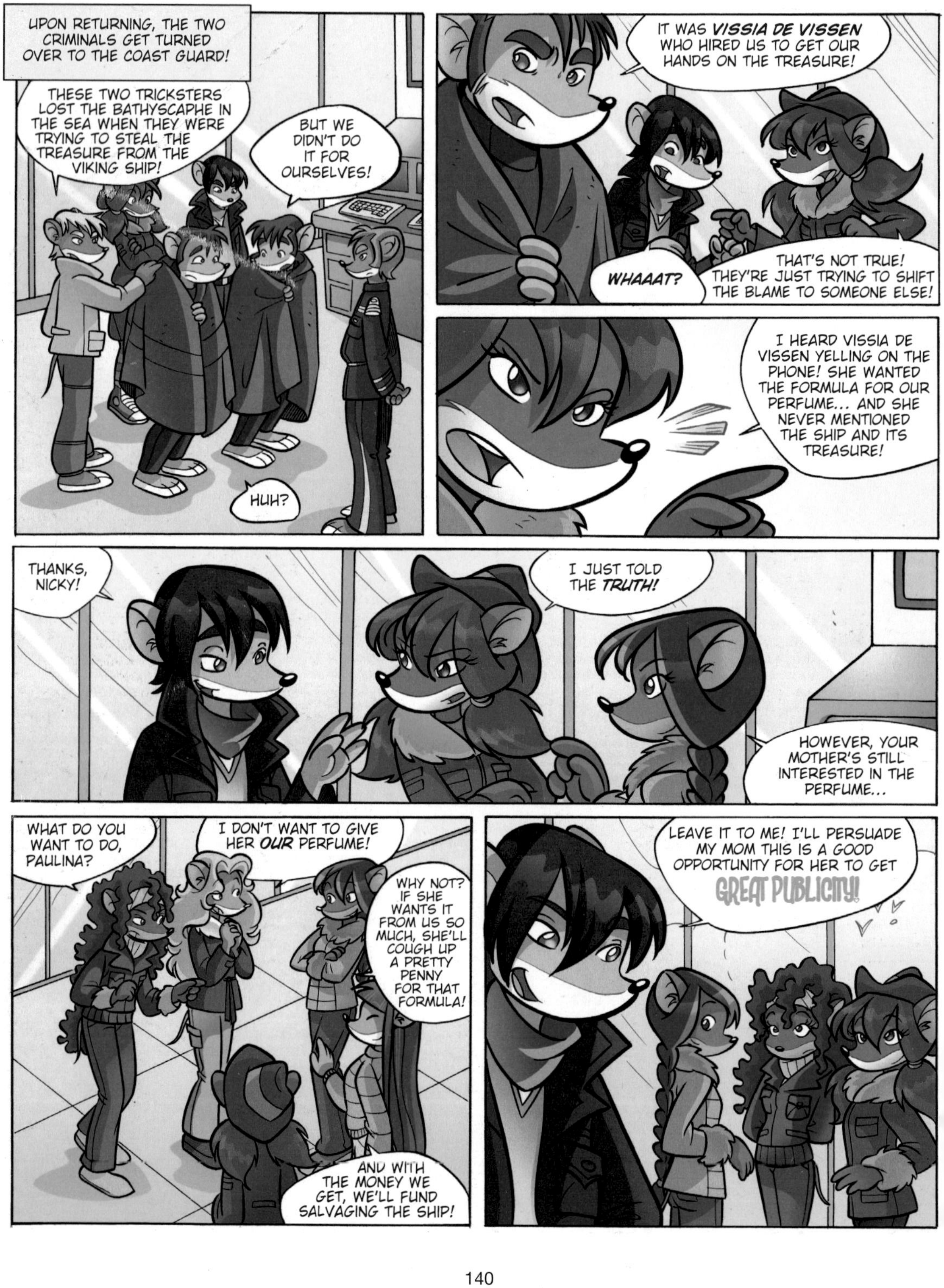
UPON RETURNING, THE TWO CRIMINALS GET TURNED OVER TO THE COAST GUARD!
THESE TWO TRICKSTERS LOST THE BATHYSCAPHE IN THE SEA WHEN THEY WERE TRYING TO STEAL THE TREASURE FROM THE VIKING SHIP!
BUT WE DIDN'T DO IT FOR OURSELVES!
HUH?
IT WAS VISSIA DE VISSEN WHO HIRED US TO GET OUR HANDS ON THE TREASURE!
WHAAAT?
THAT'S NOT TRUE! THEY'RE JUST TRYING TO SHIFT THE BLAME TO SOMEONE ELSE!
I HEARD VISSIA DE VISSEN YELLING ON THE PHONE! SHE WANTED THE FORMULA FOR OUR PERFUME... AND SHE NEVER MENTIONED THE SHIP AND ITS TREASURE!
THANKS, NICKY!
I JUST TOLD THE TRUTH!
HOWEVER, YOUR MOTHER'S STILL INTERESTED IN THE PERFUME...
WHAT DO YOU WANT TO DO, PAULINA?
I DON'T WANT TO GIVE HER OUR PERFUME!
WHY NOT? IF SHE WANTS IT FROM US SO MUCH, SHE'LL COUGH UP A PRETTY PENNY FOR THAT FORMULA!
AND WITH THE MONEY WE GET, WE'LL FUND SALVAGING THE SHIP!
LEAVE IT TO ME! I'LL PERSUADE MY MOM THIS IS A GOOD OPPORTUNITY FOR HER TO GET GREAT PUBLICITY!

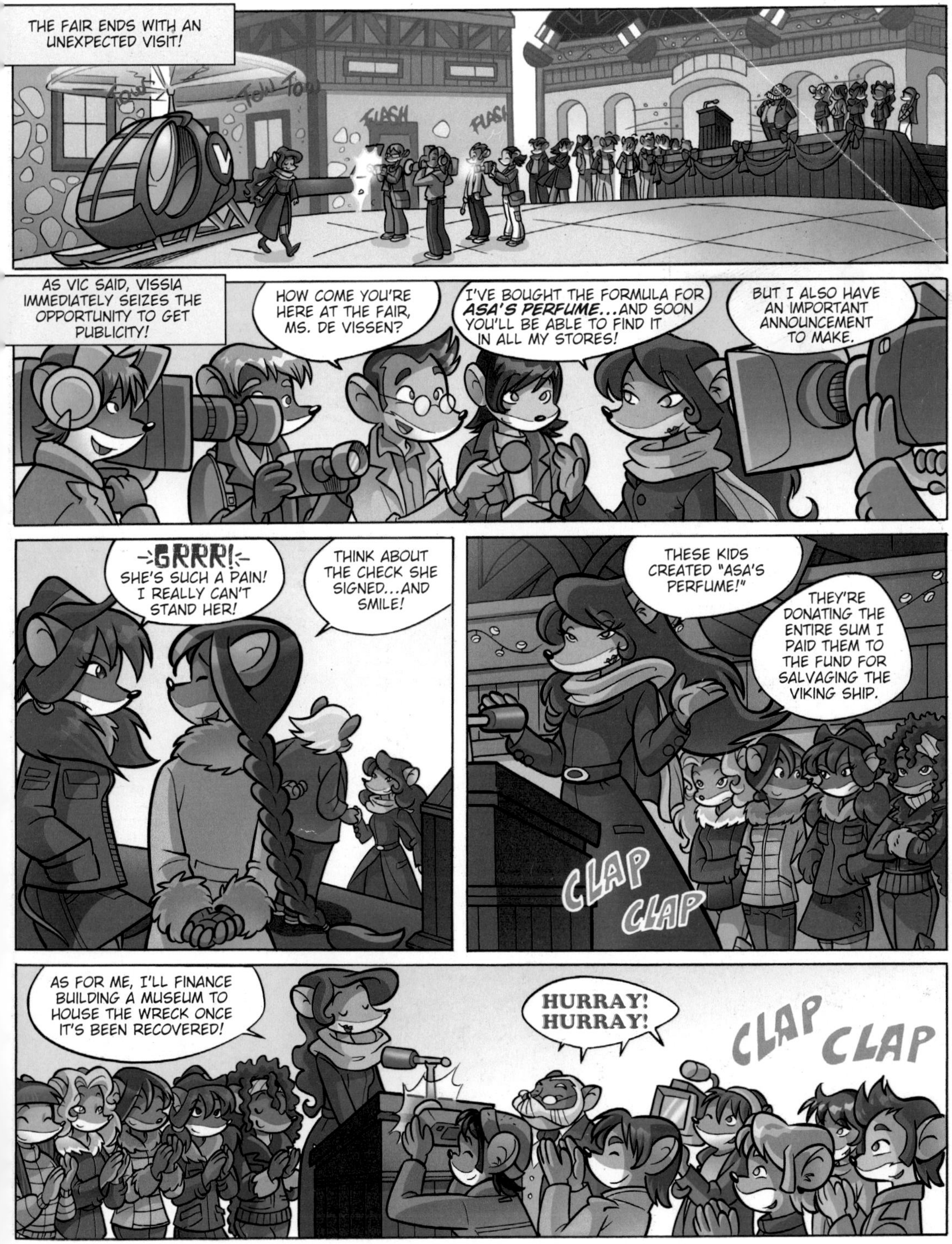
THE FAIR ENDS WITH AN UNEXPECTED VISIT!
TOW TOW TOW
FLASH
FLASH
AS VIC SAID, VISSIA IMMEDIATELY SEIZES THE OPPORTUNITY TO GET PUBLICITY!
HOW COME YOU'RE HERE AT THE FAIR, MS. DE VISSEN?
I'VE BOUGHT THE FORMULA FOR *ASA'S PERFUME*... AND SOON YOU'LL BE ABLE TO FIND IT IN ALL MY STORES!
BUT I ALSO HAVE AN IMPORTANT ANNOUNCEMENT TO MAKE.
-GRRR!- SHE'S SUCH A PAIN! I REALLY CAN'T STAND HER!
THINK ABOUT THE CHECK SHE SIGNED... AND SMILE!
THESE KIDS CREATED "ASA'S PERFUME!"
THEY'RE DONATING THE ENTIRE SUM I PAID THEM TO THE FUND FOR SALVAGING THE VIKING SHIP.
CLAP CLAP
AS FOR ME, I'LL FINANCE BUILDING A MUSEUM TO HOUSE THE WRECK ONCE IT'S BEEN RECOVERED!
HURRAY! HURRAY!
CLAP CLAP

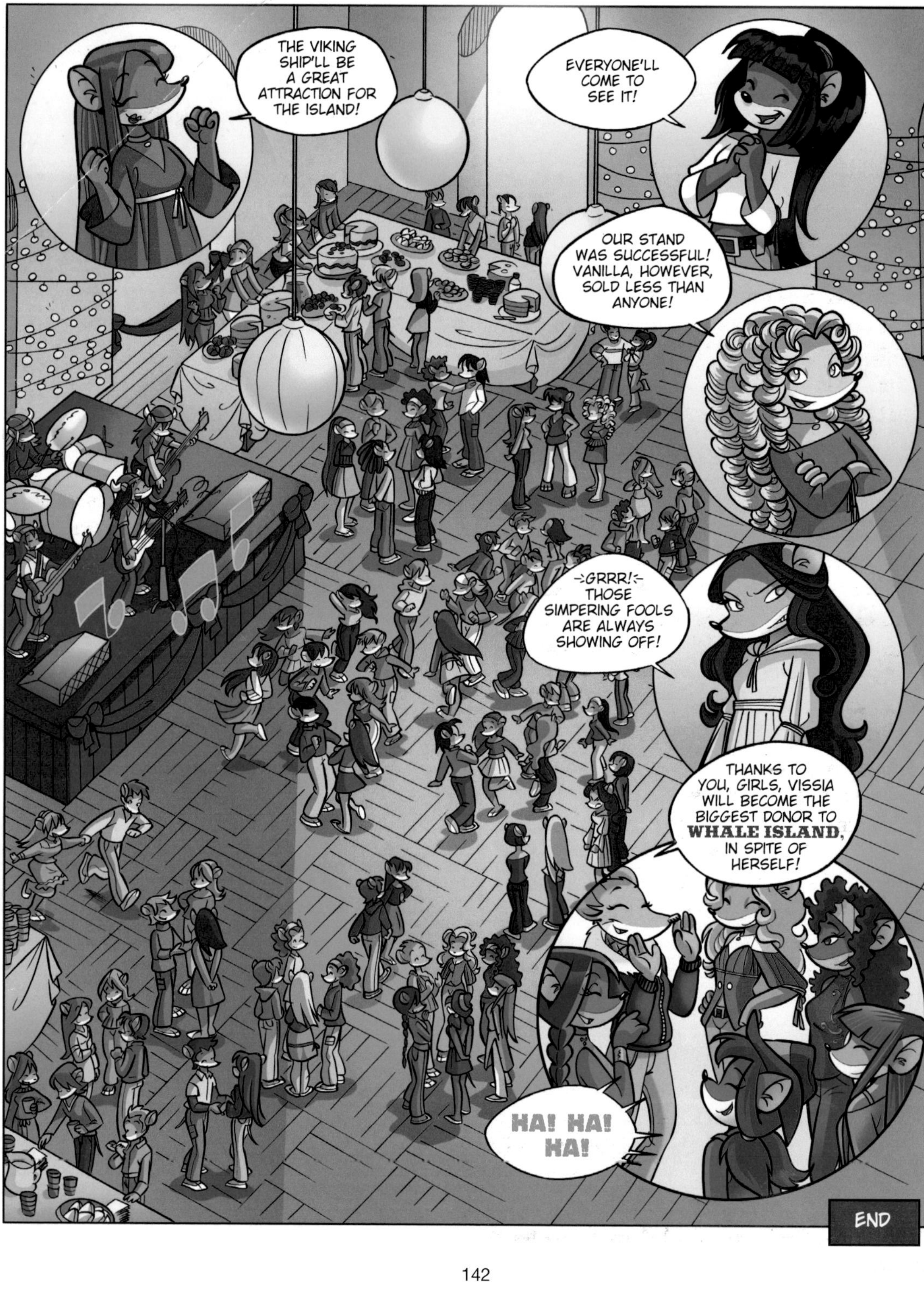
THE VIKING SHIP'LL BE A GREAT ATTRACTION FOR THE ISLAND!
EVERYONE'LL COME TO SEE IT!
OUR STAND WAS SUCCESSFUL! VANILLA, HOWEVER, SOLD LESS THAN ANYONE!
-GRRR!- THOSE SIMPERING FOOLS ARE ALWAYS SHOWING OFF!
THANKS TO YOU, GIRLS, VISSIA WILL BECOME THE BIGGEST DONOR TO WHALE ISLAND, IN SPITE OF HERSELF!
HA! HA! HA!
END

Watch Out For PAPERCUTZ

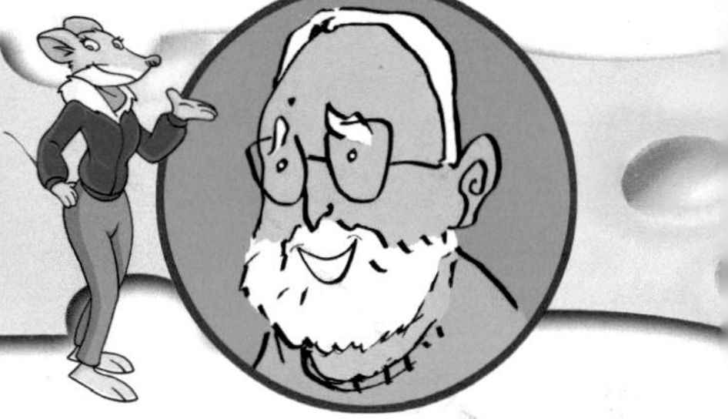

Welcome to Whale Island! Er, no, no I meant, welcome to Freshman Orientation at Mouseford Academy! Wait, that's not it, either! Oh, I remember now… welcome to the premiere THEA STILTON graphic novel from Papercutz, the furry folks dedicated to publishing great graphic novels for all ages! I'm Salicrup, *Jim Salicrup* the Editor-in-Chief of the Rodent's Gazette. Oops! That's not right either! Geronimo Stilton is the Editor-in-Chief of the Rodent's Gazette! I'm the Editor-in-Chief of Papercutz!

The previous nine sentences are from my *Watch Out for Papercutz* column from THEA STILTON #1 from 2013. It was my pleasure then to introduce North America to the graphic novel incarnations of the Thea Sisters—Colette, Violet, Pamela, Nicky, and Paulina. Actually, I had help from Thea Stilton herself! She wrote this letter that explained what the THEA STILTON series was all about…

> Ciao, I'm Thea, special correspondent to the Rodent's Gazette, the most famouse paper on Mouse Island! I teach journalism at Mouseford Academy, where I've gotten to know five very special students! They're top notch kids who've developed a real friendship for each other. They formed a group that they named after me: the Thea Sisters. I've decided to tell you about their adventures at Mouseford Academy: you'll have a blast!

And now, I'm proud to re-present the first three THEA STILTON graphic novels in this special collected edition, THEA STILTON 3 IN 1.

But that's not all! Now that you've met these five students from Mouseford Academy, and enjoyed three of their wonderful adventures, I'm eager to introduce you to five female students from Destiny, another special school—Electra, Selena, Cora, Maya, and Cleo. Just as the Thea Sisters aren't exactly like the students you'll find at your local college, these five girls are a little different too. They are winged unicorns called Melowies. Allow me to explain…

The world of Aura has four ancient realms where everyone lives in peace. In this world, a few winged unicorns are born each year with a special symbol on their wings, a sign that they have a special hidden power. These unicorns are called Megas and Melowies.

At a certain age, Melowies go to school at Destiny, a legendary castle hidden in the clouds. Here is the place where each Melowy finds her path as she masters the great power she has inside.

Coming soon from Papercutz is MELOWY, an all-new graphic novel series starring Electra, Selena, Cora, Maya, and Cleo. I suspect you'll love it just as much as you do THEA STILTON. For more information on MELOWY visit us at papercutz.com.

The Thea Sisters will return in THEA STILTON 3 IN 1 #2 coming soon. Until then, school's out!

Jim

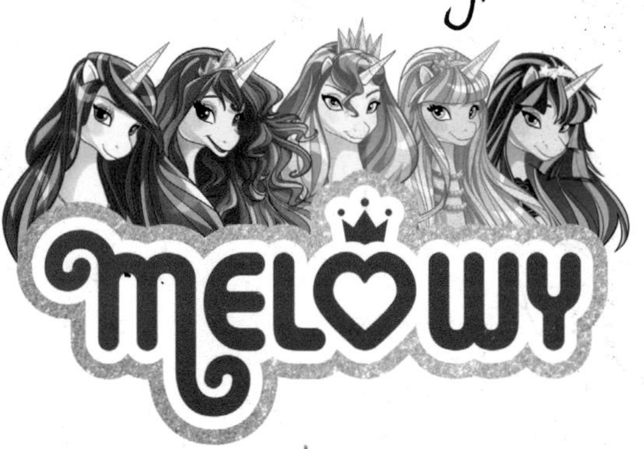
MELOWY

From left to right: Cleo, Electra, Cora, Maya, and Selena.

STAY IN TOUCH!

EMAIL:	salicrup@papercutz.com
WEB:	papercutz.com
TWITTER:	@papercutzgn
INSTAGRAM:	@papercutzgn
FACEBOOK:	PAPERCUTZGRAPHICNOVELS
FAN MAIL:	Papercutz, 160 Broadway, Suite 700, East Wing, New York, NY 10038

Geronimo Stilton

GRAPHIC NOVELS AVAILABLE FROM PAPERCUTZ

...ALSO AVAILABLE WHEREVER E-BOOKS ARE SOLD!

#1
"The Discovery
of America"

#2
"The Secret
of the Sphinx"

#3
"The Coliseum
Con"

#4
"Following the
Trail of Marco Polo"

#5
"The Great
Ice Age"

#6
"Who Stole
the Mona Lisa?"

#7
"Dinosaurs
in Action"

#8
"Play It Again,
Mozart!"

#9
"The Weird
Book Machine"

#10
"Geronimo Stilton
Saves the Olympics"

#11
"We'll Always
Have Paris"

#12
"The First Samurai"

#13
"The Fastest Train
in the West"

#14
"The First Mouse
on the Moon"

#15
"All for Stilton,
Stilton for All!"

#16
"Lights, Camera,
Stilton!"

#17
"The Mystery of the
Pirate Ship"

#18
"First to the Last Place
on Earth"

#19
"Lost in Translation"

papercutz.com